D1291853

MR CAMPION'S ABDICATION

Margery Allingham's
Albert Campion returns in

MR CAMPION'S ABDICATION

by

Mike Ripley

This first world edition published 2017
in Great Britain and the USA by
SEVERN HOUSE PUBLISHERS LTD of
19 Cedar Road, Sutton, Surrey, England, SM2 5DA.
Trade paperback edition first published
in Great Britain and the USA 2017 by
SEVERN HOUSE PUBLISHERS LTD

British Library Cataloguing in Publication Data
A CIP catalogue record for this title is available from the British Library.

ISBN-13: 978-0-7278-8735-1 (cased)
ISBN-13: 978-1-84751-847-7 (trade paper)
ISBN-13: 978-1-78010-907-7 (e-book)

All Severn House titles are printed on acid-free paper.

Severn House Publishers support the Forest Stewardship Council™ [FSC™],
the leading international forest certification organisation.
All our titles that are printed on FSC certified paper carry the FSC logo.

MIX
Paper from
responsible sources
FSC
www.fsc.org   FSC® C013056

Typeset by Palimpsest Book Production Ltd.,
Falkirk, Stirlingshire, Scotland.
Printed and bound in Great Britain by
TJ International, Padstow, Cornwall.

For Daniela and La Pergoletta
(the real ones)

Author's Note

I have taken numerous liberties with the geography of Suffolk but hopefully in the same spirit which Margery Allingham did. Once again, I am grateful to Roger Johnson of the Margery Allingham Society for his cartographic skills.

As this story is set in early 1970, I have used *Sutton Hoo* by Charles Green, originally published in 1963, for background on boat burials in East Anglia. A comprehensive study detailing more modern excavations can be found in Professor Martin Carver's *Sutton Hoo: Burial Ground of Kings?* 1998, London: British Museum Press.

Although this novel does not directly concern itself with the 'Abdication Crisis' of 1936, the writing of it coincided with research by Dr Jennifer Palmer into papers in the Allingham Archive at the University of Essex, which revealed Margery Allingham's thoughts as the crisis came to a head in December. In a letter to her American agent, Margery gave her reasons why many in Britain did not wish to see the king abdicate. These were: '(a) he had got the makings of the best king we ever had, popular at home and abroad; (b) it would leave us with the Duke of York who stammers, is very shy and is not known anywhere except in Austria and Australia; (c) thousands of pounds have [already] been sunk in the Coronation [planned for May 1937]; (d) it would hurt our prestige, but this did not carry much weight as Mrs S. had done a lot of harm already.'

Allingham was in London during the crisis, describing 'a week of silent crowds' in Whitehall as news of the abdication became official. Margery ended her correspondence on a more upbeat note as Edward was replaced by his younger brother who became George VI: 'There is a strong feeling that this lad will make a better constitutional monarch than his brother, and having a family certainly does help.' On that latter point, Allingham was spot on.

Contents

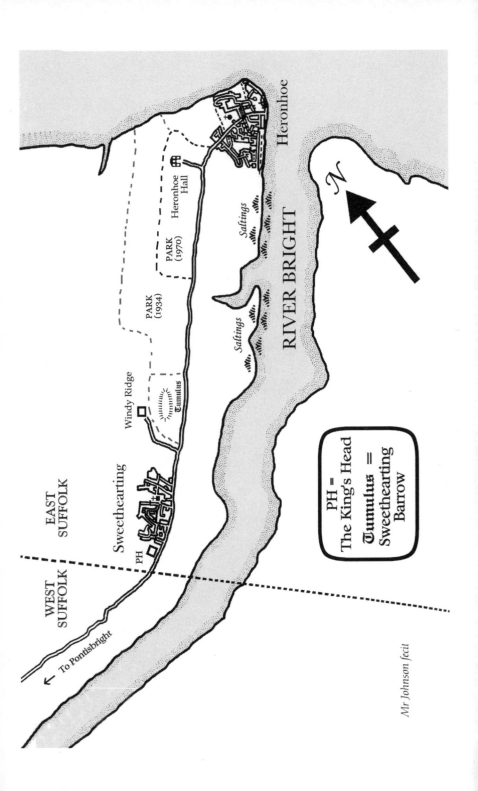

WEST
SUFFOLK

EAST
SUFFOLK

← To Pontisbright

Sweethearting

PH

Windy Ridge

Tumulus

PARK
(1934)

PARK
(1970)

Heronhoe Hall

Heronhoe

Saltings

Saltings

RIVER BRIGHT

N

PH =
The King's Head

𝕿𝖚𝖒𝖚𝖑𝖚𝖘 =
Sweethearting
Barrow

Mr Johnson fecit

ONE
Lords Temporal

'So where exactly did Albert Campion stand on the Abdication?'

'Behind the throne, slightly to the left?' suggested Luke.

'I honestly don't know, Lord Breeze. The subject never came up.'

'Well, it wouldn't, would it? You're not of our generation, the generation who lived through it; you'd be too young to be worried by such things. And it's Gus to me friends, by the way. The title comes in handy in restaurants, but in this place every bugger's got one, so it's nowt special.'

Commander Charles Luke, being a very senior officer in the Metropolitan Police, was naturally wary of complete strangers who insisted on first-name terms, even if they were members of the House of Lords. Perhaps especially if they were Lords, even self-deprecating ones.

'As I'm on duty, Lord Breeze, I'll keep it formal, if you don't mind.'

'Nay, lad, there's no need to stand on ceremony,' said Lord Breeze. 'Don't let this place intimidate you.'

Luke suppressed a snort of mild disgust at the suggestion that he could be intimidated by the sedate comfort of the peers' bar when he had survived Friday night fights with broken bottles down the East India Docks and had once had to act as the lone keeper of the peace between two warring Chinese restaurants disputing the right of way in a dark alley off Brewer Street. On both occasions the antagonists there had all wanted to call him 'friend', and somehow he had remembered those nervous incidents as less disconcerting than his present situation. If anything did make Luke uncomfortable, it was Lord Breeze's increasingly thickening Yorkshire accent and bluff camaraderie, both of which were no more than a politician's props; the umbrella, the cigar and the black briar pipe of yesteryear updated to the age of the television interview or panel game.

'I am quite familiar with the House, Lord Breeze,' Luke said politely. 'In my position, one has to be.'

'Matters of national security, that sort of thing, eh?'

'Certainly those, but when an arrest has to be made . . .' Luke paused mischievously, '. . . it helps to know the lie of the land, so that we can be discreet and cause the minimum of disruption.'

'You've had to make arrests? *Here?*' Lord Breeze was definitely shaken, if not stirred.

'Oh, yes,' said Luke quietly, but did not volunteer the information that the arrest in question had been that of a junior kitchen porter who had been diverting joints of beef to a series of Indian restaurants in Brick Lane.

'Well, I suppose it takes all sorts,' said Lord Breeze, not before time as it was one of his favourite catchphrases when asked a difficult question by a journalist; not that Lord Breeze was often questioned by members of the press, but when he was the questions tended to be difficult. 'Good job you came in uniform, then, in case you have to feel another collar.'

Charles Luke flexed his shoulders and neck muscles so that the material of his blue serge jacket rippled gently across his chest.

'Unless you have information to the contrary, my Lord, I am not expecting to make an arrest today. The uniform is because I have a formal dinner engagement this evening, so I am afraid this meeting will have to be a brief one.'

'Nah, lad, tha's got time for a snifter, surely?' The faux Yorkshire accent grated on Luke like gravel and he tried his best not to wince. 'Tha' money's no good in 'ere, you know. Only peers get to pay. Mind you, upside is we're not troubled by licensing hours.'

'I'm sorry, Lord Breeze, but I must decline,' said Luke, now tired of this particular charade. An end-of-the-peer show, he thought and allowed himself a private smile. 'Perhaps it is best that we get down to business. I still have no idea why you have summoned me here.'

'But you came anyway, a busy man like you.'

Lord Breeze had piggy eyes at the best of times. Now, after a good lunch (a bottle-and-a-half-if-not-two lunch if Luke's guess was right), and with a senior policeman seemingly waiting on his grace and favour, they had become the eyes of a weasel or a ferret.

'It was . . . suggested . . . that I should come,' Luke said carefully.

'And that suggestion came from a rather interesting place, did it not?'

'I think you know very well where it came from.' Luke clenched his teeth to stop them grinding and wished that the peer would either stop fencing or take a long walk off a short . . . well, pier.

'And one can't ignore a suggestion from the Palace, can one? Neither of us can, not that we'd want to, eh? I mean, we've both sworn oaths of loyalty.'

'I certainly have sworn to keep the Queen's peace,' said Luke, taking a deep, calming breath, 'but I am at a loss to see how I am performing that duty at this particular moment.'

Lord Breeze smiled the wincing sort of smile associated with indigestion and adopted his second-best condescending tone.

'I know what you're thinking, lad . . .' Luke sincerely hoped he did not, '. . . you're wondering why the Palace should have chosen little old me, old Gus Breeze, a life peer of nobbut four years' standing and a socialist to boot, to act as messenger boy.'

Luke nodded his head slightly, inviting an explanation. It seemed the most likely way to get the little man to stop rambling and get to the point. For the moment, he would keep his powder dry on the fact that he knew that 'old Gus' had been christened Gabriel Augustus St John Breeze and that, if he had been born in a tied cottage, then it was a cottage in the grounds of his father's estate in North Yorkshire. As Gus – never Augustus and certainly not Gabriel – Breeze he had earned his peerage from a grateful Labour government for his services to house building, having sold the estate he had inherited and ploughed his capital into other types of estates: crowded, red-brick ones with standard metal-framed windows offering better plumbing but little else in the way of improvements when compared to the Victorian terraced houses they replaced. The provision of much-needed social housing, however quickly and cheaply erected (and some Breeze Homes estates had been completed in suspiciously quick times) in desolate areas of the north had brought not just the ermine cloak but substantial profits. Some would say as suspiciously substantial as the rapid completion times of some of his housing estates.

Lord Breeze continued without the need for prompting, raising a forefinger to tap the side of his sharp, whiskery nose.

'Family, that's why they sent me to talk to you,' he said with a satisfied smirk.

'I'm afraid I simply don't follow you, Lord Breeze. The Home Office has perfectly good channels of communication with—'

'Come on, lad, don't pretend to be slow. You should have twigged by now that this was not something for normal channels.'

Luke allowed himself a glance around the bar – its deep-brown leather armchairs, low tables and dark oak-bevelled wall panelling – which was empty apart from the two of them and a bored white-coated barman strangling a pale ale glass with a crisp white tea towel.

'I'll grant you that these are not my normal channels,' said Luke, pointedly consulting his wristwatch, 'and for once I do not have to pretend to be slow on the uptake as I sometimes have to when dealing with political situations. I assume that is what this is.'

'That's better, lad. Showing a bit of gumption – that's more what I was told to expect.' Breeze turned to the barman and made a flamboyant hand gesture which would not have looked out of place on a race course. The barman, grateful for something to do, began to rattle bottles and glasses as officiously as possible. 'Sure I can't tempt you, Commander?'

'Lord Breeze, I am on duty, in uniform and due somewhere else very soon, so would you mind awfully getting to the point and sharing this message you say you have been intrusted with?'

'I was told you could be blunt,' said the peer, taking a balloon of brandy and soda from the silver tray proffered by the barman, who had slid silently up to the table.

'So you had me checked out, as the Americans say.'

'Of course,' said Breeze. 'First rule of business: know who you're dealing with. I'd be surprised if you didn't ask around about me as well.'

'Oh, I did,' said Luke, deadpan.

'Did you find owt? Any muck worth raking?'

'Little mysteries, that's all,' said Luke. 'The Yorkshire accent, for instance. Did you develop that at Stowe or wait until you got to Oxford?'

Lord Breeze hid his face in his glass but Luke's sharp eye, conditioned by a thousand witness interviews, detected a pink glow in the drinker's cheeks.

'It comes in useful sometimes,' said Breeze, lowering his glass.

'When booking tables in restaurants?' suggested Luke innocently.

'When I'm playing the part of a Labour peer with a background in the building trade, it does. It's what's expected, but if the Tories get in at the next election, I will call myself a property developer and hopefully never have to sit on another arbitration committee with gruesome trades unionists again. Is that too cynical for you, Commander Luke?'

'Too honest for a politician,' said Luke, 'though I doubt you'd repeat that outside the House.'

'You're not wrong on that, and I'll deny every word of it should you ever think of writing your memoirs.'

If I ever did, thought Luke, *you'd be lucky to get a footnote, though at this rate I might reach retirement before the noble lord gets to the point.*

'Needless to say,' Lord Breeze continued, 'none of what I am about to divulge will go in your memoirs, either.'

'I can think of nothing which could go in a memoir, Lord Breeze,' said the policeman solemnly. 'All you've asked me is a rather obscure question about Albert Campion and the Abdication which happened thirty-three years ago, if my maths is up to scratch.'

'A third of a century, indeed, but not forgotten. Still news; still scandal in some quarters. It's a story which simply will not . . . go away.'

Dies, thought Luke, *you meant to say the story that never dies.*

'It was a story which had everything,' he said. 'The aristocracy, scandalous behaviour, outraged politicians and a king giving up a throne for the woman he loved. It's the stuff of a thousand romantic novels and a million women's magazines and it could have made a Disney film if it hadn't been for his fondness for Hitler.'

'I can see you were not a fan.'

'As you said, I was too young to have an opinion when it happened, but looking back I'm totally convinced we got the right king for the war.'

'Good,' said Lord Breeze, placing his empty glass on the table between them and slapping both hands on his thighs. 'We are on the same page on that. The point is does Albert Campion sing from the same hymn sheet?'

'I really don't know. It is not a topic I can remember ever having discussed with him.'

'But you are aware of his connections to the Palace?'

'I'm as aware as anyone, which is to say rather vaguely. He has never volunteered information on that subject and certainly never boasted about it, but then he never boasts about anything. Well, nothing serious. I think he once claimed to be a tiddlywinks grand master and that he would captain the British team if it was ever allowed at the Olympics.'

'Mmm . . .' Lord Breeze scratched his chin as he ruminated. 'I've heard he's a bit of a clown, which is why he's been kept on the sidelines.'

'When it comes to Albert Campion, both those statements are completely false, and many a reprobate who shared those views has found they have made a dangerous mistake. The loveliest trick of Mr Campion is to persuade you that he is totally harmless.'

'You think quite highly of him, Commander, don't you?'

'More to the point, Lord Breeze, I like him and count him a friend, so perhaps you should tread carefully if you are asking for my help with anything to do with dear old Albert.'

Lord Breeze took a deep breath. 'Very well, I will tread carefully, for the friendship of a good policeman is to be valued, but I am not asking you for help as such, rather a character reference. One that I might pass on – pass on upwards, if you get my drift – to reassure certain personages.' He caught Luke's unblinking eye. 'Oh, I know what you're thinking – you're thinking what is this jumped-up bricklayer doing acting as a go-between with Scotland Yard for the Palace?'

For once, Lord Breeze had accurately read Luke's mind.

'I admit, I was surprised to get the call – from an equerry or a private secretary, of course. I mean, I'm as loyal a monarchist as the next man and have always done my best for queen and country as I saw it, but I'm under no illusions. I got my title for political services, for being useful to the government, not for slaying dragons or raising levies to go fight the French. So I'm the least likely person the Palace would turn to, unless they wanted a three-bedroom semi in Doncaster or similar, except for the fact that Lavinia's husband is involved.'

'Lavinia?'

'My daughter. Her husband is that wastrel Oliver Grieg Bell.'

'I'm sorry, Lord Breeze, but could you be clearer?'

'Well, my involvement in this affair is all because of my son-in-law Oliver and his rather bizarre ideas about the Abdication Treasure.'

'Treasure?' Luke spoke far more loudly than he had intended, glanced automatically towards the bar and was reassured that the three basic tenets shared by diplomatic barman and wise monkeys, to neither hear, see, nor speak evil were being observed. Nonetheless, he lowered his voice. 'Abdication Treasure? What on earth is that?'

'Clearly it's all nonsense; a myth, a legend, no more than scurrilous gossip, but it hangs around the house like a problem with the drains. Of course, I knew the *stories* when I bought the place – dirt cheap as it happens, as it was in a terrible state of repair and death duties would make sure there would be no money to spend on it – but I didn't pay them any mind as I intended to raze the place to the ground and slap up a few dozen semis with garages, all mod cons and a river view for those buyers willing to cough up the premium. And that's what I would have done except the County Council Planning Department – or the Gestapo as we in the trade call them – plus the tweedy county set, local historians, wildlife lovers and the National Trust brigade all started to object; historic building and all that. Trouble was my flaming daughter sided with them and threatened to go to the press. That would have been a nice story for the Sunday rags, I don't think. So I thought I'd cut my losses. I sold off some of the land to the local farmers – there were no objections there, I can tell you – and I gave Lavinia the hall as a wedding present when she got hitched to Oliver. That's Oliver Grieg Bell, by the way. Not heard of him? Don't worry, neither had I until I was called on to give Lavinia away, but the point is Oliver fell for this Abdication Treasure fairy story hook, line and sinker.'

Luke held up a hand; a hand which had brought traffic to a halt on the Holloway Road during rush hour in its day.

'For the sake of my poor policeman's brain, could I clarify a few things, Lord Breeze?'

'Of course.'

'Then let me ask questions and you give simple answers that I can understand. Fair?'

Lord Breeze raised his eyebrows in resigned acceptance of his guest's clear lack of intelligence and semaphored for another drink until the Easter Island statue behind the bar sprang in action. Luke took his silence as agreement.

'The house you gave your daughter is supposed to contain this "Abdication Treasure" whatever that is, correct?'

Lord Breeze nodded as he drank.

'Am I to assume that your son-in-law, Mr Bell, is actively looking for it?'

Another nod.

'Yet he doesn't know *what* this treasure is, let alone *where* it is?'

'Small details like that would not worry Oliver. The boy's a moron.'

'So what are his chances of finding this mysterious treasure?'

'Middling to none, I would say, if he was on his own. He's been busy ripping up floorboards and knocking holes in the walls, though he could pull the hall down about his ears for all I care – that's what I would have done if I'd had my way.'

'Hall? You've called it a hall twice now. Where exactly is this place?' Luke twisted his neck muscles against his shirt collar to ease the tingling sensation as hairs began to stand on end, a feeling every policeman knew was not an old wives' tale.

'Heronhoe Hall,' said Breeze. 'A dreadful dump, terribly run-down, good for nothing except redevelopment in my opinion; formerly the manor house of a place called Heronhoe. You'll never have heard of it. It's . . .'

'In Suffolk, near the coast, down the road from Pontisbright,' said Luke.

Lord Breeze looked surprised – Luke doubted he could ever look impressed by anything other than a balance sheet.

'That's right.'

'And it explains Campion, I suppose. He never could resist a treasure hunt.'

'Ah, yes, you would know of the Pontisbright connection. Campion married the sister of the earl, didn't he?'

'I believe the first time they met was in Pontisbright,' said Luke thoughtfully. 'It's the sort of place where one can meet a future wife.'

Lord Breeze ignored the poignant pause the policeman had introduced and galloped on.

'Naturally, the Earl of Pontisbright would have – should have – been the natural go-between on this matter, but he can never be found when he's needed. I don't think he's ever been into the House, let alone made a speech here and he lives abroad mostly. South Africa, I think.'

'Last reports were that Hal, the "young earl" as they used to call him, had moved to South America,' said Luke.

'Africa got too boring for him, eh? Well, good luck to him. The upshot is that as the father of Lavinia, who is now Mrs Oliver Grieg Bloody Bell, I have drawn the short straw and got involved in this stupid treasure business, and I'm now getting you involved too.'

'How?'

'You're the one who is going to have to lean on Campion.'

'But you still haven't told me how Campion is involved.'

'He's down there at Heronhoe at this very moment; supposedly, he's with the film company but . . .'

'What film company? Are they looking for this treasure as well?'

'Oh, damn the treasure! There is no treasure! It's all just a story. Look, it all stems from the Thirties. Long before anyone in this country knew that the Prince of Wales was carrying on with that divorced woman Mrs Simpson, the pair of them slipped out of London to do their carrying-on at Heronhoe Hall as guests of the then owner, a chap called Wemyss-Grendle – Captain Wemyss-Grendle – who had been in the Household Cavalry, I believe, and used to go point-to-pointing with the prince. Anyway, Heronhoe provided a nice little love nest as there was also a useful cover story on hand if the prince needed it. You see, they'd just discovered an interesting bit of archaeology on the edge of the Heronhoe estate, an Anglo-Saxon boat burial.'

'And that's where the treasure was?'

'No, no, no, I told you there is no treasure and there certainly wasn't any found in that boat burial. God knows, I paid enough cash out on surveys and reports when I bought the place to be sure of that. It wasn't like the famous one up the coast at Sutton Hoo that they found in 1939, this was a boat burial where the

only thing they buried was the flaming boat! Still, archaeological
digs were all the rage back then, and the prince naturally took
an interest. If anyone spotted him lurking about the place he
had a good excuse to be there, but nobody ever did, or if they
did they didn't tell the press. The locals round there must have
known but they kept quiet, and the prince was grateful for that.
When it came to the Abdication Crisis in 'thirty-six those dirty
weekends in Heronhoe were quickly forgotten, except not by
the prince. The story goes – and it *is* a story as far as I'm
concerned – that when he married Mrs Simpson, in 1937, that
would be, he actually sent a valuable thank-you gift to Heronhoe.
That was what became known as the Abdication Treasure,
although there's no record of anything going to Heronhoe Hall,
or of anybody ever receiving anything from the Duke of Windsor,
and nobody anywhere claims to have actually seen anything
resembling treasure.'

'So how is Albert Campion involved?'

'He's in thick with the damned film company,' said Lord Breeze
in a tone which suggested Luke had not been listening carefully
enough. 'A foreign one as well, though why the Eyeties are involved
I really don't know.'

'Eyeties . . . Italians? What have they got to do with it?'

'You may well ask.'

'I just did,' said Luke without a smile.

'I don't know why but all those countries who've got rid of
their monarchies – Italy, Spain, France . . .'

'America?'

'Worst of the lot. Anyway, all these so-called modern republics
can't get enough of our royal family and this Italian bunch are
making a film about Edward and Mrs Simpson. They're filming
at Heronhoe, recreating the visit the prince made to the archaeological dig just before he snuck off with Mrs Simpson. Funnily
enough, the boat burial is on the estuary and it's nearer to the
village of Sweethearting than it is to Heronhoe, which sounds just
the place for a romantic tryst, doesn't it?'

'If you say so, Lord Breeze, but what part is Campion playing
in all this?'

'Ah, well, that's the point, isn't it? That's the cause for
concern . . .' he jerked his head, presumably indicating the direction

of Buckingham Palace, though he was several points of the compass out, '. . . up the road. Campion's got himself involved with these film people as some sort of technical advisor and he's wangled leading roles for that son of his and his daughter-in-law.'

'Rupert and Perdita? What are they doing there?'

'Didn't I say? It's what they call a dramatized documentary, so they have actors playing the roles of the real people. Young Campion is playing Edward VIII, or the Prince of Wales as he was at the time.'

'Don't tell me . . . Perdita's playing Mrs Simpson.' Luke allowed his eyelids to droop.

'She is indeed, which hasn't pleased you-know-who one bit.' Again Lord Breeze flicked his head in the direction he thought The Mall lay. 'Not a good career move, if you ask me, but that's not really the point.'

'Is there a point to all this?' Luke snapped more sharply than he had intended.

'Of course there is. Nobody can possibly believe that Campion is down there for anything other than the Abdication Treasure, and this filming business is just to disguise his true purpose. I've done my best to try and stop my daughter and her idiot husband hunting for it – now you're needed to lean on Campion and make him stop looking.'

'But you're not sure he is, are you?'

'He must be. You said yourself that treasure hunting was right up Campion's street.'

'And you said the treasure doesn't exist.'

'It doesn't,' Lord Breeze said firmly, 'and I have been instructed to tell *you* to tell Campion that unless he wants to risk embarrassing the Palace he'd better lay off. There's no such thing as the Abdication Treasure, so there's nothing to find and Campion had better make sure he doesn't find it!'

TWO
Night Crow

Not even the most optimistic of estate agents – a profession which by custom and training always looked on the rose-tinted side of life – would have described Heronhoe Hall as a lucky house. Not, at least, for its owners down the years.

Built at the very sunset of the first Elizabeth's reign for an Ipswich merchant who then found he had invested too much money and far too much hope in a disastrous venture in the New World, the house passed almost immediately on completion to one John Weems, sometimes known as Johannes Wiems (the documentation is patchy, the signatures erratic). The new owner prospered under the new king James, possibly by changing his signature, yet again, to John Wemyss and thus claiming some distant association with the Scottish clan of that ilk. No careful scrutiny of every twig of the branches of that proud family tree, however, has ever confirmed a connection.

Whatever the provenance of John Wemyss, he acquired a sturdy manor house and some 300 acres of park land for hunting across, which was to become his downfall, quite literally, as he was thrown from his horse while riding to hounds. One of his sons, another John, also died falling from a horse at Marston Moor in 1644, though not before being shot by a Royalist musketeer. A younger son, clearly influenced by the family's unfortunate relationship with horses, opted for the safety of a naval career only to find, at the hands of the Dutch during the Battle of Sole Bay in 1672, that safety was a relative concept. Undeterred, when a Wemyss was called upon to support king (or queen) and country, he would answer bravely, though the casualty rate among the lords of Heronhoe manor suggested perhaps too recklessly. The inheritors of Heronhoe Hall fell with appalling regularity in numerous foreign fields at the hands of a wide variety of enemies: at Ramilles (the French) in 1706, at the siege of Gibraltar (the Spanish) in 1727 and in the forests of the Ohio Valley in America (a Delaware or possibly a Shawnee native) in 1757.

By now the Wemyss male line was exhausted and it was a daughter, Pamela Wemyss, who not only inherited but married well, which is to say richly. Her husband, Henry Grendle, who suggested the family name of Wemyss-Grendle, was no man of action and happy to stay close to home, if only to keep an eye on the vast number of workmen he employed. It was he who financed the rebuilding of the hall, adding an imposing Georgian frontage faced with tall sash windows looking out on a walled rose garden, an Orangery, perhaps more in hope than expectation and, internally, an elegant curving staircase and several water closets. Henry Wemyss-Grendle, having endured his first winter in Heronhoe and exposure to the winds which swept in over the salt marshes direct from Russia, also insisted on installing, in every room, one of the fashionable iron-hob grate fireplaces from the Carron Foundry in Falkirk. It was said that Heronhoe Hall was the biggest single order Carron supplied outside of London in 1785 and that Henry had been one of their most valued customers. It was therefore somewhat ironic that the eldest Wemyss-Grendle son was killed by a shot from a short cannon known as a 'Carronade' at the Battle of Plattsburg (Americans) in 1814, the Carronade being a successful diversification in the product portfolio of that noted Scottish ironworks and one sold with impunity to those pugnacious ex-colonials.

Wemyss-Grendle males fared little better than their Wemyss/ Weems forebears when it came to following the flag away from Heronhoe. There was further pruning of the root stock at Inkerman (Russians) in 1854, Isandlwana (Zulus) in 1879 and Peking (Chinese Boxers) in 1900.

It was a local saying that a new owner of Heronhoe Hall got the best view of a sunrise over a salt marsh estuary anywhere on the east coast – but not for long.

Amazingly, the childless bachelor Gerald Wemyss-Grendle survived two world wars, one as a young cavalry lieutenant under Allenby in Palestine (Turks) and one as a Home Guard captain (Germans), only to be forced, in 1966, to sell the hall and the estate to Lord Breeze, not entirely because of the lack of an heir but rather the catastrophic mismanagement of his finances, primarily and ironically due to a long series of misjudgements when it came to the horses on offer at Newmarket race course.

Heronhoe Hall did prove lucky for Lord Breeze in the sense that Captain Wemyss-Grendle was forced by circumstances to accept a low valuation of the house and park and, though denied planning permission for his more expansive plans, selling half the parkland off to local farmers did recoup the noble lord's cash outlay as well as providing him with a ready-made wedding present for his daughter. The magnificent profits he had envisaged did not materialize, but he contented himself that he had managed to break even on the deal. His self-satisfaction lasted until his daughter Lavinia began to entreat him in ways in which only a favourite daughter could for assistance with the few necessary extras which Heronhoe Hall needed in order for it to be habitable and a suitable place in which to raise – at some future time yet to be determined – a grandchild or two.

As Lavinia was Lord Breeze's only daughter, her requests were impossible to refuse despite their frequency, and at first they seemed eminently reasonable. All the sash windows on the hall's Georgian frontage – a considerable number – would need replacing, ideally with double-glazed replacements or at the very least ones which closed properly. Those heavy black iron Carron fire grates would have to be ripped out during the redecoration; even the Victorians thought them old fashioned. They would, in any case, have been made redundant by the oil-fired central heating which would be installed, along with a new kitchen range with all modern labour-saving devices as the new occupants of the hall could not afford to employ any staff.

Nor, as Lord Breeze grumbled to himself, did it appear they could afford to repair the extensive roof, repoint the numerous chimneys, install a damp course where there had never been one and replace the wall plaster in the rooms where it was all too obvious there had never been any. As for the gardens, Lord Breeze's advice to his daughter was that she and her new husband should roll up their sleeves and do the spadework, quite literally, them-selves. He had presented them both with sturdy leather gardening gloves and the encouragement that they should begin with the kitchen garden rather than the rose garden, as that way they could grow something to eat.

Not that there was any likelihood that Lord Breeze would allow his daughter to starve. Her husband, however, was possibly another matter.

Oliver Grieg Bell would not have been Lord Breeze's first choice as a husband for Lavinia – not that he had the slightest say in the matter, for Lavinia was an adult who knew her own mind and had done so for many years. Indeed, Gus Breeze had told his fellow noble Lords, in the members' bar rather than the chamber, of course, that the government had not needed legislation to lower the age of majority to eighteen as his daughter had automatically assumed it at thirteen. Long before she even contemplated marriage, it was clear that the choice of a husband would be Lavinia's and Lavinia's alone, and when she did choose Oliver Grieg Bell, no one else had a say in the matter, possibly not even Oliver himself.

Not that Oliver was an ogre, a philanderer, a drug addict or white-slaver; he was rather a good and kind man. True, he was a musician, but not a long-haired, guitar-scraping loud one; in fact, quite the opposite, as his instrument of choice was the gentle harpsichord and his repertoire limited to the late eighteenth century – sadly a repertoire also limited in its twentieth-century demand. Which was at the heart of the problem with Oliver – or the problem as perceived by Lord Breeze: he was virtually penniless and, with the exception of the ability to give piano (or harpsichord) lessons or to teach music in elementary schools, he had no visible means of earning a living.

Oliver was the sort of young man unlikely to be bothered a single jot by such considerations. He was of modest intelligence, modest tastes and little ambition, who floated through life without, seemingly, the need to dirty his hands scrabbling for money or possessions. His soulmate, Lavinia, also floated through life but for different reasons. Thanks to the wealth of Lord Breeze, his only daughter would never have to chip her nail polish in the sordid scrum of gainful employment and certainly had never expected to. Much to the surprise of those who knew them, the differences in their respective financial circumstances and prospects did not appear to be a sleeping policeman on the road to a secure marriage, for the couple clearly adored each other and there are some things which cannot be expressed on a balance sheet.

That was why, when Lavinia nudged Oliver sharply in the ribs just after four a.m. on a cold and frosty February morning and hissed, 'Darling wake up! There's somebody rummaging around downstairs!' Oliver did exactly that.

He woke but, apart from his eyelids, he did not move a muscle. The fireplace in the master bedroom had been removed and the central heating still not fully installed, and Oliver was determined to remain in the cocoon he had created with his half-share of the five blankets and the car rug under which the couple sheltered from the draughts of the yet-to-be-replaced sash window.

'It's probably one of the archaeologists pottering around making tea,' said Oliver, straining his ears for any sound out of the ordinary night-time concerto of rattling window panes, creaking floorboards and settling roof tiles.

'Nonsense,' said his wife firmly, 'they're all in the Orangery,' adding pointedly, 'because it's warmer than this damned house, and anyway they have their own kettle. Besides, it's the dead of night and they're never around before dawn. Listen!'

Next to her, Oliver used his shoulder blades to move his head infinitesimally up the pillow until his chin was clear of the blankets. The bedroom was in pitch darkness, any moonlight repelled by the heavy curtains hung to minimize draughts, but Oliver imagined he could see his breath frosting, which only added to his conviction that it would be foolish to leave the snugness of his nest. But, dammit, his wife was right. He had heard a noise, a distinct thump, which could not be explained by the house easing its old bones.

'Dining room?' he whispered out of the corner of his mouth.

'More like the study, I think,' Lavinia replied calmly and quietly across the surface of a white, ice-cold pillow.

There was another muffled *thud* and Oliver felt his wife stiffen. He knew by instinct that her delicate fists would be clenched tight.

'Do you think it's an animal that's got in?' he said slowly, hoping to diffuse the tension.

'The wildlife around here isn't stupid,' whispered Lavinia. 'They know it's warmer out there on the saltings than inside this house. It must be an intruder.'

Oliver smothered the urge to giggle. 'A burglar? What have we got worth stealing?'

'Only Hattie,' Lavinia said softly, the mischief in her voice muffled by the blankets she was quivering under.

'Hattie? Burglars don't steal harpsichords, darling, unless they've got a truck parked outside.'

'I know that, dearest, but now you simply have to go and look, don't you.'

It was not a question, nor a proposition up for debate; it was a statement by a wife who knew her husband only too well. Oliver carefully peeled back the blankets and swung his legs out of bed, his toes urgently seeking shelter inside the wool slippers parked strategically on the carpet and his fingers scrabbling over the bed to retrieve the woollen dressing gown spread there as an extra blanket.

Once insulated, but still shivering, he slid across the bedroom, his hands outstretched in front of him until he located the door handle, turned it and eased the door open. On the landing there was some light as the tall, rectangular window here was un-curtained and Oliver paused at the top of the staircase, allowing his eyes to adjust before he began to walk carefully down the steps, pausing only once when he heard another distinct bump and what could have been a muzzled oath. Lavinia had been right: whatever or whoever the intruder was, they were in the study, just across the hall, the door nearest the hall's front door.

But at the foot of the staircase, Oliver turned back on himself and edged his way along and under the run of the staircase until, by touch alone, he located the cupboard under the stairs where the inevitable jetsam of any household is stored. For a moment, Oliver paused, then took the risk of reaching into the cupboard, locating the light switch and flicking it on. It was, he knew, only a twenty-five-watt bulb in there and any spillage of light would be unlikely to be noticed under the door of the study further along.

It took Oliver longer than he had hoped to locate what he was looking for, as he had to carefully move several pairs of Wellington boots, four walking sticks, an empty picnic hamper, a croquet mallet and an ironing board he had never seen before to one side and without making a noise. At last, he could reach what he wanted without the contents of the cupboard spilling out into the hallway: a battered duffle bag hanging from a bent nail hook. He took it and stepped carefully backwards into the hall, working the draw-strings with both hands to stretch the neck of the bag open.

Plunging his right arm deep into bag, he located two three-inch cartridges, one of which he slipped into the pocket of his dressing gown; the other he put to his lips and clenched the brass base cap between his teeth. Then he drew from the bag a Belgian folding .410 shotgun with a skeletal butt, a remarkably light, single-barrelled weapon which he had been assured was useful for eradicating rats assuming they came within range, moved slowly and were feeling suicidal. Oliver straightened the gun until it clicked into one long piece, pressed the side lever to open the breech and loaded the cartridge he had held between his chattering teeth. He gently closed the breech and thumbed back the hammer. With the gun at port arms, he advanced on the closed door of the study.

He strained to hear anything which might provide a clue as to what was behind the door, pressing the side of his head up against its solid oak panelling. He was instantly rewarded, but in a way he least expected, and it took his brain several seconds to decipher the sound which reached his ears. In any other circumstances, the tumble and click of a key being turned in a lock would have been a perfectly normal, almost comforting sound, unless the ear hearing it belonged to someone in prison. In these circumstances, it was bizarre. The intruder had turned the key from the inside; the burglar was not breaking in but *locking* himself in.

Without thinking, Oliver grabbed the handle and rattled the study door, and was rewarded by a bump and a curse from the other side, followed by a discordant screech which he recognized as coming from the base keys of Hattie the harpsichord as some-body or something fell against them. Oliver's brain registered the sound of his beloved harpsichord and immediately felt a flush of anger that some criminal might be blundering about in the dark damaging it, then came another familiar domestic sound, that of the sash window squeaking in protest – as all the windows in the house did – as it was opened. That meant, Oliver realized furiously, the intruder was standing on his beloved Hattie in order to haul up the sash window. A further two or three seconds passed before it sank into Oliver's brain that this meant the intruder was in the process of escaping.

'Oh, no you don't!' he shouted at the study door then loped towards the front door. As he slammed back the bolts top and bottom and then turned the large iron key in the impressive lock, he heard Lavinia's voice from the upper storey.

'Oliver, are you all right? What's going on down there?'

'Stay upstairs, darling, don't come down.'

Oliver heaved the door open, levelled his gun and stepped out into the cold, inky night. He registered that the sash window of the study was pushed up and fully open and a shadowy figure like a tall, flapping crow was running down the path through the wintry stubble of the rose garden towards the drive and the road beyond.

Oliver brought the shotgun up to his shoulder and let fly, to be rewarded by a distant cry of 'Bloody hell!' but no slowing in the pace of the fugitive. He pressed the side lever to eject the spent cartridge and fumbled in his dressing-gown pocket for a replacement, but before he could reload the lights in the hallway behind him came on, spilling out through the open door, illuminating him as if he were an attacking soldier caught in a searchlight.

'Was that the breakfast gong I heard?' asked a languid voice from inside the house. 'Or are we actually hunting for our breakfast? As we're still months off the grouse season and it's the middle of the night, I can only assume that it will be either bat or owl on the menu. Frankly, I think they're both overrated and I will probably stick to Corn Flakes.'

'Nope,' said the American girl, 'we didn't hear diddly-squat.'

'Sound sleepers, are you?' asked Mr Campion.

'We had help.' The girl smiled broadly at her elderly passenger. It was a beautiful smile, full of perfect teeth, but Mr Campion would have preferred the smiler kept her eyes on the road. 'Not dope or pills, if that's what you're thinking.'

'Nothing was further from my mind,' Campion lied politely.

'We'd been drinking,' the girl said with relish, 'and in this country it's legal! Where I come from you have to be twenty-one to buy booze.'

'And yet you can drive at – what – sixteen? Interesting.'

'Not as interesting as being able to buy beer without some guy demanding ID. That was fun! I think I'm gonna enjoy this vacation.'

Mr Campion pressed his glasses more firmly into his face and wondered if his driver would be insulted if he fastened the seat belt provided. She seemed blissfully unaware of this safety feature so thoughtfully fitted by Volkswagen.

'So where,' he said, to take his mind off the vehicle's increasing speed on the narrow lane running alongside the salty mud banks of the River Bright, 'did all this imbibing take place? No doubt there was carousing as well. Was it the Hythe Inn at Heronhoe, which I am told is the haunt of old sea-dogs and pirates, or the half-timbered, if faded, charms of the King's Head in Sweethearting?'

'Neither,' said his chauffeuse, twisting the steering wheel dramatically. 'Was that what you guys call black ice? We didn't go pub crawling as you limeys would say – hey, you don't mind me calling you limeys, do you?'

'Not at all, Yank,' grinned Campion, 'though by virtue of my great age and the rules of chivalry I feel obliged to call you Miss Aird.'

'Precious.'

'I wouldn't say that, merely good manners.'

'No, you must call me Precious – it's my name: Precious Simcox Aird.'

'How interesting, and you must call me Albert.'

'Like the memorial?'

'Exactly so. In fact, Memorial is my middle name. Now, tell me, Precious, how long have you been an archaeologist?'

'About six months, off and on, with breaks.'

'Breaks? Would those be study breaks, the sort of thing we would call reading week? My son went to Harvard and he was always talking about breaks. I think spring break was his favourite.'

'I've not actually started college yet,' said Precious, flicking back a long blonde fringe which, to Campion's concern, did nothing but obscure her view of the road ahead. 'Pop thought I should take a year out to consider my options, which for my mom means looking around for a husband, but Pop signed me on as a volunteer on a dig in New Mexico on an abandoned Navajo village. There was no way I would find a husband there,' she ended triumphantly.

'I am sure it was good practical experience and your breaks were for more theoretical study, I presume.'

'Heck, no! The breaks were for surfing. I'm a California girl, after all.'

Mr Campion looked suitably impressed.

'You must find England very dull.'

'Little bit, but buying the beer yesterday, that was cool.'

'So our pubs meet with your approval, do they?'

'Ain't been into one yet – hey, maybe you could show me a few – but we found this liquor store in Heronhoe. What do you call them? Off-licences . . . something like that? They had these really big cans of beer, called them Party Sevens, so we took one back to the hall and had a party. I was the most popular person there since I had a church key.'

'I'm sorry, did you say church key?'

'Yeah, an opener. You know, those pointy metal things for punching a hole in the top. Everyone has one in the States for opening cans of soda.'

'Fascinating,' Mr Campion said to himself. 'I can see your fellow diggers would have been impressed. How are you getting on with your team?'

'We haven't had much time to get to know each other but Si and Dave seem OK; not sure about Cat, though. She's not a party girl, at least not on last night's performance, and she says her prayers every night before turning in. I think she must have got religion.'

'But you all get on all right, sleeping together in the Orangery?' Campion asked in his best I'm-not-really-prying voice.

'Oh, sure – boys at one end, gals at the other, all dead respectable; no monkey business going on.' The girl turned and flashed her smile again. 'It's so goddam cold in there at night nobody dares get out of their sleeping bags. So what did we miss last night?'

'Actually it was earlier this morning, about four o'clock.'

'I thought in England four o'clock was teatime; I didn't realize there was a four o'clock *in the morning*.'

Mr Campion laughed out loud. He was definitely warming to this girl.

'So what happened at four a.m.?'

'Oh, something and nothing,' said Campion smoothly. 'Just a bit of a kerfuffle.'

Now it was the girl's turn to laugh, and as she did she beat out a short drum roll with the palms of her hands on the van's steering wheel, somewhat to Mr Campion's concern.

'Kerfuffle. Is that a word?'

'A perfectly good one,' said Campion, 'which I think we borrowed from the Gaelic or perhaps the Irish; it means a minor confusion. Our host, Oliver, was disturbed from his slumbers by some local wildlife which had got in through a downstairs window, so he got out his little rifle – what you would call a "vermin" gun, I suppose.'

'Varmint,' drawled Precious Aird.

'Quite so. Anyway, Oliver took a pot-shot but didn't hit anything.'

'What was it? A fox?'

'No, probably a badger. You have badgers in America? Usually quite harmless chappies though they have a reputation as burglars because of their black-and-white markings, like the traditional burglar's jersey.'

The white-haired man trained his spectacles on the girl's face for a reaction but there was no discernible change in her expression.

'Yeah, we have badgers, but don't you mean raccoons?'

'An animal with similar felonious mimesis thanks to their little masks. We don't have raccoons over here.'

To his consternation, Mr Campion's otherwise charming young driver gave a most unladylike nasal snort of laughter, and for a moment Campion thought the aftershock would swing the Volkswagen over to the American side of the road.

'You talk funny,' giggled Precious as she recovered both her and the VW's composure. 'And I don't get most of it, but I think you could be cool if you weren't a Brit. Is this where we turn?'

Mr Campion gave the road ahead his full attention on the grounds that one of them really ought to.

'No, keep right on into Pontisbright. That road leads down to the river and The Beckoning Lady.'

'Is that a pub we could visit?'

'No, it's not a public house,' said Campion quietly, 'it's a private house, quite a well-known one. I used to know the people who lived there rather well.'

'But not any more?'

'No, sadly, not any more.'

There were clear signs of habitation now, with cottages,

bungalows and the occasional barn to the right of the road and water meadows to the left leading down a slight slope to the river lined with trees which looked stark and faintly menacing in their leafless wintry state.

'This is Pontisbright,' said Campion, assuming the role of navigator. 'We need the first right turn alongside the heath. It should be signposted to a place called Great Kepesake.'

'If there's a Great Kepesake, what's Lousy Kepesake like?'

'Oh, very funny,' said Campion with a smile. 'If I had a guinea for every time I'd heard that, although it is usually a less-polite version, then I would be a very rich man.'

'What's a guinea?' asked the girl with an almost straight face.

'Oh, just drive, woman! Here's the turning – don't forget to indicate. That's it, now straight up here, past the pub – it's called The Gauntlett for future reference, and you'll see the church at the top of the hill.'

'Who is it we're meeting?'

'*I'm* meeting an old friend,' Campion said firmly, 'and while I think you'll be interested in meeting him, we may need to have words in private, so forgive us if we are rude and ignore you for a few moments. Perhaps you could take the opportunity to explore the church. Would you mind awfully?'

'No, sure, I can make myself scarce but it's gonna cost you when you eventually take me to a pub that's open.'

'It's a deal, though I have a feeling that might prove to be an expensive exercise.'

'Is this old friend of yours the priest or the vicar or the *padre* or whatever you call them?' asked the girl, accelerating as the stone-and-flint church tower came into view.

'Oh, no,' said Campion. 'Much better than that. He's a policeman.'

THREE
In a Country Churchyard

Though he had known him for many years, Mr Campion was always slightly surprised how tall Charles Luke was when standing next to him. From any distance at all, the width of his shoulders and the breadth of his chest gave him the appearance of a much shorter stature, a physicality which must be an irritant when purchasing his shirts.

Campion was thinking this as he walked up the path to the church because his friend now seemed even shorter than usual, his rain-coated figure bent over a gravestone. Campion had no need to guess whose grave the policeman was visiting.

As Campion and Precious Aird approached him, Luke drew himself up to his full height and turned to face them as he spoke.

'Traded in your car for something more youthful, have you, Albert?'

Campion's head turned automatically to the road where Precious had parked – rather casually – the lime-green Volkswagen campervan.

'Needs must, Charlie, needs must. Amanda has the Jaguar this week, showing some bigwigs round a factory in Bristol or Birkenhead or somewhere beginning with "B". Didn't think I'd need transport of my own once I was snuggled in at Heronhoe, but then I got your message yesterday and fortunately I was able to thumb a lift with this charming young lady. Allow me: Precious Simcox Aird, this is Commander Charles Luke of New Scotland Yard, though there is absolutely no need for you to curtsy.'

Luke pulled off his trilby and held out a hand for Precious Aird's far daintier one to disappear into. Campion noted that the girl, with her American height and self-confidence, was not in the least intimidated or overawed as the pair locked eyes.

'Sincerely pleased to meech-ya, sir,' announced Precious, showing off her perfect teeth. 'Albert here has told me how you're the top cop in all the land and the Queen's personal bodyguard.'

'I have told you no such thing!'

'My point exactly,' said Precious smugly. 'You've told me nothing and I've driven you halfway across the county.'

'It wasn't halfway,' Campion said quietly. 'It just seemed like it, but you're quite correct, I have been unforgivably rude. Charles is indeed one of our top cops as you so succinctly put it, but despite that he happens to be an old and distinguished friend and we both have fond connections to Pontisbright.'

'I see that now,' the girl said respectfully, pointing a long fore-finger at the gravestone Luke had stepped away from. 'Was Prunella your wife?'

The big policeman seemed to deflate slightly inside his raincoat.

'Briefly,' he said, 'but it's been a while now.'

Campion took a moment to observe the American girl. She had quickly spotted the marble headstone and its unsentimental inscription: Prunella Luke (née Scroop-Dory), Wife and Mother, 1931–1962.

The girl was sharp. 'Mother?' she asked.

'We had a daughter – Hattie.'

'The same pretty name Oliver Bell has given to his harpsichord,' said Campion, 'and the one bright thought in this rather melancholy venue. I'm afraid Charles and I have many – too many – friends and acquaintances in this churchyard.'

'It's a sure sign of old age,' said Luke, 'when you meet at a church for more funerals than weddings.'

'In my case perhaps,' said Campion, 'but you're still a spring chicken, Charlie, and Miss Aird here is hardly out of the eggshell.'

'I'm almost twenty,' pouted Precious, 'which makes me old enough to try one of your English pubs, doesn't it, Mr Policeman?'

'This is something of an *idée fixe* with my young friend, Charles. Perhaps we should drop into The Gauntlett when we're done here. That should cure her.'

Luke grunted in agreement.

'There's still a good half-hour to wait till opening time,' he said without consulting his wristwatch, 'and that's if they're operating on Ipswich licensing hours. From what I remember of the landlord when I first came here, he opened when he felt like it, and that was neither regular nor often.'

'Honesty Bull,' said Campion dreamily. 'That was his name, but that was fifteen years ago. He's probably retired by now.'

'Or he's taken up residence here.' Luke waved an arm indicating the crop of gravestones.

'Hey, look, you guys have catching up to do and I've got my orders about three being a crowd, so I'll get my camera out of the wagon and take a few pictures inside the church to send back to Mom and Pop, show them I'm behaving myself.' Precious pulled on the hood of the padded parka she was wearing. 'At least it'll be warmer inside the church than out here. Nobody told me it would be this cold in England.'

As she strode off, Campion took a pair of leather gloves from his overcoat pockets and pulled them on while Luke jammed his hat back on his head.

'I'm afraid Precious is drastically underestimating the hardiness of the average congregation as well as the ambient temperature in an English country church,' said Campion. 'I hope she keeps her coat on. Shall we take a stroll among the tombstones?'

'Is her name really Precious?'

'Apparently so, and it took me by surprise because stupidly I never checked. Her father kept saying "my precious daughter", or so I thought. Turns out he meant "my daughter, Precious". Not that it matters. She's a lovely girl, knows her own mind, is resourceful and she can do the job.'

'And her job,' said Luke, sounding like the policeman he was, 'is what exactly? Driving you around East Suffolk in that hippy-mobile? Is that your idea of going undercover, Albert?'

'Ah, yes, the campervan – they call them Dormobiles, don't they?' said Campion as if he was observing the VW for the first time. 'Yes, I believe they are quite popular among the young and free-spirited. I certainly wasn't expecting Miss Aird to turn up in it but I'm jolly glad she did. It comes in very useful for transporting my merry band of archaeologists and their tools, and it has a little cooker in there which runs on bottled gas – very handy for making tea.'

'You are not an archaeologist, Albert,' said Luke firmly.

'Never said I was, old chum, just that I have a happy band of them; in my employ, you might say. But then, you're not here for the brass-rubbing, are you?'

Luke plunged his hands deep into his coat pockets as they rounded the corner of the church, which brought them head on into chill wind.

'First place I thought of to meet. I like to call on Prune now and then but it seems we always end up here when we come to Pontisbright.' He nodded towards the far corner of the graveyard. 'We were here when they put Minnie Cassands over there next to old Uncle William Faraday and again when Tonker followed her last year.'

'It was so sad about Minnie,' said Campion, remembering the extrovert owners of The Beckoning Lady. 'Was it really three years ago?'

'Nearer four, and Tonker started to fall apart bit by bit. Minnie's death took him hard, and that surprised a lot of people given that their relationship had been pretty stormy over the years. There were times Tonker drove her to distraction and nobody would have blamed her if she'd planted 'alf a brick in his skull but, by heaven, he missed her badly.'

Campion felt a twinge of compassion for his friend; compassion which he knew must not come across as pity.

'Nobody knows what goes on in a marriage, Charlie, least of all the people in it. They were an odd pair but they were certainly a pair. Minnie left me a painting, you know, a real, genuine Miranda Straw in oils painted on what appeared to be one side of an old tea chest. It was her heart, wasn't it, in the end? I never got a chance to talk to Tonker properly after Minnie went.'

'Heart attack following pneumonia and high blood pressure according to Tonker, but the doctors said cancer. Tonker just couldn't bring himself to say the word.'

'People are strange that way. It has an evil ring to it: say it and you get it is what many folk still think. It got Tonker in the end.'

'Technically what got Tonker were complications following an operation for lung cancer, brought on by him smoking eighty untipped ciggies a day since he was about twelve. He used to boast about it.'

'He could be very stupid at times,' said Campion. 'Still, neither of them were any serious age. And don't look at me like that,

Charlie Luke. They were both younger than me, so I am allowed a morbid moment or two.'

'Feeling your years, are we?' Luke grinned. 'I knew the day would come when you'd be flicking through retirement homes' brochures.'

'Don't be cheeky! I have not yet reached my three-score-and-ten. Well, not quite yet, still a few months to put up with. Anyway, wise old owls like me don't retire; people just stop consulting them.'

They had walked the length of the church, and like well-drilled soldiers they wheeled left around the bell tower perfectly in step. The gravestones were older here, white-pitted by the weather and more than one stone angel leaned at an obtuse angle.

'You once asked me,' said Luke thoughtfully, 'and I think it was here in Pontisbright, if it ever occurred to me that nothing you did in your meanderings among the criminal fraternity could not be done better by the police.'

'I do remember,' said Campion, 'and I remember being rather hurt by the alacrity with which you replied that of course it had.'

'But I qualified that by saying you were a sort of expert – someone people or the police could consult, like a doctor or a pathologist. The question is what exactly your expertise is and who is consulting you over in Heronhoe?'

'Those are very good questions. The first, regarding my magical expertise – well, that has mystified man since the dawn of time and to give it a name would smack of a professionalism I would be most unhappy with, for it would be claiming something under very false pretences. As to your supplementary question – my business in Heronhoe – well, I rather think that is my business and mine alone unless, of course, this is an official interrogation, in which case I demand my full civil rights, the telephone call one is always allowed in American films, several lawyers, a copy of *Teach Yourself Law* for when I fire them and a pint mug of police station tea. Milk and four sugars, unless you have Earl Grey, in which case, just the lemon.'

'Finished?'

'Exhausted but ready to do a bit of trading. You tell me why my little holiday in Heronhoe is of interest to Scotland Yard and I'll spill the beans. Straight up, guv, I'll do meself up like a kipper and slip the bracelets on me wrists meself.'

Luke stopped walking, turned his back to the wind and faced his old friend. The two men, one tall and broad, the other thin and not quite as tall, their coats tightly buttoned and their hats firmly secured, would have appeared a pair of mismatched bookends from a distance.

'You know the expression "don't shoot the messenger"? Of course you do,' said Luke. 'You probably know the Latin for it.'

'I seem to recall it had its origin in Plutarch, or perhaps earlier with Sophocles, and it probably referred to beheading rather than shooting, but I totally understand the sentiment. You have been tasked with delivering bad news and you have my sympathy, but my ears are always open to you, Charlie.'

'Then pin those lug-holes back and pay attention because I don't like playing the second-hand messenger boy.'

'Second hand?'

'The message comes from a highly respected source via Augustus Breeze.'

'Lord Gus? The millionaire property developer and television socialist?'

'The same; and not my favourite person, either,' grunted Luke.

'Can't say I know him,' said Campion, 'though I can see a thread beginning to unravel here because I'm actually staying with Lord G's daughter and her hubby over at Heronhoe Hall. But you implied that the message I promise not to shoot you for delivering came *via* Lord Breeze, so who was he relaying the message from?'

'The big house at the end of The Mall.'

'Oh, dear,' said Mr Campion, 'what have I done now?'

'As far as I know, nothing, and the message is that you should keep it that way.'

Sixty miles away from where the two men faced each other in the lee of a church and shivered in an east wind, Rupert Campion, the son of one of them and adopted godson of the other, and his wife Perdita were taking their clothes off in a room above a wholesale greengrocer's just off the Farringdon Road. Even in their relatively short careers as thespians, it was far from the most unusual rehearsal room they had experienced.

In fact, Rupert was beginning to suspect that their agent, the flamboyant Maxim Berlins, was perhaps not taking their careers seriously, at least not his. He had found Perdita a tiny part as a housemaid in a war-horse of a murder mystery play on a limited run at the Fortune and encouraged her with the prediction that as the theatre was old and damp, a leading cast member was bound to fall ill or trip over a loose fitting and break an ankle, and Perdita, assuming she knew the entire play off by heart, would be able to take on any part. When Perdita had made the point that all the lead parts were male roles, Maxim Berlins had twiddled his brightly coloured silk bow tie (which Rupert was convinced was made out of a tricolour) and told her that could only show her versatility, and versatility was a marketable commodity in show business.

For Rupert, or so he was assured, Maxim had 'pulled out all the stops' and got him an audition at the Victoria Palace for a chorus part in the Black and White Minstrels' Show. Rupert had said, far too quickly, that he could not sing a note, and Maxim had pointed out that on his résumé it distinctly said that he could, and then scowled when Rupert said if everything on an actor's résumé was supposed to be truthful then many would be very short documents. If Rupert was going to be picky about this, Maxim had pronounced, then he must take what was offered or starve, which was the natural lot of the actor, although he was able to offer Rupert four weeks' work as an understudy in the pantomime Dick Whittington at – and here he paused dramatically, then said with a flourish 'the Palladium'.

Perdita had squirmed with excitement and hardly any professional jealousy when Rupert had told her and had asked, breathlessly, if he really was understudying the star of the show, Tommy Steele. Soberly, Rupert had admitted that he was not, as Mr Steele's under-study was a rather talented (and altogether too handsome) young chap called David Essex. Rupert was actually understudying an assistant stage manager who had been whipped into hospital to have his appendix out. Still, Perdita had consoled him, he would now be able to add the Palladium to his résumé and honestly so.

When Mr Berlins had called to say he had a perfect opportunity for both his clients to work together playing a couple in love as the stars of a television programme, it seemed too good to be true; and, therefore, probably was.

Well, yes, Maxim admitted, it was a one-off and not a regular series, but the advantage of that was that it wouldn't take up much time. And no, that didn't mean they were small parts – they were the main parts; in fact, they would be the *only* actors in it, so they were guaranteed top billing. The script? No difficulty or lengthy speeches to learn as there wasn't a script – no dialogue at all. What could be easier? Filming would be done in the country and who could resist working in the beautiful Suffolk countryside? Yes, even in February. And no need to worry about rehearsals – they would be done on location with the director, though there would be a costume fitting in Clerkenwell; tomorrow, actually. Oh, and by the way, did either Rupert or Campion speak Italian?

'Stop staring at my legs!' ordered Perdita, snapping the last dangling suspender strap into place and then using the palms of her hands to twist the stocking into place. 'Are my seams straight?'

'How can I tell without staring at your legs, darling?'

'It doesn't matter anyway,' said Perdita, smoothing down the woollen skirt from where it had been bunched around her waist. 'No one will see them. I don't think I've ever worn a skirt this length below the knee, nor one so tightly nipped in at the waist. Pass me the jacket.'

Rupert held the eel-grey matching jacket open so that his wife could slot her arms into the sleeves and pull it over the high-necked white cotton blouse.

'Well, I think I look quite dapper,' said Rupert, holding the wide shoulders with fingers and thumbs until Perdita pulled the curved lapels together and fastened the three tortoiseshell buttons. She turned to face her husband and gave him a quick once-over; a far swifter survey than he had given her.

'Very smart, dear, but a bit old fashioned. Still, that's the point, isn't it? Is it heavy? It looks heavy.'

Rupert took a pace back and did a dancer's turn on toe and heel.

'Brown herringbone tweed would not have been my natural choice – the trousers flap about a bit and the turn-ups are deep enough to carry a packed lunch – but it has a certain style and at least it will be warm out there on set. I wonder how they got my measurements so quickly.'

'And our shoe sizes. These fit perfectly.' Perdita hitched her skirt an inch or two higher up her calves, though the hem line was

still almost a foot below current fashion in order to admire the
two-tone lace-up Oxfords with Spanish heels.

The shoes – brown brogues for Rupert – had been in plain
shoeboxes, wrapped in tissue paper at the foot of a metal coat
rack, one of the long, wheeled ones found in department stores
and dry cleaners'. This one had only two wooden coat hangers,
one holding the eel-grey woollen skirt and jacket and the other
the three-piece suit hung over a laundered white shirt and tie of
unidentified regimental origin. On arrival, the Campions had found
the room empty apart from the rack, a full-length mirror on a
beech-wood frame and a single chair, on which lay a white
suspender belt and the tan-coloured stockings in a packet which
was branded *Ballito – they wear so well!*, Rupert had held it aloft
and commented, 'Advertising doesn't lie for once.'

There were no instructions, other than the cursory ones they
had received from Maxim Berlins, which had basically consisted
of an address, a time and the need to identify themselves as 'here
for the fitting'. This they had done, but were unsure that the rather
grizzled old man in a brown smock and flat cap smoking a half-
inch of Woodbine who had shown them through the greengrocers'
stores to a staircase leading to the upstairs room had understood
English. He had certainly made no attempt to speak it, but he
grunted quite fluently.

The Campions were not unduly perturbed as *Monsieur* Berlins
had in the past dispatched them to auditions and costume fittings
in deconsecrated churches, church halls, youth clubs, a bomb
shelter, saloon bars during afternoon closing and, on one memo-
rable occasion, a bingo hall while a tense, high-stakes game was
still in progress.

They posed side by side in front of the standing mirror.

'Don't we look a couple of swells, Miss Browning,' said Rupert,
using his wife's maiden and stage name. He formed a D with his
right arm, fist on hip, and Perdita slipped her left arm through it,
though not before leaning across to straighten her husband's tie.

'I agree. We look the part – we just don't know what the part
is. We don't even know who provided these clothes.'

'Morris Angel, of course, costumier to the stars of stage and
screen!'

The Campions swung round to follow the voice that had taken

them by surprise. Mounting the last few steps of the open staircase leading to the shop below with the stealth and precision of a cat was a woman perhaps ten years older than either Campion but the only one dressed in the latest fashion. Her long blonde hair was scraped back from her face and tied in a long ponytail which hung down over a black leather overcoat. The coat was unbuttoned and swept back almost like a cape by virtue of the woman clasping her hands behind her back.

She stepped up the last stair and into the room, planted her feet apart and looked the Campions, who instinctively moved slightly closer together, up and down and then leaned to one side to view their reflection in the mirror. She wore knee-high boots with stiletto heels – how had she climbed the stairs so quietly in them? Perdita wondered – shiny black tights and pink velvet hot pants with bib and braces over a tight white cashmere sweater.

Perdita jerked at Rupert's arm and murmured, 'Close your mouth, dear, you're drooling.' Then she smiled sweetly at their visitor.

'Good morning, I'm Perdita Browning . . .'

'No, you are not,' said the woman with a lilt of an Italian accent. 'You are Mrs Simpson and this handsome chap is His Majesty the King.'

It had not taken Precious Aird very long to realize that the freezing gloom of a nineteenth-century Suffolk church – she had never been in a building colder on the inside than outside without the intervention of air conditioning – was not her 'thing'. She had taken photographs of a dull stained-glass window, an unremarkable pulpit and a plain but moving commemorative memorial to the dozen or so villagers, seemingly drawn from only two families, who had fallen in 'The Great War 1914–1918' by which she assumed they meant the conflict of 1917–18, but perhaps she would ask Mr Campion about that.

He was a curious old bird that Campion, unlike anyone she had ever met. Perhaps there was no American equivalent of a Campion – well, maybe there was something like him among the Boston Brahmins, but she had never met one of them.

Having forsaken the church, she took shelter from the wind in the oak-framed porch from where she observed the two men who now seemed to be wandering aimlessly among the gravestones, deep in conversation. Campion's friend was quite something too – a big man who could move powerfully fast; probably something of a hunk in his younger days. Certainly not what Precious had expected of an English 'bobby' but then she had not expected to be introduced to one. In fact, she had promised herself that she would not do what most American tourists did as soon as they deplaned, which was to rush up to the nearest uniformed policeman and ask, 'Gee, is it true you don't carry guns?'

This friend of the old man's, Luke something-or-other, looked as if he could handle himself without recourse to firearms. He was worth a photograph and she raised the camera hanging round her neck and surreptitiously snapped the two men deep in conversation across a gravestone.

She would send that one to her mother to prove, despite her dire warnings about Teddy Boys and Mods and Rockers, that all the males in England were old enough to be her father or grand-father and hung around in churchyards.

No wonder they were interested in archaeology.

'It was thirty-five years ago,' said Campion. 'There wasn't any "Heronhoe Horde" or treasure then and there isn't now.'

'So where did the stories come from?' asked Luke.

'Where they always come from, the four-ale bars and the snugs of all the pubs within a fifty-mile radius after too many pints of Bullard's Mild.'

'So what were you doing sniffing around?'

Campion pulled off his gloves and thrust them into his coat pockets, then produced a large white handkerchief from his trou-sers, carefully removed his spectacles and began to polish them. Luke knew Campion's habits of old and recognized this one as a ploy to gain time in order to give a considered answer.

'I would hardly call an amateur academic interest in what could have been an important archaeological find "sniffing around". Ship burials don't come round like buses, you know. There had been one found up at Snape back in the last century – 1862, I think – which yielded a ring and a glass beaker; no doubt the local soaks in Snape and Aldeburgh called that a treasure trove back then but it was still an event of national interest. Not as much, I admit, as the Sutton

Hoo find just before the war, and if I'm being truthful the Heronhoe excavation was a bit of a damp squib when it came to antiquities and a dead loss if you were a treasure hunter.'

'But you still made the effort to come down here, didn't you?'

'Couldn't resist, not with it being on the doorstep of Pontisbright, so to speak, which was always Lugg's favourite place on earth, so there was no trouble getting him into the car like an enthusiastic Labrador, and I was on nodding terms with the Mad Major, as we used to call him.'

'And he would be . . .?'

'Actually not a major at all, more a captain really but he did love riding horses, quite dangerously as I remember, and betting on them equally badly, so the nickname seemed to fit. Better known as Captain Gerald Wemyss-Grendle, the owner of Heronhoe Hall at the time and last of the line of Wemyss and Grendle, the chap who sold the place to Lord Breeze and who is probably living in Switzerland on the proceeds.'

'Frinton,' said Luke. 'I checked. There were just enough proceeds to pay off his bookies.'

'Ah,' sighed Campion. 'That doesn't surprise me, but Gerry was our host that week – the week I suppose you're interested in.'

'Which week would that be?' asked the policeman rather than the friend.

Mr Campion faced Luke, expressionless. 'The week in 1935 when the boat burial at Heronhoe got a visit from HRH you-know-who and his retinue, which is what I suspect this third degree is all about.'

'Third degree? We're nowhere near one-and-a-half degrees yet. Were you and Lugg in the prince's retinue?'

'Not really; we were a sort of advance guard, checking the place out, doing a bit of reconnaissance. The Mad Major, as his name implies, wasn't the most reliable of chaps and I was there to vet the other visitors. Lugg was there to chuck out any journalists or photographers.'

'Of course,' Luke said, nodding to himself, 'the great unwashed public knew nothing of the king and Mrs Simpson, did they?'

'David wasn't king at that point and the British public were pretty much in the dark, though in other countries their relationship was well known.'

'And your job was to keep it that way?'

'As I said, I was merely the reconnaissance party, Charlie the advance guard. There's always one for a private royal visit, whatever the occasion. I knew the area and I happened to know Gerald Wemyss-Grendle and when it was time to hide the gin bottle. Being the loyal and trustworthy sort of chap I am, I was volunteered.'

'So what happened?'

'Nothing,' said Campion firmly. 'Lugg and I arrived a day or two in advance, had a talk with the archaeologists on the site, checked the surrounding bushes for booby traps and liaised with the local constabulary who seemed to have everything well in hand. The prince and his valets and bodyguards turned up and we had a decent dinner at the hall. Next morning, bright and early, Lugg and I were on our way back to London.'

'Done your job, had you?'

'We were dismissed . . . surplus to requirements. David knew his way around Heronhoe; he'd stayed at the hall several times before. He and the Mad Major shared a love of point-to-pointing, it seems, and they wanted to get some riding in while he was there. Wemyss-Grendle used to have a well-stocked stable in those days.'

'So did you see Mrs Simpson?'

'No.' Campion shook his head. 'Not then and I only heard she'd been there later. I find it difficult to imagine her being a guest of the Mad Major at the hall.'

'Wemyss-Grendle didn't approve of divorcees?'

'Gerry certainly didn't approve of marriage but he had pretty liberal views about married women, if you get my drift, and I wouldn't have thought he had any prejudices against divorcees. One got the impression that no woman was completely safe when under the same roof as the Mad Major.'

'So nothing untoward happened back in 'thirty-five when the royal personage visited the Heronhoe boat excavation?'

'Not that I'm aware of, old chum,' said Campion, brightening. 'No shenanigans, no lurid stories in the press and absolutely no treasure found, lost or stolen.'

Luke planted his feet apart and, with a forefinger under the brim, pushed his hat to the back of his head.

'Then, *old chum*, can I ask just what the hell you're doing in Heronhoe now?'

Campion's face slipped into an expression which a stranger might have mistaken for genuine shock and outrage.

'Didn't I tell you, Charlie? I'm a film producer.'

FOUR
Boat Burial

When Lord Breeze purchased Heronhoe Hall and Park from the impecunious Captain Wemyss-Grendle, he had little knowledge of the history of the house. He was aware, thanks to the land agent's prospectus, that John Constable had been asked to paint the hall in 1816 but the then owners had baulked at the 100 guineas' fee he had demanded and, as a consequence, the artist had taken his brushes and easels down the road into Essex and painted Wivenhoe House near Colchester for the Rebow family. Lord Breeze openly admitted that he knew little about art, but he recognized a failed investment opportunity when he saw one.

Until he attempted to get planning permission for some – preferably all – of the associated parkland, Breeze was also totally ignorant of the boat burial which had been found by local antiquarians in 1934 at the very western edge of the estate where it bordered the village of Sweethearting.

At the time of the discovery of 'a Barrow of archaeological interest', the then owner, Gerald Wemyss-Grendle, expressed an active disinterest in the find when it was reported to him by the vicars of both Heronhoe and Sweethearting, two well-meaning gentlemen who shared an interest in the topography and history of the east coast. On the day this clerical delegation had called at the hall to impart the news, it so happened that the captain had many other things to occupy his mind which was, by common consent, not one of the largest in Christendom. He had just added a new four-year-old to his small stable of horses and was keen to get into the saddle; there was a new housemaid to 'break in' to the routines of the hall and he was expecting a delivery of port and claret from his new wine merchant in Ipswich while simultaneously devising ways of avoiding the final demand which his previous wine merchant in Hadleigh was attempting to deliver. As a consequence, and with hardly any thought at all, he waved the reverend gentlemen away with a barked instruction that they could do what the blazes they liked as long as the smooth workings of the estate – raised eyebrows and knowing looks on the faces of the two vicars at that! – were not disrupted.

Archaeology in the Thirties was still seen, despite the efforts of Mortimer Wheeler, as a pursuit followed by the gifted amateur with physical support from the labouring classes when it came to moving earth. The problem with the dig at Heronhoe was that it rapidly became a contest between the two vicars who, while friends and allies in theology and religious practices, rapidly became rivals once out in the field. First there was disagreement over whether their find was a tumulus or a barrow and, as the parish boundaries had never been exact, whether it should be called the Sweethearting Barrow/Tumulus or the Heronhoe Tumulus/Barrow. Then there was a long debate about the best way to dig into the Barrow. Under a cloud of well-mannered acrimony, the dig proceeded thanks to the muscle power of parishioners from both churches, with the vicar of Sweethearting claiming the moral high ground by supplying a tea urn and scones for the diggers courtesy of the Mothers' Union. When the Barrow had been excavated from two sides (to keep the warring vicars apart) and it became clear that what had been buried there was a boat, further energy was expended on whether to call it the Sweethearting Boat or the Bright River Boat, on the assumption that it had got where it had by travelling along the nearby river.

That particular debate was firmly concluded by Captain Wemyss-Grendle on his first visit to the site, which he had totally forgotten about until he noticed two of his part-time gardeners carrying spades and hoes walking along the river's edge while out riding one day. On being told he had a site of some interest on his lands, he immediately proclaimed it to be henceforth known as the Heronhoe Boat and, should any treasure or grave goods be found in there, they were naturally the property of the owners of Heronhoe Hall.

Little of interest, and nothing of value, was found that summer, the dig starting late because of the unseasonal snowfalls in May – 'hardly even a boat' as one local wag observed to a local newspaper reporter. The acidic soil had consumed the timbers of a boat approximately twenty feet in length with a beam of six feet (the two vicars recorded wildly differing measurements in their reports), leaving only an outline in the sand and clay. If there had been a body in the boat when it was buried, it too had dissolved and the only artefacts the rival teams of diggers managed to harvest were a few rusted iron nails or rivets, some fragments of broken pottery, a bent and rusted knife blade and some fragments of *briquetage* suggesting that the boat or its owner had something to do with the salt trade, a perfectly logical assumption given the importance of that industry and the proximity of the saltmarsh estuary.

A disgruntled Captain Wemyss-Grendle was heard to mutter that he could not understand why the Vikings had gone to the trouble of burying a boat with nothing valuable on board. His mood was not lightened by being told (by both vicars, agreeing on something at last) that it was not a Viking boat but undoubtedly a much earlier, possibly sixth-century vessel built and sailed by Angles in the process, historically speaking, of becoming the English.

All-in-all, Gerald Wemyss-Grendle found the whole thing uninspiring and there was not even the opportunity to charge a penny admission to visitors, partly because there was nothing much to see but mainly because most of the population of Sweethearting and a sizeable proportion of that of Heronhoe had already been there to look and be disappointed for free. The owner of Heronhoe Hall was only grateful for the fact that the site was at the furthest reaches of his land and could not be seen from the hall. If it had any use, it might be as a snippet of small talk to impress his friends in London on a quiet evening in one of the few clubs where his credit was still welcome.

Which is exactly what happened.

'It turns out,' said Oliver Grieg Bell, 'that old Wemyss-Grendle moaning about "bloody archaeologists" and "meddlesome vicars" came to the attention of King Edward – or should I call him the Duke of Windsor?'

'He was not yet king,' said Mr Campion, 'but the Prince of Wales, and known as David.'

'Why wasn't he called King David, then?' asked Precious Aird innocently.

'It's the English tradition of regnal names, something you rebellious colonials long since gave up bothering about.' Campion smiled. 'Edward was one of the prince's names and I think it was his mother who chose that one as his regnal moniker. His brother, who became George VI after the Abdication, was actually Albert Frederick Arthur George, but everyone knew him as Bertie. Well, perhaps not everybody. I'm sorry, Oliver, pray continue.'

Their host continued to saw thick slices from a loaf of wholemeal bread the size of a draught excluder and pass them clockwise around the table as his wife Lavinia circulated in the opposite direction with a large china tureen balanced on her hip, from which she was ladling out chicken and potato soup the colour and consistency of wallpaper paste.

'From my researches and the local folklore,' said Oliver, 'it seems that the prince was interested in the Sweethearting Boat even if Wemyss-Grendle wasn't. Of course, back then it was called the Heronhoe Boat, but since Lavinia's father sold off half the park, including the site, to the farmer at Windy Ridge, it's no longer on Heronhoe Hall land, and anyway, it was always much closer to Sweethearting than Heronhoe.'

'So the dig site is not actually on your land?' asked Precious, tearing a slice of bread into more manageable chunks.

'Technically, the land now belongs to the farmer, Thomas Spark, but he hasn't cleared the trees or anything, he's kept the area around the Barrow pretty much as it was and doesn't mind the locals walking their dogs there.'

'Has Farmer Spark not been tempted to go treasure hunting on the site?' said Campion, his spoon hovering twixt bowl and lip.

'Thomas Spark's father, sadly no longer with us, was one of the volunteer diggers organized by the vicar of Sweethearting and Thomas swears blind his father never found a thing of value there except for some bits of pottery which the museum in Ipswich got excited about but nobody else did. He said the most interesting thing about the original excavation – the only interesting thing – was the visit of the prince and Mrs Simpson.'

'So he was an eyewitness,' murmured Campion.

'According to Spark family tradition, he was, and he knew them well enough from previous visits. Of course, everyone was sworn to secrecy, or at least discretion, as the visit was very unofficial, and of course Wemyss-Grendle as lord of the manor would have laid down the law on that as he and the prince were great pals when it came to point-to-pointing.'

'Came to what?' spluttered Precious Aird through a mist of breadcrumbs.

'A sort of horse racing for amateurs,' said Campion, grateful for an excuse to lay down his spoon. 'You'd probably call it steeple-chasing, but I am no student of the turf. And neither, as I remember, was Gerald Wemyss-Grendle, or at least not a very good one. Do we know if he is the only surviving eyewitness to that visit back in 'thirty-five?'

'Apart from yourself, Albert,' said Lavinia, threatening to reach for the tureen. 'More soup? There's only more bread and some mousetrap cheddar for dessert, though I've got jam . . . but no butter.'

'Not for me, thank you,' Campion said quickly, 'and I was not here when the prince was; I was merely the advance party. In fact, I was the advance party *for* the advance party, making sure the rooms were aired, the bedsheets not damp and there were enough fish forks to go round, that sort of thing.'

'Then you may well be right about Wemyss-Grendle,' Oliver agreed, 'as he was their host after all, though he wasn't forthcoming on the subject.'

'You've spoken to him? I'm told he's still in the land of the living, or at least in Frinton. I mean, he can't be *that* old.'

'Seventy-seven, something like that, but he hasn't grown old gracefully.'

Precious Aird's lips formed a perfect O and allowed an almost silent whistle to escape. Mr Campion did his best to furrow a brow in her direction.

'Why, that's no age at all, but as I recall the Mad Major never did anything gracefully.'

'You limeys! There you go again!' exclaimed Precious. 'You can't decide on a name for your archaeological find, you have kings called David and Albert but you call them Edward and

George, and now you have this Captain Gerald guy and suddenly he's a major. Who promoted him?'

'I suppose we must be very confusing for the foreigner,' Campion said cheerfully, 'which is why I'm here.'

'It is?'

'Of course. Not so much for your benefit, Precious, but to advise the film crew who will be descending upon us tomorrow. You see, they're Italians – and what do Italians know about archaeology?'

'Film crew? Tomorrow? But we've only just scratched the surface of the site,' wailed Precious Aird. 'Literally, my diggers are still clearing the underbrush and I really should get over there to help out, having had my morning disturbed by playing chauffeur for certain persons.'

Mr Campion studied his soup bowl, suitably shamefaced.

'We all had a disturbed morning, one way or another,' Lavinia observed through tight lips.

'Pity you weren't here, Albert,' said her husband. 'I called the police station in Heronhoe to report the break-in and they sent one of their finest in a smart new Panda car. He made a few squiggles in a notebook, though he didn't actually appear to know which was the business end of his pencil, and said it was probably a local tearaway or a biker boy. We do have them in Heronhoe, you know, but I couldn't give him a decent description. The bobby said it was a pity I hadn't used a twelve-bore instead of my little .410. That way there might have been a blood trail to follow.'

'Hmmm . . .' Campion mused. 'I'm not sure I approve of that advice. However, I have, purely by chance, been told by an old friend that, should there be any further incidents, the man to talk to is Inspector Robert Chamley of Suffolk CID.'

Campion and Precious exchanged meaningful glances across the dining-room table – the sort of glances which signalled that all there was to say about Mr Campion's friend had been said.

'This film crew of yours,' said Lavinia, eyeing Campion carefully, 'we're not expected to feed and house them as well, are we? Precious and her three diggers are of course very welcome to camp in the Orangery. That was agreed at the start, but we weren't expecting . . .'

Mr Campion put down his spoon as if lowering a dumbbell.

'My dear child, worry ye not. My film people do not have any Hollywood airs or graces about them and they have found suitable digs in Heronhoe. There are only three of them – a cameraman, a soundman and a director, and they have their own transport, which could be useful until my wife allows me the use of my car again.'

'I don't mind driving you around in the VW microbus,' said Precious, 'that is, if you don't mind being seen riding in it.'

'Not at all,' said Campion. 'It seems to be the perfect vehicle for transporting the diggers to and from the site and, as for myself, I rather like the idea of being mistaken for an ageing hippy.'

'I'm sorry we don't have a car to put at your disposal, Albert, but the running costs are beyond us at the moment. Lavinia and I get around on bicycles in the summer . . .'

'And in the winter months we simply don't go anywhere,' Lavinia said with a grimace, 'except to the shops.'

'That reminds me,' said Mr Campion, rising from the table. 'May I borrow your telephone?'

'Of course, it's in the study.'

'If it's still connected,' said Lavinia, adding a weary postscript to her husband's offer.

'What I meant to say,' said a blushing Oliver, 'was that it was a good thing you thought of hiring that VW for Precious and her gang, otherwise they would have had a torrid time pushing wheelbarrows and their shovels and things over to Sweethearting and back every day.'

'Oh, I didn't hire it,' said Campion, walking out of the room, 'Precious' father had the foresight to buy it for her. Not sure how he did it but it was waiting for her, properly taxed and insured, keys in the ignition at Heathrow the moment she stepped off the Jumbo last month. He was really very generous when it came to kitting out his daughter. Those rather unflattering boots she wears are the latest issue for US airborne forces, I'm told, though I had no idea they did them in small sizes for such dainty feet. Very intelligently, she wore them on the flight over rather than attempt to pack them in her suitcase. Now please excuse me for a moment; shan't be a tick.'

There was a moment of heavy quiet in the dining room after Campion had made his exit. Precious Aird could tell from the way

Oliver and Lavinia were staring at her that something she had done had brought down the embarrassed silence which lay across the dining table like a fog. She tried a weak smile while frantically thinking of something to say that did not involve her shoe size, but Lavinia saved her.

'You came over on the Jumbo Jet?' she said with awe.

'Yeah, that's right,' Precious breathed again, 'it was the first one to land in London. Caused quite a stir, I understand.'

'It was on the news,' said an enthusiastic Oliver. 'What was it like?'

'The flight? Oh, kinda long because there were delays in New York before we took off. Sure were a lot of people on board.'

'Was it expensive?' Oliver asked and then winced under his wife's warning glance.

'I honestly don't know,' answered Precious, listlessly stirring her cold soup with her spoon. 'Pop fixed it all up for me. He's kinda rich and knows people in the airline business, people like Al's wife.'

'Al?'

'Albert – Mr Campion. His wife Amanda and my father are on the boards of some of the same companies. I guess that's how Albert got to hear about my interest in archaeology and thought of me when this project came up. Pop stumped up for the plane ticket, topped up my allowance in your pounds sterling rather than dollars and bought me the VW with strict instructions to remember to drive on the left and to ask for petrol rather than gas at a filling station.'

Anxious to change the subject from the generosity of fathers, Lavinia asked, 'So where did you qualify, Precious?'

'Gee, I'm not qualified, leastways not in archaeology.' She winked at Oliver in a most unseemly way, thought his wife. 'I spent last summer in Navajo territory in New Mexico helping out on some *hogans* – the mud huts the Indians lived in – or what was left of them. It was completely different to what you do over here. I mean, trowels and spades and *mattocks*, whatever they are . . . Out in the desert all we had to do was a bit of dusting with a paint brush.' She smiled at the Bells, showing off her perfect American teeth. 'This "digging" everyone talks about sounds like real hard work.'

'I'm sure the boys will do all the heavy lifting,' said Lavinia. 'Simon and David are from good local farming stock and used to working outdoors, and Catherine—'

'She prefers to be called Cat.'

'Catherine,' Lavinia continued, uncorrected, 'is a studious girl who has hopes of going to university and thinks this will look good on her application. I'm sure she'll pull her weight. Are you all settled in in the Orangery?'

'There was one thing,' Precious hesitated, 'and I guess it's up to me to tell you as I seem to be in charge of the hired hands.'

'We haven't hired them,' said Lavinia quickly. Then she glanced at Oliver. 'Have we?'

Her husband coughed nervously.

'I believe Albert is paying them a small stipend. Pocket money, if you like, just as he's making a small donation to our running costs. So what's the problem, Precious? Are they going on strike for a pay rise?'

'No, it's not that, it's just all three of them are locals – they have families in Heronhoe.'

'Yes, we know that – we know their parents.'

'Well, thing is all three of them are thinking of staying at home and just coming here during the day, to dig. The say it's warmer at home and the food's better.'

'Well, really!' breathed Lavinia. 'You'll have to tell Albert and hope it doesn't spoil his plans.'

'I hear my name taken in vain,' said Mr Campion, re-entering the room, 'which is always a good sign as it is so tiresome to be forgotten so quickly, but now I'm back, so please continue talking about me. Oh, and Oliver, thank you for the use of the telephone, and Lavinia, would you be so good as to be here tomorrow morning, probably just before noon. I've taken the liberty of ordering in a few hampers of iron rations to keep us going for a few days.'

'Rations?'

'Just a few basics to help out feeding the workers, stock the larder, that sort of thing.'

'And they're being delivered here?' Lavinia looked as if she was waiting for a translation rather than an answer.

'Oh, yes,' said Mr Campion. 'Harrods are very good that way.'

* * *

At least Rupert had stopped drooling, thought Perdita, although he was still breathing through his mouth and had not taken his eyes off the striking blonde woman. He was acting the village yokel seeing a horseless carriage for the first time, or the schoolboy caught smoking behind the Fives Courts, or at least she hoped he was acting.

The woman who stood before them – auditioning them, inspecting them? – was certainly impressive in every sense of the word. She impressed herself on the younger couple, her presence dominating the shabby room just as she would, no doubt, dominate a cocktail party in a Venetian palazzo or, come to think of it, a stage. But that was Perdita's home ground.

'I do not believe,' she said with crystal clarity, holding out her right hand, palm downwards, as if expecting it to be kissed, 'that we have been formally introduced, *Signora*. My name is Perdita Browning.'

'So you have already said, and this most handsome young man must be Rupert Campion.' She shook rather than kissed the proffered hand but her eyes and her smile never left Rupert, whose name she positively purred as 'Rooopert'.

She took a step to her left so that she was directly in front of 'Rooopert', far closer than was necessary as far as Perdita was concerned, but at least the woman resisted the temptation to click her booted heels in salute even if her bosom was standing to attention.

'You are the son of a lady,' said the woman, tilting her head to one side as if to get a better view of Rupert's face.

'Aren't we all?' said Rupert with a nervous smile, though not, his wife thought, quite nervous enough.

'I mean a lady with a title, of course. Lady Amanda, yes? I, too, where I come from, have a title. I am Donna Daniela Petraglia.'

'Are you from the costumiers?' Rupert blurted and Perdita glowed with loyalty and pride and just a twinge of jealousy that she hadn't thought of that first.

Donna Daniela, already as tall as Rupert in those heels, drew herself higher, as if a rope travelling up her spine and through the top of her head was being pulled taut.

'I,' she said breathily, 'am your film director.'

'I love Italian cinema,' said Rupert.

You little liar! Perdita glared at her husband, who seemed not to notice.

'I am a great fan of the films of Fellini, Rosellini and Pasolini . . .'

Rubbish! You had trouble following A Fistful of Dollars.

'Have you worked with any of them?'

The blonde woman turned her head slowly as if easing an ache or strain in her neck.

'I did work for Mario Bava once but now I do more serious work: documentaries for television.'

Donna Daniela planted her fists on her hips and bent forward even closer to inspect Rupert's face from the left and then the right. The only sound in the room was the creaking of her long black leather coat, which Perdita was later to say she could hear over the thunder of her husband's breathing.

'Yes,' said the woman firmly, 'you will do perfectly.'

'We come as a pair,' said Perdita.

The woman reached out her right hand and gently cupped Perdita's chin, angling it so she could study her profile.

'And you will do too,' she murmured, 'with make-up and a benign camera.' She released Perdita's chin and clapped her hands, applauding them.

'*Si, si, perfetto!* Now get changed and please do not spoil or stain the clothes and do not wear them again until we are on location. You have a car? You can drive to this 'Eronhoe?'

'Yes, we have our own transport,' said Rupert, 'but no one has said anything about where we will be housed.'

'Housed?'

Donna Daniela leaned her face in towards Rupert's with the curiosity of a cat wondering why the mouse it had been tormenting had suddenly stopped wanting to play.

'Accommodation,' squeaked Rupert. 'Where will we be staying?'

'There will be no need for hotels. You will drive up from London on the days you are required, and that depends on the natural light and the weather. It is not the best time of the year, so we are in the hands of the gods.'

'Do we get petrol money?' sniped Perdita.

'Petrol?'

'Travelling expenses.'

'Ah, yes. I mean, no. Your agent, *Signor* Berlins, said that would not be necessary as television would be good exposure for your careers.'

'But we do get paid, right?'

'Of course. *Signor* Berlins was quite insistent about that. You will get the agreed union rate for the days when you are filmed.'

'And when will filming start?' Rupert intervened before his wife could ask a more sensitive question.

'In perhaps two or three days' time.'

'And we will be required for how many days?'

'One day, if the sun shines. But in this country . . .' she shrugged her shoulders, her leather coat creaking in protest, '. . . we have allowed for two.'

'When do we see the script?' Perdita asked professionally.

'Script? There is no script. I am the director. I will tell you where to stand. You are actors. You will act.'

Mr Campion had not meant to give a lecture, not even a pep talk. He did, however, feel obliged to give his digging team something of a background brief and, as he had arrived at the Sweethearting Barrow, as he preferred to call it, armed with Thermos flasks of hot, sweet tea and packets of chocolate biscuits, his diggers were more than happy to take a break from their labours.

Precious and her three young assistants – Simon, known as Si, Dave and Catherine, or Cat, rather – had all cheerfully downed tools and crouched in a circle in the bracken and sparse grasses around Campion on the top of the Barrow. Having borrowed an ancient and slightly pungent duffle coat and a pair of Wellington boots from Oliver Bell at the hall, Mr Campion had no illusion that he was delivering the Sermon on the Mount despite the attentiveness of his audience. He was realistic enough to appreciate that these days young people would prefer any brief distraction to the thankless task of chopping and hacking back the undergrowth covering a bump of earth in the corner of a windswept Suffolk field, even if it included an address by (in their eyes) an ancient schoolmasterly type. The tea and biscuits did help, though.

So Campion told them the story of the Sweethearting Barrow which had given rise to the legend of the Heronhoe Horde, which was, of course, pure fantasy, probably created in the wake of the discovery of the much more famous Sutton Hoo ship burial in 1939. Now *that* was a horde of archaeological treasures to be sure, as it had clearly been a royal boat burial, arguably the rather elaborate grave of a king – the king of the East Angles, from which was derived East Anglia and, in the final analysis, the English. There had been no body in the burial chamber constructed in the Sutton Hoo ship – as that had dissolved into the sandy soil, and there had been no convenient sign or inscription stating who it was who 'lies here'; the identity of the noble deceased had been a matter of some controversy, though the hot favourite was always the seventh-century Angle king called Raedwald.

Mr Campion could not resist embellishing his narrative with the story of how an elderly professor of Old English from Cambridge had stamped his authority on the identification. Although, now he thought about it, Professor Hector Munro Chadwick of Clare College had been almost exactly the same age in 1939 as Campion himself was now. But the story went that once he heard of the Sutton Hoo discovery, he ordered his wife to get the car and they set off from Cambridge making steady but stately progress at twenty mph, a speed which Professor Chadwick (a non-driver and nervous passenger) firmly insisted his wife did not exceed. Arriving, eventually, at the Sutton Hoo dig site, the professor alighted from his car once he had ascertained that his wife had applied all the brakes and surveyed the scene of activity, drawing quite a crowd as several of the diggers were from Cambridge and recognized him. They waited for him to introduce himself or announce the purpose of his visit. Instead, the professor simply declared 'Raedwald!' in a loud, imperious tone. Just the one word, then he tipped his hat at the crowd, got back in the car and instructed his wife to drive back to Cambridge at twenty miles per hour. From that magic moment, the body in the Sutton Hoo ship burial, even though there wasn't actually a body, was identified as Raedwald, King of the East Angles.

Realizing that his anecdotes about ancient professors of Old English on low-speed archaeological missions across East Anglia over thirty years ago were not exactly entrancing his young audience, Campion decided to tempt them with treasure, for unlike the Sweethearting Boat, the Sutton Hoo ship had carried plenty. In fact, it had been stuffed to the gunnels if, that is, seventh-century

Anglo-Saxon ships had gunnels. The grave goods found in that royal ship burial had come from far and wide: a sturdy shield boss from Sweden, a sword and drinking horns from Germany, a cauldron from Byzantium, silver bowls and spoons, intricate gold buckles and Merovingian gold coins. Most famous of all, of course, was the warrior's helmet, that fearsome metal mask which had become even more famous when it had been used on the cover of the Penguin paperback edition of *Beowulf.*

At this point, Mr Campion noticed that the circle of young faces around him had started to glaze over and he made one last attempt to rekindle their enthusiasm. The dramatic finds at Sutton Hoo, he told them, had been made on the very eve of the outbreak of the Second World War and the treasure trove, which had been rushed to the British Museum for safety, was almost immediately hidden away in a disused London Underground tunnel, where it stayed for the duration. At least there it was not damaged by the war, unlike the site itself, which, as with much of east coast, found itself on the frontline.

At last, there was a question from the pupils of this impromptu tutorial.

'I'm American,' said Precious Aird, 'and therefore have no knowledge of geography, but how do you reckon the Suffolk coast to be "on the frontline"?'

Campion straightened his back and raised his right arm to the horizontal, pointing, he was fairly confident, due east. 'My dear girl,' he said, 'back in 1940, when Britain stood alone against the Nazi hordes – you chaps in America took a bit of persuading to come to our aid, I seem to remember – this part of the coast, from Heronhoe down to the Blackwater in Essex really was the frontline because over there, across the North Sea, was Holland. In fact, Holland's still there, but back then it was occupied by the enemy and the enemy had lots of aeroplanes and airborne troops in gliders, or so we thought they did. The water meadows and saltings around the estuaries of south Suffolk and north Essex were flat and soft and perfect as landing grounds for invading troops. People were so worried that the Ministry of Something-or-other ordered an anti-glider ditch dug across the Sutton Hoo site in a rather bizarre and brutal example of reverse archaeology, digging a trench with a bulldozer to protect a trench carefully dug by hand to uncover a grave dug twelve hundred years before by Angles, who we would, of course, call Germans today.'

'But they didn't bother digging an anti-Nazi trench here, did they?' observed Precious. 'Pity; might have saved us a job re-excavating it.'

'Oh, don't worry, you don't actually have to excavate anything,' said Campion, grinning broadly. 'Well, not properly. You just need to clear the ground, rake up a bit of soil and make it look as if you're excavating – for the film cameras. And, by the way, they didn't put in an anti-glider trench here because they built pillboxes in the field over there so the Home Guard could provide a cross-fire over possible landing grounds. Look, there's one over there, beyond the trees.'

To the bemusement of his students, Mr Campion raised his right arm to the perpendicular and waved it furiously.

'Is it normal to wave at inanimate concrete objects in England?'

'I'm merely being friendly,' said Mr Campion. 'Just saying hello to the chap over there *behind* the pillbox who has been watching us through binoculars ever since we arrived.'

FIVE

'Arrods' 'Ome Delivery

Oliver Grieg Bell would never have admitted to having had a sheltered upbringing but he was intelligent enough to realize that his experience of the world had been somewhat filtered; not by wealth or position but by a series of happy accidents. He had won a scholarship to a minor public school where his natural talent for music was not only nurtured but ensured that he was protected from the rougher educational advantages offered on the school's playing field. An organ scholarship took him to Oxford, where he embarked on a love affair with the harpsichord and was much cherished by a cabal of dons who shared a love of Baroque music. He emerged with a creditable second-class degree in music and a total ignorance of anything resembling politics or philosophy and certainly economics. He had studiously failed to remember the names of, let alone cultivate friendships with, fellow students from his college, who had by 1970 become merchant bankers, Members of Parliament, a lead writer on *The Times* and a prize-winning mathematician.

With wealth and position he had no conscious personal contact until he had met, and fallen for, Lavinia and her fearsome father, Lord Breeze. The first experience had been fortuitous and pleasant, the other inevitable and far less so. Lavinia had cared not a jot that he had no money, no job, no career plan. She had seen and fallen in love with his unworldly innocence and genial, somewhat Micawber-ish something-will-turn-up attitude. The fact that Oliver seemed totally unimpressed by, and uninterested in, her father's fortune and his ambitious plans to increase it only endeared him to her. The fact that her father disapproved of their marriage sealed the deal.

When Lavinia received Heronhoe Hall as a wedding present, along with a twelve-inch-high porcelain bust of Lord Breeze, Oliver accepted it as a 'something' that had 'turned up' fortuitously, negating the need to apply for a mortgage or find regular employment. His future would be dedicated to the upkeep of the hall although he was, in practical terms, totally unsuited to achieving such an objective. To put it kindly, Oliver was not exactly focused when it came to understanding such matters as electrical rewiring, damp courses, sewage and drainage, woodworm treatments, the intricacies of plumbing or the ability to understand a professional report or estimate on any of them.

Such domestic concerns were never going to trouble Oliver unduly but the legend of the Heronhoe Horde which came with the hall fascinated him and he demonstrated a level of enthusiasm for uncovering the mystery which Lavinia noted had been previously reserved only for Hattie, his beloved harpsichord.

He soon discovered that the very words Heronhoe Horde were a myth, almost certainly created by Gerald Wemyss-Grendle, for there was no horde of treasure in the boat burial excavated. Oliver had combed the archives of the *East Suffolk Courier and Hadleigh Argus* for contemporary reports of the excavation, which were covered in some detail that summer of 1935 by a reporter called Samuel Salt, who quoted both the vicars of Sweethearting and

Heronhoe on the dearth of finds. There had, of course, been no public precedent as the treasures of Sutton Hoo were not discovered until 1939, and the one grainy picture used in the newspaper coverage showed a finger and thumb holding a piece of what was said to be pottery but could, to the untrained eye, have been just about anything.

Yet the excavation of the Sweethearting Barrow or Tumulus – or whatever the warring vicars called it – had been newsworthy enough, apparently, to attract the attention of the Prince of Wales and his paramour, the then un-divorced Mrs Simpson. Or so local legend had it, although Oliver was rather curious that local journalist Samuel Salt had made no mention of the royal visit. Plenty of local residents had confirmed that the visit had happened although, at the time, the British public was kept deliberately uninformed of the future king's dalliance with a twice-divorced American woman.

At some point in history, or at least in Oliver's research, the 'Heronhoe Horde' underwent a metamorphosis and became the 'Abdication Treasure'. It was equally nebulous in the sense that no one had actually seen it, or knew its worth or even form. The residents of Sweethearting – at least the ones Oliver talked to in the public bar of the King's Head – were, however, convinced that the prince who then became a king and then a duke had bestowed some elusive 'treasure' on the village following his abdication in recognition, it was presumed, of the hospitality shown by the locals during his visit. Oliver's researches in his other personal reference library, the public bar of the Hythe Inn in Heronhoe, elicited no supporting evidence whatsoever for this rumour, although even an innocent incomer such as Oliver had quickly realized that Heronhoe folk would rarely admit to the Sweethearting population of possessing anything they did not, other than perhaps swine flu.

As both vicars who had actively participated in the 1935 excavation had long since left their parishes – one seeking a more adventurous life in retirement on Alderney and one to commune more closely with his employer – reliable sources were no longer available, Oliver having discounted Gerald Wemyss-Grendle as reliable on their first meeting. Not even local journalist Samuel Salt had pursued the story, or at least Oliver could find nothing in the archives of the *East Suffolk Courier*. In fact, Samuel Salt, after his initial enthusiasm for the Sweethearting excavation in 1935, seemed to have lost interest in the story completely, and his journalistic byline disappeared from further reportage of local news.

A simple soul at heart, Oliver was convinced that as so many local inhabitants so firmly believed that there was a treasure of some description connected to Heronhoe Hall, then it must in fact be true. That no one had ever actually seen anything which could be valued, weighed or measured as treasure; that the previous owner of Heronhoe Hall had not enjoyed any sort of financial windfall (although it was whispered that the turf accountants of Newmarket may have); and that Lord Breeze, when buying the estate, had insisted on in-depth legal searches and valuations, did not deter Oliver in the slightest. He rummaged in lofts, explored cellars and outbuildings, tapped panelled walls, uprooted floorboards, even stripped wallpaper looking for a safe or hiding place for valuables, to the complete distraction of his wife Lavinia. He spent weeks pouring over documents in the county land registry, parish records, old parish magazines and newspaper cuttings in search of clues, all to no avail. What had begun as a hobby – and a harmless one, or so his wife thought – had become almost an obsession, and Oliver had been on the point of despair when Mr Albert Campion appeared out of the blue and on to the scene.

The genial Oliver Grieg Bell had never thought to ask exactly why Albert Campion and Lady Amanda had turned up unannounced that wintry afternoon just after Christmas, claiming that they had 'been in the neighbourhood visiting family'. To be perfectly honest, Oliver had no idea who the Campions were, but he was old fashioned enough to accept that the proprietorship of a manorial hall brought responsibilities of hospitality, or at least tea and a plain digestive biscuit. He was relieved to discover that his wife had no objection at all to his inviting these particular strangers into the hall at a moment's notice, even though she was wearing her oldest jeans and one of Oliver's moth-eaten pullovers, no make-up and had been in the middle of painting a skirting board in the kitchen. Unlike her ethereal husband, Lavinia had certainly heard of the Campions and regarded Lady Amanda as something of a heroine and an exemplar to women. She allowed Amanda to make herself comfortable in their one presentable armchair and even take an exploratory sip of her tea before she simply had to congratulate her on her achievements in the aero-nautical industry, an industry dominated by men.

Amanda had accepted the adoration with good grace, saying, 'It all began right here in Suffolk, you know, over in Pontisbright, fiddling about with mechanicals. Sometimes, though, I wish I had chosen a more credible career.'

Oliver, meanwhile, was displaying a similar sort of hero-worship once Mr Campion had volunteered the information that not only had he visited Heronhoe Hall during the excavation of the Sweethearting Barrow in 1935 and had heard the stories of missing treasure, but he was also genuinely interested in Oliver's theories on the subject.

Six weeks later, here was Mr Campion based in Heronhoe Hall with a team of young archaeologists who were to recreate the 1935 dig for the television cameras and, although the naturally vague Campion had been less than forthcoming about the actual details, Oliver was convinced that a treasure hunt was underway. Even if nothing physical were found nor a speculative theory proved, Campion's offer to pay a reasonable rent for the rather basic accommodation to his young diggers and the part-decorated, half-furnished bedroom he himself occupied was a welcome deposit in the echoing coffers of Heronhoe Hall. He had even offered to pay a fee for permission to dig the Sweethearting Barrow but Oliver had come clean and admitted that technically, since the disposal organized by Lord Breeze brought on by the refusal of building permits, the site was now on land owned by Thomas Spark of Windy Ridge Farm.

Whatever Campion's motives, as long as they were likely to result in the outcome Oliver desired, Oliver was content and, in any case, Campion was clearly a man of wealth and taste, having already endeared himself by enthusing about harpsichord music and not just the populist composers such as Bach and Scarlatti but also those earlier pioneers, William Byrd and François Couperin. He had also shown his generosity to the cash-strapped Bells in very practical terms, as witnessed by the arrival at the hall of a delivery van in green livery with the signature *Harrods* emblazoned in gold lettering.

Lavinia rushed out of the front door to meet the arrival with the speed of a child waking on Christmas morn and the same

air of barely concealed mercenary interest. Campion had materialized, as if from nowhere, at her side and Oliver joined them
as two middle-aged gentlemen wearing brown bowler hats and
long brown coveralls – the ubiquitous warehouseman's coat which
Lord Breeze with his northern heritage would certainly insist on
calling a 'smock'– dismounted from the cab and proceeded in
stately fashion to the rear doors of the van, which they opened
with a flourish.

Whatever cornucopia of delights Oliver and Lavinia Bell had
envisaged would be revealed, the interior of the delivery van took
their breath away, but not in a way they might reasonably have
expected. Of the three, only Mr Campion's jaw remained in place
and his facial expression remained blandly untroubled.

The bowler-hatted, brown-smocked footmen held the van doors
open to their full extent, revealing, in regal pride of place among
the crates, boxes and shopping bags overflowing with fruits and
vegetables, a throne.

It was in fact a Chesterfield Queen Anne wing-back armchair
in grey leather, secured to the floor and frame of the van by a
system of canvas straps, buckles and bolts. In it, blinking sleep-
filled eyes in the sunlight, yawning until his jowls quivered with
the effort and stretching his arms out in front of him like an overfed
cat, was Mr Magersfontein Lugg.

'So it's true,' breathed Campion. 'Harrods really do sell
everything.'

'I sees a bit of comfort goin' spare and so I takes advantage of it.
There's no 'arm in that, though I suppose you'd 'ave preferred it
if I'd ridden up front with the staff.'

'Not at all, old boy,' said Campion. 'A chap your age needs to
conserve his energy, especially after a hard morning's shopping.
Did you make sure they filled my list?'

'They take great h'offence at 'Arrods if you question their
integrity, you know,' said Lugg, 'and if you pays for top-class
service, you gets it there. They didn't bat an eyelid when I thumbed
a lift with 'em, and as that armchair was on its way to a certain
party up in Hadleigh it seemed a shame to waste it. I think you'll
find you've got everything you ordered.'

'I don't remember requesting a crate of brown ale.'

'You said on the blower that you was getting in iron rations for this campaign; well, them's my iron rations.'

'Fair enough,' said Campion. 'Let us away to the kitchen and find some glasses and a church key.'

'A wot? Bit late for Matins and too early for Evensong, ain't it?'

'I meant an opener, a bottle opener. "Church key" was just an Americanism I heard yesterday.'

'Americans in the vicinity, eh? More bloody foreigners,' grumbled the bald fat man.

'You don't know the half of it, old fruit. I take it your stately progress from Knightsbridge was comfortable enough? It certainly looked that way.'

'At our age, yer takes yer bits of comfort where yer can, though I would've preferred one of them electric vans they used to run before the war. Remember them? Top speed nineteen miles to the hour, now that was stately.'

'Of course I remember them, but I suspect they are all in museums now, as perhaps we should be.'

Campion led the way into the kitchen where the Bells were unpacking boxes of groceries into cupboards and a bulging refrigerator with puppy-like glee. Lavinia broke off from cataloguing what she clearly regarded as her personal Heronhoe Horde to forage for glasses and a bottle-opener and Campion played barman after selecting two pint bottles of Watney's Brown Ale from a green plastic crate.

'Do Harrods give you fourpence back on the empties?' he mused as he poured.

'Dunno,' said Lugg, raising his glass religiously to his lips. 'I'm sure I saw a couple of ham and egg pies in one of them 'ampers.'

Mr Campion raised his glass in salute.

'I'm sure you did, but they are not for your waistline, which is quite ample enough. These victuals are for the members of my little archaeological expedition who are being quartered here at the hall. You will not be staying here, old chum, you will be . . .' he paused for dramatic effect, '. . . going undercover.'

The bald man inhaled another draught of beer, one quizzical eyebrow raised, then dabbed his lips on the back of the hand surrounding his glass. He nodded his huge head towards Oliver and Lavinia, who were still as busy as squirrels in late autumn, and it was only when Campion nodded, indicating that he had no objection to speaking in their presence, that Lugg continued.

'Good job I packed me country casuals then, so's I can blend in with the yokels, though I've always said it lowers yer dignity if you dress too comfortable.'

Mr Campion's large round spectacles scanned Lugg from shiny dome to equally shiny size-twelve brown brogues, taking in the full ensemble of a black blazer with an unidentifiable badge stitched on to the breast pocket, a worsted waistcoat, its buttons stretched to bursting point, and pinstriped trousers from a morning suit which had presumably passed high noon.

'I thought you *had* come in character,' said Campion, 'though I should have known you have not yet plumbed the sartorial depths you are capable of.'

'Don't you worry about yours truly. I can blend into most places except nunneries and temperance meetings. I've come wiv some old clobber in my traps so I can be either a poet or a peasant, as circumstances demand.'

'I think I would be intimidated by both *personae*,' said Mr Campion, 'but for the moment I simply want you to do what you do best, which is hang around and keep your ears wide open down in Heronhoe.'

'Is that where I'm to be billeted then?'

'It is, in a wonderful, olde-worlde hostelry offering the finest food and wines as well as panoramic views over the estuary – you do realize I am lying through my dentures, don't you? It's called the Hythe Inn. They have rooms – well, one room – and I'm sure you won't mind sharing with the odd lascar or cast-adrift pirate if need be. But do be wary if they offer you a pull on their opium pipe.'

'Hhhhrumph!' Lugg snorted. 'So what am I listening out for wiv my ears akimbo?'

'Oh, the usual sort of public bar gossip which seems to flow to you like iron filings to a magnet. The words "treasure" and possibly "Heronhoe Horde" should go straight into your notebook, though of course I don't expect you to actually carry a notebook. Don't want you mistaken for an off-duty Peeler.'

'Perish the thought! Anything specific on your radar I should be aware of?'

'We had a little break-in here the other night but Oliver saw him off very sharply.' Campion glanced towards his host but Oliver was too busy stacking tins of ham and salmon as if they were chips on a roulette table to eavesdrop.

'Bit of a botched job,' Campion said, lowering his voice. 'Didn't get anything and I'm sure our burglar was a local.'

'Get a look at 'im?' asked Lugg with professional interest.

'Only from behind, in the dark, tearing down the drive pursued by some .410 buckshot, none of which hit as far as I could tell. Medium height, thin, dark coat flapping – made me think of a crow running across a lawn. I know that would not stand up in court, not even a court of crows, if you'll allow me a *bon mot*.'

'I'd rather not,' said Lugg, then he too dropped his voice. 'You going to tell me what's really going on here?'

'Remember when we were here together the last time, back before the war?'

''Course I do, I remembers all my trips out to this neck of the woods. It's me getting back to nachure comin' out 'ere, and I've always loved nachure. That'd be the time we were on point patrol for you-know-who. Year before the Abdication, weren't it?'

'Exactly. Just keep that in mind, will you? And also, if you can manage to hold two thoughts simultaneously, keep an ear out for anything that reminds you of our adventures in Clerkenwell.'

'Clerkenwell? What's that got to do with the price of fish?'

Campion smiled beatifically. 'I hope something and also nothing, but don't worry, my faithful gundog, all will become clear within the week and – who knows? – you might get a part in the film.'

'Film? Nobody said anything about a film. Who do I play?'

Lugg drained his glass and plonked it down on the kitchen table, then he straightened his great bulk, fastened the middle button of his blazer and stood at what, at his time of life, passed for attention.

'A bit part is all you're likely to be offered, I'm afraid,' said Mr Campion, 'as a Thirties' amateur archaeologist climbing up and down the Sweethearting Barrow, perhaps doing a bit of digging in the background. In long shot, I think they call it.'

'Do I get appearance money?' The big man's eyes had become slits.

'Board and lodging, and your bar bill at the Hythe Inn paid for.'

'I see. How about a stunt double for the dangerous bits?'

'A double? For you? Where on earth would we find one of those?'

'Oh, Mr Campion, could I ask about this film crew?' Lavinia turned from a high cupboard now happily groaning with victuals. In her arms she clutched six large tubes of chocolate digestive biscuits to her chest. 'Will they be joining us here at the hall?'

'I'm not expecting them to, Mrs Bell; in fact, I'm told they have made their own arrangements to stay in Heronhoe.' Campion exchanged glances with Lugg. 'Where their arrival will almost certainly be noted in the newsroom that is the Hythe Inn.'

Lugg tapped his nose with a sausage of a forefinger, indicating 'message received'.

'They will certainly want to film the exterior of the hall, I would imagine, but I hope they won't trouble you too much. Most of their work will be done over at the dig site at Sweethearting, which is where Rupert and Perdita will be staying.'

'Rupert?' asked Oliver as if just tuning in to the conversation. He had been emptying a vegetable box and the last items – a pair of cabbages – he held balanced, one in each hand rather like a pantomime scales of justice.

'My son-and-heir-to-not-very-much,' beamed Campion, 'and his wife. They are both aspiring thespians, which I think comes from the Greek for unemployed.'

'They the stars of the show, then?' grunted Lugg.

'Of course they are. If a film producer can't exercise a little bit of nepotism now and then, who can?'

At approximately the same moment but seventy-five miles away to the south and west, the unpacking of a delivery of a different kind was also taking place in a kitchen – the kitchen of a small, unobtrusive Italian restaurant in Clerkenwell called La Pergoletta.

It was the sort of Italian restaurant which neither claimed nor aspired to be on the same level as Mario and Franco's *Terrazza*, a fashionable world away in Romilly Street, and its menu certainly never aspired to offer anything as exotic as *vitello tonnato* or *fegatini di pollo alla Siracusa*, but then neither did it have main courses costing over sixteen shillings nor a half-crown cover charge. A peripatetic restaurant critic – a rare sight indeed in Clerkenwell – might have sarcastically suggested that the Pergoletta, with its Formica tables, dusty wallpaper and faded watercolours showing Vesuvius, the Colosseum and the leaning tower of Pisa, was more suited to a clientele which believed that spaghetti only came out of tins in a sweet neon sauce or, in its raw state, grew on trees.

The restaurant, with its frontage of peeled paint and cracked plaster, did however enjoy a location which, with a kindly eye, could be seen as picturesque. Situated on the corner of Exmouth Market, where market traders specializing in fruit, vegetables and flowers provided a colourful backdrop, and in the shade of London's most Italianate church, Holy Redeemer, with its own personal campanile and an interior based on Santa Spirito in Florence, gave the area an air, albeit a shabby one, of a Little Italy abroad. The only thing spoiling that impression was the giant GPO sorting office known as The Mount to those who worked there, across the Farringdon Road, but hungry and fortunately undemanding postal workers provided the Pergoletta with a regular delivery of customers.

With lunchtime service now over the restaurant was empty and the kitchen staff had finished their cleaning chores in double-quick time and dispersed, having been told that 'Donna D' required the kitchen for stocktaking purposes, though the stock that was being checked had nothing to do with the restaurant business.

Two men, dressed alike in tight blue jeans and black leather jackets, had unloaded metal cases from the back of a left-hand drive Citroën Ami 6 with French number plates. They now stood, surrounded by their shiny luggage in the restaurant's kitchen where Daniela Petraglia leaned against a cold cooking range, her high-heeled boots crossed at the ankles, smoking a Sobranie Black Russian cigarette.

'Gianfranco, Maurizio,' said the woman, acknowledging their arrival.

Both men nodded respectfully and said together: 'Donna Daniela.'

'Did you have any trouble crossing the Channel?' she asked in Italian.

'No problem at all. The French customs guys are always happy to see foreigners leave their country,' said the man called Gianfranco.

'And the car is clean?'

'We bought it legally, but it cannot be traced back to our family,' answered Maurizio.

'Good, very good,' said Daniela, blowing a smoke ring towards a faded *Vietato Fumare* sign stuck to the side of a tall upright fridge. 'What about the English at Dover?'

'They were only interested in how many cigarettes we had bought in the duty-free shop on the ferry. They come down much harder on their own people and they take pleasure in frightening British drivers. *Stronzi*, all of them.'

'Well then, open up.' The woman waved her cigarette to the kitchen work surface next to the sink and, after moving a large pockmarked chopping board, Maurizio lifted one of the metal cases on to it, snapped the fasteners and lifted the lid. Inside, nestled in cut-out segments of a black foam plastic block, were a variety of camera lenses and filters.

Maurizio pushed his fingers down the sides of the foam lining and ran them down the width of the case, releasing some hidden mechanism. He lifted the pliant foam block out of the rigid case and laid it carefully on the work surface to reveal a second layer of cushioning in which lay three small automatic pistols, each in its own perfectly sculptured shallow grave.

Donna Daniela plucked one of the guns from the foam and examined it expertly, releasing the magazine and working the slide, along which was stamped P Beretta 6.35 BREVETTATA.

'Ladies' gun,' said Gianfranco sourly.

The woman flashed him the sort of steely look that any male should be wary of, let alone when a female was holding a weapon.

'Good thing I'm a lady, then,' she said. 'You have a problem with them?'

'They have no stopping power,' said Gianfranco nervously. 'The British call them the Beretta .25 and it was James Bond's favourite gun until they made him change because it was only effective if used at very close range.'

Daniela weighed the gun in her right hand, reinserted the magazine and looked carefully at the pistol's safety catch as if wondering whether it was worth engaging it.

'James Bond wasn't real,' she said, 'but I am, and I am very good at getting into close range. Now, check the camera and the sound gear. Make sure everything is working. We have to look professional and I do not want to come back to London for any reason. If we are successful, we will use the air ferry from Southend to Calais. It is the quickest way back to Europe.'

'Will we be leaving in a hurry?' asked Maurizio.

'Who knows? We will have to see how our little drama plays out.'

'Have you checked out the actors?'

Donna Daniela nodded and unslung her soft brown leather shoulder bag.

'They are young, pretty and stupid,' she said. 'And, other than needing their hair to be dyed, they are therefore perfect for their roles.'

'You are not expecting trouble from them?'

'Not a bit,' said the woman, slipping the Beretta into her bag and zipping it shut.

'So why do you need the gun?'

'Oh, that's not for them . . .'

SIX

Royal Welcome

The younger Campions left London in Perdita's red Austin Mini Cooper, taking the Epping New Road through the Forest and reflecting on the local names – The Warren Hill, Cuckoo Pits, the Ching river, Almshouse Plain and Fairmead (not 'Fair Maid') Bottom – which reflected an antiquity not long for this world. The signs were everywhere: large, earth-moving machinery parked at the side of the road, dormant but ready to roar into life at any moment, advertising hoardings giving dire warnings of the advent of new desirable homes, and everywhere the temporary site offices in which surveyors and contractors made their campaign plans.

They cut across country to Chipping Ongar and then picked up the old Roman road at Chelmsford. Between there and Colchester Rupert gave a running commentary as he drove, pointing out that settlements along the way such as Witham and Kelvedon would, he guaranteed, be eight miles apart as that was the distance between Roman staging posts on a major itinerary, as they would have called it. Going the other way, it was also the road which Boadicea, the vengeful queen of the Iceni tribe, had lead her army south towards London in order to sack and burn the city as she had done in Colchester, which was of course the capital of Britain at the time.

Perdita had listened patiently for twenty minutes before advising her husband that it was now accepted that the queen of the Iceni who rebelled against the Romans was called Boudicca, which experts in the field spelled with one 'c' rather than two, and not Boadicea, which was a Victorian affectation. More to the point, she wondered why her husband was taking such an interest in ancient history, to which Rupert replied it was a question of getting into character. They would be filming on an archaeological dig, so he had been mugging up on archaeology.

With the sympathetic patience that recently married women perfect remarkably quickly, Perdita pointed out that any archaeology they encountered was likely to be Anglo-Saxon rather than Roman in period, but in any case as Rupert would not be playing an archaeologist but a famous member of a royal family on a sightseeing tour instead, she added sweetly that all he had to 'mug up' on was being royal.

Beyond Colchester, they stopped for a ploughman's lunch in a smart, timber-framed pub in Stratford St Mary and, between chunks of bread, bites of strong cheddar and the dissection of a giant pickled onion, Perdita asked her husband if he knew of the King's Head in Sweethearting, their next stop now they had crossed the border into Suffolk.

Rupert admitted that although he had visited Pontisbright as a lad, he had never ventured as far as Sweethearting or Heronhoe or, if he had, he had no viable memory of either place but he was sure that the locals there would be similar to the inhabitants of Pontisbright.

When Perdita had asked him in what way they would be similar, Rupert had replied simply, 'They'll be interesting.'

                              *   *   *

The King's Head, the first dwelling of Sweethearting as approached from Pontisbright, was not Perdita's idea of a village pub in what parliamentary supporters of the Development of Tourism Act (though perhaps not Lord Breeze) might have generously called 'Constable Country'.

This was not a thatched-roofed, roses-around-the-door village pub with its plasterwork painted in traditional 'Suffolk pink'. It was an angular, brick-and-tile building, its windows and doors badly in need of a coat of any colour of paint. It was both ugly and out of proportion; clearly too big for the needs of the village of Sweethearting, which was visible in its entirety along the road from the empty pub car park. Perhaps it had been built when an influx of tourists – possibly cycling clubs – were expected in the summer months, but then the First World War had intervened. Whatever and whenever its origins, it had seen better days and even the pub's sign hanging over the road from a free-standing pole was faded and tinged with mould. Fortunately the king it depicted was a generic medieval one and so badly painted that the sign's condition would hardly be a matter of public concern, though it would probably find favour among republicans.

'We should have got here during opening hours,' said Perdita as the pair of them, luggage in hand, approached the front door of the pub, framed by a slightly leaning porch which seemed to do little except shelter a thin white sign announcing that Joshua P. Yallop was licensed to sell alcohol both on and off the premises. 'The place looks deserted.'

'Don't worry,' said Rupert, rapping his knuckles on one of the panes of glass in the upper half of the pub's door, 'the English country pub, and especially the East Anglian country pub, is famed for its hospitality, and the staff are probably busy roasting chestnuts or baking bread for us, or slipping hot warming pans into our bed.'

Behind the glass a dark curtain was whipped aside and a face appeared: a round, female face wearing pink plastic-framed National Health spectacles repaired at the bridge with a plaster. Beneath the spectacles a toothless mouth opened, and from it a muffled voice made its feelings known through the door.

'We now be closed, so bugger off till six-a-clock!'

*   *   *

'You must forgive my wife,' said Joshua P. Yallop (licensed to sell, etc.). 'Edna is from Norfolk and not used to strangers.'

Perdita smothered a giggle, unsure whether this tall, thin stick of a man, who reminded her of a nervous Maths teacher, had spoken in jest or not.

'We should have phoned ahead,' said Rupert, playing the diplomat, 'rather than disturb your rest period.' He had been coached in his youth by that authoritative figure on such matters, Mr Lugg, that the hours of closure in the afternoon – a piece of cruelty imposed on good Englishmen by Mr Lloyd George, a Welshman, during the First World War – were now regarded as sacred by many publicans.

'Don't worry about that, we've put you in the Royal Suite, as we call it, and the other Mr Campion, who booked the room, did phone to say you were on the way. He also said to tell you to report to Heronhoe Hall tonight for dinner and rehearsals in costume, whatever that means, but he was quite specific.'

'I think I understand,' said Rupert. 'I hope that doesn't put you out at all.'

'Kitchen don't open in the evenings,' said Mrs Yallop who, having disappeared through a door to the side of the main bar once her husband had appeared to receive their guests, had now silently reappeared at his side having spent her time absent wisely, running a brush through her hair and reinserting her false teeth, although her feet remained shod in a pair of red furry slippers which were moulting badly.

'What Edna means is we don't do bar food in the evenings during the winter. There's no call for it, you see.'

'Not much call in the spring or the summer either,' said Mrs Yallop, resigned and unsmiling. 'This place is past its prime, just like we are, Joshua.'

Mr Yallop loped a long arm around the shoulders of his diminutive wife, where it hung loosely like an unwanted scarf.

'Now then, Edna, not so glum – not on our night off,' he said, though Edna did not seem cheered by the news.

'Going anywhere nice?' asked Perdita, feigning both joviality and interest.

The small woman looked up at the younger woman as if she had suggested something unspeakable.

'It's our night in front of the box, now we've got colour,' said Mrs Yallop. And then, convinced that Perdita had not understood, added, 'The box, the gogglebox.'

'Tonight is our one night of television viewing,' said Mr Yallop to clarify things, 'and now we have a colour set, we aim to get the good of it, whatever programmes are on. But don't worry, the bar will be open as usual and Sonia will see to you if you need anything as long as it's not food or room service. Sonia doesn't climb stairs these days.'

'Sonia?'

'She's our cleaner and barmaid and a positive gem, a one-in-a-thousand, a really precious asset to the place. She's been the life and soul of the King's Head for years. Worth her weight in gold is Sonia.'

'But she doesn't do stairs,' said Mrs Yallop.

Having discharged his duties as quartermaster and seen Lugg trudge down the modest slope towards Heronhoe, Mr Campion donned his overcoat, hat and a white cashmere scarf and set off in the opposite direction along the road to Sweethearting.

He adopted a long stride and a brisk pace as the chilly, bleak afternoon was not conducive to a gentle country ramble and the view over the saltings lining the Bright estuary, which Campion knew on a misty summer morning could be intensely beautiful, was now offering only a featureless steely grey canvas.

He could see the rooftops and the square church tower of Sweethearting and wondered if Rupert and Perdita had arrived yet, but if his message to the King's Head had got through – and of that he was not absolutely certain as the woman who had answered the telephone had given him the impression she was handling a small, venomous animal – he would see them that evening.

Precious Aird's lime-green VW microbus was parked at the side of the road by the small copse of leafless trees which in summer hid the Sweethearting tumulus. Campion stepped delicately over a single sagging strand of barbed wire and crunched through the stubbly undergrowth until the outline of the Barrow was revealed to him.

As an earthwork, as ancient earthworks went, it was far from impressive and, before its 'discovery' by two inquisitive and competitive parish priests, it would probably have been dismissed as just another lump or bump in the rural landscape. At its highest it was no more than ten or twelve feet above ground level and the slope was gentle enough that Campion was confident he could scale it without recourse to crampons, an ice pick or a walking stick, even at his advanced age.

Plodding his way carefully to the summit, such as it was, he heard the banter of youthful voices. Precious Aird and her 'diggers' were wisely working on the northern side of the Barrow, out of the wind stinging over the saltings, and only ceased their heated debate over the merits of a new pop group (of whose existence Campion was blissfully unaware) when he appeared above them.

'Well, hi there, Mr C. To what do we owe this honour?' Precious sang in greeting.

Campion would have recognized the American girl even before she spoke, thanks to the blue and red baseball cap she was wearing, but he was unsure that he could identify even the sex of her three companions, so tightly muffled were they in layers of pullovers, woollen hats, scarves and thorn-proof gloves as large and thick as a medieval knight's gauntlets. They were armed with a variety of implements including mattock, pruning shears, hoe and scythe.

'Just passing through,' said Campion cheerfully, 'to see how the archaeology's going.'

Precious expelled a scoffing laugh. 'Archaeology? This is more like aggressive gardening.'

'But necessary nonetheless,' said Campion. 'The site has to be cleared of vegetation before you can put in a trench and pretend to be the original diggers back in the Thirties for the film people.'

'Do we actually get to be in the film?'

'I'm not sure they've allowed for extras as I think they call them, but I'm sure they'll need some. You'll all have to look like Thirties' farm labourers or vicars, though, at least from a distance, so we'll still have to find some dog collars and flat caps and gaiters from somewhere to get you into character.'

'Do we get extra pay?' beamed Precious.

'I'll have to discuss that with the producer.'

'I thought you were the producer.'

'So I am,' said Mr Campion thoughtfully, 'but I can't dawdle just now as I'm on my way over to Windy Ridge Farm, but I would appreciate a lift back to the hall before it gets dark as I foolishly forgot to bring a torch. I'm assuming you'll be packing up before the light goes?'

'That's the plan, Mr Producer. Don't worry; we'll hold the bus for you.'

Campion took his leave of them and walked on through the copse until he reached the single-track lane leading to the farm called Windy Ridge, which surely contravened the recent Trade Descriptions Act as nowhere in Suffolk really deserved the title 'ridge'. It was, though, Campion mused, a more attractive name than 'Windy Up A Slight Hillock Farm' and it did, like Heronhoe Hall, have terrific views over the Bright estuary and its saltings.

It was a Victorian brick-and-tile farmhouse in its own courtyard in which it nestled against the standard collection of outbuildings in various states of disrepair, the obligatory tractor which had not moved for two decades or more and those unidentifiable bits of agricultural machinery which seemed to have been made out of rust. There were chickens underfoot and a warm, earthy smell in the air which suggested that at least one outbuilding had porcine tenants, but then where would a Suffolk farm be without eggs and ham on the breakfast menu?

To Campion's eye, the farmer, Thomas Spark, had certainly enjoyed a regular diet of such breakfasts. He was a broad, ruddy-faced man, half Campion's age and triple his girth, with fair curly hair and wispy sideburns which suggested a man who had attempted to grow a beard, then changed his mind and settled for what in a previous age would have been called mutton-chop whiskers.

Farmer Spark had appeared at his front door before Campion was halfway across the farmyard, as if some inherited agricultural sixth sense had alerted him to trespassers.

'Good afternoon, Mr Spark,' Campion hailed him, lifting his hat in greeting as he approached. He was gratified to see a pair of bushy eyebrows raised in surprise.

'Do we know each other?' the farmer asked politely, stepping out to lessen the distance between them.

'Only through the lenses of your binoculars,' said Campion, offering a handshake and an idiotic grin. 'You were keeping an eye on my young archaeologists from behind a pillbox, as you have every right to, it being your land, but I can assure you that they are not causing damage to anything except possibly some unwanted vegetation. At this time of year I can't think they will be disturbing much wildlife and I am assured that if and when they get down to the boat burial, they will leave it in perfect condition for the next occupant. My name's Campion, by the way.'

'You were here, back then, in 'thirty-five, when the royals came, weren't you?'

Campion was taken aback slightly, but he had long since perfected the art of keeping his trusty mask of vagueness in place.

'I was, and that is because I am very old. You are not, and could not have been more than a lad.'

'I was a schoolboy in Heronhoe and we had a talk from the vicar about the old kings of East Anglia, but I can't say we paid much attention. All we were interested in them days was Spitfires and stamp collecting. But my dad did a bit of digging, even though it wasn't our land then.'

'You purchased it from Lord Breeze relatively recently, I understand.'

'I bought a few acres of the old parkland from him when he found he couldn't build houses there and the Sweethearting Barrow came with them. His Lordship knew he'd never get planning permission, what with it being an ancient monument or whatever they call it, and he was happy to offload it.'

'Lord Breeze can't build on it, but you can't farm on it either, can you?'

The farmer shrugged his shoulders as if adjusting a yoke.

'It keeps the boat burial in the village,' he said. 'Not that there's any boat left or anybody buried there, but it's a bit of local history and it does keep any curious villagers from straying over my farm, so I think of it as a *cordon sanitaire*. My old man would have preserved it. He thought it might attract tourists but of course it didn't. Sutton Hoo and Woodbridge got all that trade after the war.'

'The old man – your father; is he still with us?'

Thomas Spark shook his head. 'He died five years ago but he was always talking about that summer they did the dig, had a load of stories about it, he did.'

'Stories about treasure?' Campion tried.

'Mebbe when he'd had a few too many down the King's Head

or he was pulling somebody's leg,' snorted Spark. 'They didn't find no treasure over there. If they had, Dad would have known about it. He used to go round the site every morning, very early, before the volunteers arrived, just to make sure they hadn't missed anything.'

'I wouldn't mind hearing some of those stories, you know.'

'I don't do guided tours; I've a farm to run.'

'Perhaps I could offer you some refreshment one evening, at the King's Head?' suggested Campion.

'I don't drink; saw what it did to my dad.'

'Then how about joining us at the hall for tea or dinner?'

'I don't think so; my wife doesn't approve of incomers to the area. She's funny that way, but that's the way she is. I'll be in the doghouse for just talking to you now.'

'But I'm hardly an illegal alien, you know. I did marry a local lass from Pontisbright – that's not too foreign, is it?'

'There's some round here would say you needed a passport to go there, crossing the border into West Suffolk, but I ain't one of them. Your missus, that'd be Lady Amanda Fitton, as was?'

Campion made an effort to appear impressed.

'Was, and still is, I hope, but how did you know?'

'Same way I knew you'd visited back before the war: my dad. He read something in the paper one day and said "that Lady Amanda's husband, he was here with the king when he came to see them dig up the boat". The local papers used to carry all the news about Lady Amanda, even when it weren't really news, more like gossip.'

'Yes, I know,' said Campion lightly. 'We consorts of important ladies have a lot to put up with.'

Thomas Spark had placed himself firmly between Campion and his front door, indicating that the farmhouse was out of bounds and, from the twitching of curtains, Campion observed over the farmer's shoulder that the place was well-guarded.

'Could we not have a private word, perhaps out of sight of your other half?' he suggested.

Spark thought for a moment, weighing his predicament on the scales of domestic justice.

'Don't suppose there'd be any harm in you helping me feed the pigs,' he said, nodding towards one of the long, low outbuildings, 'as long as you don't mind their table manners, as they ain't got none.'

'My dear sir, I was at Cambridge and had to eat at High Table three days a week. I doubt very much that your livestock can shock me.'

If anything, Campion thought, the pig sty with two lines of pens each containing half-a-dozen pink and squealing porkers was warmer than he remembered his college dining hall and it amused him to speculate that the level of discourse taking place between the diners was higher at Windy Ridge. Once the pigs heard the rattle of pellets in the feed bucket Thomas Spark was filling, the squealing rose in volume and dozens of stubby noses were poked between the metal bars of the pens, eagerly awaiting service. As the farmer poured the feed along the line of their troughs, the pigs set to with a will and the shrill squealing was replaced with a subdued snuffling and dedicated chomping.

Now they were out of sight of the farmhouse, Spark's attitude softened and he became more forthcoming.

'Farmers get a bad name when it comes to archaeology,' he said. 'They're always seen as obstructive and having run-ins with professors and museum people, but my father wasn't one of them. He was all for the excavation back in 1935 because it was part of the local landscape and its history. It wasn't Windy Ridge land, of course, not then, but when the chance came to buy it with some of the parkland, I jumped at it. Dad would have approved, even if the wife didn't, but then she never wanted to have any dealings with the toffs at Heronhoe Hall.'

'Bit of a socialist, is she, Mrs Spark?' Campion grinned. 'They're not all bad, I hear.'

'No socialists in Suffolk,' grunted the farmer but smiling as he did so, 'leastways not south of Ipswich. No, the wife has her own reasons for disliking them up at the hall; personal reasons, nothing political. She worked up there for a while, after the war and before we were married, as a cook for Wemyss-Grendle. Didn't stick it for long. Friend of yours, was he?'

'The Mad Major? No, not really,' said Campion.

'Good, though it wouldn't stop me telling you what I think of him if you were. That old devil had wandering hands. That's why my wife didn't last long up there – she couldn't stand the pestering.

And it was the same with every female from the village that went to work up there. He had a right reputation for being always on heat. "Groping Gerry" they used to call him. We were glad to see the back of him when he had to sell up. Probably doing his lechery in Soho or Paris or one of them places now.'

'Hardly,' said Campion. 'I understand he's in a nursing home in Frinton.'

'Then heaven help the nurses – that's all I can say. If one of the beasts on my farm behaved like that he'd know what was in store for him.'

'I can imagine. Did your father ever talk about Wemyss-Grendle's attitude to the boat burial?'

'Said he didn't take much notice at first, just let the locals get on with it. Then he got the idea into his head that there might be something in there worth hard cash and he insisted it was called the Heronhoe Barrow even though it was properly in Sweethearting. That ruffled a few feathers, but when there was no buried treasure to spend down the bookies he lost interest until he discovered he could show it off to his posh friends. Not that it did him much good in the long run. In fact, nobody came out of it well. There was no treasure, the archaeology was nothing to write home about and soon forgotten once they did the Sutton Hoo dig. My dad broke his ankle falling into a trench and never walked straight again, and Sam Salt never got his big story.'

'Sam Salt?' Campion said carefully. 'Should I know that name?'

'Doubt it, not unless you were a regular reader of the *East Suffolk Courier* back then. He was the local reporter and covered the dig from the start. Dad used to say Sam believed it would be his big story, one that would get him into the national papers. Even had a bet with Dad that he could get Sweethearting on to the front page of the *Daily Mail*. The wager was a flitch of bacon from the farm against Sam's pocket watch – he use to wear a big Hunter type on a gold chain across his waistcoat. It was probably worth a lot more than a side of pork and my father always had his eye on it.'

'I take it he didn't win – your father, that is.'

'Neither of them did. Well, Dad never saw Sam's name in the *Daily Mail*, or anywhere else for that matter. In fact, he never saw Sam again after the dig; said Sam must have stayed clear of

Sweethearting because he didn't want to lose that watch when he didn't get his big scoop. Dad never got his name in the papers, which I reckon he would have liked.'

'But he got to meet the future king of England, didn't he?' Campion asked. 'That must have been a proud moment for him.'

Thomas Spark shrugged his broad shoulders again, tipping the last pellets of feed in the bucket on to the head of an overenthusiastic pig.

'Not especially. He'd seen the prince in Sweethearting many a time.'

'How interesting,' said Campion quietly, and rather absent-mindedly reached out to pat the nearest pig on the head, then, remembering just in time that pigs had teeth, withdrew his hand. 'How very interesting.'

Their room at the King's Head had the luxury of a private bathroom and a hair-dryer, so Perdita insisted that as they were expected to appear in character that evening they might as well go the whole hog and use the hair dye she had bought. It would be a painless – though messy unless Rupert stopped fidgeting and kept a towel round his shoulders – process and the results would be spectacular. She would achieve the impossible and be able to pass for thirty-nine, whereas Rupert would no longer be a redhead which, she teased, would make him look at least forty-nine.

Feeling more than a little foolish, Rupert dutifully sat on the edges of the bed with a towel round his shoulders for the half-hour recommended by the manufacturers of the evil-smelling dyestuff while Perdita bent over the bathroom sink and tackled her own coiffure.

'I'm quite surprised they have such mod cons as hair-dryers,' said Rupert, watching his wife's pert derrière. 'Did you see the collection of dusty old beer bottles behind the bar? They look positively Victorian: London Porter, Oyster Stout, King's Ale . . . They surely can't be fit to drink.'

'I didn't notice,' said Perdita, her voice distorted by the sink bowl in which her face was buried. 'Perhaps Mr Yallop is starting his own beer museum. You never know, it could make the pub a tourist attraction.'

'It would take more than a display of dusty bottles,' scoffed

Rupert, 'and if this is the Royal Suite, then I hate to think what the steerage accommodation is like.'

'Don't be such snob. You're only *playing* a king, you know, you're not really going to ascend the throne. It's called acting, just try to remember that.'

'Yes, ma'am,' said Rupert to the rear view of his wife, an aspect which seemed to be able to move with a momentum which had nothing to do with the laws of gravity.

They dressed in the clothes they had tried on above the Clerkenwell greengrocer's, and when Perdita had applied her make-up and straightened Rupert's tie, they left the room with arms linked in stately progress. It was now after six thirty, and through a window on the landing they could see that it was fully dark outside.

From below them came the sounds of a bar coming to life – the clink of glassware, the scrape of furniture being rearranged, the mechanical clang of a cash register being primed – in expectation of the first eager customers of the evening.

'That'll be the faithful Sonia,' Rupert whispered as the couple began to descend the stairs which lead to a door into the main bar. 'The ancient barmaid who can't manage the stairs; the landlord warned us about her.'

'Why are we whispering? If she's completely doddery then the two of us creeping about might give the poor old thing a heart attack.'

'You're right, my dear,' Rupert said loudly. 'We're paying guests after all, not burglars.'

He curved his left arm so that Perdita could hook her right arm through it and opened the door and, like animated figurines of a bride and groom atop a wedding cake, they stepped into the bar only to find it completely deserted.

'Hello?' Rupert called out, determined not to skulk.

From behind the bar counter came a thump of something heavy being dropped or closed and a frail female voice said, 'Be right with you, my dears. What'll you be having?'

The owner of the voice appeared, or at least the head and shoulders of the owner, peeping round a trident of black wooden beer pump handles. The face, the shape and whiteness of a china side plate belonged to an elderly lady with a blue-rinsed perm.

Even across the width of the bar, Rupert could see her eyes widen and her mouth drop slowly open as if she was seeing her first-ever customers. He raised his right hand in a sort of limp wave and was about to reassure the woman that no service was required when she began to speak.

'Oh my good God above! *It's you again!*'

Then the woman's eyeballs turned up into her head and she fainted, falling sideways out of sight behind the bar, only a loud, unhealthy *thump* signifying the exact moment she hit the floor.

SEVEN

Unit

'I've often wondered what a film producer actually *does*,' said Oliver Bell airily.

'So have I,' said Mr Campion. 'Let's find out together, shall we?'

The two men stood at the front door of Heronhoe Hall and watched the small, angular Citroën bounce up the driveway, its hydraulic suspension system reminding Campion of the gait of a drunken frog. As it drew nearer and sighed to a halt, it was clear that the car needed all the suspension it could get as it appeared to be packed from footwell to roof with equipment as well as three people.

'A left-hand-drive French car,' observed Oliver, 'how cosmopolitan.'

'It gets even more so, as the film crew is Italian,' said Mr Campion. 'We must keep in with all our European neighbours if we're ever going to join the Common Market.'

The driver's door of the car opened and a long, leather-clad leg emerged, then a matching black leather-clad female body followed almost immediately.

'*Buona sera, Signora Petraglia, come sta?*' said Campion, nodding formally.

'*Bene, grazie. E lei?* But please, Mister Campion, call me Daniela.'

'Of course. Daniela, can I introduce Oliver Grieg Bell, the . . .'

'Ollie, please call me Ollie,' said a quivering Oliver, offering a hand which was already shaking.

'Mr Bell,' said Campion firmly, 'is the owner of the hall and will be delighted to allow you the run of the place. You'll find him very hospitable.' His voice took a more serious tone. 'As is his charming wife, Lavinia, whom I think is making coffee for us all as we speak.'

'Er . . . yes . . . she is. Please come into the kitchen. It's only instant, I'm afraid, but you and your associates are very welcome.'

Signora Petraglia smiled graciously.

'Please do not go to trouble on our behalf, Mr Bell.' She smiled again and Campion was sure he saw Oliver's knees buckle slightly. 'We have had our coffee this morning but we would like to see this famous house. This is Gianfranco, my cameraman, and Maurizio, our sound engineer. I am afraid neither of them speaks English very well.'

Campion had watched the two sallow-skinned, dark-haired young men emerge quietly from the Citroën and take up positions behind and to each side of the leather-suited Valkyrie currently hypnotizing Oliver Bell. They were already scouring every inch of the front of the house with their eyes, although Oliver did not seem to have registered their presence.

'Let's not keep Lavinia waiting,' said Campion. 'Shall we go inside?'

'Have you thought about a music soundtrack for your film?' Oliver asked hopefully as he opened the front door for his awesome guest.

Lavinia Bell's reaction to their Italian visitor was less enthusiastic but possibly entirely predictable, and Campion locked his jaw to prevent the progress of an uncouth smile. The tinkling of Oliver's harpsichord floated through from the front room while Lavinia played a timpani accompaniment of sorts, spooning instant coffee granules out of half-a-dozen mugs and back into a glass jar, angrily rapping the teaspoon on every rim.

'What is he doing now?'

'Auditioning, I think,' said Campion. 'Perhaps he sees a new career ahead writing film music.'

'She doesn't look the sort of woman to be wooed by Oliver's

sweet tinklings on his darling Hattie – as if she wasn't competition enough!'

'I really do not think you have cause to be jealous of either, my dear,' Campion soothed. 'Oliver is highly unlikely to stand a chance with *Signora* Petraglia, and if he is unfaithful with Hattie then at least you'll hear him being so.'

'Oh, I'm not seriously worried,' said Lavinia, screwing the top back on the coffee jar with more force than was necessary. 'That woman would eat Oliver alive and spit out the gristly bits. Isn't she a bit too old for the bank holiday motor-biker look? Mind you, she has the figure for it. Where do you think she gets all that leather?'

'Florence would be my guess. It's quite the 'in' place for leather fashion, or so my wife tells me, and I bow to her expertise in all such matters.'

'Yes, well, Italians are supposed to be stylish, aren't they? I just wish that one would go and style somewhere else.'

'Don't worry, my dear, they'll be out of your hair soon enough.'

'What exactly is she doing here anyway?'

'Checking out the hall as a suitable location for filming,' said Campion, 'although it's her minions who seem to be investigating the house while she is being serenaded.'

Lavinia opened a drawer in the kitchen cabinet and produced a packet of Silk Cut cigarettes and a box of matches. She placed one between her lips and offered the pack to Campion, who waved it away.

'No, thank you; I gave up when it was still unfashionable to do so.'

Mrs Bell was not deterred. She lit up and exhaled smoke with feeling.

'If they're using the hall as a location, does that mean Edward and Mrs Thing were . . . doing their thing, so to speak, under this very roof?'

As she concentrated on sucking on her cigarette, there was a lull in the rather ethereal harpsichord music and Campion strained to hear another noise coming from upstairs: the sound of feet on floorboards.

'Daniela's minions would seem to think so as they appear to be checking the bedrooms for clues,' he said.

'How dare they? The cheeky little swines! I'll soon settle their hash, as my father would say.'

She dowsed her cigarette under the kitchen tap and inserted the soggy remains into one of the empty brown ale bottles lined up on the draining board.

'I'm sure Lord Breeze would have them out on their ear toot sweet,' said Campion, 'but I crave your patience. For my sake, please, allow them to do their job.'

'I suppose I must as you're paying the bills, but I thought the main action was supposed to be down at the Sweethearting Barrow?'

'It is,' Campion reassured her. 'There's no evidence that Edward and Mrs Simpson stayed here at the hall together, or none that I'm aware of yet.'

'So why are those people crawling all over my house?'

'I haven't the faintest idea,' said Mr Campion dishonestly.

They both reacted sharply to the click of high heels and turned to face the kitchen doorway where the frame was filled by the statuesque Daniela Petraglia, hands on hips, her leather jacket and trousers creaking softly.

'We should be going to the boat burial,' she announced firmly. 'Your Ollie has offered to guide us there.'

'Oh, he has, has he?' breathed Lavinia.

'It's really not far,' said Campion, stepping between the two women in case a buffer was needed. 'Your actors are waiting their call to rehearsal at the King's Head in Sweethearting. We saw them last night for dinner and they absolutely look the part.'

'That is good,' said the leather lady, 'and we will see them this evening to go over their moves, but first my crew needs to examine the site, to decide the best angles for our camera and to judge the light quality.'

'Of course,' said Campion seriously, 'and at this time of year, you don't have much daylight to play with. What a pity we couldn't do this in the summer when the original dig actually took place.'

The Italian leather jacket creaked loudly this time as its wearer spread her arms in hopeless supplication.

'What can we do? The deadline is not of our making, but the television company. That is why we need to plan our shots with the camera, to fool the watcher.'

'So the camera does in fact tell lies?'

The woman pouted as if thinking carefully then smiled.

'Almost all of the time, and we women are often grateful for it. Do you not agree, Mrs Bell?'

'I really wouldn't know about that,' said Lavinia.

Oliver appeared in the hallway, shrugging his way into an ancient, faded Barbour coat while holding a pair of Wellington boots.

'Just off over to the dig, darling, to show the crew the lie of the land. I'll grab some lunch in Sweethearting but be back in plenty of time for dinner.'

'Do have fun, my dear,' Lavinia responded unenthusiastically, though her husband failed to register the icy chill in her tone.

'I say, Albert, do you think I should take them by way of Windy Ridge Farm and introduce them to Mr Spark?'

'I wouldn't if I were you,' said Campion. 'Farmer Spark seems quite relaxed about what we're doing and I got the distinct impression that unannounced visitors are not exactly welcome at Windy Ridge.'

'Happy to take your advice on that. Can't say we've had much to do with Spark – doesn't seem interested in being neighbourly at all. We've even invited him and his wife over for dinner a couple of times but couldn't get them to rise to the bait. Still, we'd better get going. Are you joining us, Albert?'

'No,' said Campion, 'not just at the moment, but you could do me a favour if you would while you're there.'

'Sure.'

'Ask Precious if she would be so kind as to pop back here with her van in about an hour, after she's met our visitors, of course.' Campion turned to Daniela Petraglia and beamed. 'Precious is our lead archaeologist and I think the two of you will get on like a house on fire.'

'She's American,' gushed Oliver, 'and female too. The women seem to be in charge all round these days.'

Only Campion, the nearest to her, heard Lavinia's muttered 'Idiot!' before he piped up chirpily, 'Oh come on, Oliver, we all know that behind every successful man there's a rather surprised woman.'

'Er . . . quite,' said Oliver doubtfully. 'Shall we *avanti* over to the archaeology?'

Campion and Lavinia watched from the front door as Oliver, Daniela and her two associates squeezed into the Citroën and the car sank even lower on its hydraulics before it bounced down the drive.

'How does that woman drive in those heels?' Lavinia asked. 'How does she even *walk* in them? And how on earth does she get out of those tight leather pants?'

'There is a very coarse answer to that,' said Campion, 'but one more suited to the music hall or a *Carry On* film than polite company.'

'Oliver seemed quite smitten and desperate to impress. Is *avanti* really a word in Italian?'

'Yes, it is, but not the right one.' Campion smiled. 'Now, can I impose upon your hospitality even further and make use of your telephone? I insist you send me your bill for this month, by the way.'

'You've been far too generous already,' said Lavinia, 'and anyway, Precious has insisted on paying for all her calls.'

'Precious? She hasn't been ringing America, has she?'

'I don't think so. I mean, she would have said if she was phoning trans-Atlantic, wouldn't she?'

'I would certainly hope so. She seems a good-hearted soul, which I intend to take advantage of today. My only *frisson* of surprise was that I'm not sure how many people she knows to phone in this country.'

'Well, she certainly knows somebody. She uses the phone every night and always makes sure nobody's about when she does. Perhaps she's a quick worker and has found a boyfriend already.'

Campion raised his eyebrows and shook his head slowly, his lips moving in silent counting.

'. . . Four . . . five. That's quite enough time to waste on me being shocked by the younger generation, now let us be shocked by the older one.'

'I'm sorry?'

'Try and avoid eye contact where possible, though he's actually quite harmless.'

'What? I'm not with you, Albert.'

'Down the drive, hiding behind one of the conifers which rather fails to conceal much of his girth. It's Lugg, waiting for the coast to clear. Like a faithful gundog he'll come trotting up with his first report in his slobbering jowls, or then again he may just be after a second breakfast.'

Lugg had made himself comfortable in the kitchen and induced Lavinia into providing him with a pot of tea and two doorstep slices of toast and Marmite while Campion was on the phone.

'Nice house you've got here,' he told his hostess, 'or it will be when it's finished. Your improvements, that is; long overdue, they are, if you ask me. The Mad Major never spent a brass farthing on the place from what I heard. Mind you, if he'd had a brass farthing to spare he would probably have put it on a nag somewhere. The Bookie's Friend, that's what they called him.'

'Did you know Wemyss-Grendle?' Lavinia asked her guest, although 'guest' seemed a loose term for the large ancient figure who had planted himself at the kitchen table and was currently overflowing the edges of a rickety wooden chair and crunching toast, occasionally picking wayward crumbs from the front of the dark-blue seaman's pullover stretched taut across his stomach.

'Do I look like a bookies' runner? Nah, I didn't know 'im and there weren't many in polite society would admit to knowing 'im, but I did stay here that once, with his nibs, back in 'thirty-five. A good year for port, that was, so I'm told; not much else, but good for port if you had the sense and the means to lay a few bottles down.'

'What are you talking about?' said Campion, gliding into the kitchen. 'This old recidivist isn't trying to sell you something, is he, Lavinia?'

'Just making polite conversation,' whined Lugg, 'to fill in the hours while others are busy with idle chitchat on the blower.'

'Filling your face and stomach by the looks of it, and neither my chit nor my chat on the telephone was idle. On the contrary, that call was quite productive.' He turned to address Lavinia. 'And there may be a call back this afternoon from an Inspector Chamley of the CID up in Ipswich. I've told him to leave a message with you. I hope you don't mind.'

'Glad to be of help,' said Lavinia.

'Yer just couldn't resist, could yer?' said Lugg, examining the empty plate in front of him as if expecting a miraculous replenishment. 'Calling in the local bluebottles, throwin' your weight about teaching them how to do their jobs. Not that most of them don't need a bit of help now and then.'

'I am merely using the official channels, as recommended by our mutual chum Charlie Luke – to gather some local intelligence,' said Campion with a sigh.

'Intelligence gathering, is it? I thought that was my billet, 'aving gone undercover for yer in Heronhoe.'

'Listen, old fruit, the last piece of word association that I would make, even if my life depended on it, would be "Lugg" followed immediately by "intelligence" but I cannot deny you have a rat-like cunning for sniffing out fellow rats. So have you anything to report?'

Mr Lugg did his best to look aggrieved at this perceived sleight from his long-time friend and sometime employer, primarily by turning his planet-sized bald head to profile and jutting out his lower lip.

''Course I have, otherwise I'd have been having a lie-in listening to the seagulls fighting over the dustbins, which seems to be the main spectator sport over in Heronhoe. I 'ear people come from miles around to watch.'

'Oh, do let's have it if there's anything to have.' Campion's face was immobile but Lavinia caught the sly wink of an eye aimed in her direction.

'Right then,' said Lugg, daintily pushing his plate, which had sadly remained empty, to one side, 'I did as I was commanded and slipped into the social 'ierarchy of Heronhoe wivout causing barely a ripple.'

'So you've spent one night there and not been arrested,' Campion remarked. 'Bully for you, that's an improvement on your usual track record. Pray continue.'

'You didn't give me much to go on, just some airy-fairy description of your burglar disappearing into the night like a crow, I think you said. Well, you hit the bullseye there, I can tell you, because the odds-on favourite if it's a bit of low-level breaking-and-entering you're after in the parish of Heronhoe is a crow: Bill Crow, to be precise. Our Mr Crow 'as a reputation for cack-handed burglaries and amateur thievery and is generally thought of as the type wot gives an honest rogue a bad name. Officially he runs a rag-and-bone

yard of sorts called the Heronhoe Emporium, though being near
the sea they probably call it salvage, but Bill Crow's your visitor
from the other night – I'd stake my name and your pension on it.
Any more tea in that pot, missus?'

'Don't indulge him, Lavinia,' said Campion. 'Once he gets his
feet under a table he's in for the duration. Any other news fit to
report?'

'The talk of all the public bars – for the saloon bars and lounges
I cannot speak – is about this treasure hunt your lot seems to be
on down the road, and you can bet five quid to a bag of toffees
that was what prompted Bill Crow's night on the prowl. Daft thing
is nobody has any idea what this so-called treasure is made of.
Could be gold doubloons or a knock-off *Mona Lisa* for all the
locals know. They're just convinced there's a treasure of some
sort, somewhere between this place and Sweethearting, though
nobody's seen it for thirty-five years, if there was ever anything
to see in the first place.

'Oh, and one piece of stop-press news: the arrival last night of
some foreign television crew. That seems to have got tongues
wagging, especially a rather tall blonde who seems to be the boss
lady. They've been put up at Heronhoe's one and only restaurant
that isn't a chip shop or a whelk stall, a place called Stephano's.
Eyetie, I reckon, does a lot of spag Bol and frothy coffee, not that
I've had the chance to patronize it yet. The telly people turned up
in one of them highly strung French cars, and you know what? It
was a dead ringer for the one I saw parked outside the front here;
that's why I thought it best to adopt a low profile and conceal
myself in the undergrowth.'

'Again, two words I would not normally associate with you,
dear Maggers: low and profile,' said Campion, 'but I have to say
that was most productive for your first night of eavesdropping.
Now, as soon as Precious gets here, we can . . .'

'Precious? A precious what?'

'Not "what" but whom – a very bright young American girl,
daughter of a friend of Amanda's. She's my archaeologist and she
will be providing our transport today.'

'Where we going, then?'

'We're off to *Statio Tranquiliatis*, as the astronauts say.'

'I beg yours?'

'Tranquility Base – on the moon – the place where the moon landing happened.'

'You're still not making sense.'

'Tranquility Base is the rather disparaging name adopted by the popular press for that admirable seaside resort of Frinton-on-Sea.'

'Aw, Gawd,' moaned Lugg.

'We'll have to smarten you up, though,' said Campion. 'Dressed like that you'll certainly frighten the horses, never mind the residents.'

Oliver Grieg Bell stood atop the Sweethearting Barrow looking down at the two rival groups of people below him at either end of the mound of earth now devoid of vegetation. This must be what a watchtower guard on the Berlin Wall experienced, he thought, or perhaps what the wall itself felt like.

He had been so taken with the tall gorgeousness of the glamorous Italian woman that it had never occurred to him that a young and presumably 'with it' girl such as Precious Aird would not also be instantly attracted, perhaps not by her voluptuous figure but by her air of supreme confidence and her fashion sense. Oliver was not, however, so naïve that he did not recognize the cold front which descended between the two females as soon as he introduced them. But that was women for you: unfathomable. And hadn't Lavinia gone suddenly rather distant when the delightful Daniela had turned up?

Perhaps Oliver had made a *faux pas* when he had introduced Precious as the 'chief digger'. Did that make her sound too menial – even agricultural? It had been rather stupid of him not to remember the names of the other diggers, especially as Simon, Dave and Cat were presently living under his roof, and certainly remiss not to recall the names of Daniela's technicians or whatever they were. As a consequence, Oliver was pretty sure he had put his foot in it from the moment they had arrived.

But he was used to people who did not know him well regarding him as bit of a fool, so it could not have been that which had lowered the social temperature. It had been something deeper, more sensory when Precious and Daniela had met on the mound – it had been almost as if two felines had found themselves suddenly whisker-to-whisker on strange ground, neither sure who had the better territorial claim. A worldlier or less-innocent man than Oliver might have sensed the tension and a more cynical one would instantly thought in terms of claws being unsheathed like flick-knife blades.

Oliver, of course, blundered on, escorting Daniela across the site, giving a running commentary on how the 1934 excavation had been undertaken by rival teams of vicar-led amateur enthusiasts. The deep central trench running north–south across the Barrow had, of course, been back-filled with the soil removed by the original diggers but, for Daniela's filming purposes, a long, deep trench edged by planks to be used as walk boards and perhaps a ladder were all that were needed to recreate the scene. Oliver offered this information as fact because he had a personal collection of Xerox copies of newspaper cuttings written by local journalist Sam Salt and the few photographs taken at the time, but failed to register Precious Aird's dry protest that perhaps such intelligence might have been shared with those actually doing the re-excavation.

Under the approving eye of the dominant Daniela, Oliver took matters into his own hands, or rather feet, and began to scrape the outline of where the trench should go with the heel of his boot. Meanwhile, Daniela had produced a small leather-bound notebook (which Precious was not surprised to find matched her outfit) and a tiny silver propelling pencil, with which she made copious notes as she strode around the Barrow, pausing every few steps to make a rectangle out of forefingers and thumbs and peer through it as if lining up a filming angle.

Her two 'assistants' circled Daniela like moons around a planet as she crisscrossed the site, speaking only occasionally and always in Italian. Eventually Daniela waved Oliver over to her and announced that the site 'was acceptable' and that he should begin digging the trench he had marked out as soon as possible. A depth of a metre would be enough 'to begin with' with the dug earth piled along the long eastern edge of the trench.

The woman slipped her notebook into an invisible pocket with the sleight of hand of a magician, folded her arms and waited for Oliver to pass her instructions on to the digging team.

As he was doing so – totally oblivious to Precious' icy glare – he remembered Campion's request for her to report back to the hall. It was a call which Precious responded to with surprising enthusiasm and, after a brief encouragement to 'get digging' to Dave, Simon and Cat, she trotted up and over the mound to the road where her VW van and the television crew's Citroën were parked.

At the hall she was greeted by Lavinia Bell and the sound of a harpsichord rendition of 'I Get A Kick Out Of You' floating from the front drawing room.

'Do come in, Precious.' Lavinia greeted her with mock weariness. 'You might as well – it seems we're having an open house this morning. Lugg has nipped across the fields back to Heronhoe to smarten himself up and Albert, as you can hear, is serenading us on Hattie. Oliver would be terribly jealous if he knew.'

'I think Oliver has a different female on his mind at the moment, if you don't mind me saying so.'

'So you've met the Italian siren, have you? Oliver was struck quite dumb in her presence.'

'Dumb is one word for it,' said Precious, 'but in America we have several others.'

'Being American, I am sure you do, my dear, but you are young and yet to experience the full ridiculousness of men.'

'How old do you have to be?' said Precious out of the corner of her mouth. 'By the way, what's a Lugg?'

'He's a friend or possibly associate of Albert's and I think he's harmless, though he looks quite fearsome: a bit like a bald orangutan although more jowly, with the face of a disappointed bulldog. I think he was once quite a colourful character and perhaps he still is.'

'Well, we surely can't have too many of those, can we? Any idea why I've been recalled to base camp?'

'I have no idea what's going on, my dear. Let Albert explain.'

Mr Campion looked up from the harpsichord keyboard as the women entered the room, but continued to vaguely hum the lyrics to the song he was playing, then finished with a flourish and a resonant final chord. Lavinia noticed with some glee that Campion had placed the bust of Lord Breeze on the floor when he had opened Hattie's lid and turned the noble lord's face to the skirting board.

'That would be one of my Desert Island Discs, I think,' he said,

'but a version done on a piano in a smoky nightclub at midnight,
perhaps. Hattie the Harpsichord is not the right instrument for
Cole Porter – far too, too *churchy*, wouldn't you say? Oddly
enough, that was the hit song of the year Lugg and I came to the
hall as advanced scouts for the royal visit. We had a great time
driving through Constable Country in the Lagonda bellowing, "I
get no kick from cocaine" when we passed a church and "Mere
alcohol" whenever we saw a pub. Quite disgraceful behaviour
really, just the sort of behaviour I would be calling the police
about nowadays.'

Campion had changed into a dark-blue faint pinstripe suit, a
white shirt and a red tie patterned with small shield motifs.

'I can't believe you were ever a young tearaway,' said Precious.

'Oh, I tore with the best of them,' Campion grinned, 'and now
Lugg and I are about to go on another madcap road trip – that's
what you call them, isn't it? – to cause mirth and mayhem in dear
old Frinton-on-Sea.'

'You are?'

'Yes indeed, but we need to steal your van to do it.'

Precious recoiled slightly. 'Steal my VW?'

'I told you we were tearaways and there's no tearaway like an
old tearaway. If I were you, I wouldn't trust us as far as you could
throw us.'

'Are you sure you can handle it?'

'My dear young thing, German engineering holds no fears for
me. I once drove a Mercedes, a Maybach and a thing called a
Kubelwagen in the space of one week, though admittedly I only
had the owners' permission for one of those. I can assure you that
I am fully insured, familiar with the Highway Code and have
considerable experience of driving on the correct side of the road.'

Precious narrowed her eyes. 'Is that a swing at my driving?'

'Good heavens, no.' Campion looked suitably offended. 'It is
just that I have need of transport today and foolishly have entrusted
my car to my wife who is, unlike myself, engaged on legitimate
business activities and far away in somewhere called the north or
possibly the west.'

'Then let me drive you.'

'A kind offer, my precious Precious, but I must decline. Much
as I am sure Lugg would find it an education to be driven anywhere

by you, Frinton is not a place for the young at heart and, while old fogies such as Lugg and myself will blend in perfectly, you would not. In fact, the last time anyone in Frinton saw an American it was probably at the controls of a Flying Fortress going overhead – and, by the way, one should never go on holiday to a place where they look skywards in wonder at aeroplanes. Besides, while I'm away I need your eyes and ears here, or rather at the Sweethearting Barrow. I want you to keep an eye on the Divine Daniela if you can bring yourself to do so.'

'You should have asked Oliver,' said Lavinia through gritted teeth. 'He can hardly take his eyes off her.'

'I need,' Campion chose his words carefully, 'a more objective view, a professional assessment of what she's up to.'

'But I don't know diddly about film making,' Previous protested.

'But you are American and Hollywood is in America.' Campion raised his eyebrows as if challenging the girl to dispute this. 'And that's close enough.'

'And unlike Oliver,' Lavinia observed, 'Precious isn't likely to get distracted so easily.'

Mr Campion diplomatically refrained from comment, especially when Lavinia added under her breath, 'So very easily.'

'OK, I'll bite the bullet,' said Precious, pulling a ring of car keys from the pocket of her jeans and handing them to Campion, 'as long as you promise to take care of the old bus and realize that you owe me one heck of a pub crawl at some point.'

Campion smiled. 'I will put my best man on it, and by that I mean Lugg. I am sure he will be delighted to plan an itinerary which is both sociologically enlightening and highly entertaining.'

'It's a deal, then, and just to prove that I already have my eye on our Italian friends, I took a good look through the rear window of their car before I came up here. It's stuffed with camera cases and microphones and the stuff you'd expect from a film unit, but why do you think they need two metal detectors?'

'I suspect,' said Mr Campion gently, 'they intend to do a bit of treasure hunting.'

EIGHT

Inside the Gates, by the Sea

B y the time they arrived outside the Hythe Inn in Heronhoe, Mr Campion was confident that he could handle the VW Dormobile, partly because Precious Aird had resisted the urge to throw herself out of the passenger door and on to the road.

Their approach was closely monitored by a figure shaped like an overweight bowling pin standing as if a reluctant sentry on the doorstep of the pub.

'Now don't be afraid,' Campion told Precious, 'it's only Lugg and he's really quite harmless. Be a dear and jump out and let him in, would you? The sliding door will completely baffle the old chap.'

Precious Aird did as she was bid, even throwing in at no extra cost a cheery 'Hi there, Mr Lugg!' which probably surprised the new passenger as much as did seeing Campion at the wheel of such a vehicle.

With a considerable amount of grunting and shuffling, Lugg settled his girth on the bench seat which doubled as a bed for the enthusiastic camper, though only one of half the diameter of Magersfontein Lugg, and rested an elbow on the wooden cabinet which housed a small sink and a pump action tap next to a brace of gas rings. As Campion turned the van in the narrow Heronhoe street, the cupboards rattled with bouncing crockery and the rattle of loose cutlery.

'If this doesn't take the dog's biscuit,' he moaned loudly. 'Yer spends half yer life below stairs and then when you gets the chance to be chauffeured to a day at the seaside, yer finds yerself back in the kitchen! You sure we're going to Frinton and not some Ban the Bomb rally or one of them pop festivals like they 'ave on the Isle of Wight – all drugs and tie-dyed blouses?'

'I assure you, Frinton it is, although I admit this isn't the most inconspicuous vehicle for such a destination,' said Campion.

'You can say that again,' grumbled Lugg. 'Now Clacton, we'd fit right in.'

Mr Campion observed his faithful companion in the rear-view mirror and expressed his approval. 'That's as may be, but I'm delighted to see you've made the effort to smarten up.'

'Thought it best to conform,' agreed Lugg seriously, smoothing down the front of the chocolate-brown squared pattern V-neck pullover. He had completed his ensemble with a bright green with black spots silk cravat and a dark-blue blazer which was fastened across his midriff, should he remember to breathe in, with shiny silver buttons bearing an anchor motif. 'If yer going to mix with the blazered buffoons, you might as well try and pass for one.'

'Good thinking,' said Campion over his shoulder, then to Precious, 'You see, he's not as oafish as he looks, if you keep one eye closed and squint a bit.'

'What's a "blazered buffoon"?' she asked, turning in her seat. 'Or is that just some patter from your double act? I mean, you two were on the stage once, weren't you?'

'You cheeky young . . . American,' scolded Lugg. Then to the back of Campion's head, 'She's saying we're Morecambe and Wise.'

'Who're they?' said the girl.

'A sort of English Martin and Lewis, though much funnier,' said Campion.

'Again, who?'

Mr Campion sighed theatrically. 'I was forgetting your youth, my dear. But to answer your question, old Lugg's description of blazered buffoons was, I suspect, a rather disparaging description of the population, or at least the male half, of Frinton-on-Sea, a coastal town popular as a retirement destination for those who like their greenswards trimmed with nail scissors and their pavements – that would be sidewalks to you – cleaned and buffed with a feather duster. It is a place where public houses are banned, motor vehicles discouraged and the trees in the municipal parks are not allowed to drop their leaves without written permission.'

'Sounds soooo exciting!' Precious put the tips of her fingers to her cheeks and mugged teenage ecstasy. 'I think I'll take my chances with the Italian bitch and join the digging crew. You can drop me anywhere here.'

They were approaching the Sweethearting Barrow and the film unit's parked Citroën, and Campion began to brake.

'Remember, you are my eyes and ears,' he said, 'and try not to antagonize *Signora* Petraglia – well, not just yet anyway. Now let Lugg out of the kitchen so he can come and sit in the front with the adults.'

As Campion applied the handbrake, Precious jumped out of the van and slid open the side door. Lugg heaved himself out, nodded his thanks and replaced the girl in the passenger seat.

Campion touched a finger to his forehead in salute as Precious crossed the road to the Barrow, then engaged first gear.

As the VW began to accelerate, Lugg, his eyes firmly on the road ahead, said, 'About the pubs being banned. That was a joke, right?'

Although he had no wish to rub salt into Lugg's perceived wound, Mr Campion could not resist pointing out the King's Head as they passed through Sweethearting, Perdita's bright red Mini Cooper being the lonely occupant of the pub's car park. Lugg muttered that the King's Head looked no more welcoming from the outside than the Hythe Inn in Heronhoe, but probably attracted a better class of clientele, it being 'country' rather than 'dockside', and it had an archaeological tourist attraction on its doorstep whereas Heronhoe could only offer a few weatherbeaten fishing boats and a swollen population of angry seagulls.

Campion reported the first impressions of the King's Head as experienced by Rupert and Perdita, who had been all too eager to share them over last night's dinner at Heronhoe Hall. If they were to be believed, Mr and Mrs Yallop, the landlord and landlady, were 'characters' though possibly not Lugg's idea of the perfect publicans. The barmaid, Sonia, however, would surely be to Lugg's taste. Being even older than he was, they must have plenty in common, although Sonia did have an inconvenient aversion to climbing staircases and the unfortunate tendency to faint dead away at the sight of strangers.

Lugg's instant reaction to this intelligence was that it was no more than the typical behaviour of the Suffolk-bred female, who were well-known for their propensity to swoon at the slightest provocation. Campion, who had married one, did not rise to that

but dangled his own bait to gently tempt the professional interest
of his companion by reporting that the King's Head possessed, or
so he had been told, a fine collection of historic bottled beers
behind the bar. Although in retirement, Lugg had accepted the
position of Beadle at the Brewers' Hall, one of the City's less
ostentatious but eminently content livery companies – a role which
he always claimed was mostly ceremonial but did involve an
element of what he referred to as 'quality control' – he feigned
disinterest in the pub's vintage ales, muttering that even if you
'swept the cobwebs off 'em' they were probably not worth drinking.

Mr Campion allowed Lugg to sulk quietly although the fat man
perked up considerably as they drove through Pontisbright as he
had not seen 'the old place' on his journey from London, albeit
in comfort, in the back of a Harrods van. For the next dozen miles,
they reminisced about adventures they had shared there and characters they had known, most of whom, Campion pointed out
sombrely, were still there in the churchyard.

By the time they crossed the border into Essex and, at Colchester,
had taken the coast road, Lugg was relaxed and sociable enough
to complain that he was hungry and even proposed, assuming there
were provisions on board, that he climb into the back of the VW
and attempt to get the little gas stove going with a view to a swift
fry-up. Mr Campion expressed horror at the prospect of Lugg
climbing over the seat while the vehicle was moving, let alone
experimenting with gas and flame, and he was sure there were
neither eggs nor bacon and probably not even a frying pan on
board. To prevent another attack of the sulks, Campion mollified
his passenger by saying that he was sure there were many excellent fish-and-chip shops in Frinton, though not – before Lugg could
ask – a single whelk stall. That, of course, grumbled Lugg, would
be common.

Assuming the role of counsel for the defence, Mr Campion
argued that Frinton really was not such a bad place and had been
much maligned by newspaper cartoonists and comedians. True,
he had seen with his own eyes the spoof, but convincingly official-
looking, sign at Colchester railway station which told the unwary
traveller that trains departed 'To Harwich for the Continent; Frinton
for the Incontinent' which had probably originated during a
students' rag week.

But with all good jokes, argued Lugg, acting for the prosecution, there was an element of truth and in his not-so-humble opinion, Frinton's louder and more colourful neighbour, Clacton-on-Sea, was a far more attractive retirement destination. It had a pier for one thing, and the most popular stars of variety appeared in the summer shows at the end thereof. Plus, it boasted a growing population of ageing East End villains and criminals who had avoided (or completed) a long vacation at Her Majesty's Pleasure and sought to end their natural life sentences in a nice bungalow with a sea view. Not surprising really, as Clacton had for several generations been a traditional destination for day-at-the-seaside outings for East Enders, just as Margate had been for south Londoners.

Campion claimed that he could call just as many character witnesses in defence of Frinton and that they would probably be of a better character than any Lugg could call for its neighbour only seven miles distant in geography but a world apart in gentility. It was well-known that there were two Frintons: Summer Frinton, which existed for between six and eight weeks each year, and Tranquil Frinton, where for between forty-four and forty-eight weeks a year the town snuggled quietly down under the security blanket of its own self-confidence with very little to worry about. There was hardly any crime recorded in the town and the municipal authorities had plenty of time to concentrate on ironing the green-sward and dusting the beach huts before the next year's invasion of summer visitors.

The invaders were not, of course, a barbarian horde but a rather civilized selection, who came by private car rather than charabanc or train and indeed, in the 'golden times' of the Twenties and Thirties, the fashionable set of holidaymakers included no less a personage than the Prince of Wales. In the past decade though, the railway – always crucial to the town since Victoria's reign – had assumed a new significance with the level crossing gates near the station forming a barrier between the old, established town and the sprawling new township which had sprung up in a fit of post-war expansionism. Now, in effect, there were two physical Frintons – one inside the gates and one outside – as well as two Frinton time zones.

Campion piloted the VW over the famously divisive level crossing and headed for the seafront and the Frinton greensward, under the many watchful eyes peering out from behind the regularly cleaned windows of stately Edwardian villas and frequent Art Deco houses. When a panorama of the grey and chilly North Sea filled the windscreen, Campion pulled into the kerb and parked. It being Tranquil Frinton, there was parking space a-plenty although the arrival of the lime-green campervan drew looks of disbelief mixed with downright suspicion from two elderly ladies sitting on the nearest park bench. They were well-muffled against the breeze coming off the deserted beach, with tartan blankets across their laps and matching red scarves tied around their heads like nuns' wimples. At their furry-boot-clad feet two shivering Pekinese dogs sat on their haunches like Chinthes – or 'Chindits' as the British army had called them – the stone lions which stood guard at the entrance to a Burmese pagoda.

As they disembarked, Campion tipped the brim of his fedora to them and Lugg strained a polite smile but both ladies and dogs remained impassive apart from a slight synchronized twitching of nostrils as if a bad smell had wafted in on the ozone.

They made their way towards the landmarks Campion recognized: the Free Church and clock tower in all their redbrick glory, the Grafton restaurant and, next door, The Galleon café and ice-cream parlour. Religion would have to take second place to more human appetites if the rumblings from Lugg's stomach were anything to go by, and so the pair veered towards the scent of frying fish.

Over a substantial portion of haddock, chips, peas and white sliced bread, followed by weak milky coffee and a rather embarrassing Knickerbocker Glory for Lugg, Mr Campion informed his companion between spoonfuls that they were about to call on Gerald Wemyss-Grendle in his new domicile, the Harbour Lights Residential Home for retired gentlefolk.

It turned out to be one of the Edwardian villas halfway along Connaught Avenue and offered no safe entry to, nor even a view of a harbour. Furthermore, according to the slightly dishevelled and clearly harassed middle-aged woman wearing a nurse's uniform and sensible flat shoes who answered the doorbell, it contained few gentle folk.

'Who? Compton? Oh, Campion. Yes, you rang, didn't you?' The nurse almost had to shout to be heard over the sound of loud military music coming from the upper floor of the house. 'You'd better come in. We're trying to get some of the residents down for their afternoon nap but one in particular is being uncooperative.'

Campion leaned in close to the nurse's ear. 'Captain Wemyss-Grendle, by any chance?'

The woman nodded violently. 'That's him – Old Grumpy. We keep hiding his records but he always finds them. He's particularly fond of the band of the Coldstream Guards.'

'So it would seem. That's Gounod's *Marche Militaire*, I think, and clearly a favourite,' said Campion as the music increased in volume. 'This is Mr Lugg, by the way,' he shouted.

Lugg took the nurse's offered hand and leaned in perhaps closer than was necessary to her starched aproned bosom.

'Be a proper angel, Matron, and go tell His Lordship that we're a delegation from Wellington Barracks come to complain about the noise. Then see if you can rustle up a pot of tea, would yer?'

The nurse wrenched her hand out of Lugg's paw and leaned back out of range of his leering face.

'Tell 'im yerself,' she snapped in a tone she would not have used to Campion but a vulgarian such as Lugg was fair game. 'I 'aven't the patience, me feet are killing me and I'm not running round after visitors – 'specially not Mr Wandering Hands up there. Up the stairs, first door on the left, or you could just follow that blasted noise. You can tell him from me where he can stick his trombone section!'

With a crackle of static from her blue uniform, she spun on her heels and stamped off down the hallway, leaving Campion and Lugg to mount the staircase in time to the music pouring down on them.

'I see you have not lost your touch with the fairer sex,' Campion said.

But Lugg merely cupped a hand around an ear and said, 'Eh?'

Captain Gerald Wemyss-Grendle, sometimes erroneously promoted to the rank of major and in many eyes fairly accurately described as mad, failed entirely to notice the two intruders until the music stopped completely and the room went silent. Even then, he remained seated in a fiddle-back rocking chair facing the window and continued to conduct the band of the Coldstream Guards *in absentia* though with a hand clutching a tumbler of orange-brown liquid rather than a baton.

Lugg had gone immediately to the portable record player balanced on the sideboard and, while he disabled the instrument, Campion took up a position in the centre of the room to distract the resident music lover when he finally realized that the band had marched on out of earshot, and turned his head.

'Who the . . .? What in God's name . . .?'

'Hello, Gerald; long time no see.'

'Campion? Well, I'll be blowed! Is it really you? I was sure that stupid mare who calls herself a nurse had got it wrong. Nobody visits me these days anyway, 'part from debt collectors and bookies' runners.'

'I can assure you, Gerald, it is me, and I can confirm I am here neither to collect debts or bets; and my apologies for interrupting your recital.'

Wemyss-Grendle propelled himself out of his rocking chair without a drop spilling from his glass, his face a picture of confusion as if he had not yet registered that the music had stopped. In fact, it was almost as if he had forgotten there ever had been music in the room.

'How long's it been, Albert? You still go by Albert, do yer?'

'It fits me like a second skin after all these years and I doubt if I'd respond to anything else now.'

The captain peered over Campion's shoulder to where Lugg was standing at ease, his bulk masking the record player and most of the sideboard it rested on.

'And that grizzled old sod,' said the captain, 'who looks like the chucker-outer at the undertakers' ball; I remember him, too, from before the war. He's your butler. Grogg, that's his name.'

'Only by absorption,' said Campion smoothly to cover the low growl being emitted by the fat man, 'and please do not call him a butler – he loathes the term and it actually does a disservice to real butlers everywhere, but I am delighted you remember him, because it is your memory we wish to tap.'

'Pah! According to the staff here – more like the Gestapo, they are – I can't be trusted to remember me own name!' He jiggled his glass gleefully in front of his face. 'I can always remember where I've hidden the bottle, though, and they never find it. Didn't bring any extra supplies with you did you, Campion? Running a bit low, so can't offer you one.'

Exactly when Gerald Wemyss-Grendle had gone to seed Mr Campion did not know, but the mental arithmetic needed to work out that the captain was not more than half-a-dozen years his elder was depressing enough. True, he had not seen Wemyss-Grendle since the war and men and women can change much in a quarter of a century, but Campion took a perverse pride in the fact that he could still fit comfortably into the officers' mess dress suit tailored for him by Dege & Skinner of Savile Row in 1940. The captain, once the same height as Campion and far more muscular in build, had not only acquired considerable poundage but the additional weight had made his body somehow slump on its frame. His natural bow-leggedness – a stance due to years of enthusiastic horse riding – added to the reducing effect. The backs of his hands were liver-spotted, he had shaved only in a cursory fashion and his hair had made only fleeting contact with brush or comb that day. In the tumbler he clutched in his right hand lay the explanation for his florid complexion.

'I am afraid I came empty-handed, Gerald,' said Campion, 'but perhaps we could arrange something before we leave Frinton, assuming they have allowed wine merchants beyond the Gates.'

'I can name three,' said the captain, his eyes lighting up, 'but it would be cash, not credit, I'm afraid.'

'That would not be a problem, but first, could we make ourselves comfortable while we discuss the reason for our visit?'

Now Wemyss-Grendle's expression changed to one of mild surprise as if suddenly remembering he had visitors. He sank back into his rocking chair and waved his drink-free hand vaguely in the direction of a rather grubby, chintzy two-seater sofa. Campion settled himself carefully and crossed one long leg over the other at the knee. Lugg preferred to remain standing, though he shifted his position so that he leaned over a small pine desk covered in copies of the *Racing Post*, in which he was taking a deep academic interest.

'I don't owe you money, do I? It's difficult to keep track sometimes . . .'

'Not at all,' Campion reassured him. 'As I said, I want to borrow something from you – your memories.'

'My memoirs? Never got around to writing them; if fact, advised not to by several lawyer types. Too many ladies with blushes to spare, even in these permissive days, if you get my drift.'

Campion replied calmly, 'I think I understand. You never married, did you?'

The captain expelled a sound which was part snort, part dirty chuckle. 'Why buy a book when there's a library on every corner? I never had any trouble with the female of the species – well, not until I fell on hard times and had to sell the hall and move into Colditz-by-the-Sea here. You got yourself hitched, though, didn't you?'

'Almost thirty years ago.'

'Bet you miss your bachelor days.'

'Honestly, Gerald, not a bit, but I want you to think back to when a rather famous bachelor visited you at Heronhoe Hall before the war – the Prince of Wales.'

'You mean the Duke of Windsor?' For a moment, it appeared that the captain was considering standing to attention as if the national anthem had struck up. 'Has anything happened to him?'

'Not to my knowledge,' said Campion. 'He and the duchess are alive and well and living in Paris. They have a very nice house in the Bois de Boulogne, given to them by the French government.'

'Typical French!' the captain spat. 'They chop the heads off their own royals then they commandeer ours. David was very shabbily treated, you know. Should have been king; would have been a popular one.'

'A popular chap, certainly,' admitted Campion, 'and very person-able, but lacking in judgement. Visiting Germany and being chummy with Hitler, Goering and Himmler and that gang was a big mistake.'

'That may be, but that was 1937, after he got the push, but perhaps you're right – he didn't show much judgement when it came to *that* woman.'

'You mean he bought the book rather than renewed his library card?'

'I don't think David ever thought of it like that. He was soft, you see, always falling in love as he saw it, though it was infatu-ation in my opinion. With Wallis Simpson he got it worse than

usual and then when people like Baldwin told him he couldn't
have her *and* the crown he went skulking off like a spoiled child.
You ever meet Baldwin?'

'Actually I did, through his socialist son. For a time we were
both members of the Savage Club.'

'What I most remember was that awful pipe Baldwin smoked.
My God, what a stink!'

'He smoked a blend called *Presbyterian Mixture* as I recall. It
was a tobacco made before the first war for the Moderator of the
General Assembly of the Church of Scotland, and dear old Stanley
had supplies of it posted down from Glasgow. But that's neither
here nor there; how did the Prime Minister cut across your bows?'

'Horses,' said Wemyss-Grendle firmly. 'It was always horses
that got me into trouble, far more than females ever did. David,
when he was Prince of Wales, loved to ride point-to-point. Trouble
was he wasn't terribly good at staying in the saddle and he took
a few serious falls, so much so the palace got worried, Baldwin
got worried and then David's mother put her foot down. She was
a formidable female by all accounts.'

'She was indeed,' said Campion automatically.

'Upshot was David had to promise to give up point-to-pointing
and was encouraged to take up golf.'

'But he still came down to Heronhoe and rode your horses,
didn't he?'

'He certainly did! He played hooky whenever he could, many
a time when he was supposed to be taking the sea air here in
Frinton. I'd get a telephone call telling me to "saddle up" and
David would turn up and we'd go charging all over the park,
whooping like drunken cowboys. 'Course, we had to keep it under
wraps and his visits were always hush-hush as the reptiles were
always on his tail.'

'By reptiles, I assume you mean members of His Majesty's
far-from-honourable press corps?'

'Damn right there, Campion. The newspaper proprietors up in
London played the game and kept things quiet. Looking after their
knighthoods most likely, but out in the provinces there was always
a reptile lurking in the bushes hoping to catch the prince and
Mrs Simpson at it. They couldn't wait to break the story, hanging
around like vultures they were.'

'Oh, I hardly think . . .' Campion started, but the captain, even though his glass was empty, was in full flow.

'Nobody knew anything about their affair – not here anyway. They might have done on the Continent . . .' Wemyss-Grendle grimaced at the thought of Europe, '. . . or in America, but apart from the society circle in London, the population was kept in the dark until that blasted newspaper in Ipswich smashed the code of silence.'

'I think it was actually the *Yorkshire Post* which broke the story,' said Campion, 'though I have heard the Ipswich version bandied about, probably because that's where Mrs Simpson was granted her divorce. That's all slightly beside the point, though. Can you remember when the prince came down to look at the Sweethearting Mound?'

'Of course I can; I'm not senile yet!' snapped the captain. 'And we called it the Heronhoe Tumulus in those days. You were there yourself – you and your pet bulldog there. Are you trying to trick me into something?'

'Not at all, Gerald, I simply want to make sure we're on the same page, so to speak. After all, it was thirty-five years ago, but you're right; Lugg and I came down as the advance party – checking for reptiles as you might say, not that we found any.'

'Pah! Didn't look very far, did you?'

Mr Campion's eyes widened behind the lenses of his large round spectacles, but the flash of surprise was quickly replaced with steely concentration. 'What exactly do you mean by that?'

The captain glanced once again at his empty glass and then, with his jaw jutting, stared up at Campion, who marvelled at how the belligerent old man was resorting to his natural state – that of the bully – even though he was in a sitting position and in a rocking chair to boot.

'You two came swanning up from London and did your sniffer-dog act looking for microphones in the bedrooms and photographers in the bushes, and then you buggered off back to your clubs and cocktail bars after a swift jaunt into the countryside to laugh at us bumpkins. Never even bothered to go into Sweethearting, did you?'

'Why should we have done that, Gerald?' Campion's voice was now as hard as his glare.

'You might have come across that snooper Sam Salt, an oily little oik who worked for the local rag, the *East Suffolk Courier*. He was hanging around Sweethearting most days, covering the excavation of the Mound, waiting to report on the finding of the great Heronhoe Horde, except there wasn't one. Not a sausage.'

Campion slowly removed his spectacles, hauled a large white handkerchief from a trouser pocket and began to polish them with careful circular movements of finger and thumb. Wemyss-Grendle did not understand the importance of the gesture, though Lugg did and he sniffed loudly as if in approval.

'I only heard about Sam Salt yesterday,' Campion said slowly, 'from Thomas Spark, the farmer, at Sweethearting.'

'That land-grabber . . .' muttered the captain, '. . . couldn't wait to get his mucky little paws on park land. I couldn't bear to sell to him and his frigid little wife.'

Campion replaced his spectacles carefully and peered over the rims down at Wemyss-Grendle, who shrank into the back of the rocking chair. For a moment, the only sound in the room was that of Lugg breathing heavily through his nose.

'Yes, I got the impression there was history there, between the hall and its neighbours.' He spoke as if pronouncing a judgement and let his words hang over the captain's head before continuing. 'Mr Spark told me that his father, who was one of the volunteers on the Sweethearting excavation back in 'thirty-five, knew this Sam Salt, even had a bet with him about what they might find in the dig – something about a side of pork against a pocket watch, I believe. What happened to our intrepid local reporter?'

'How should I know? I haven't seen him for years, not since that summer as a matter of fact. Didn't like the fellow – he was always sniffing around the girls in the village, and it wasn't tit-bits of news he was after.' The captain's face twisted in an uncertain combination of a grin and a leer. 'Very fond of the young females he was, if you get my drift.'

'Must be something in the water up there,' mused Lugg.

'Any female in particular?'

'Oh, there were plenty of willing young girls back then. They say this is the decade of free love and permissiveness but they don't know what they're talking about. Lots of ripe girls with little chance of snaring a husband, stuck in a backwater village with no cash even if there had been anything to spend it on. A lot of them were grateful for any hint of a good time.'

The captain's face had taken on an unhealthy glow and the hand holding his empty glass was shaking, but Campion's disapproving stare broke what was in danger of becoming a reverie.

'Salt was dead keen on one of the barmaids at the King's Head in Sweethearting; used to hang around her like a lap dog with its tongue out. Mind you, you wouldn't blame him if you'd known Elspeth; she was a little cracker with all the curves a man could want and all in the right places, and old enough not to know better.'

'Elspeth?' Campion asked with a sharpness which Lugg noticed but Wemyss-Grendle did not.

'Very popular, Elspeth was, if you know what I mean,' the captain smirked. 'Poor Salt didn't stand much of chance with her, though it didn't stop him trying. Elspeth always went for something a bit more glamorous, a bit more romantic than a provincial scribbler who wrote about garden fetes and flower shows.'

'The sort of girl who would fall for a dashing horseman and country squire?'

Wemyss-Grendle stiffened, unsure whether to feel insulted or be frightened.

'I can't deny I had my way with Elspeth Brunt – and I won't, so don't look at me like that. She was more than willing and there was no harm done, and anyway, I wasn't the only one, especially during the war years. I even sent her a bottle of bubbly after she married that wop back in 'fifty-six.'

'Would you please clarify that remark,' said Campion with the severity of a cross-examining barrister.

'I sent Elspeth a wedding present when she tied the knot with that Eyetie POW to show there were no hard feelings between us. Decent thing to do, I thought, given the fun we'd had.'

'Had you offered marriage?'

'Good God, no! Just fond of the gal, that was all, though I didn't think she was showing much sense falling for that Italian Romeo, but at her age she wasn't going to do much better.'

'Italian?' prompted Campion.

'There were thousands of them in Suffolk, all prisoners of war from the North Africa campaign, and most of 'em were a damn sight happier to be over here rather than over there. They were put to work on the land and a lot of them stayed on after the war, married local girls and opened restaurants, like Stephano did.'

'There's a place called that in Heronhoe,' said Lugg in a voice which brooked no argument.

'That was his,' said Wemyss-Grendle, 'until a year ago. Now it's run by a cousin of his called Rosario. Poor Elspeth died, you see. A stroke took her, sudden like, which is always the best way. Stephano said he couldn't go on without her, leastwise not in Heronhoe, so he sold the restaurant and buggered off back to Italy to retire. Salerno, I think he said. He was going home to Salerno – yes, that was it, the place where the Allies landed during the war.'

'This Stephano wouldn't have been around in 1935, would he?' Campion pointed out.

'Not around here. Back then he'd have been goose-stepping for Mussolini somewhere. I told you, Elspeth didn't meet him until well after the war's end. Before then she was open to offers from British, Canadians, Free French and Americans alike – 'specially Americans. They were very popular with ladies looking for a good time.'

'But Samuel Salt wasn't that popular, at least not with Elspeth?'

'Wouldn't know, old boy – never saw him after the excavation. He'd built up the story, you know, expecting some sort of buried treasure, and when there wasn't any he just sloped off somewhere with his tail between his legs. Mind you, we'd all hoped there would be treasure; would have come in very useful, I don't mind admitting, but there was nothing there. It was a complete waste of time.'

'You acquired an interesting bit of archaeology.'

'You can't take that to the bank, can you?' said the older man peevishly.

'Or the bookies,' muttered Lugg in the wings.

'But you could show it off to the Prince of Wales and Mrs Simpson,' said Campion.

The captain shrugged his shoulders and wrinkled his nose as if trying to put a value on such an asset.

'True, but David never really needed a formal invitation to come down to the hall to go riding and he was always wandering off into Sweethearting; said he felt duty-bound to drink in any pub called the King's Head.'

'That day he came to the excavation with Mrs Simpson,' Campion said quietly and deliberately. 'Did he bring her to the hall?'

'Of course, you'd sloped off back to London, hadn't you? Missed all the fun – well, fun for the locals. They were over the moon when the Prince of Wales turned up to watch them digging a trench – couldn't tug their forelocks hard enough and split their sides when he joked that if they found any treasure he would claim it by royal prerogative or some such nonsense. He was just kidding them on, of course, when he said he always knew there was a treasure in Sweethearting. They didn't find anything though, dammit.'

'But Wallis Simpson,' Campion pressed, 'did she stay at the hall?'

'No, she didn't. The day after you'd done a bunk, David turned up with his detective and his driver and we had a bit of lunch, then walked across the park to the dig. Mrs Simpson joined us there. Must have come under her own steam. When it was time to go, David said he would give her a lift back to her car and off they went.'

'I see,' said Campion.

'What do you see?'

'I can see how the local legend of the Heronhoe Horde grew. A local newspaper reporter starts the speculation because he's after a big scoop, then the Prince of Wales makes a joke about treasure in front of a group of enthusiastic diggers who are really keen to find some and it becomes a sort of self-fulfilling prophecy.'

The captain raised his glass an inch and slammed it down on the arm of his rocking chair.

'Dammit, how many times? There was no flaming' treasure! Why won't people listen? I even had that wop Bolzano going on and on telling me there must have been. Sitting right where you are, telling me to my face I must have found treasure on my own land, and him a foreigner who was not even in the country in 1935.'

Wemyss-Grendle recognized that something in the atmosphere within the room had changed but had no idea what. The large, bald gorilla – Grog or Log or whatever his name was – had at least stopped rocking on his heels like a bored policeman and become solidly stationary, his eyes fixed on his shoes as if in contemplation or even prayer. Campion, too, was immobile, sitting on the sofa, one long leg crossed over the other, his hands cupped over his knee, his eyes gleaming behind those round tortoiseshell frames.

'Stephano Bolzano?' Campion asked softly but deliberately.

'Yes, Stephano – Elspeth's Eyetie husband. Came calling last year to tell me she'd died and he was packing up and going back to Eyetie-land. Too late to go to her funeral, of course, not that the Gestapo here would have let me go. They keep me on a tight rein, you know. There again, I hadn't seen Elspeth for quite a few years. Best to keep the married ones at arm's length is what I always say. Don't know why Stephano suddenly got this thing about treasure in his head, but he seemed more interested in that old fairy tale than he was about his wife dying. But then, who can understand the mind of foreigners?'

'Who indeed?' Campion uncrossed his legs and stood up until his thin frame towered over Wemyss-Grendle. 'I thank you for your time, Gerald. It has been most useful.'

'It has? Can't quite remember what it was you came for.'

'Oh, just to reminisce and fill in a few blanks in my sieve-like memory, that's all. We'll get out of your hair now and leave you to the nice nurses.'

'Huh!' snorted the captain. 'Fat chance of a sympathetic hearing there; bunch of ice maidens the lot of them and mostly as ugly as sin.'

'Perhaps you should take up another hobby, Gerald.'

'Bit difficult, being virtually a prisoner here. By the way . . .' the captain waggled the empty glass he still clutched as firmly as a rosary, '. . . you said you would consider smuggling in some extra supplies for me.'

'Oh, I'll consider it,' said Campion. 'You can bet on that.'

As they trooped down the wide staircase, Lugg expelled breath and invective in equal proportions.

'Now there's a gent wot don't deserve the title gent. If that was the h'officer class, it's a wonder the revolution didn't happen years ago. You ain't going to get his whisky, are you?'

'I told him I'd consider it, I just didn't say when.' Campion turned towards the fat man. 'You heard that name, I take it?'

'Yus.' Lugg nodded. 'Thought it best not to react.'

'Well done, though I don't think it meant anything to dear old Gerald.'

'He's old but he's not very dear.'

The nurse had materialized at the foot of the staircase to see the visitors off the premises with a stern expression.

'If I'd spent as long in there with him as you have, I'd come out black and blue in places I don't like to think of.'

Lugg stepped towards her, holding out his hand. 'Just a little something to make your life more bearable, my dear, along with my 'umble apologies for treating you like a skivvy earlier on.'

The nurse looked at the small, plastic, rectangular object with tiny wires protruding from one end which Lugg had placed in her palm and asked, 'What's this?'

'It's the stylus cartridge from his nibs' record player,' said Lugg through a grotesque smile. 'And for your information, he's got a half bottle of Scotch stuffed into the cover of a Vera Lynn LP, should you be interested.'

The nurse closed her hand and nodded her thanks. 'Now you, sir, are a proper gentleman,' she said and Lugg beamed with pride, but only for a moment as she continued, 'and if you should decide to see out your days in Frinton, you'll be welcome here at Harbour Lights.'

Lugg was still grumbling, and Campion still chuckling, as they re-crossed the Greensward to where they had left the Volkswagen. The two old ladies and their Pekinese were still occupying the bench and all four faces were examining the lime-green vehicle with curious distaste.

As Lugg opened the passenger door and began to heave himself in, he fixed ladies and dogs with an icy stare and snapped: 'So we're a pair of ageing hippies. Wot of it?'

NINE
Lights, Camera, Inaction!

'I don't care if this skirt makes my waist look good – I'm freezing.'

'It's supposed to be summer,' said Rupert, taking off his jacket and draping it over his shivering wife's shoulders.

'But it's February,' wailed Perdita, 'and I'm fed up with all this hanging around. We could have stayed back at the pub until they needed us. They wouldn't have kept the real Prince of Wales and Mrs Simpson waiting while they dug what looks like a giant grave.'

'At least the diggers are keeping warm,' said Rupert, who was now chaffing his jacketless arms.

'I can find you a shovel each,' said a female voice behind them, 'but you'll get those swanky outfits all dirty.'

The young Campions turned to see a girl some ten years their junior. She was tall, with long blonde hair held captive in a ponytail by a scrap of red silk and had a fresh, rosy outdoors complexion. Under the bulky, mud-spattered anorak she wore over a fisherman's jersey, Perdita suspected she had a very decent figure and, hidden by tight black jeans and shiny soldier's boots, enviably long legs.

'I'm Precious Aird, your tame archaeologist,' said the girl cheerfully, 'and I guess you must be our guest stars, Ed and Wally.'

'Actually it's Rupert and Perdita,' said Rupert, 'but we are playing, or at least pretending to look like, Edward, Prince of Wales, and his paramour, Barnes Wallis.'

'Rupert! Behave yourself! You'll have to forgive my husband, Precious, he's an idiot, or at least does a good impersonation of one.'

'I'm sorry, darling, it's just that since you told me her name was Bessiewallis Simpson, at least after her second marriage, I can't get "Barnes Wallis" out of my head. You must admit, it's an unusual name.'

'So's mine,' said Precious, 'but I don't mind it. She, on the other hand, hated hers and she was always "Wallis", though the newspapers back home called her Wally.'

'I can tell by your accent that you ain't from around these parts.' Rupert turned on his best cowboy charm and tried to stop shivering in the wind coming off the saltings, sniping at his shirt sleeves.

'See what I mean, Precious; my husband, the idiot,' said Perdita.

'Oh, I don't think he is,' said the American girl. 'I think he's just a good actor, like his father.'

'You've met Dad?'

'Me and your Pop . . .' Precious held out her right hand, the long, slim middle finger crossed over the forefinger, '. . . are like that. I even gave him the loan of my van today for some errand he had to run.'

'That garish campervan?' blurted Perdita, her hand flying quickly to her mouth. 'I'm sorry, I meant colourful.'

Without a trace of irony, Precious said, 'Yeah, it is cool, isn't it? Albert said it would pop a few eyeballs in Frinton – wherever that is.'

Rupert mouthed *Frinton?* silently, and with horror, to his wife.

'We saw it last night when we had dinner at the hall,' said Perdita, 'but we didn't see you.'

'I was with my digging crew.' Precious pointed to the three hunched figures digging in the trench running across the top of the Mound. 'We're camping in the Orangery at the rear of the hall and, as my dad always says, when in the field, a good general always bunks with his men.'

'An army man, is he?' asked Rupert.

'Uh-huh, he was Air Force through and through and now he's in the aircraft business, which is how he knows your mom, Lady Amanda and, I guess, how I got this job.'

'Interesting,' said Rupert, containing his surprise. 'How's the job going?'

'Well, it's going . . . but it's not archaeology, it's more like set dressing. All we're doing is digging out the backfill of the 1935 excavation to make it look like it did when the stars of the show came to visit. That's you two, by the way. You're the stars of this show, not the archaeology.'

'Haven't seen much evidence of anyone being star-struck in our presence, apart from Sonia round at the pub last night,' said Perdita. 'Otherwise, everyone seems to be ignoring us.'

'Your moment will come when Cruella de Vil shouts "action" and the camera starts rolling.'

'Cruella . . .?' spluttered Rupert, 'I take it you mean Daniela, our beloved director.'

'She's a piece of work, isn't she? She's very good at directing others: dig here, throw dirt there, no, not there, just one side of the trench, keep the pile neat, dig deeper . . .'

The trench which had been outlined by Oliver Bell was roughly eight yards long and two wide and ran approximately north–south over the Barrow, the dug earth piled on the long eastern edge. The three diggers in the trench were, from the state of their clothing, already veterans of trench warfare, an image that was reinforced by the lone figure in jeans and a leather jacket who was patrolling the growing spoil heap of excavated soil wearing headphones and holding what at first sight appeared to be a metal broom, sweeping the ground in front of his feet.

'Isn't that our sound man?' said Perdita distractedly.

'He's certainly listening for something,' said Precious. 'The film crew brought metal detectors with them and just started detecting. They didn't ask my permission. Maybe he's just an enthusiastic amateur checking the spoil to see if the diggers have missed anything.'

'Is that usual?'

'Maybe it's standard practice in Europe. In the States we tend to fine sieve the dirt we take out, though we don't wait thirty-five years to do it.'

'Excuse me?'

'Don't you see, darling?' said Rupert. 'What they're digging out now was dug out in the first excavation in 1935 and then put back in when the dig was over. I told you I'd been reading up on this stuff. When will you get down to the level they found the boat burial?'

'We probably never will, not unless you give me another ten diggers, some shoring timber, some wheelbarrows, maybe a bull-dozer and a month of fine weather. Even then, I couldn't guarantee we'd get to the right level of the archaeology. There were no detailed plans or measurements made at the time – it was amateur hour, after all.'

Rupert grinned as Precious pronounced it 'hammer-chewer hour'.

'And even if we found the exact place where the boat was buried over a thousand years ago, we know there's nothing left of it to find. The timbers had rotted into the soil, we know that, and if there had been a body buried with the boat, that would have gone too by now.'

'So why the mine detector?' Rupert asked.

Precious corrected him gently, '*Metal* detector. We're not expecting to find any ordnance here. Could be our Italian friend over there is looking for loose change dropped by the original diggers. He might get lucky and pick up a couple of pennies with your head on them.'

'My head? Oh, I see what you mean. I don't think Edward VIII was on the throne long enough to have coins minted. If he was, they'd probably be quite valuable now.'

'He lasted less than a year, didn't he? Became king in early 'thirty-six and then abdicated in December – what was the line? "To be with the woman I love"?'

Precious grinned broadly. 'See, I've been reading up on stuff too. And all because she'd been divorced.'

'Twice,' said Perdita curtly.

'Then I guess that makes you the scarlet woman in British eyes! We have a far less starchy attitude to divorce in the States.'

'Or perhaps we Brits just take marriage more seriously,' said Perdita, linking arms with her husband.

'Hey, he's your king. We opted out of kings a while back, but if we were ever looking for a handsome couple of young royals to help out President Nixon then you two would surely fit the bill. Now I'd better get down in that ditch and help with the digging. We've still got a way to go, we're losing the light and my team keep giving me the evil eye. If I don't pull my weight they'll be demanding *my* abdication.'

'Has our beloved director abdicated?' Perdita asked her. 'She seems to have disappeared.'

'You could ask Maurizio over there, but he pretends not to speak English. Last I saw her she was sneaking off with the cameraman towards the village.'

*   *   *

Daniela Petraglia and her cameraman, Gianfranco, had slipped
away from the Barrow dig unnoticed and had hoped, somewhat
optimistically, to sneak into Sweethearting the same way. But
Sweethearting was a small village and its only street on that chilly
afternoon was devoid of vehicles and pedestrians; workers were
at work, schoolchildren were in school and housewives were far
too busy to stand on doorsteps gossiping or sit on guard behind
a twitching net curtain. If a cottage window curtain had twitched,
it might have provided more than a moment's interest, allowing
sight of the imposing leather-clad woman with a slim, leather-
jacketed young man in tow (brother, lover, surely not son?)
marching through the village checking the names or numbers on
the gates or doors of the cottages.

Halfway along the twisting street, beyond the small under-
attended church and the even smaller Victorian primary school,
the woman and her companion stopped on the narrow pavement
in front of a triptych of cottages facing out over the bleakness of
the River Bright and its saltings, their Suffolk Pink paintwork
pock-marked and fading, the thatch of their roofs in need of
refreshment.

At the third gate, as the road curved right and left from the
village towards the King's Head, the Italian woman paused and
looked around slowly and carefully. Satisfied that they were unob-
served, she pushed open the small garden gate and she and her
companion strode the three strides needed to reach and knock on
the dark oak door where the varnish had warped and flaked and
two white plastic numerals, a 4 and a 9, dangled from rusty screws.

Had there been an observer, perhaps secreted in the privet hedge
across the road – a poor, municipal attempt at a windbreak – they
would have seen the door to number 49, High Street open a tentative six inches, and after a flurry of conversation the visitors had
eased – no, pushed – the door aside and entered. They may even
have caught a glimpse of a small figure with a blue rinse perm
being squeezed to one side.

For almost an hour that hypothetical voyeur would have witnessed
a pretty dull spectacle, with only the occasional glimpse of an
indistinct figure flitting across the window frames. As the afternoon
darkened, lights came on in number 49, both downstairs and upstairs
and curtains were drawn, quite clearly this time, by the tall Italian

woman and there was nothing more to be seen from the outside. But had the inquisitive snooper moved closer, right up to the cottage's front window, and pressed an ear rather than an eye to the pane, they would have heard raised, albeit muffled voices, the thump of footsteps travelling angrily from room to room, the crash of furniture being overturned and then the unmistakeable sound of flesh being slapped several times in succession.

But there were no witnesses to see or hear when the Italian woman opened the front door and she and her young companion stepped out, leaving the sound of loud sobbing behind them.

As daylight fades, so do archaeologists, and shortly after three o'clock Precious Aird called a halt to the digging. Bemoaning the fact that they had no groundsheets or planking to protect the trench, now eighteen inches deep, she offered a brief prayer to the rain gods to refrain from visiting the site during the night, otherwise, in her words, they would have created a 'mud wallow' and not a trench.

Without instructions from their still-absent film director, Perdita announced that she and Rupert would join the diggers as they retreated to the shelter of Heronhoe Hall, and to that effect she shouted across the site to Maurizio, the sound engineer turned metal detectorist. Her news was acknowledged by the Italian only in that he pushed back his headphones, nodded, replaced the headphones and continued to sweep the ground with the circular metal disc of the detector. Perdita thought young Maurizio's behaviour odd to say the least; as part of a film crew he seemed distinctly disinterested in making a film and, as a young Italian male, strangely uninterested in making advances to any of the three females in his line of sight. An educational visit to Florence long before she met Rupert had educated Perdita in the wiles of male Italian youths, if not the wonders of Renaissance art or the legacy of the Medicis.

As the afternoon failed, the Barrow troops retreated along the road towards Heronhoe and the hall in single file, Rupert with his arm around Perdita bringing up the rear, Precious Aird leading from the front, the diggers carrying spades and shovels at the slope and stamping their feet to dislodge muddy earth from their boots. Their heads bowed with tiredness, they failed to appreciate the stunning desolation of the view over the saltings and the Bright estuary and, out beyond Heronhoe on the incoming tide, the pair of fishing boats heading home.

The lights were on in the ground-floor rooms of the hall, offering a welcoming orange glow as the file of Barrow veterans turned into the drive. At the front door, the column divided, Precious leading the diggers around the side of the hall to the Orangery, explaining to Rupert and Perdita that hot water was limited in their unconventional dormitory and she wanted to get her fair share. The Campions said they would take their chances in the kitchen where their interest in hot water would be confined to the teapot, assuming that Oliver and Lavinia Bell were familiar with the laws of hospitality as applied to cold and dispirited strangers in a strange land wearing the fashions of the pre-war era.

Lavinia, being a product of the best finishing school education her father could buy, was eager to play the role of hostess to the young Campions, especially as her larders had been so generously replenished by the senior Campion. She assured them the kettle was already on, biscuits were available and they should make themselves comfortable in the front room where Oliver was lighting a fire prior to his daily practice session on Hattie, his beloved harpsichord, though she did confide to the new arrivals that once the hall's finances improved Hattie would find herself in competition with a brand-new colour television. It would mean, however, finding a new home for the hideous porcelain bust of her father which rested on the lid when the harpsichord was not being played. Treasonously, Lavinia expressed the opinion that their burglar could have done them both a favour by knocking the thing over and smashing it while making his escape.

Once settled in front of a fire which seemed destined to disperse warmth at any moment and armed with tea and biscuits, Rupert and Perdita were treated to the first few bars of a tune Oliver had composed to accompany the finished film of the Sweethearting dig, a melody he was anxious to play to Daniela.

It was Perdita, not Rupert, who noticed Lavinia's sharp intake of breath at the sound of the word 'Daniela' and quickly declared her colours by saying loudly that if their beloved film director did deign to join them at any point in the near future, her time might be better employed telling her actors what they were supposed to be doing before she started worrying about post-production effects.

Rather than being at all offended by Perdita's forthrightness, Oliver became enthusiastic and informed the Campions that he could tell them exactly what they were going to be asked to do as he had discussed it with Daniela. Rupert had resisted the temptation to reach out with his fingers and gently close his wife's lower jaw, which had drooped in surprise, and asked Oliver to explain, preferably without musical accompaniment.

Oliver had been more than delighted to do so and had enthusiastically produced a battered scrapbook from inside the piano stool he had been warming as he played Hattie.

The scrapbook – a converted photograph album with triangular corner sticker mounts dotted randomly over the pages – was the product of Oliver's three-year search for what had, over time, been called the Heronhoe Horde, the Abdication Treasure and, by Lavinia Bell, 'Father's Folly', the elusive rumour of something – anything – valuable which Lord Breeze might have overlooked.

There seemed to be no chronological order to the entries in the scrapbook, which were mostly cuttings from newspapers and magazines, the odd scrap of map, a few photographs, several dog-eared handwritten letters and certainly no index, but Oliver knew what he was looking for.

He held the book open in front of the Campions to display the yellowed and crumbling top half of a broadsheet page of newsprint taken, according to a handwritten caption, from the *East Suffolk Courier* for 18 July, 1935. Over a landscape picture traversing four columns was the headline 'Heronhoe Antiquarians Prepare to Greet Their Prince by Samuel Salt' but if there had been any text to accompany the photograph it was now missing. Fortunately, in the true spirit of photo-journalism, the picture was relatively self-explanatory, showing the Sweethearting Mound surrounded by trees in full leaf, with the heads and shoulders of half-a-dozen men peering over the lip of a trench, the edge of which was decorated with bunting made up of Union and assorted naval signal flags. The men all wore flat hats and waistcoats, their shirt sleeves rolled up. Most had carefully trimmed moustaches and several had pipes clenched between teeth, which made it impossible to determine if any of them were actually saying 'Cheese!' to the camera. There was a strange, almost funereal quality to the whole pose.

'Why Heronhoe Antiquarians and not Sweethearting?' asked Perdita.

'At the risk of sounding cynical,' Oliver began, though no one in the room would have thought of accusing him of such a thing, 'my guess is that the *East Suffolk Courier* sold more copies in Heronhoe than Sweethearting, it being the bigger place. Plus, I suspect it was the vicar of Heronhoe who called in the local press, being keener on public relations than his rival the vicar of Sweethearting, and he would have insisted on calling them "Antiquarians" as "diggers" would have been too agricultural, or common, for him. I think he was a bit of a snob. Anyway, that is more or less the scene Daniela wants to recreate for her television programme.'

Both Oliver and Rupert were blissfully unaware that Lavinia had silently repeated the word 'Daniela wants' while rolling her eyes wildly, a gesture to which Perdita had indicated resigned agreement by raising her eyebrows in mock exasperation.

Oliver, who for once had a captive audience, warmed to his subject. 'This article appeared in the paper the day before the Prince of Wales, as he was then, was due to visit. I get the impression that there had not been much warning of the royal visit, as it was an informal one and not listed in the Court Circular or mentioned in any of the national newspapers as far as I could discover, though of course there was a good reason for that.'

'Me!' said Perdita perkily. 'I mean, Mrs Simpson.'

'Quite. The newspaper proprietors had agreed to keep a wall of silence around Edward and Mrs Simpson ever since the affair had started in 1934, thinking that once he became king he would do the decent thing and keep her as a mistress . . .'

'Oliver, please!' Lavinia was convincingly outraged. 'Keeping a woman as a bit on the side is not doing the decent thing, even for a king!'

'I'm sorry, my love, but that's just the way they saw it back then; in fact, it was regarded as something of a historical tradition, just one you didn't talk about.'

'Was she such an awful person they had to pretend she didn't exist?'

'I don't think she exactly endeared herself to the powers-that-be,'

Perdita offered. 'I've read that she was described as the sort of woman who, when entering a room, expected to be curtsied to or at least not at all surprised if it happened.'

'Haven't you ever felt like that?' suggested Lavinia, sensing an ally.

'Often,' whispered Perdita.

'Anyway,' Oliver resumed, 'the result was that newspaper readers in America and Europe knew far more about Mrs Simpson than anyone here did and probably why there was never a photograph of the actual visit. Which was odd, because Sam Salt of the *Courier* followed the excavation right from the start. Apart from the parish magazines, it was just about the only publicity the boat burial got, though if they'd found anything it would have been a different story – or at least a story. There was nothing about the royal visit in the following week's edition.'

Rupert dared to ask the question everyone had avoided so far. 'So are we sure there actually *was* a royal visit?'

'Of course there was!' Oliver was indignant at the suggestion. 'The vicars of both Heronhoe and Sweethearting referred to it in sermons, which were reported in their parish magazines, though neither mentioned Mrs Simpson. Of course, it could well be that no one here knew who she was then. It was more than a year later that the affair became public knowledge and then everyone knew who she was and there were plenty of locals who saw them together on that visit. By all accounts, the prince didn't stay long, just peered over the edge of the trench, made a few polite remarks and shook hands with the diggers. That's all Daniela wants you to do, I think.'

'She could have told us that instead of leaving us hanging around all afternoon,' Perdita moaned.

'Apparently she and her cameraman had some additional research to do in Sweethearting,' Oliver said in Daniela's defence, 'and in any case, the trench isn't yet as deep as it was back in 1935.'

He pointed to the faded newsprint image of the diggers clearly standing in a depression shoulder-deep.

'If that photograph was taken the day before the visit, why wasn't one taken *of* the visit?' Rupert asked suspiciously.

'I told you, it was not in any way an official visit and Mrs Simpson was definitely off limits to the press. Wasn't that why your father and the charming Mr Lugg' – Rupert and Perdita exchanged wry looks – 'came down a day early, to make sure the coast was clear?'

'He wasn't here when the prince was, but I was thinking that one of the locals might have taken a few snaps as souvenirs.'

Oliver shook his head and smiled patronizingly. 'These were rough and ready country folk and it was the middle of the Great Depression. Few people would have had access to a camera and film.' He paused, then drummed his fingers on the scrapbook page just above the picture of the trench. 'Come to think of it, it is odd that the paper ran this picture with a caption advertising a royal visit yet never reported that it had taken place. Even Samuel Salt, who had been following the dig from the start, stopped reporting on the Sweethearting boat burial. Mind you, the dig, as a dig, was pretty much over by then. In fact, they would have started back-filling had it not been for the visit.'

'Did you say Samuel Salt, dear?' Lavinia sounded bored, more interested in squeezing another cup of tea out of the pot on the tray in front of her.

Oliver Bell reacted with pleasure that his wife had been taking interest in what she had previously dismissed as his 'obsession'.

'Yes, darling; Samuel Smith, the journalist who worked for the *Courier.*'

'That's the one the inspector rang about.'

'Inspector? What inspector?'

'A policeman. Inspector Chamley, I think he said his name was. He rang earlier and left a message for Mr Campion. Said he'd made a few enquiries, as asked, and it seems that Samuel Salt left the *Courier* in July, 1935. In fact, he just didn't turn up for work one Friday, which was unusual because it was the day the reporters claimed their expenses. It was only the following week that someone checked his digs in Hadleigh, found him gone but his belongings still there and thought to tell the police. He was over twenty-one, unmarried and with no debts and no relatives to report him as a missing person, so the police probably didn't look very hard.'

'And Pop had asked this policeman chap to investigate Samuel Salt?' asked a puzzled Rupert.

'I guess so. He told me to expect a call from Inspector Chamley and take a message before he and Mr Lugg shot off to Frinton.'

Lavinia sipped delicately from her cup. 'I've no idea what it means, but the gist of the message seems to be that Samuel Salt disappeared around the time of the prince's visit and hasn't been seen since.'

Mr Campion and Lugg were clear of the bright lights of Frinton and negotiating the country backroads between the Bentleys (Little and Great) and the Bromleys (Great and Little) before either of them vocalized what they had both been thinking.

Campion took a deep breath and said simply, 'Bolzano. You remember?'

'Yes,' said Lugg grimly, 'Little Italy.'

TEN

Little Italy

The ancient central London parish of Clerkenwell, named, one presumes, for a well patronized by clerks taking a break from their literary duties, had been a proud component of the borough of Finsbury until a municipal takeover in 1965 by the less-fashionable borough of Islington.

It is unlikely that either the existing residents, or the ghosts of previous ones, objected to this snippet of local government reform, if indeed they noticed it, for Clerkenwell was an area which had long looked after itself socially and politically and had never been afraid to encourage the dissenter, the protestor or indeed the law-breaker. From the network of brothels housed there in Elizabethan times, to political street demonstrations by Lollards and, later, Chartists, to offering a domestic sanctuary away from Westminster to Oliver Cromwell and editorial offices for Vladimir Lenin for his newspaper *Iskra* in 1903, Clerkenwell had seen its fair share of colourful residents. It was a local legend that Lenin had gone drinking with a young Stalin on a youthful visit to London, in the Crown and Anchor, later renamed The Crown, on Clerkenwell Green.

Yet it was beyond dispute that the most colourful inhabitants of Clerkenwell were the Italian immigrants who migrated there in the early part of the nineteenth century.

London had always attracted its fair share of huddled masses seeking a better life, and though some of those early Italian settlers might have been tired and poor, many were skilled tradesmen and technicians attracted by the opportunities of the industrial revolution. The overwhelming majority of that first wave of invaders came from the Tuscan walled town of Lucca, where Julius Caesar, Crassus and Pompey had once met to split Roman political power three-ways. They brought with them an expertise in the making and repair of watches, telescopes, lenses and thermometers, and they prospered to the extent that they could import those Italian necessities they missed and which soon became part of the fabric of Victorian Clerkenwell: Catholic churches, restaurants, wine and ice cream, whose sellers with their cries of '*Ecco un pocco*' to tempt customers into trying 'a little taste' became known in the parlance of the indigenous Londoner as 'the Okey-Pokey Men'.

London embraced 'Little Italy' as it would a comforting hot chocolate on a frosty morning, although the residents referred to it is simply as 'The Hill' after the climb up the Farringdon Road from Farringdon and High Holborn station. Until 1940, that is, when Winston Churchill issued his infamous 'collar the lot' order to round up and intern enemy aliens.

In the Fifties, normal service was resumed to Little Italy with an influx of fresh blood for the returning diaspora, mostly from the region of Emilia-Romagna this time, though it became a staging post providing early orientation for new arrivals from all over Italy, including the generation of chefs who were to make Soho the hub of the *trattoria* revolution.

And, through family connections and recommendations from the church, Clerkenwell was also the first port of call for many a young, female Italian visitor travelling alone to London.

Seraphina was one of those.

Before it became fashionable for city-dwelling middle-class couples with large houses and growing families to employ an *au pair* girl – more often than not as a status symbol rather than an indispensable domestic assistant – every 'decent' home in London with children aspired to have an 'Italian girl'.

Their duties were varied and normally non-technical. They were not, of course, expected to be able to drive a car, but they might be required to learn how to use the latest electric washing machine with built-in mangle and to appreciate whether the lady of the house preferred Persil or Tide as the bespoke soap powder. Similarly, tuition might have to be provided for the household's beats-as-it-sweeps-as-it-cleans Hoover, for the poor dears would surely never have seen anything like one back in the slums of Naples or wherever it was they hailed from. The kitchen was an area of some importance for them as they would spend much of their time in there, not cooking (what did Italian girls know about food?) but doing the washing-up, drying and putting-away and cleaning down the recently installed wood-effect Formica work surfaces. Their busiest time would be early morning, getting children out of bed and breakfasted on Puffed or Shredded Wheat once the differences between these two essential cereals had been explained – the production of boiled eggs and toast soldiers only being entrusted to the most reliable girls, usually after a trial period in the house of at least a year. Having walked children to their nearby primary schools – though little instruction was ever provided in the strategic art of crossing a London road at rush hour, the theory being that if they had, as children, survived Anzio and Monte Cassino, they could cope with the Ladbroke Grove traffic – a girl's morning routine would then revolve around whatever cleaning or laundry tasks the mistress of the house delegated to her and which she could complete before, after a solitary lunch, usually of cold cuts from the family dinner the night before, she could retire to her own room, invariably at the top of the house, as close to the attic as possible, for two hours of personal reflection or study. Then it was collecting children from school, getting their tea ready and assisting in the more menial tasks of the production of dinner for the man of the house returning from a hard day at the office. Contact with this rather austere and distant figure was deliberately restricted by an unspoken protocol dependent on the age and attractiveness of the girl, a protocol strictly enforced by the lady of the house. Only when all chores were completed would the Italian girl be invited to join the family as they gathered around that wonder of 1950s Britain, the television set, an activity seen as a tutorial aid to help the girl learn English rather than entertainment.

With one day off a week, invariably Sundays so that Catholics could do whatever they had to, and a meagre allowance of 'pocket money', the opportunities for any sort of social life for the average Italian girl were limited. The suggestion, by many of them, that they supplemented their meagre incomes by offering to give Italian lessons to English gentlewomen or children was dismissed as fanciful.

It was not therefore surprising that with whatever spare time an Italian girl was allowed she would gravitate to Little Italy in search of the companionship of her own language, culture and traditions. Unfortunately, those traditions were not always lawful. The heyday of the organized gangs involved in criminal extortion had been the pre-war years – when the protection rackets which blighted every race course in southern England were run from Clerkenwell – but in Little Italy, old habits die hard.

Seraphina Vezzali was just seventeen when she arrived in London to be the Italian girl for the Knighton family and their grand Victorian terrace townhouse with six bedrooms over five floors on tree-lined Northumberland Place. Her hosts, or perhaps guardians or even mentors – certainly nothing as crude as 'employers' – were a well-to-do couple with four children aged between ten and three; Jonas Knighton worked long hours as a subeditor on a Fleet Street newspaper (sadly, not *The Times*) and his wife Alice had considered careers in the musical theatre and as an author of romantic fiction before settling on marriage and motherhood.

Being liberal with a small 'l' in outlook, and Jonas having served briefly in Rome on a British army newspaper towards the end of the war, it seemed only logical to offer bed and board in exchange for light household duties to an Italian girl. Besides, in 1955, live-in servants were almost impossible to afford or even find and absolutely *all* Alice Knighton's friends in her bridge and tennis clubs had one, even if they didn't have four kids to deal with.

To Seraphina, who had arrived with one pair of shoes and two threadbare summer dresses, the grey, smoky cold of an austere London was a colourful, light-filled box of delights when set against memories – and persistent nightmares – of her own hungry and dangerous childhood in bomb-scarred Naples. For the first time in her life, she felt secure and was guaranteed warmth and food in exchange for the tasks set her by Mrs Knighton, and she was happy with her lot. She was also clever enough never to admit to the Knightons that, whatever duties she was asked to perform for them, they were light work indeed compared to the responsibilities for looking after the five brothers, a widowed and wheelchair-bound mother (both thanks to Allied bombing) and the two ageing grandmothers which she had left behind in Italy.

Yet Seraphina had no desire to become English or abandon her heritage, and almost by osmosis found her way to Little Italy. On her days off, when the Knightons assumed, if they assumed anything, that Seraphina was sightseeing or at church, she would take the underground from Notting Hill Gate to Chancery Lane and Gray's Inn and then walk 'up the hill' and over the Clerkenwell Road.

She never told the Knightons about the friends she made among the Italian community there, or the hours she worked as a waitress in a restaurant called La Pergoletta, for she needed the extra money and was not afraid of hard work.

Seraphina was good at keeping secrets, up to and including her death.

Alice Knighton valued her membership of the Holland Park Lawn Tennis Club almost, her husband would complain to his Fleet Street chums, as highly as the annual fees. It was, Alice maintained with some force, her only luxury in life, at which point Jonas would sigh and reach for his chequebook.

It was not that Alice was a good or even enthusiastic tennis player, or that she lusted secretly after any of the tennis coaches, but she did enjoy what she regarded as a certain social exclusivity by being a member, especially when it gave her the chance to play a set against or take tea with the likes of fellow members such as Lady Amanda Campion.

She could not claim to be close friends with Lady Amanda, as Amanda's visits to the club were irregular and she was not the sort of woman who encouraged social mountaineers. Alice's coterie of tennis friends tended to be women of her own age with young children (although Amanda, at forty-one, could easily have passed as one of the youngest of that group) with whom she could exchange gossip and advice on the trials and tribulations of family life in West London. A constant topic of concern for Alice's circle was how to entertain children at weekends and during school holidays, a problem Alice had solved by having an Italian girl, making her the envy of the other mothers. It seemed only polite for Alice to share her good fortune with her dear friends and offer the services of Seraphina as an occasional babysitter and child-minder when her duties at Northumberland Place allowed. Financial remuneration was, of course, unnecessary as Seraphina would be grateful to meet new people and improve her English, which really was quite good, but occasionally a dress or a coat might be an appropriate reward as the poor dear had little money and her wardrobe was positively bare.

It was towards the end of the heatwave summer of 1955 that Alice Knighton began to have concerns about Seraphina, though it was coincidental that when she finally voiced those concerns aloud it was in the presence of Amanda Campion, and even then only prompted by the fact that she had been eavesdropping.

Alice had called in at the tennis club for afternoon tea and a sociable chat with any of her friends who happened to be present, expecting the range of gossip exchanged to be no more sensational than the ongoing drought in the north of England and the imminent first broadcast of independent television in the London area.

Not recognizing any of her usual circle of friends, Alice ordered the club's 'Short Tea' – a pot for one, bread, butter and jam – and, while she sat at a table waiting to be waited on, buried herself in the latest *Good Housekeeping*. She became aware that the table next to hers in the club bar was being occupied, but she had the good manners typical of a certain class of the English – something other nationalities referred to as aloofness – not to look up from her magazine.

Out of the corner of an eye, she was aware that two people wearing white tennis kit had sat down and could not avoid hearing a male voice loudly order two glasses of 'your finest lemon squash' with instructions 'not to stint on the ice cubes' which were 'as rare as hens' wisdom teeth' that summer. It was only when she heard a soft female voice say, 'Oh, Albert, do behave!' that she realized she was in the proximity of Lady Amanda Campion and, more interestingly, her husband.

Alice Knighton had heard of Mr Albert Campion through her husband's subediting job in Fleet Street. Jonas Knighton had on numerous occasions described Mr Campion; not physically, but as a presence. He was a man, her husband judged, behind many a headline, but his name was rarely mentioned in any story. He was thought to be 'well-connected', as the saying went, not just within the upper strata of society but also within the police.

The fact that she had exchanged several 'good afternoons' with Lady Amanda and had once even complimented her on her backhand was all the confidence Alice Knighton needed.

'Forgive the intrusion, Lady Amanda, but might I take a moment of your time?'

'Of course. Mrs Knighton, isn't it?' Amanda replied politely.

'Please, call me Alice. We have met, briefly, here at the club. I hope I am not intruding.'

'Intrude away, dear lady, just don't mention tennis,' said the man at the table. 'Our family is famous for being bad losers.'

'And also incredibly lucky winners,' said Amanda without missing a beat. 'This is my husband, Albert.'

Alice Knighton appraised the man as he stretched his long, thin frame until he was standing and offering a handshake. He was older than his wife – perhaps by a dozen years or more, she guessed – with the sort of fair hair which would go a gentle white but never grey with old age. Oddly, the large round tortoiseshell glasses he wore did not notably enhance the features of his pale face, rather they added to the overall air of him being innocently unmemorable.

'I do hope you don't find this inappropriate, Lady Amanda, but could I ask if you have an Italian girl?'

Mr Campion raised his eyebrows but bit his tongue and remained silent as the question had been clearly posed as a woman-to-woman matter in which mere males had no valid opinion.

'No,' said Amanda, 'our son is beyond the nanny stage now and we have always managed a small household without much trouble, and though my husband does require a disproportionate amount of care and attention, I would not wish that on anyone. Are you trying to find a home for an Italian girl?'

Alice Knighton shook her head. 'It's nothing like that, Lady Amanda.'

'Just Amanda, please.'

'Well, you see, Amanda, we have given a home to an Italian girl and I can honestly say we've – that is, my husband and I and our children – have all been very happy with her.'

She paused and it was Mr Campion who gently filled in the gap.

'But? I thought I sensed a "but" coming.'

'You did, Mr Campion, you did. Seraphina – that's her name – seemed such a good girl, I thought nothing of recommending her to some of my friends here at the club. You know, women of like mind, who wouldn't take advantage but perhaps could use a bit of help occasionally, picking children up from school, taking them for a walk in the park, babysitting on the odd night, that sort of thing.'

'The girl was happy to be loaned out, so to speak?' asked Amanda.

'She seemed perfectly happy and never complained and the houses she went to were delighted with her. They were all good families, of course, who thanked her with little presents and it wasn't as if she had to travel far as they all lived nearby. Bayswater, Kensington – all good addresses.'

'So what exactly is the problem?'

'This is very delicate, Amanda, and I'm not sure how to put this, but over the past two weeks I have had telephone calls from the police asking me to give them Seraphina's whereabouts on certain days.'

'You'd better start calling me Mrs Campion,' said Amanda.

'I'm sorry?'

'I think it is my husband's attention you desire rather than mine.'

Alice Knighton blushed and averted her eyes to her teacup, but her embarrassment was fleeting.

'You're absolutely right,' she said, 'and I should not have so rudely interposed, but I understand that Mr Campion has some influence with the authorities.'

'Reports of my authority and influence,' Campion said, examining his glass of lemon squash as if it were a perfectly mixed cocktail or a fine wine, 'along with those of my magical powers and prowess on the cricket field have all been terribly exaggerated, but it is true that I have friends in low places. May I ask if these official enquiries were anything to do with your Italian girl's passport or work permit, or perhaps some dubious political affiliations?'

'No, nothing like that. The police were checking up on certain dates when Seraphina had been helping out the Blenkinsops – you must know them, Nigel and Sarah. He's something in the City and they love the theatre but their usual sitter had let them down.'

'So you loaned them the services of this Seraphina? I must say, that's a jolly fine name.'

Alice Knighton could not decide whether Mr Campion was mocking her or being deliberately slow. 'Well, you could put it that way. The only problem was that a few nights later the Blenkinsops were burgled while they slept. Luckily they slept through the whole thing. Just imagine if they had woken up and come face-to-face with a burglar!'

'A frightening prospect,' Mr Campion agreed, exchanging a suspiciously innocent glance with his wife. 'Are you saying that the police were suggesting that Seraphina was somehow involved?'

'I have no idea what they were thinking, but on the night in question Seraphina was at home at Northumberland Place, with us, watching television.'

Mr Campion thought for a moment and said, 'Television – yes. I was thinking we ought to get one of those . . . but I digress. So you were able to provide Seraphina with a cast-iron alibi; moreover, a genuine one, yes?'

'Of course it was. Seraphina was not out of our sight that evening and I will swear on a stack of Bibles that she never left the house during the night. I told them that, and then I told them exactly the same thing when they rang again and asked about the Symingtons' and the Warnocks'.'

'Let me guess,' said Mr Campion, 'you had loaned Seraphina to the Symington and the Warnock households, and they too had subsequently suffered burglaries.'

'Exactly!' Alice Knighton was delighted that Mr Campion at last seemed to be paying attention. 'But on both those occasions, Seraphina was at home with us; I swear she was, and I told the police that.'

She looked to Amanda for support but Amanda remained non-committal and, with a gracious bob of the head, deferred to her husband.

'Does your Seraphina have any family or friends in London; Italian ones, that is?'

'She's never brought anyone to the house, but I know she spends her days off over in Clerkenwell in what they call Little Italy.'

'Oh, dear,' said Mr Campion.

Mr Campion explained patiently and repeatedly to Alice Knighton that he was not a policeman and had absolutely no more influence on police matters than the average rate-paying citizen, He did, however, have more than a nodding acquaintance with a certain senior officer, Chief Superintendent Yeo, who might be persuaded to reveal the current state of police thinking on the matter. He could not, of course, make any promises and Mr Yeo would be firmly within his rights to tell Mr Campion to withdraw his inquisitive nostrils.

Good as his word, Campion telephoned Yeo that very evening and was mildly surprised, though of course he did not show it, to find that the chief superintendent was fully conversant with the domestic problem of Mrs Knighton's friends and neighbours.

'Yes, we've had a real spate of house-breaking in Bayswater and Notting Hill over the last month or so, properties belonging to Blenkinsop, Symington and Warnock off the top of my head and maybe one or two others that have gone unreported. The thieves were very careful, in and out very fast, leaving no mess, almost like they knew what they were looking for. Quite selective, they were – going for jewellery, silverware, even a mink coat which the lady of the house only noticed was missing after we asked her to check, her not having the need of it what with the heatwave this year. Put my best divisional inspector on it, son of an old colleague of mine and one of our rising stars, chap called Charlie Luke.'

'Him I have come across,' Mr Campion said, 'and I could not think of a better man for the job. For any job, come to think of it.'

Chief Superintendent Yeo, always happy to hear his protégé praised, promised that Luke would ring Campion with an update on his investigation, which the Divisional Detective Inspector duly did three days later, though when he did it was with a heavy heart and grimness in his voice.

'I understand you were making enquiries about an Italian national, a female by the name of Seraphina Vezzali. I'm afraid I have to tell you that she was found in the early hours of this morning on the pavement outside St Peter's Church on the Clerkenwell Road. It looks as if she's been beaten to death.'

'Stop kicking yerself,' said Lugg.

'You didn't know the girl,' said Amanda.

'She was only seventeen,' said Mr Campion.

A week after breaking the news on the telephone, DDI Charles Luke called on the Campions to update them on his investigations.

Luke's divisional CID team had already suspected that the Bayswater break-ins had been if not an 'inside job' then a job with insider information and had, with painstaking police thoroughness, searched for the common thread which would link the homes of the victims. The usual suspects were the first to be vetted – milkmen, postmen, window-cleaners, dustbin men, meter-readers, newspaper boys and anyone whose visit to the property would go unremarked but who would have the opportunity to spy out the lie of the land. And, as usual, those suspects turned out to be invariably honest and, for the purposes of the investigation, unrewarding. Next came the occasional visitor or passer-by – delivery drivers, market researchers and door-to-door salesmen known to have been working the area, even rag-and-bone men (Bayswater offered rich pickings) – and again they turned out to be an innocent lot. Finally came that most difficult of categories, the irregular and infrequent or unique visitor to a suspicious number of the houses which had been robbed.

But in two households, and then three and then four, one name did crop up: Seraphina, that charming Italian girl who lives with the Knightons in Northumberland Place – so good with children, so polite, so . . . innocent.

'It's a trick as old as Dickens,' Charles Luke told them, having refused a fine malt whisky on the grounds that his anger needed no fuel.

'Are we talking Ikey Solomon here?' asked Mr Campion.

'I see you've done your history homework.'

'Never mind 'is nibs' akker-demicals – who's this Ikey Solomon and does he need a bit of a sortin' out?' Lugg contributed to the discussion.

'Ikey was a legendary fence who dealt in stolen goods in the early nineteenth century and got gangs of kids to break into houses or pick pockets for him. He was the inspiration for Dickens' character Fagin in *Oliver Twist*, which is a book, so you've probably never heard of it, though there was a jolly good film of it not long ago with a rather controversial portrayal of Fagin by a young chap called Alec Guinness.'

'Guinness, eh?'

'Yes, I thought that might get your attention. Now please be quiet and let Mr Luke continue.'

'Well, you can guess, can't you, Mr Campion?' said Luke. 'Young Italian girl in London all alone, naturally seeks out other Eyeties. Where does she find them? Where else but Clerkenwell: Little Italy. 'Course, it's nowhere near what it was before the war when most of them were interned, but a few of the bad eggs have found their way back and some new bad eggs have arrived in the last few years, from down south: Salerno, Naples, places like that. They're the sort who have a twisted sense of family values, if you know what I mean.'

'I think I do,' said Campion.

'They trade in pressure, putting the squeeze on Italians over here by threatening their families back home. They get them to thieve for them or distribute smuggled goods – booze, cigarettes, drugs – and the centre of the fencing operation, or one of them, is a restaurant up near the Mount Pleasant sorting office, run by a family called Bolzano. Seraphina Vezzali has been identified as working there as a waitress odd days, cash-in-hand, of course. It would have been easy enough to snare her into helping out the other side of the family business.'

'Is your intelligence reliable?'

'I stand by it. Westminster Division actually recruited a couple of young Italian lads back in 'forty-eight, children of long-term residents who'd been interned, though they'd never had any truck with Mussolini and wanted to be British. They've come in very useful, keeping an eye and an ear on Little Italy for us.'

'And they are aware of this Bolzano family?'

'Very much so. There's a pair of brothers, Marco and Stephano, running the restaurant – it's called the Pergoletta, by the way – but they're just foot soldiers. Thank you.'

Luke took a cigarette from the silver case offered by Campion and then a light from, he noticed, a well-manicured but slightly shaking hand.

'The Bolzanos aren't the kingpins, they're part of a bigger family business based in Italy, a business based entirely on crime and involving ties of loyalty so tight they make some of our East-End gangs look like strangers on a morning commuter train into London Bridge. Everything is run on a code of silence so nobody peaches or informs, at least not to us, but maybe the chaps in Interpol will have better luck.'

'Interpol?' grunted Lugg. 'What's that then?'

'ICPO,' said Campion, 'the International Criminal Police Organization based in Paris. The telegraphic address is INTERPOL and that became their nickname. They're going to make it official next year, not that anything they can do is going to help poor Seraphina. Do we know how it happened, Inspector?'

Luke breathed out smoke like a dragon. 'Nobody's talking, but we have a theory – well, I have a theory. Some Fagin character – for my money one of the Bolzanos – was using the girl, wittingly or unwittingly, to pass on information about the big houses she visited, though obviously not the place she lived herself, what valuables they had, if the owners had regular nights when they went out, that sort of thing. Maybe she realized what she was being used for – and we've no evidence she made any money out of the burglaries – and decided enough was enough. There again, she might have got wind of our enquiries, especially after she showed up on our radar and we contacted Mrs Knighton, and got into a blue funk. Either way, I reckon she went to Clerkenwell to hand in her resignation, so to speak.'

'But her resignation was not accepted,' said Campion softly.

Luke shrugged his oak beam shoulders. 'Tempers flared; perhaps she threatened to come and tell us what had been going on, who knows? But some nasty sod thought Seraphina needed a good slapping to shut her up and it went too far. That's me being chari-table, by the way.'

With venom, Mr Campion crushed his cigarette into a glass ashtray and said, 'Charity is not a consideration in this case.'

'Albert, please do not make this personal,' Amanda pleaded.

'I can't help it, my darling. My help was asked for and I failed to respond quickly enough.'

'I think the die was already cast by the time Mrs Knighton approached you,' said Luke. 'Whether the girl had a change of heart or realized she'd be played for a dupe or was just scared, we'll never know. She did the worst thing she could have and went to Little Italy where she thought she was among her own people. They beat her to death and dumped her body on the pavement in front of St Peter's Church.'

'Do you have any suspects?'

'My money would be on Marco Bolzano. He's the brawn of the outfit, but truth is we've got no hard evidence and certainly no witnesses. We'll keep looking, though, Mr Campion, I'll make sure of that. Seraphina didn't have much of life but she won't be forgotten.'

'No,' said Campion slowly, 'she will not.'

After several false starts, Mr Campion had discovered how to dip the headlights on Precious Aird's VW campervan and he was negotiating the narrow country road between Pontisbright and Sweethearting before Lugg, after a long period of contemplative silence, returned to the subject.

'So yer thinking – an' I know you are 'cos I can hear the cogs whirring – that the Bolzano that visited the Mad Major was one of the Bolzano brothers back in Little Italy in 'fifty-five.'

'I suspect it was.'

'And now he's gone home to the real Italy.'

'So it would seem, if dear old Gerald is to be believed.'

'And you had no idea this Bolzano bloke had been living in Heronhoe for what, ten years or more?'

'Honest Injun, I did not.'

'Pah!' Lugg scoffed. 'Don't credit that with a bag of toffees. You've never forgotten that poor girl's murder and you told me to keep an ear open for any gossip about Clerkenwell more or less the minute I arrived here.'

'So I did,' Campion agreed, 'and you are perfectly correct

about Seraphina Vezzali, but I wasn't thinking about the Bolzanos specifically, rather the real power behind the Clerkenwell throne: the Italian family business that the Bolzanos worked for.'

In the darkness of the VW's interior, Mr Campion thought he could actually hear, even above the chugging of the engine, Lugg's face contort in puzzlement.

'Then answer me this,' said Lugg eventually, 'what's the connection between some Italian villains, all this digging in fields and a treasure linked to the Abdication which hardly anybody really believes exist?'

'Elspeth,' said Mr Campion, keeping his eyes on the road ahead and the pools of light from the van's headlamps. 'Who is also, sadly, dead.'

ELEVEN
Tales from the Tap Room

T he return journey from Frinton and driving in the dark had tired Campion more than he would care to admit and he was grateful to see the lights of Heronhoe Hall as he turned into the driveway. Lugg, in contrast, had a spring in his step once he realized he had arrived in time for dinner and, even if it was a meal of cold cuts, they were, after all, Harrods' cold cuts.

Perdita and Lavinia busied themselves in the kitchen where they were joined by Lugg, who proved more a hindrance than a help, while Campion and Rupert settled in mismatched armchairs near the fire in the front room and Oliver Bell rattled glasses and blew the dust off a bottle of dry sherry.

Campion asked if Precious was around as he wished to reassure her that he had returned her van intact from his expedition into darkest Essex.

'I've asked her to join us for dinner,' Oliver said, pouring sherry. 'She's using the telephone at the moment. Which reminds me: Lavinia took a message for you from an Inspector Chamley this afternoon about Sam Salt, the journalist who covered the original dig. It seems he simply disappeared the day after the visit of Edward and Mrs Simpson and nobody's seen him since.'

Mr Campion replied with a non-committal, 'Interesting,' and then turned to his son. 'But how are things with our thespian versions of the famous lovers?'

'We spent an afternoon being cold, bored and forgotten. Our beloved director disappeared with the cameraman and we came back here when the diggers packed in,' Rupert said grumpily. 'God knows when we'll do any actual filming.'

'I'm told it can be a long and boring process,' said Mr Campion, taking off his spectacles and massaging the bridge of his nose with finger and thumb, 'but that doesn't sound like any way to treat their stars.'

'We're hardly stars, Pop; we don't even have any lines. According to Oliver, we just stand on the lip of the trench looking regal and pretending to chat with the diggers. We're set dressing, that's all we are.'

'Some of us have always felt like that,' muttered Lugg, 'or even salad dressing, come to think of it.'

Oliver laughed politely but Campion said, 'Don't encourage him.'

'Did your trip to Frinton bear fruit?' Rupert asked and Lugg could not resist.

'Found a real old fruit. Overripe, yer might say.'

'Ignore him,' said Campion. 'Those aren't really words; they're the sound of his stomach rumbling.'

'I'll see if dinner is ready,' Oliver offered. 'It's pot luck, I'm afraid, but the pot is of very high quality and thanks to your generosity, Mr C., we have wine as well.'

'Please don't open a bottle on our account,' Campion demurred. 'Lugg and I are going out later on a bit of a pub crawl.'

Lugg's face contorted briefly. 'We are? Fair enough.'

'Not without me, you ain't.' The voice was young, female, fearless and undoubtedly American. 'That was the deal, remember? You had the use of my van on condition you took me to one of your Great British pubs.'

Campion levered himself out of his chair and handed his sherry glass to Rupert, then turned to address the girl who had just entered.

'A deal is a deal, Precious, and I will be abstemious and refrain from alcohol in order to act as your chauffeur while my elderly friend here, who has far more experience in these matters than I, will be your guide and mentor on how to behave in an English public house.'

'It'll be a pleasure to show you the ropes, m'dear,' said Lugg, smacking his lips, 'just as soon as we've had a spot of grub to take the edge off.' Then turned on Campion with his best indignant scowl. 'And less of the "elderly", thank you very much.'

'Do you have anywhere exciting in mind?' asked Rupert.

'Only the King's Head in Sweethearting,' replied his father, 'but at least you'll get a lift home.'

'Before we go anywhere,' Precious announced, 'you'd better get to the phone, Mr C. There's a call for you and it's your wife. Don't worry, I haven't told Lady Amanda you're taking us out drinking.'

'Thank goodness for that. I wonder what she wants? Hey-ho, better not keep the boss lady waiting. Do excuse me.'

Thirty seconds after Campion had left the room, Lugg caught Rupert's eye.

'I didn't hear the phone ring. Did you?'

If Precious Aird had a pre-conceived notion of what comprised a typical night in an English country pub – a sing-song around an upright piano, the odd Morris Dancer flitting across the bar waving a pig's bladder, perhaps a guest appearance by a pair of Pearly Queens – she was to be sadly disappointed. The arrival of the party of five from Heronhoe Hall at around nine o'clock that evening more than doubled the population of the saloon bar.

Warming to his task as Precious Aird's appointed guide, bodyguard and mentor, Lugg had patiently explained that 'saloon' in the instance of a British pub meant the more comfortable and slightly more expensive of the two bars usually on offer, the word deriving from the French *salon* rather than anything to do with a hostelry found in Dodge City or other parts of the Wild West. Normally, of course, he and the senior Campion would be found slumming it in the 'public' bar, especially in a city like London, as that was where the gossip was at both its freshest and ripest, but with ladies in tow and out here in the sticks, it was probably safest to stick to the saloon.

If his pupil insisted on drinking beer, then Lugg's advice was the same, he claimed, as he would give a visitor to Scotland asking for recommendations on which Scotch to drink: follow the example of the locals, who would know what was the best quality and value on offer. When it came to beer, Precious must not expect anything like 'that fizzy Yankee stuff' which was ice cold and weak as water (on which point he was only half right). In the King's Head she should expect the Suffolk regulars to drink mild ale or, if they were feeling adventurous, a brown-and-mild combination, at least during the winter months. After the spring equinox, this heady cocktail would be replaced by light-and-bitter, which was, said the cynics, the only way Suffolk folk knew the seasons had changed.

He had added one last piece of superfluous advice. 'And if the yokels speak in a funny way in an accent which yer might find h'unintelligible, don't worry. Your young ears'll soon pick up their foreign lingo and you'll be able to translate for me.'

Precious Aird's first observation on entering the saloon bar was that there was no dart board – that stalwart component of the English pub as seen in every Hollywood incarnation. Lugg explained that dart boards were usually confined to the public bar but that, as a novice to pub etiquette, it would be best to get the lie of the land before engaging in a combat sport.

The licensee himself, the skeletal Joshua Yallop, was on duty behind the bar, though if he was pleased to see five additional customers to boost his evening trade he hid it well. The image which sprang into Mr Campion's mind was that of a curate with indigestion and he decided that a considerable portion of false jollity was called for if the evening was not to be a complete damp squib.

'Good evening, mine host, five pints of your finest draught beer, please. No, wait, make that four as I'm driving.'

'And I'd prefer a whisky,' Perdita whispered in his ear.

'Three.'

'Me too,' said Rupert with the certainty of someone who already knew the quality of the pub's draught ale.

'Very well, then. Two pints of mild, two whiskies and a tonic water please, and don't spare the sliced lemon. What a charming establishment; have you been here long?'

Joshua Yallop strained a sinewy arm and bent one of the plain dark wood beer pumps towards him, producing a gurgling sound of liquid gushing into a glass somewhere out of sight.

'Ten years this year,' said the landlord without emotion. 'Edna and me took the licence in 1960 when we'd had enough of life in the big city.'

'Ah, Londoners, are you?'

'No, Norwich. The city was getting too big and too busy. They were even talking of building one of them new universities on the golf course, of all places.'

'I believe they have,' said Mr Campion smoothly, 'and it is attracting some bright young talents from what I hear. My name's Campion, by the way. I'm the one who booked the room for my son and his wife. We're all down here to do some filming, recreating the Sweethearting Barrow dig.'

'We never get to the pictures,' said Mr Yallop, 'so we won't see it.'

'It's actually for a television programme,' said Campion, and then quickly added, 'an Italian television programme, so I probably won't see it either, but it's a good thing to do, I think, to commemorate the dig. You wouldn't have been here back then, in 1935?'

Joshua Yallop pushed two pint jugs filled with flat liquid the colour of treacle toffee towards Campion and turned to the whisky optic to dispense the legal nugatory measures.

'Long before our time. The pub would have been run by Arthur Aldous back then. Did you want an ice cube in the tonic?'

'Only if it's not too much trouble,' said Campion, reaching for his wallet.

'I'll have to get some from the kitchen,' sighed Mr Yallop.

'Now that sounds like far too much trouble. It's too cold for ice anyway.'

At his side, Perdita whispered, 'You should try the bedroom.'

Campion proffered two pound notes across the bar, and even though Yallop acknowledged Campion's instruction that he should 'have one yourself' with good grace, producing the correct amount of change still seemed to be something of an imposition.

As they settled around a solid wood table kept level by a folded beer mat under one leg, four pairs of eyes swung on Precious Aird, whose face was masked by the pint pot of mild ale she was attempting to consume in one single gulp. About sixty per cent of the way through, she put her glass down.

'What?'

'How are you enjoying our quaint English pub?' asked Rupert as he and Perdita clinked glasses.

'It's kinda quiet. Don't they have a jukebox?'

'That would be in the public bar,' said Lugg, 'if they 'ave one an' if they do it'll be bound to 'ave the very latest Henry Hall or Victor Sylvester.'

'Who?'

'They are Lugg's favourite pop stars,' said Mr Campion. 'He's not as with it as the rest of us.'

Mr Lugg made a noise with his fleshy lips which would have reminded a country sportsman of the sound a partridge makes taking off.

Rupert attempted to cheer him up. 'Have you seen the pub's collection of bottled beers? Some of them are ancient and may be worth something. You should cast your expert eye over them and educate your American pupil in the wonders of the brewhouse.'

'There's no peace for the wicked,' grumbled Lugg, good-heartedly straining his bulk into the upright position. 'Come on, Yank, let's get you educated. Have you noticed how good the young master is getting at giving orders? The apple don't fall far from the tree.'

Precious emptied her glass at one gulp and had jumped to her feet before Lugg was anywhere near vertical.

'Let's go, Teacher. We can get more beers on the way back.'

Mr Campion allowed himself a beatific smile as he watched the odd couple – the fat, bald old man with the young, slim girl – drift across the bar arm in arm. Once they were out of range, Rupert leaned across the table towards his father.

'What did Mother want when she rang just before dinner?'

Mr Campion sipped at his tonic water. 'Oh, this and that, wanting to know how you were getting on being film stars,' Rupert sniffed loudly at the thought, 'and bits of general housekeeping, that's all. Sends her love, naturally, and she's promised to bring my car back in one piece.'

'That all?'

'Yes, that was all,' said Mr Campion, his face inscrutable.

He hated telling even the whitest of lies to Rupert but he saw no point in worrying his son with Amanda's forceful instruction down the telephone line: 'Albert, you be very, very careful, and just remember – it was not your fault.'

'Now that, top left, is a bottle of Maxim Stout. Comes from a brewery up north and is named after the Maxim machine gun,' said Lugg, gesturing rather grandly over the bar to the bottle display. 'The chap who owned the brewery did his bit for queen and country by paying for a machine-gun regiment to serve in the Boer War in South Africa. That's where my name comes from,' he ended proudly.

'You fought in the Boer War?'

'Hardly,' said the fat man indignantly. 'I was named after the battle.'

'There was a battle of Lugg?' Precious tried but failed to keep her face straight.

'The battle of Magersfontein, if you must know, and I think you *do* know.'

Precious giggled. 'Mr Campion warned me. I think I shall call you Maggs.'

'Don't. Next to it is a local speciality; well, near enough. That's the famous Colchester Oyster Stout which they used drink at the Oyster Festival there. It had real oyster juice in the brew, though it went a bit wrong just before the war when they used tinned oysters from New Zealand and they must have been off. But that there' – Lugg pointed a sausage of a finger towards a large, black, broad-shouldered bottle with a faded reddish label – 'is a real collector's item. That's a King's Ale, from 1902, when the king – that would be Bertie, Edward VII – went to the Bass brewery and started the mash for that particular brew. Special bottles which were embossed with the words King's Ale and sealed with a cork and wax. Still drinkable after all these years, so they tell me.'

'You ever tried it?'

'Not officially. That one next to it is even rarer now and, funnily enough, very relevant to our business here in Sweethearting; that's Prince's Ale, a brew mashed – that means started – on July 23, 1929 by the Prince of Wales at the same brewery.' Precious peered at the shelves and identified a large quart bottle with a yellowish label sporting the *fleur-de-lis* feathers. 'That was the Prince of Wales who the lad Rupert plays in this film. O'course, it wasn't a popular beer once he'd abdicated but it wasn't a bad drop. Drank some meself during the war; mind you, we were grateful for anything we could get then.'

'Would that be the Boer War?' grinned Precious.

'You cheeky so-and-so. Just for that, it's your round. Come on, if you're old enough to be in here you're old enough to stand your round.'

From their table, the Campions observed the mismatched pair propping up the bar with benign astonishment.

'Those two are really hitting it off,' said Perdita. 'Who would have thought it?'

'Not me,' said Rupert. 'I would have thought she would have him down as a dinosaur within the first two minutes.'

'A jovial, not-very-fierce, rather rotund dinosaur, perhaps,' said Mr Campion. 'I'm sure there must have been one like that, and Lugg was always good with children.' He looked at Rupert. 'He didn't drop you on your head more than twice.'

His son laughed. 'And it never did me any harm.'

'The jury's still out on that one,' observed his wife, patting her husband's hand affectionately.

Mr Campion had always considered himself fortunate in his son's provision of daughter-in-law but his self-satisfied reverie at that particular moment was interrupted by a blast of cold air to the back of his neck as the pub door opened. His ears pricked when Joshua Yallop hailed the pub door opening with the words ''Evening, farmer Thomas,' and he turned his head to greet the incomer.

'Mr Spark, how nice to see you again; may I buy you a drink?'

Thomas Spark closed the pub door behind him but kept hold of the door handle and surveyed the room, nodding to the few villagers there sitting in silence in front of their drinks before accepting.

'I don't see any reason why not,' he said, unbuttoning his overcoat, 'unless I'm interrupting something.'

'Just a family gathering,' Campion said, rising to his feet. 'This is my son, Rupert, and his wife, Perdita. Over there, appraising the publican's bottle collection is an old family friend – that would be the portly, less attractive one – and a new acquaintance, the young, attractive and far more intelligent one, who happens to be

American. She's also in charge of the archaeology at the Barrow so you really should meet her as, technically, she's digging up your land. Now, what can I get you?'

'I don't drink beer, wine or spirits,' said the farmer.

'I remember you saying . . .'

'But I'll take a glass of cider from you.'

'Cider?' Campion was momentarily confused.

'They do small bottles,' said Spark as if explaining to a child, 'and there's not much alcohol in cider, is there?'

Noticing that Joshua Yallop had already placed a bottle and a glass on the bar, Campion declined to argue the point.

'I defer completely to your agricultural expertise, Mr Spark. Please, take a pew.'

Perdita volunteered to assist with the drinks and Lugg, who had run out of things to say on the history of beer and decided that consumption was the better part of education, joined them. Campion formally introduced Thomas Spark as the owner of Windy Ridge Farm and, by default, the Sweethearting Barrow and also someone who had a close family connection with the events Rupert and Perdita were recreating.

'You were there?' blurted Precious, somewhat to the embarrassment of everyone else around the table apart from Thomas Spark himself.

'Not me; I was just a kid but my father was a volunteer digger, one of the Sweethearting lot, not one of them the vicar of Heronhoe brought in.'

'I take it there was considerable rivalry in the two camps,' Campion observed.

'There's not much love lost betwixt the parishes,' conceded Spark, 'and Sweethearting always had the edge in the bragging rights when it came to visits from the royals.'

'You rather gave me the impression that your father had seen the Prince of Wales in Sweethearting more than once.'

'That he had; leastwise, that's what he used to tell us, especially when he'd come staggering back from an evening in this place. Used to be proud to drink in a pub where royalty drank, a place where they knew how to look after a prince of the realm, if you know what I mean.'

'I don't,' said Precious Aird, and Campion issued a silent prayer of thanks for the useful innocence of the young American. 'Understand, that is. What do you mean by "look after"?'

'I'm sure it means that the staff of the pub were very accommodating,' Campion said quickly, 'and looked after the prince's every need efficiently and discreetly.'

'They certainly were discreet,' agreed Thomas Spark, 'and nothing ever got in the papers.'

'No, the whole affair with Mrs Simpson was hushed up,' said Campion. 'A conspiracy of silence, you might say, organized by the highest in the land.'

'That's as may be,' said the farmer, wiping cider from his lips with the back of a red-haired hand, 'but there's plenty that thought there was an indiscretion which brought him to this particular pub before he started with that American woman.'

'Is this American woman missing something?' demanded Precious.

'She ain't the only one.' Perdita supported her in a stage American accent.

It was clear to Campion that Thomas Spark was uncomfortable in having to exchange this particular piece of saloon-bar gossip in front of a female audience and he nodded encouragement even though the farmer was clearly nervous as Precious and Perdita leaned forward across the table to hang on his every word. Even more disconcerting was that Lugg, with a distinctly satanic leer on his face, was doing the same.

Spark cleared his throat and pressed on valiantly. 'You know the prince used to come to the hall to go riding with Wemyss-Grendle?' He acknowledged the nods of agreement from Campion and Lugg. 'Well, he used to drink here on occasion and was particularly taken by the barmaid, Elspeth Brunt, who was what the newspapers would have called "vivacious" if they'd ever cottoned on to her. They said the prince took quite a shine to her; mind you, he wasn't the only one. Wemyss-Grendle had his eye on her as well, even tried to get her to work up at the hall, but that didn't last long.'

Campion held up a finger to make an interjection. 'I'm told the journalist, Samuel Salt, had a bit of a thing for her as well.'

'He could have, according to what my old dad used to say – plenty of men did, but Elspeth played the field and ended up marrying an Italian, an ex-POW who stayed on in Heronhoe after the war.'

'I'm not sure he was ever a POW,' said Campion, exchanging looks with Lugg, 'but that's not relevant to the period in question. Would Elspeth Brunt have been working here in 1935 when they were digging the Barrow?'

'Well, remember I was only a kid meself, but in his cups my dad used to laugh about it and say it was a good job Elspeth had moved on to pastures new that year because otherwise there could have been a bit of an embarrassing situation, what with him bringing that Mrs Simpson here.'

'Are you sure about that?' asked Campion. 'Here, to the King's Head?'

'My dad was. He used to have a laugh at the thought of Elspeth having to serve them breakfast in bed if she'd still been working here. Wicked sense of humour, my dad had.'

'We thought they were joking when they called it the Royal Suite,' said Rupert, his mouth open wide. 'We're sleeping in it.'

'The landlord calls it that?' Lugg faked indignation. 'That's a bit rich, i'n'it, after all this time?'

'Josh Yallop treats it all as a bit of joke,' said Spark, 'good for the tourist trade, he says, as if he had any. He wasn't the landlord back then, o'course – it was Arthur Aldous in them days. Him and his wife ran the place in the Thirties up to 1939 when the war came and Arthur tried to join up, as he was the patriotic sort – really patriotic. I've seen pictures of the pub from Arthur's time and you could hardly see the place for bunting and Union Jacks on high days and holidays. Anyways, Arthur was too old to get a uniform so he decided to do his bit on the fishing trawlers out of Heronhoe. Folks had to eat, after all, and the navy was dragging off the younger blokes, so it seemed like Arthur was contributing to the war effort.'

'Pity running a pub wasn't made a reserved occupation,' muttered Lugg. Then, when he saw several disapproving faces looking at him, he added, 'Just saying . . .' and reburied his face in his pint pot.

'He didn't contribute much,' Thomas Spark ploughed on, ignoring the interruption, 'and probably would have been better off staying here and running the pub. It was only his second trip

out when his boat was machine-gunned by a lone Dornier trying
to find its way home. There was only the one casualty: Arthur
Aldous, who took a bullet to the head. They say his body was
landed at Heronhoe quay along with six boxes of herring.'

'But this was 1939, you say?'

Spark nodded in answer to Campion's question. 'Very early on,
in the first months of the war, I think.'

'By which time the Abdication was done and dusted and the
Prince of Wales had become King Edward and then the Duke of
Windsor, and the Sweethearting Barrow had been totally forgotten
and overshadowed by the finds at Sutton Hoo.'

'Because those boat burials were full of treasure,' said Spark,
'not like our very own Sweethearting one. My dad followed the
story and often moaned about how they found nothing worth
talking about in our one.'

'And yet people did talk about it, didn't they? Still do, in fact.
Sometimes it's the Sweethearting Treasure and sometimes it's
the Abdication Treasure because the Barrow dig coincided with
the Mrs Simpson affair in people's minds, though of course the
Abdication crisis was a year later, 1936 not 1935.'

'Do we 'ave any idea what this so-called treasure was? All I've
'eard sounds as if this was the treasure that never was.' Mr Lugg,
now anticipating his third pint, found himself in a loquacious
mood. 'I mean, nobody can tell me what it looks like, what it's
worth, where it came from, who found it or where it is now. Is it
portable? Can it be fenced? Or would an honest pawnbroker take
one look at it and keep you talking while he phoned the law?'

Campion removed his spectacles and, with a handkerchief the
size of a white flag which could have graced any major military
catastrophe, began to polish the lenses.

'There are two theories to explain the rumoured treasure, old
friend. One is that something valuable came out of the Sweethearting
dig at the time of the visit of the Prince of Wales; a theory which
seems to have been comprehensively denied by everyone who was
around at the time and unproved by everyone who has looked for
it since. The other theory is that the treasure was some sort of gift
from the Prince of Wales during or immediately after the Abdication
crisis for . . . well, for services rendered, shall we say?'

'Services?' asked a puzzled Thomas Spark. 'What services?'

'You have more or less described them this evening, although no doubt in all innocence,' said Campion, replacing his glasses. 'If the prince had been using the King's Head as a private love nest when he was in the area – and I can quite understand his reluctance to take his lover to Heronhoe Hall and suffer the hospitality of that lecherous old goat Gerald Wemyss-Grendle – then he may have made some gesture of *largesse* to a pub which had kept his secret. Once his secret was out, as it were. He may have, belatedly, thanked the pub and its landlords for keeping his residency here discreet and out of the spotlight of press coverage. You told me yourself that there was a local journalist sniffing around here.'

'Aye, that'd be Sam Salt, but he never did write a story about that.'

'Nor about the rumours of the Abdication Treasure after the dig was finished. In fact, I'm told he didn't write anything after the day of the visit of the prince.'

'And we can't ask the landlord, can we?' observed Lugg drily. 'Not with him dead on the fish dock. Did he leave a will with a few OBEs and the odd Crown Jewel in it?'

Campion flapped a hand to dismiss Lugg's fanciful suggestion. 'What happened to the pub, Mr Spark, after the death of Arthur Aldous?'

Spark scratched his chin. 'The licence passed to his widow – there was a war on, after all. Afterwards the brewery let her stay for what they called her official "widow's year" but they must have really valued her as that year turned into ten or more. They let her stay on all through the Fifties, when it was rare to have a woman licensee.'

'Still is,' grunted Lugg.

'Sonia retired in 1960 and the Yallops took over.'

'Sonia?' exclaimed Rupert.

'You know her?' asked Mr Campion.

Rupert and Perdita nodded in unison, then Perdita said, 'She doesn't do stairs.'

TWELVE

Supporting Cast (Present)

Mr Campion's day began with a cup of tea placed on his bedside table and Lavinia Bell's voice whispering a polite wake-up call, which to any other ears would have been quite startling.

'Sorry to disturb you, Mr Campion, but there's a policeman waiting to see you downstairs.'

Campion rolled over on his pillow and reached with his eyes still shut for his spectacles on the table, his hand instinctively, almost magically, avoiding the hot cup and its saucer.

'You know you are getting old when the policemen are up and about before you,' he said, sitting upright and applying the large round tortoiseshell frames to his face. 'Does this early bird go by any name other than worm-catcher?'

'It's Inspector Chamley, the one who rang and left a message for you yesterday,' Lavinia said, determined to show her efficiency as a hostess. 'I've put him in the front room with Hattie and a cup of tea, though I've no idea if he's musical, but it's more comfortable than the kitchen where Precious is organizing breakfast for the diggers.'

'And here's me luxuriating in my silk pyjamas while the world works.' Campion smiled. 'Let me throw some togs on and I'll stumble into action.'

Dressed but unshaven, Campion was downstairs within three minutes and within four was offering his apologies to the visiting policeman.

'No call for that, Mr Campion, except perhaps on my part for disturbing you so early. It's just that I've been working the night duty and I knock off at eight – well, that's the theory, anyway – and I wanted to clear something up for the report I have to leave for the day's shift. It's only a small matter.'

'I am at your disposal, Inspector, and in your debt for the information you supplied yesterday.'

Inspector Chamley waved away any obligation of debt. 'Happy to be of assistance to any friend of Scotland Yard and Mr Luke and I only hope the information was helpful. Now, perhaps you can return the favour.'

'Naturally, if I can.'

'It's about the break-in . . .'

'You've made an arrest?'

'No, we have not,' Chamley turned the hat he was holding nervously by the brim, 'although we are of course continuing our enquiries into that one.'

'*That* one? The one here at the hall the other night?'

Chamley nodded silently, allowing Campion to make the connection.

'You're talking about another one, aren't you?'

'Yes, sir, I am. Last night, or rather earlier this morning, someone broke into the King's Head in Sweethearting but they were disturbed before they could take anything; disturbed by a gentleman who claims to be your son.'

'Rupert? Good heavens above! He has every right to claim me as a parent, though often he would possibly prefer not to have to. Is the boy all right?'

'He had his night's sleep disturbed,' said Chamley as if reading from his notebook, 'and made several references to having an early morning call "on location", whatever that means.'

'Strangely, Inspector, that makes perfect sense – trust me.'

'If you say so, sir. Your son heard the intruder rummaging around in the bar and came downstairs to investigate instead of doing the sensible thing and waking the landlord.'

'We are not,' said Campion seriously, 'a family noted for doing sensible things.'

'Well, however unwise, your son stumbling upon the intruder did the trick and scared him off empty-handed as far as we can tell, though not after a bit of damage was done. When young Mr Campion confronted the chap there was a bit of a scuffle and some beer bottles got smashed. I'm afraid your son, who was in pyjamas and bare feet, trod on some broken glass. His wife is looking after him and she seems to know what she's doing.'

'Oh, she does; he's in safe hands. While I'm grateful for the news, Inspector, I'm not sure how I can help you. I was in the King's Head myself last night, but I was on chauffeur duty and drove everyone home. In fact, we called it a night quite early, about ten o'clock, I think. Do I need an alibi?'

'Of course not, sir, but you could help with an identification.'

'Really? I assure you I am happy to identify my son and fairly confident I can do so at the drop of a hat.'

'No, no, sir, you misunderstand. Or is that the Campion sense of humour I was warned about?'

'Almost certainly the latter, I'm afraid, Inspector.'

Chamley steeled himself to the task in hand. 'There are, at first sight, certain similarities with the break-in here at the hall and we are looking at anything out of the ordinary that's happened locally, which includes checking up on strangers and suspicious characters. I was wondering if you could vouch for one such stranger who has been acting somewhat suspiciously in Heronhoe.'

'If I can,' said Campion.

'He's an elderly gentleman, bald and a bit portly by all accounts, talks like a Londoner. Doesn't sound like a burglar but I have to ask.'

'Do not fret yourself, Inspector. Your suspect certainly doesn't look like a burglar – well, not since he let his figure go – and I am ashamed to say I can vouch for him. His name is Lugg – he's quite harmless and he was with us in the King's Head last night until we left, whereupon I gave him a lift to his lodgings at the Hythe Inn in Heronhoe. Once there, he seemed set on laying the groundwork for this morning's hangover. I doubt very much he would have had the inclination or the energy to go breaking into the King's Head in Sweethearting in the early hours, and in any case he has no transport and cockneys are well-known for their fear of Suffolk country lanes after dark.'

Chamley seemed mollified but remained in official mode. 'There's a possibility that the intruder at the King's Head left the village on a bicycle, heading in the direction of Heronhoe.'

'That certainly can't be Lugg, then. An inebriated salmon would display better balance on a bike than Lugg. These days a sedan chair would be his preferred means of escape.'

'Well, thank you for that, Mr Campion, and your forbearance at the intrusion. I'll let you get to your breakfast.'

Campion smiled but made no attempt to move, anticipating the policeman's standard 'one last thing' question, which was not long in coming.

'One last thing, sir,' said Chamley, pulling on his hat. 'Given your experience, if you don't mind me saying that, and the fact that you were present in both places, do you have any theories as to who might have done these break-ins?'

Campion beamed innocence. 'I have absolutely no idea, Inspector.'

That Daniela Petraglia had a stunning figure, especially when displayed through a second skin of fluid black leather, was not in question. That she herself knew this for a fact was also beyond doubt and she had long realized that she possessed a weapon which could disarm, intimidate and, at the very least, confuse an enemy or even a friend, as long as they were men. As a director very much of the dictatorial school of film making, she was dressed for the part even though only fifty per cent of the audience she was dictating to was male.

'Keep in character,' Perdita had hissed to Rupert. 'You have at your side the woman you love – the woman you will give up the throne for. You are not on the lookout for a quick fling with the hostess of one of those strange clubs in Soho where they make you scream for their kisses.'

Rupert could, in all honesty, have denied knowing of even the existence of such establishments in Soho, let alone the etiquette of patronizing them, but thought it safer to let the matter lie.

'Best foot forward, darling,' he said. 'Let's hit our mark and dazzle a smile for the cameras.'

'Camera – singular,' Perdita reminded him. 'This isn't *Dr Zhivago*, you know, though I'm so cold it could be. Why wouldn't Madame Strict let us wear our coats?'

'Because it's supposed to be the summer of 1935, my love, which is why we're standing on this side of the trench, so they don't get the trees in the background.'

'Trees? Did you say trees? I can't hear you very well over the sound of my teeth chattering.'

'The trees would have been in leaf in summer. We have to pretend it's summer but we're good at make-believe; we're actors.'

'So I suppose I have to wear these stupid sunglasses to complete the illusion, though I can hardly see where I'm putting my feet so I'm sure I'll trip and end up in that damned ditch.'

'It's called a trench, dear.'

'That makes it sound like the First World War, which fits with all this mud, I suppose. I'm bound to go over in these shoes – they have absolutely no grip.'

'Don't fall and ladder those fabulous stockings, whatever you do. You haven't got a spare pair.'

'I'll be careful.' Perdita sighed. 'I know; the show must go on. I just wish it would get started.'

To give her her due, their beloved director, the leather-clad Daniela Petraglia, was far from idle and seemed as determined to get things going as was the shivering Perdita. She stalked the site with Gianfranco the cameraman snapping at the high heels of her boots, stopping every few yards to size up potential camera angles, having explained to her two 'stars' that they had to make sure to avoid leafless trees (at which Rupert had nodded wisely) and also, in the far background, the television aerials spiking up from the roofs of the nearest houses in Sweethearting. Not having thought of that, Rupert was suitably impressed at Daniela's professionalism, but Perdita grumbled that perhaps they should have thought of that before – possibly at some point in the intervening thirty-five years between the historical event and its fanciful recreation.

The sound man, Maurizio, was likewise wandering over the site with a heavy tape recorder the size of a suitcase slung over his shoulder, headphones clamped to his ears and holding a bulbous, fur-covered microphone on a yard-long metal pole. Occasionally he would stop dead in his tracks, put his head on one side, hold the microphone rigid out in front of his body and fumble with the controls of his machine.

'Background noise – sound effects,' Rupert said knowingly to Perdita, who wrapped her arms around herself, shivered and remained unimpressed.

Almost all the 'background' noise on the Sweethearting Barrow was coming from a level below Rupert and Perdita's feet, where Precious and her three assistants were digging furiously to deepen the rectangle they were standing in, throwing the soil they excavated behind them, forming a ridge running along the long western edge of the trench.

Rupert could tell (for he had 'read up' on these things) that Precious, Si, Dave and Cat were, in effect, creating a classical ditch-and-rampart defensive position. Attackers would be expected to clamber over the ridge of piled-up soil where they would be exposed to the spears and arrows of defenders, the survivors sliding down the slope into the ditch where defenders would pound them with stones and slash them with swords.

Fortunately, the only invaders Precious and her team would have to face that day would be Rupert and Perdita inhabiting their 1935 personae, standing delicately on the rampart and smiling, possibly waving regally down on the diggers who were, in case the camera caught them in close-up, dressed as contemporary muscular farm labourers turned volunteer archaeologists. Or at least the top halves of their bodies would be costumed. From somewhere Daniela had acquired jackets, frayed white collarless shirts, pairs of braces (which Precious called 'suspenders'), neckerchiefs and elasticated armbands ('garters'), all items having been much lived-in and infrequently cleaned, along with a selection of greasy flat caps, squashed trilbies and a couple of briar pipes.

By adding these props and layers to their existing clothes, the diggers – at least in long shot – would pass without too close an inspection as representatives of the 1935 Sweethearting workforce ready to cheer, on cue, their royal visitors. The hats would, of course, not only add authenticity to the scene but help disguise the sex of Precious and Cat and the long, girlish locks of the self-conscious Simon who had grown his hair in anticipation of a university place later that year.

Perdita knew that the younger, non-thespian members of the supporting cast would object to having to dress up in second-hand clothes which did, she admitted, look far from sanitary, but they at least would manage to stay a damn sight warmer than she was.

By the time Mr Campion had bathed, shaved and made himself thoroughly presentable, the archaeologists had departed for Sweethearting and Oliver Grieg Bell, dressed in a white painter's overalls and armed with paint scrapers, sandpaper and a large bottle of white spirit, was wandering the corridors of the hall in search of decorating tasks. Lavinia Bell had clearly decided that Oliver's time would be better spent on minor domestic repairs, of which she had a comprehensive list, than 'hanging around' a film set gawping at the metronomic rear view of the director.

At Lavinia's insistence, Campion fortified himself with a cup of coffee and a slice of bread and honey, also accepting from her a long, bright red woollen scarf as he was buttoning his overcoat and pulling on his hat and leather gloves. He was, he informed her, embarking on a brief route march into Heronhoe, where he would attempt to purchase a newspaper for himself and the latest *Beano* or *Dandy* for Mr Lugg, assuming the latter had actually risen from his pit and greeted the dawn yet. Unlike Mr Campion, who preferred to step out and meet each day with his hat at a jaunty angle, his venerable and really quite ancient friend often required a considerable amount of gentle coaxing these days.

The morning was a chill and clear one with a hint in the air that a frost had considered forming but had thought better of settling on the muddy saltings and moved inland seeking a more sheltered target.

As he strode down the road, Campion enjoyed the desolate view over the saltings and the Bright estuary, which belied its name as the outgoing tide had left large slabs of mud exposed. He shared that view with a squadron of noisy gulls which had, as usual, found something to squawk about, two passing cars and a post office van. As he entered the precincts of Heronhoe proper he saw his first human: a middle-aged woman in a pinafore dress beating a doormat against the step of a terraced cottage. Automatically he made to raise his fedora in polite greeting but the woman withdrew as quick as a squirrel into the cottage, closing the door firmly behind her.

Campion sighed and rationalized the woman's reaction, somewhat fancifully, by the fact that because he was on foot and coming from that direction he must have been mistaken for a resident of Sweethearting. He was well aware that, in rural Suffolk, local rivalries had long memories.

He meandered through the narrow streets of the town, noting a grocery, a post office, a Methodist church, a ship's chandlers' and hardware store, a tiny street-corner pub called the Rising Sun which had clearly seen better days some time ago, an even smaller red-brick building no bigger than a garage which claimed to be the Sailors' Reading Room and then, as the main street gave way to the small harbour and the quayside, two fishmongers, a fish-and-chip shop and the Hythe Inn with its distinguished – and only – visitor booked in on a bed-and-breakfast basis.

Campion found Lugg, having availed himself of the bed, taking full advantage of the cooked breakfast on offer. He was the sole occupant of the public bar – to which Campion only gained admittance by knocking plaintively on the frosted-glass window – seated alone at a table designed for four diners of normal girth. He was paying homage to a plate in front of him which appeared to display a model of a Norman castle made out of substantial rashers of Suffolk ham and several sausages, topped with a brace of fried eggs and surrounded by a moat of baked beans in an orangey tomato sauce. To help lay siege to this castle, on a separate plate were battering rams of thickly sliced toast. The gusto with which Lugg was tackling the plate in front of him augured that the siege would not last long and that the outcome was inevitable.

'I see they're feeding you up,' said Campion. 'They must have taken pity on a poor waif from the big city. Perhaps they thought you'd come straight from Bernado's without passing Go.'

'Less of the dark sarcastics,' said Lugg through an explosion of toast crumbs. 'Just keeping me strength up against the rigours of the day. You had rigours in mind, I suppose, to bring you here at the crack of dawn?'

'Dawn cracked some time ago, old fruit, so I would be obliged if you would put your boots on, polish up your best knuckle-duster and introduce me to Bill Crow at his emporium, though I wouldn't be at all surprised to find Mr Crow was having a bit of a lie-in this morning.'

'Lucky bloke. Been out on the tiles, has he?'

'Not in the way you might think; then again, you probably would. There was a break-in at the King's Head during the night, a pretty ineffective one by all accounts but with similarities to the one at Heronhoe Hall. You'll be proud to know that the local constabulary immediately had you in the frame for it until I stepped forward and committed perjury by giving you an excellent character reference.'

'Much obliged, I'm sure,' mumbled Lugg through his last mouthful of sausage. He allowed his knife and fork to clatter on to an empty plate. 'So you've got Bill Crow tagged for it?'

'I am merely following your instincts in this matter. Instincts which, when it comes to matters nefarious, have proved reasonably accurate in the past, so let us pay the man a visit and submit him to your considerable charms.'

Anyone who might have conjured a mental picture of an emporium as being something akin to an Arabic *souk* would have been instantly disillusioned by the Heronhoe interpretation of the concept. Down a dingy side street at the side of one of the quayside fishmonger's there was no high Moroccan sun reflecting off multi-coloured silks and burnished copperware; nor was the air pricked with the sharp scent of exotic spices or the warm notes of coffee brewing with cardamom pods. This emporium was dark and dingy, the overwhelming colour scheme made up of many shades of brown and the dominant smell was of a damp mustiness augmented by the fishiness wafting in from the quay.

The emporium's thick oak double doors, arched like church windows, were propped open with a pair of ancient, heavy flat irons – the sort of smoothing iron which Campion's mother, although rarely using one herself, had always insisted on calling 'sad irons' after the old English term 'sad', meaning solid.

The shape of the doors and the solid brick construction of the single-storey emporium suggested that it had originally been used as a warehouse or possibly, Campion thought, the sort of service shed usually associated with the railways. Perhaps Heronhoe had once boasted a rail line but if it had, Campion's view was that it had disappeared long before Doctor Beeching had swung his axe.

A single, low-wattage light bulb hanging from a twist of brown cable was the only source of illumination of the interior and it took Campion a full minute for his eyes to become accustomed to the gloom. Lugg, on the other hand, blessed with suspiciously good night vision, quickly located the sole proprietor of the establishment behind and through a forest of old furniture, bicycle parts, washing machines, a snooker table, hat stands and what could have been the fishing gear from a trawler or the centre nets of a full-size tennis court.

'Mr Crow, is it?' announced Campion once he had identified the small human shape sitting on a three-legged stool beside an oil-fired stove, on top of which a battered aluminium kettle wobbled precariously.

'Does I know yer? People round here call me Bill.'

'Until I know you better, I will stick with Mr Crow.'

'Suit yerself,' said the small man while his hands – in fingerless black gloves – performed a complicated dance which resulted in a straggly, rolled-up cigarette being fashioned, put to his tongue to wet the gum of the paper and, with a final twist and a flourish, find its way to the corner of his mouth. A match flowered and a flicker of light showed a dark, saturnine face which quickly dissolved behind a cloud of blue smoke.

'I've seen 'im before.' Bill Crow aimed the glowing cigarette at Lugg like a gun. 'Hanging around the town the last couple of days.'

'I thought the town would appreciate the tourist trade, especially out of season,' said Campion equably, 'as there seem to be relatively few ways for a man to earn a living here. How is business, Mr Crow?'

'It comes and goes, if it's any of yours – business, that is.'

'Forgive my natural nosiness, but the rag-and-bone man has always fascinated me as a stalwart British character. Do you have a horse and cart, may I ask?'

'I ain't no rag-and-bone man!' snarled Crow. 'I'm a trader in used goods and do house clearances, offering fair prices to the recently bereaved.'

'I am more interested in the house clearances you attempt where there have been no bereavements, the residents are all hale and hearty and are often enjoying a good night's sleep.'

'What the hell are you talking about? Just who are you anyway?'

Bill Crow got to his feet and glared pugnaciously at Campion, though his rat-like eyes flicked beyond Campion towards the open doors leading to the street. He was a small man but wiry and at least a dozen years younger than his interrogator. Campion was under no illusions that if Crow decided to make a break for it the clutter of furniture and bric-a-brac between him and the door might slow him down more than Campion could hope to.

'My name is Campion and my associate is Mr Lugg, and we are here merely as concerned citizens seeking information.'

'You've got a nerve, coming into my place of business and threatening me.' Crow jutted out his chin and clenched both hands into fists, his eyes darting about the jumble of his stock and settling rather obviously on a set of golf clubs in a threadbare canvas bag which was temptingly within his reach.

'Please do nothing you may regret, Mr Crow,' said Campion. 'I am sure Inspector Chamley and the local police will take a dim view of an assault on two respectable pensioners who have merely wandered into your establishment lured by the Aladdin's cave of goods you have on offer.'

'Are you barmy?'

'It has been said, Mr Crow, but I should warn you that I am also armed.'

Campion pulled off his left glove slowly and dramatically and Crow watched, mouth gaping, as he plunged the hand inside his coat as if reaching to a shoulder holster.

Bill Crow shrank where he stood, then shuffled backwards until his thighs and buttocks came up against the oil stove, causing him to straighten involuntarily.

Mr Campion pulled off his right-hand glove with his teeth and opened the leather wallet he was holding in his left.

'As you can see, I have brought plenty of ammunition,' he said, rifling through a wedge of notes with his thumb, 'as I appreciate you must be a busy man. Now what can you sell me that would be worth an hour of your time and some answers?'

'That depends on the questions,' said the small, dark man, his eyes never leaving Campion's open wallet, and the hypnotic effect it produced blinkered Crow to the fact that Lugg had moved away from Campion's side and, with impressive silence and stealth for a man of his size, was threading his way through the clutter in a flanking movement.

'An easy one,' said Campion, demanding Crow's full attention, 'would be what were you after last night when you broke into the King's Head over in Sweethearting?'

Crow pulled on his glowing cigarette and blew smoke down his nose. 'That would be incriminating myself and you can't pay people to incriminate themselves; I know the law.'

Lugg cleared his throat loudly to attract their attention. He was holding a black man's bicycle by its frame at chest height as if practising weight-lifting, though in his hands the bicycle appeared no heavier than a feather.

'Exhibit A, M'Lud,' he announced proudly.

'So that's a bike, so bleedin' what? I sell lots of bikes,' said Crow pugnaciously.

'Lights in working order,' said Lugg, shaking the bicycle so that something jingled and rattled, 'a variety of useful tools in the saddlebag which the suspicious mind might think were suitable equipment for burglary and, wiv a stretch of the h'imagination, I'd say the seat was still warm.'

'You can't prove a thing!' Crow spat the words along with shreds of loose tobacco.

'We have a witness who saw that bicycle in Sweethearting last night and, more to the point, we have two witnesses who will swear in court that you were also the miscreant who broke into Heronhoe Hall. One would be the daughter of a peer of the realm and the other would be me. Despite all appearances to the contrary, I do have a reputation for respectability in certain circles. Now, do we go to the police or do you think you could find something to sell me?'

Rupert and Perdita had at last been put through their paces in what Daniela Petraglia had called a technical rehearsal. She had positioned Gianfranco, the cameraman, to the east of the trench and rehearsed the slow, traversing shot he would use across the heads and shoulders of the diggers – who were suitably disguised as 1935 volunteers – and then pan up to the spoil heap rampart running along the west side. Over the top of the rampart would appear – taking care not to slip and fall headfirst into the archaeology – the Prince of Wales with Mrs Simpson at his side to acknowledge their patriotic cheers.

'You should talk to each other,' Daniela had told Rupert and Perdita in a rare directorial instruction. 'It does not matter what you say because the microphone will not pick up the words, but you must not appear too . . . familiar . . . too cosy. No touching, no hand-holding; that would not be done in public back then. The affair was still secret, so it must be formal but . . . *warm*. There must be passion there, but passion which is . . . how do you say . . . in a jar or a bottle?'

'Contained,' suggested Perdita through chattering teeth. 'I can do contained.'

'Good girl,' said Daniela with a broad smile. She raised a hand to Perdita's cheek and withdrew it sharply. 'But you are so cold! I thought it was the make-up, which is very good, I must say.'

'I am cold,' Perdita said grimly. 'It's all this hanging about with nothing to do, along with having my beauty sleep disturbed by the burglary.'

'What?' *Signora* Petraglia's hand rose automatically but this time stopped short of Perdita's cheek.

'There was a break-in at the King's Head last night, or rather early this morning, while we were all sleeping,' Perdita explained feeling, for some reason, on the defensive. 'My gallant husband here foolishly went downstairs in his bare feet, there was a scuffle, bottles were broken and Rupert trod on some glass. You may not have noticed but Rupert's been limping all morning.'

'What was taken?' demanded Daniela without any sympathy.

'Nothing, as far as we could tell,' said Rupert, drawing the Italian woman's gaze on to him.

'Nothing? Are you sure?' The woman's face was suddenly uncomfortably close to Rupert's and she was not smiling.

'Certainly not money,' he said nervously. 'The till drawer was locked away in Mr Yallop's safe.'

'Then what was the purpose? What were they after?'

'The policeman said the only thing disturbed was the pub's collection of historic beer bottles, which I managed to cut my foot on.'

The Italian woman's face contorted in fury. 'Police? You sent for the police?'

'Of course the police were called, *Signora*,' said Perdita in her best schoolmistress voice. 'A crime has been committed, so the police were called. That's what happens in this country.'

Signora Petraglia did not seem convinced.

THIRTEEN
Supporting Cast (Past)

'All right then, I was looking for the Abdication Treasure, just like a lot of others round here are just at the moment, even if they pretend to be kindly old gentlemen who wouldn't say boo to a goose.'

Bill Crow had not admitted defeat. His interrogation had turned into a negotiation and he was not going to give ground gracefully.

'And what exactly do you think this Abdication Treasure consists of?' Campion remained cool and seemed more interested in counting the notes in his wallet than in the rodent seated on his three-legged stool glaring up at him.

'I dunno. Nobody does, could be anything,' said Crow.

'You might already 'ave it in stock,' said Mr Lugg, who had worked his way around and behind Crow through the minefield of junk and was holding aloft a badly chipped statuette of the cloaked figure of the 'Sandeman Don' famous from the sherry adverts.

'I doubt that's it,' said Campion, 'but keep looking and you might find the Maltese Falcon in here. And speaking of black birds, let us get back to you, Mr Crow. If you honestly have no idea what the Abdication Treasure is, or what it is might be worth, why on earth are you attempting to find it?'

'It's like I said, everybody else is looking so there must be something in the old stories.'

Campion produced a crisp ten-pound note from his wallet and flicked it between his finger and thumb. 'Now you have my interest, Mr Crow. I have not yet seen anything which takes my fancy in your emporium but I am always in the market for a good story, so please tell me one.'

The general manager and sole proprietor of the Heronhoe Emporium considered his options carefully. He was unsure who the tall, thin man in the spectacles actually was. A toff, certainly, and a clever one – not like some of the stuck-up types that used to visit the hall in the rare days when old Wemyss-Grendle had money and hosted raucous house parties much to the trepidation of the female servants there. Nor was he one of those weekend yachtsmen, the sort the locals called 'cloth-cap admirals', who put into Heronhoe in the summer hoping to find a picturesque coastal hideaway they could brag to their friends in Hampstead about. That lot usually left disappointed, and quickly. Clearly he was not a policeman, nor any sort of official Bill Crow could bring to mind; officialdom had never been known to open its wallet to the likes of Bill Crow.

As for the older and considerably heavier half of this odd part-nership, now he was a type Bill Crow could recognize as a bit of a kindred spirit. He may have gone fat some years ago but he hadn't gone to seed and could still move swiftly and quietly when he wanted to. If there were not some boxing in his history then there was certainly some rough-housing and it would not do to be too close to the older man if things turned ugly.

Yet for all the bald man's bulk and intimidating swagger, it was the tall, thin one – a gentleman through and through for sure who looked harmless – who was the one to be careful of. Bill Crow was no psychologist or dedicated student of human nature, but a life lived on the edge of legality had given him the survival skills to assess opponents and weigh up the odds. In his own mind he was in no doubt that this well-spoken gent with his good tailoring would fight dirty if it came to it, but at the moment there was cash money rather than violence on the negotiating table.

'The stories have been around for years, since before the war.'

'Since the excavation of the Sweethearting Barrow, in other words,' said Campion.

'We called it the Heronhoe Boat round here.'

'Of course you would. May I ask how old you were back then, Mr Crow?'

'I'd be twenty-three, twenty-four, something like that. Why? What's it to you?'

'Not terribly much,' said Campion equably. 'You weren't tempted to join in the dig?'

'That was a game for mugs, that was,' scoffed Crow. 'I had a good job on the boats back then and we used to land fish up at Lowestoft and down at Harwich. I had girls in both places so I didn't have a lot of spare time.'

He treated Mr Campion to a wolfish grin, or a grin which would have been more convincingly lupine if it had been accompanied by a full set of teeth.

'Not that anybody had treasure in mind when they were digging. We hadn't had the Sutton Hoo find then and nobody round here knew much about archaeology – that was something the vicars and schoolteachers were interested in, not the man in the street – and times were hard back then, a lot of unemployment. There were plenty of blokes willing to do a bit of digging to keep the vicar happy if he was putting on some free food and maybe slipping them the odd half-crown. The rumours started after the visit of King Edward.'

'The Prince of Wales, as he was at the time,' Campion corrected him.

'My old mother, Gawd rest her, always called him King Edward and Mrs Simpson was "the woman who stole our king". He was quite a favourite round here, as plenty of local folk had seen him out riding up at the hall or having a pint over in Sweethearting.'

'Ah, yes, I understand he was something of a regular at the King's Head,' said Campion, casually examining his fingernails as if the bank notes he was fanning had stained them.

Bill Crow curled a lip into a lascivious smile. 'He certainly was when Elspeth pulled the pints there.'

'That would be Elspeth Brunt, would it not? Now tell me about her.'

'She was a cracker, Elspeth was, the life and soul of the party. Younger sister of the landlady but the customers, being mostly men, always thought of it as Elspeth's pub, not Sonia's or Arthur's. Every man who saw her gave her the eye and more often than not he'd get a come-hither wink in return, as long as he had a few bob in his back pocket. She was good for attracting business, that's for sure, though it was Sonia who did all the work. A proper diamond, Sonia was. Elspeth liked a good time too much and she never made any secret of the fact.'

'Did that include a good time with the prince in his days as a bachelor gay?'

'We all had our suspicions but Elspeth never boasted about that one, though she was not slow to gossip about her other conquests, like that crazy captain up at the hall.'

'Yes, dear Gerald remembered her fondly – possibly too fondly. Didn't I hear that she once worked for him at the hall?'

'Everything in a skirt with their own teeth was offered a job in service at the hall during the captain's day but none of them lasted long. Wandering hands, you see. Elspeth was more used to that than most so she stuck it out longer, but when the war came there were plenty of blokes around to take her out and give her a good time.'

'Were you one of them?'

Crow flapped away the suggestion. 'Not me. Elspeth wouldn't have anything to do with a smelly trawler-man and, in any case, I had other fish to fry, as it were. She could be choosy at times, though it didn't stop her marrying an Eyetie ice-cream seller. Still, that was after the war – her good-time days were over by then and her looks were going.'

'I have heard that Elspeth was the object of desire for a local journalist, Samuel Salt,' Campion prompted.

'Sammy Salt.' The name struck a chord in Crow's memory, as betrayed by his widened eyes and uplifted chin. 'I remember Sammy. Wasn't much older than me and fancied himself because he was a scribbler on the Hadleigh paper, as if reporting on flower shows and regattas was a really important job. He used to zip around on an old motorbike and sidecar combination, like he was running messages to the frontline. Bit of a prat if you ask me, but yeah, he had the hots for Elspeth when she worked at the King's Head, though even after she quit the pub he still drank there rather than in Heronhoe.'

'There's no accounting for taste,' murmured Campion. 'You say Elspeth left the King's Head. Would that be at the time of the dig?'

Crow shook his head and a lock of dark, greasy hair slid over one eye. 'No, she went the year before. Maybe she was offered more money – and fringe benefits, if you know what I mean – to work up at the hall, or maybe she'd tried it on with Arthur Aldous and Sonia threw her out.' He shook his head. 'No, it wouldn't have been that – Elspeth was too choosy, like I said, and Arthur wasn't her sort. Anyway, the job at the hall didn't last long and she came here to Heronhoe and worked in shops until the war broke out and she went off to the NAAFI.'

'So Elspeth, whose name keeps cropping up, wasn't actually in Sweethearting at the time of the royal visit?'

'No. As I said, she'd left the King's Head by then and didn't show the slightest interest in the royal visitors until after the war.'

'For someone who was never romantically involved, if I can put it like that, you seem well-informed of Elspeth's movements,' said Campion, ignoring the ill-concealed snort of derision which came from Lugg somewhere in the dark, dusty recesses of the emporium, 'and her thoughts.'

'Just 'cos I wasn't one of her fancy men doesn't mean I didn't know her for nearly thirty years!' Crow's voice rose in pitch as if he had been accused of some heinous crime. 'I used to see her round the town all the time, and for a while she lived just round the corner and I was able to get her the odd bit of furniture for her house. I even supplied one or two bits and pieces for the restaurant after she married the Eyetie.'

'That would be Stephano Bolzano, yes?' Campion asked.

'That's right.' Crow looked at the older man suspiciously.

'Do you happen to know when that was?'

'Be around 1956, I reckon. We had quite a few Eyeties floating around the town then, former prisoners who had saved up a bit of cash working on the land since the war and were looking for businesses and property to buy. Elspeth got friendly with some of them and would disappear off to London with them. She used to call it "visiting Little Italy" like it was going on holiday.'

Across the showroom, Campion and Lugg exchanged glances, though Crow failed to notice.

'When she came back married to one of them, it was a bit of a surprise, I grant you. I hadn't pegged her for the marrying kind and never knew she was a Catholic, though I doubt she was a good one. Getting wed seemed to suit her, though – settled her down – and she helped Stephano run the restaurant right up until she died suddenly. He took it badly, sold up and moved back to Italy.'

Campion palmed two ten-pound notes from his wallet and held them to his chest like a winning hand at Pontoon. The gesture had the desired effect of cementing Bill Crow's attention.

'Shortly before he decamped for *Bella Italia*, Stephano Bolzano went to see Gerald Wemyss-Grendle and quizzed him about this somewhat ethereal concept of an "Abdication Treasure". The captain, of course, knew nothing, but where did Bolzano get the idea there might be something?'

'That would be Elspeth, for sure. She was convinced that the king, when he was abdicating, sent gifts to them that had helped him get through the crisis; his sort of version of an unofficial Birthday Honours list. Elspeth, and plenty more round here, were convinced he'd sent a little bit of royal treasure to the area because he'd enjoyed coming here and those that knew about him and Mrs Simpson had kept their mouths shut.'

'And the obvious candidates for this royal generosity were Heronhoe Hall and the King's Head, both places he frequented.'

Campion paused and locked eyes with Crow.

'Those would be the places worth looking,' Crow said slowly, 'if a person was looking, that is . . .'

His right arm twitched involuntarily as if the hand was about to reach out for the bank notes Campion held, but something warned him that the old man could make the money magically disappear until it had been fully earned.

'And a person who was looking – one who was in no danger of incriminating himself – would be looking for exactly what?'

'That's just it, nobody knows. Nobody cared about whether there was any "treasure" in the Sweethearting Barrow, as you call it, when it was being dug. It was just a bit of local history and it kept the vicar happy. It was only when those buggers up at Woodbridge found all that stuff at Sutton Hoo that people started talking about treasure – and why didn't we have any? Somebody must have found something and squirrelled it away. Somehow, that idea of a lost "treasure" got mixed up with the idea of the king and Mrs Simpson being here and being grateful, and that became the "Abdication Treasure", but it was all pie in the sky.'

Try as he may, Crow could not read Campion's impassive face.

'Look, it stands to reason, don't it? If the old king had dished out a bit of treasure then it would have been to the captain up at the hall *or* to Arthur Aldous at the King's Head, right? But old Wemyss-Grendle is in some old people's home or a poorhouse somewhere and Arthur's widow is living in an almshouse and still having to work as a cleaner and barmaid even though she'll not see seventy-five again.'

Campion allowed himself a wry smile. 'For some of us, seventy-five is a target not a memory, though I take your point and, rather begrudgingly, admire your logic. Nobody who might have seems to have prospered from any sort of "treasure", which begs the question: why now?'

'Why now what?'

'Why, after all the time that's gone by, was it suddenly worth it for somebody – no names, no pack drills, at least not yet – to go breaking and entering into Heronhoe Hall and the King's Head, the two likely locations you have just identified?'

Somewhat to Campion's surprise, Bill Crow did not hesitate. 'It was them Italians stirred it all up again!'

'Please be more specific.'

'That gang of Eyeties who turned up here a week ago, said they were from Italian television "scouting locations" or some such nonsense for a film about the dig in 1935. Three of them in a left-hand-drive Frog car, one of them bouncy ones, stuffed with equipment. The ringleader is a woman – tall, blonde, curves in all the right places and probably quite a looker in her day, but fierce as hell. A right bitch who could scare the trousers off a man at twenty paces, if you ask me.'

'I didn't,' said Campion smoothly, 'but I would not argue the point. You seem, as usual, to be well-informed.'

'Strewth!' Crow exhaled loudly. 'You couldn't miss a woman like that in a place like Heronhoe if you wore a sack on your head; long leather coat, leather boots and short skirt, stomping around like she owned the place. Gawd, any bloke with a pulse would notice her! They all fetched up at the restaurant – Stephano's – where they seemed to be expected and straight away they were chatting up the locals in the Hythe Inn and round the Rising Sun, buying rounds and asking if anyone knew any stories about hidden treasure connected to the dig at Sweethearting and the royal visit way back when.'

'And naturally you kept your ear-lugs akimbo, listening in,' Lugg said darkly, and Crow realized that the big man had moved uncomfortably close.

'I didn't have to do any eavesdropping.' Crow was indignant.

'They came to me and introduced themselves. The woman told me to call her Danny and she wanted me to sort out some old jackets and hats – props, she called them – so that she could dress people up like they were in the Thirties.'

'And you, of course, obliged,' observed Campion.

'Business is business and she paid cash money.'

'I bet she also asked for a bit of local knowledge as well, about Heronhoe Hall and the King's Head, for instance?'

'She might have mentioned them.'

'And in doing so, planted the idea in your head that there might be something in this treasure story after all?'

'Where there's smoke there's usually fire,' Crow said smugly. 'Otherwise, why would people like you be sniffing around? I reckon we're not that different, us two.'

Lugg gave a loud snort of derision which startled Crow and made him wince. Campion placed the two ten-pound notes he had been holding on to the dusty surface of a teak-effect radiogram. Then he picked one of them up again and replaced it in his wallet.

'Hey, that's not fair!' complained Crow.

'No, it's probably not,' said Mr Campion, 'but then we're not that different, you and I, are we?'

'That was not too bad,' said Daniela Petraglia. 'Now we need to move the camera so Gianfranco can film our loyal diggers, so make like you are digging.'

Rupert and Perdita descended carefully from the spoil heap – it would hardly do if a future king of England and his lover slipped and slid down the slope on their backsides, even if this was all make-believe.

'I think that went well,' said Rupert once they were on terra more firm.

Perdita pulled off the white-framed sunglasses she had been told to wear. 'I wouldn't know. I couldn't see a thing and my teeth are chattering so much I couldn't hear anything you said.'

'Your reactions were perfect, darling,' Rupert played the gallantry card with the ease of someone familiar with the frailties of actors, 'and that's what matters on film. It's not acting, like in the theatre, but reacting for the camera, and I am sure the camera simply loves you.'

With the spoil heap rampart between them and the film crew and the diggers, Rupert embraced his wife and moved in to kiss her, only to be met by the pressure of her white-gloved palms on his chest.

'To hell with the camera, show me that you love me and get my coat out of the car.'

In the trench, Daniela Petraglia was organizing her extras into what would have been the crowd scenes in a biblical epic, as long as four bodies constituted a crowd. It was not a problem, the director explained to her cast, as because with a low camera angle and a 'tight shot' on their heads and upper bodies, the trench would look crowded with enthusiastic volunteers. As most of the real volunteers were men, however, it would be best if Cat – the smallest and most girlish – worked furthest away from the camera at the far end of the trench.

Precious, the tallest, had 'a fine, broad back' and a big hat to contain her hair. Therefore she could be nearest the camera which would, in any case, only capture her shoulder movements as she dug.

But the digging movements were important; they must throw themselves into it and dig furiously as soon as she gave the word. And they should, please, do it in silence, or at least the girls should. It would, however, be acceptable if the boys, Dave and Simon, were to grunt occasionally.

'Positions, please. Action!'

As they marched out of Heronhoe on the road to Sweethearting, Mr Lugg, his hands thrust deep into his pockets, became quite ruminative.

'What you said back there, to that nasty little oik, about 'im bein' identified by two witnesses of unimpeachable character, to whit: the daughter of a peer, which would be Mrs Bell, I suppose, and somebody who could pass in a dim light for a respectable gentleman, which . . .'

'Yes,' said Mr Campion, 'that would be me.'

'Well, did yer?'

'Did what?'

'Did you and Lavinia really see enough of Bill Crow the other night to be able to stand up in court, hand on heart, and identify him?'

'Of course not,' said Campion jovially, 'but the scabrous Bill Crow wasn't to know that.'

They walked on in silence, and it was not until they were at the drive entrance to the hall that Lugg spoke again, as if the house coming into view had prompted him.

'This Elspeth bird, who married the Bolzano, she worked at the hall for a while?'

'So it would seem.'

'And from what Billy Crow said, she was here when the dig was on?'

'That was the implication.'

'So she was here, in service, the night we was here when we did that recce?'

'That is entirely possible, and I am ashamed to say I have absolutely no memory of her. We should have paid more attention to the staff but back then we took them for granted and treated them as if they were invisible.'

'We 'ardly 'ad time to check up on all the locals, did we? I mean, we was called off, weren't we?'

'Yes, that always struck me as odd, sending us up here and then the phone call to say that our services were no longer required after less than a day. It's clear now that the prince had no intention of staying at the hall that night. He had other plans in Sweethearting.'

'But you've still got that girl on yer conscience, 'aven't you?'

Campion expressed surprise.

'Elspeth Bolzano? No, it's not her who haunts me. Come on, let us stretch our legs properly and amble down to the Barrow; see how the dig's going or, more to the point, the filming. Who knows, you might get a part as an extra with that noble profile of yours.'

Lugg shrank his bulbous neck into the collar of his coat and narrowed his eyes against the salty breeze coming off the estuary as he fell into step. Campion enjoyed the fleeting impression that he was walking in the company of a relatively well-dressed bipedal giant turtle. It was a turtle in contemplative mood.

'I fort you was supposed to be retired,' said Lugg after five minutes of silence, 'taking it easy, putting your feet up, all that sort of malarkey, but you just can't resist, can you?'

'Resist what, me old mucker? If I'm doing something to increase your blood pressure then how can I resist?'

'Don't be a smart-mouth with me – I've heard it all before. You know what I'm talking about: this private narking. I always said it was a bit common, but for a man of your age and standing it's positively undignified.'

Campion allowed himself a smile. 'Private detection, as I think you so colourfully put it, implies a client and a service for hire. I can assure you I am pursuing this particular investigation for purely personal reasons. I am merely satisfying my curiosity and surely that's a reasonable and harmless occupation for a retired gentleman of a certain age.'

'You make it sound on a par with reading an improving book, like you're always on at me to do. And are you sure it's your curiosity you're satisfying and not your conscience?'

'A fine distinction and a very good question,' Campion conceded. 'You really are a wise old owl. Though you conceal it very well.'

'No call to be rude,' snapped Lugg. 'I was only thinking of your health and happiness.'

'Well, that's most considerate, old fruit, but I've never been healthier, and you will note that my hat is at a jaunty angle, signifying a modicum of happiness.'

'But 'ow long would that 'ealth and 'appiness last if Lady Amanda were to find out you were consorting with low-life villainy such as Bill Crow? She'd say you were back to your bad old ways and you would never 'ear the end of it.'

At the mention of his wife, Campion allowed his grin to broaden. 'You may well have a point, and so I must appeal to your discretion. On the other hand, though, don't be too hard on Bill Crow. He may be a chancer and a sneak but he's not a die-hard villain – not like some we know.'

He paused and raised a finger as if the thought had just occurred. 'And think about it. There's a great deal of overlap between the callings of the rag-and-bone man and the private detective. They both sift through vast amounts of rubbish and end up picking through the remains of the dead.'

FOURTEEN
Old Bones

The two elderly gentlemen engaged in some preprandial exercise (much needed in one case), striding down the virtually traffic-free road, turned a curve on the outskirts of Sweethearting and saw a line of vehicles parked on the verge nearest the small copse of trees which marked the Barrow. There was Precious Aird's familiar Volkswagen campervan, then the film crew's Citroën nose-to-nose with Perdita's bright red Mini Cooper.

'It seems the gang's all here,' said Mr Campion jovially.

'Which gang?' Lugg teased.

'Now, now,' Campion chided, 'let us be positive, especially in front of the children. Do you think you can you raise your leg enough to get over this barbed wire or are your high-kicking chorus line days behind you?'

'You'll catch yer death of cold if you hang around waiting for me.' Lugg threw a far-from-shapely leg over the sagging strand of barbed wire and balanced precariously on one foot for a disconcerting amount of time until a sufficient amount of weight had shifted its polarity, enabling him to complete the transverse.

Mr Campion followed, if not with a skip and a jump then at least with a nimbleness which belied his age, and the two men began to walk around the end of the spoil heap rampart which, Campion realized, masked all activity on the dig site from anyone passing by on the road.

'Cut!' The shout stopped them in their tracks.

'Oh, dear,' said Campion, 'I think we've walked into shot.'

'Who's been shot?' Lugg glanced around him rapidly, his face a combination of bemusement and pure fury.

'I am so sorry,' Campion pronounced, raising his hat in apology. 'Have we mucked things up?'

They had rounded the rampart of spoil from the dig at the southerly end of the trench and were looking down the length of it on to the heads of the four diggers posed with the spades in mid-dig as if they were in freeze frame. Campion thought he could identify them all, but it took a few moments of concentration as all four were disporting headgear not normally seen on the youth of today, nor indeed the youth of thirty-five years ago. But if the camera concentrated on what Campion believed was called a 'head shot' and stayed above the waist (those ubiquitous blue denim jeans were so not Suffolk in the Thirties!) then a swift traverse across collarless shirts, waistcoats, flat caps and scarves might just fool an unwitting audience. He particularly liked the finishing touch supplied by – who else? – Precious, who had a lit briarwood pipe clenched between her teeth, and although she was blowing smoke rather than inhaling, seemed to be entering into the spirit of things. The other diggers appeared less enthusiastic, all three of them shivering having exchanged their coats and gloves for shirtsleeves, the two boys, Dave and Si, quietly swearing under their breath, already disillusioned by the glamour of being on television. Only Cat, the smallest of the ensemble cast and the nearest to the end of the trench, seemed to be content with her lot, though it was difficult to discern her expression as she kept her gaze downward to the floor of the trench and her head was encased by a bowler hat at least three sizes too big.

At ground level down at the other end of the trench stood Daniela Petraglia and next to her Gianfranco, leaning over a film camera mounted on a tripod, his face glued to the rubber flap of the eyepiece. Behind them, dressed as if for a cocktail party in a pre-war drama apart from the coats draped over their shoulders, were Rupert and Perdita. Their faces lit up when they caught sight of the intruders and Perdita stepped completely out of character to wave frantically and shout 'Cooeee!'

'*Signor* Campion, how nice to see you!' Even at that distance, Campion could see the Italian woman's face was set grim. 'We were just doing a retake because of a hair in the gate. Now we will do it again.'

'What's she on about?' Lugg breathed in Campion's ear. 'Who's caught in a gate by the hair?'

Out of the side of his mouth, Campion said, 'It's a technical term, my dear old Luddite. They check the lens of the camera after every shot and if a piece of fluff or dirt or leaf has got in there they call it having a hair in the gate and they have to retake the shot. Thanks to our surprise cameo appearance, they now have to retake the retake. Are you following? I had to mug up on all this, so I'm glad it's come in useful.'

'Mumbo-jumbo,' scoffed Lugg dismissively, 'it's all just make-believe.'

'Very possibly,' said Campion, striding away from his companion just as Daniela Petraglia began to march towards him along the 'clean' edge of the trench which had been kept free of the backfill spoil being excavated.

They met almost exactly at the halfway point, where Precious Aird was blowing smoke from her pipe and leaning, in character, on the handle of her spade. From her position below them, the two figures who shook hands as they met – the woman in her open long leather coat over a figure-hugging black cashmere sweater and the thin, bespectacled man in his buttoned-up woollen overcoat, scarf and fedora – presented a pose which reminded her of photograph she had seen in a school history book. The scene it had brought to mind was the meeting of the American and Russian armies on the Elbe in 1945: two allies celebrating victory over a common enemy on the eve of becoming enemies themselves. What on earth had made her think of that?

'Is everything going to plan, *Signora*?' Campion asked the Italian woman, but his smile was downward towards Precious.

'We have completed several establishing shots of our principals – our actors – and I must say your son looks very convincing from a distance. He is too young, of course, and we have had to colour his hair. Your Prince of Wales was not *un rosso*.'

'No, he was not,' conceded Campion, 'and it is perhaps a good thing his mother cannot see him betraying his Fitton redhead heritage. I have to say, though, that Perdita is a more accurate doppelgänger from a distance; very convincing in those clothes, very stylish, which of course Mrs Simpson was.'

Signora Petraglia shrugged her shoulders with an audible creak of leather. 'The girl is pretty, that's for sure. Perhaps too pretty for this role, but we have used a lot of make-up to make her face white and she has strict orders not to smile.'

Campion turned his attention to Precious Aird, whose head and eyes were at the level of his feet. 'And how are the troops in the trenches?'

'Grateful that it didn't rain last night, otherwise we'd have been knee-deep in mud and it really would have looked like the First World War round here.' Precious removed the briar pipe from between her teeth, grimaced in disgust and wiped her mouth with the back of a hand. 'Yuck! What a disgusting habit. You don't have any mouthwash on you, do you?'

Campion's smile broadened. 'I'm afraid not, though I am sure Lugg over there has a hip flask of brown ale about his person. I wouldn't put it past him.'

Precious waved away the offer. 'Forget it; I'll survive until lunch break.'

'Have you found any archaeology down there?' Campion crouched down on the edge of the trench.

Now it was Precious' turn to shrug. 'Not really expecting to. I think we're still a couple of feet off the bottom of the original excavation. No sign of "natural" yet – the stuff we're digging out is still all backfill. Plus we're not even sure if we're on the right orientation. If we could clean around and follow some edges we'd have a better idea, but that wouldn't look neat for the camera.'

'We are creating a picture for our viewers,' said Daniela. 'They are not interested in this boat burial, as you called it, but in who visited it.' She pointed towards a shivering Mrs Simpson who was leaning closely into the chest of the Prince of Wales. 'In any case, this will be on screen for only a few minutes and the commentary will tell the real story to the viewers, who will be Italians and therefore will be more interested in Mrs Simpson's clothes rather than archaeology.'

'They do have rather a lot of archaeology of their own,' conceded Campion. 'The Italians, that is; and it wasn't just Mrs Simpson who was a trendsetter in fashion in the Thirties. The prince was too, you know. His casualwear was widely copied and he introduced turn-ups on trousers. Well, if he didn't introduce them he certainly made them popular much, as I vaguely recall, to the dismay of his father who thought they were rather . . . dangerous.'

Precious threw back her head and laughed with such violence that her oversize flat cap – lined with a folded newspaper, Campion noticed – fell backwards and released her long blonde hair.

'You Brits,' she said as she struggled to pack her hair back inside its asexual covering. 'Only you Toff Brits could think of trouser turn-ups as dangerous . . .'

'It's part of our national charm,' grinned Campion, 'and now I must, as a loyal Toff Brit, go and swear my allegiance to the Crown over there in the personage of my dear son-and-heir-to-not-very-much and his beautiful wife, whose teeth I can hear chattering from here.'

'Don't forget to curtsy,' Precious called after him before clamping the pipe between her teeth and shuddering at the taste of it.

'Let us get out of your way,' Campion said to Daniela Petraglia. 'Where should we stand?'

'Behind the camera, please.' The Italian dismissed him and then addressed the inhabitants of the trench. 'Now we will go again. Heads down; do not look at the camera and plenty of digging when I give the order.'

Campion looked around the Barrow site and located Lugg shuffling through the bracken and the trees, making a wide arc to avoid the trench almost as if he was trying to outflank an enemy position. Campion was in two minds as to whether Lugg was simply extremely camera shy or merely trying to stay well out of the way in case he was dragooned into becoming a fifth digger in the trench. Given the fat man's oft-voiced grumblings that his days of manual labour were both behind and beneath him, and that he was now a gentleman of leisure, Campion thought the balance of probability lay with the latter explanation.

He, too, picked his way carefully to the far end of the trench, keeping out of the tripod-mounted camera's line of fire, until he was able to stand with an arm around the shoulders of both Rupert and his wife.

'So how are my film stars doing? Should I be asking for autographs?'

'Well, it's not exactly Hollywood,' said Rupert, 'or even Pinewood.'

'Let's be honest, it's not even Cricklewood,' chirped Perdita, 'but thankfully we're almost done and, to look on the bright side, we can now say we've done telly.'

'Italian telly,' Rupert pointed out.

'Which is good, because nobody here will ever see it. That's a win-win situation as far as our careers go.'

Mr Campion gently squeezed his daughter in law's shoulder. 'That's the way to look at it, my dear. Always find the bright side under the layers of dark, glowering clouds. Speaking of which, here comes Lugg, who I am sure will share his vast experience as a television critic. In some circles, you know, he is as highly regarded as that chap Philip Purser on the *Telegraph* and he never misses an episode of *Blue Peter*.'

'This is all a bit of a palaver, inn'it?' Lugg introduced himself to the assembled Campions. 'It's all play-acting.'

'See what I mean?' said Mr Campion. 'Erudite, incisive and devastatingly honest in his opinions; everything one rightly hates about a critic.'

'What's he on about now? Wandering, is he? It happens when you gets to his age. Don't suppose he's asked how you are after your bit of night-time crime-fighting?'

'I haven't, which is remiss of me,' said Campion, 'but I shall do so now.'

'It was all rather farcical,' said Rupert. 'Our room, the so-called Royal Suite, is at the front of the pub and Mr and Mrs Yallop sleep in a room at the back, so I heard him first. He jemmied one of the sash windows and got straight into the bar where the stairs to our room come out, so I was on him fairly quickly.'

'Foolish boy,' Campion scolded gently.

'Exactly what I said,' added Perdita, 'only with more feeling and a few swear words.'

Rupert held up his palms in mock surrender. 'I know, I know, it was rash of me; he might have been belligerent.'

'Or armed,' said Perdita severely.

'Well, he wasn't. He was actually quite clumsy – we both were really. I sort of bumped into him. It was dark, you see, and neither of us had a torch. He had an armful of bottles which he'd taken from behind the bar, we collided and they went all over the place. One of them smashed when it hit the floor and I trod on it. While I was hopping on one foot trying not to bleed to death, the little sod ran across the bar and jumped out of the window quick as a flash. Perdita roused the Yallops and the hunt was on for TCP and plasters.'

Exerting his own area of expertise, Lugg asked, 'Did you get a good look at him?'

'Hardly any look at all. I think he was more scared than I was.'

'He is now,' said Lugg, quickly silenced by a severe glance from Mr Campion, who changed tack.

'He was stealing bottles, you said; bottles of what?'

'Not what you might think,' said his son, anxious to help. 'You and I would certainly have gone for the brandy or the gin, whereas Lugg would have made a beeline for the rum.'

'Nothing wrong with a drop o'rum,' growled Lugg, 'unless that's a sideswipe at me being some sort of pirate.'

'Oh, don't be so sensitive! We all know that with a better education and a pair of sea legs you'd have been a pirate! Now, Rupert, was your clumsy burglar messing about in the pub's display of old beer bottles by any chance?'

'Yes, he was; how did you guess?'

Campion looked towards the backs of Daniela Petraglia and Gianfranco, who were both leaning over the camera a few yards away, and lowered his voice. 'Oh, just something somebody said earlier,' he said vaguely. 'Mr Yallop seemed proud of his collection. Were any broken?'

'Just the one, and of course I had to put my foot on it.'

Campion glanced towards the camera again and lowered his voice to little more than a whisper. 'Let me hazard a wild guess. It was the bottle of Prince's Ale.'

Rupert, speechless, nodded enthusiastically. 'You don't think that was the famous Abdication Treasure, do you?' Then his face fell in dismay. 'And I've gone and broken it.'

'Mebbe Bill Crow thought that was the treasure too.' Lugg jutted a conspiratorial jaw into the huddle of Campions. 'But he's way off beam there. I was telling our cowgirl friend, Precious the Yank, abaht it. Nice drop o'beer an' all and a collector's item these days but hardly worth getting yer collar felt for. We can't be talking much more than twenty quid.'

'I agree that even Bill Crow might think that beneath him when it came to treasure hunting,' said Campion, 'though I suspect his standards are breathtakingly low.'

'Who is this Bill Crow?' Perdita asked him.

'A local rogue who trades as a rag-and-bone man in Heronhoe;

almost certainly the hot favourite in the frame for the break-in at the hall and Rupert's little scuffle last night. Not that he's confessed completely but he has shown a considerable interest in the Abdication Treasure.'

'He's not the only treasure hunter round here,' hissed Lugg. 'Coming through them trees just now I almost turned my ankle on a bit of metal lying in the scrub. Turns out to be one of them mine detectors!'

'Yes, Precious told me the sound man did a bit of metal-detecting in his spare time,' said Campion.

'His name's Maurizio,' confided Perdita, 'and he's done his detecting thing all over the site. I don't think he's found anything but he doesn't say much. I don't think his English is very good.'

'No, he hasn't found anything yet,' said Mr Campion enigmatically. 'Of that I'm quite sure. Look out! Here we go.'

Daniela Petraglia was turning on the impressive heels of her leather boots with one arm raised vertically. 'Ready for one more take,' she shouted, 'with background sound only. So actors, please keep quiet!'

'She means us,' whispered Perdita in Rupert's ear.

Mr Campion's retort was also barely audible. 'Don't be too sure. You two are not the only actors in this field today.'

It should have been a simple exercise for the film-makers: a slowly rising panning shot taking in the upper section of the trench and the diggers – from the waist up, at least – happily doing what diggers do, having been carefully instructed not to look up into the camera lens and thus hopefully preserve the fiction that they were a fine example of robust Suffolk agricultural workers from the Thirties rather than a quartet of students and school-leavers, two of them female, feeling slightly ridiculous in second-hand clothes their parents would have thought unfashionable. Precious Aird, situated nearest to the camera, was designated 'Number One' followed by the two boys trying desperately to look like their grandfathers doing the garden, as 'Two' and 'Three' and then, at the far end of the trench, the diminutive Cat was a hopefully unidentifiable 'Four'. In fact, Cat had received specific instructions from Daniela Petraglia not to dig too effectively as if she lowered the level of the trench where she stood much further she would sink completely out of sight behind Number Three.

Il Regista, taking her directing duties seriously, patted her cameraman on the back and issued her final orders to the extras.

'OK, diggers, start digging. Camera rolling. Action!'

'Is that it, then?' Lugg grumpily asked no one in particular. 'Not much to it, this filming lark.'

'That's one shot,' Rupert explained, 'and quite a long one as it happens. Now they'll move the equipment and do a closer shot or one from a slightly different angle, once they've checked the gate and made sure the sound has taken.'

Lugg looked deliberately confused until he remembered he had already been told about checking the camera lens for obstructions and the sight of the sound man, Maurizio, just out of shot, wearing headphones and carrying a bulky tape recorder on a long strap around his neck and shoulder giving a thumbs-up gesture elucidated things further.

'It looks like that was a take,' Rupert explained. 'It does take an awful long time to create the magic of what you see on the screen.'

'Just listen to David Lean here,' Perdita said sarcastically, 'you wouldn't believe it was his first time in front of the camera.'

'But it's true, darling. Even on such limited experience, it's clear to me that film-making involves hours of hanging about . . .'

'Hours and hours.'

'And then a few minutes of frantic activity to provide a few seconds of screen time.'

'Plus,' Lugg observed philosophically, 'you 'ave to dress up in all that old clobber, though I admits you both look quite smart, apart from the hair. What *have* they done to your ginger locks?'

'It's called make-up, to add realism,' said Perdita, 'and you should try wearing the amount of slap I have to. All Rupert has to worry about is if it rains and the dye leaches out.'

'Now that I'd pay to see,' said an immediately cheered Lugg. 'That'd look like something out of an 'orror film. *Masque of the Red Hair*, we could call it.'

'Very droll,' said Mr Campion, whose eyes had not left the activity in and around the trench. 'You have raised the art of curmudgeonliness – if that is a word, and I'm pretty sure it should be – to a profession.' He pointed a finger, drawing their attention towards the trench. 'While you three have been engaging in caustic persiflage – another splendid word by the way – nobody seems to have noticed that digger Number Four has disappeared.'

'Where is Number Four?' demanded an irate film director, peering into the trench.

Diggers One to Three turned their heads to the southern end of the trench and automatically took a step back towards the side. In doing so, they opened a line of sight for Daniela Petraglia who was now standing on the northern lip, hands on hips, bending forward and peering down the length of the trench.

'I'm still here.'

It was a plaintive, childlike voice, muffled by the fact that its owner was on her knees, bowler-hatted head bent, scratching at the dirt on the trench floor.

'Are you OK back there, Cat?' Precious dropped her spade and gently pushed Number Two and Number Three further into the wall of the trench. 'You haven't hurt yourself, have you?'

'No, I've found something,' said Cat, still flicking soil away with her hand. 'I felt something in that last spit of earth I dug. It didn't feel right and . . . Oh, goodness! I think I'm standing on some old bones!'

Then Cat gave a small, kitten-like scream, but it was enough to make diggers Two and Three jump and attempt to push past Precious to get to the far end of the trench.

By then, Mr Campion was moving quickly towards the trench and Daniela Petraglia was issuing orders loudly in fast Italian.

FIFTEEN
The Hound of the Press

'Are you sure you felt something?'
'I'm very sure.'
'Something solid?'
'Very solid and it looked like . . . bone.'

'Out of the trench! Everybody out of the trench. Maurizio, *Andiamo a lavore!'*

Any filming done in public, whether for a television news bulletin or a big-budget drama, invariably attracts a crowd of fascinated onlookers drawn to the process as if by magnetism. As long as the crowd remains out of shot, do not shuffle their feet too loudly, cough, sneeze, or make political comments or exclamations of love to the presenters or the actors soon to be 'on screen' (usually known, often erroneously as 'the talent'), then film-makers tend to tolerate them, though invariably wishing that the unwashed, rubber-necking populous had something better to do and somewhere else to be.

At the Sweethearting Barrow that day, the usual crowd of gapers, gawkers and snoopers surrounding a film unit and the assembled 'talent' was made up of the unit itself. Only Mr Campion and Lugg could, technically, be classed as civilians or innocent bystanders, and they too were keen to get in on the rubber-necking.

While Daniela Petraglia was clearly in command at ground level, a few feet below her spikey boot heels in the trench itself it was Precious Aird who was organizing things. She pulled Dave and Si out of the way so she could get to where Cat was kneeling and ushered them unceremoniously towards the other end of the trench. She pulled off her hat and flung it on to the spoil heap, the briar pipe following its trajectory, and sank down beside Cat, whose face was white and shocked beneath the rim of the ridiculous bowler hat.

'I felt something solid under the spade,' said the girl. 'I thought it might be a stone, but look, that's not stone, is it? It's bone and I don't want to touch it.'

'Whatever it is, the best thing to do is leave it alone.' Precious put a hand on the girl's shoulder and gently squeezed. 'Let me take over. You go to my backpack and get me a trowel, OK?'

Cat nodded, the rim of the bowler hat almost catching Precious across the bridge of her nose, then climbed out of the trench like a swimmer leaving the pool.

Precious realized that she was alone in the trench and had an audience in a semicircle above her. This must be the view gladiators on the arena sand had of the baying crowd in the amphitheatre, she thought; and there, looming over her as if with the power of life and death of an emperor, was the Italian woman.

'What is it?'

'I don't know yet. Let me clean the area with a trowel and see if I can find some edges.'

Cat appeared at the trot and had to squeeze through the onlookers, which now included diggers, film crew, actors and interested civilians in the form of Mr Campion and Lugg, to hand Precious a shining new four-inch builder's pointing trowel as if passing over Excalibur.

'Wait!' It seemed that Caesar was not pleased with the idea, and had a better one of her own. 'We must let Maurizio in there first.'

Daniela Petraglia's next utterances were in Italian and Maurizio jumped clumsily into the trench, almost knocking Precious over. Unnoticed by everyone except Mr Campion, he had exchanged his tape recorder and long black microphone for the metal detector and, once in the trench, busied himself connecting the battery and clamping the headphones to his ears.

'Charming!' Perdita said loudly, offering a hand to Precious to help pull her out of the trench and up to ground level.

Campion sidled quietly round the lip of the trench to stand next to her. 'Are you all right, Precious?'

'Hey, sure.' She flashed a brilliant smile full of American teeth as she slid the trowel, blade first, into the back pocket of her jeans. 'Thought for a minute I was going to be called on to do some real archaeology. Phew! That was a narrow escape.'

Campion leaned in to her and spoke softly. 'What do you think is down there?'

'I didn't get much of a chance to look properly but Cat was standing on something, that's for sure. I got a glimpse of what could be bone; then again, it might be a stone or a piece of rubbish left by the last lot of diggers.'

'Could it be from the boat burial?'

'No. Hey, I'm making most of this up as I go along, but I have read up on the basics and we are still digging out the backfill that was put back in after the original dig.'

'So whatever Cat found went *into the ditch* when it was being filled in.'

'Yeah, it's in the backfill, like I said. That give you a clue?'

'It gives me a date,' said Campion.

Below them in the trench, Maurizio became the focal point for the ten pairs of eyes following his every move with rapt attention and bated breath. Once the machine was working to his satisfaction, he began to waft the circular head in slow, sweeping motions across the floor of the trench where Cat had been working. The action of the silvery detector head hovering a few inches above the black earth was hypnotic and Campion was reminded of a Greek word, dredged from ancient memory – *boustrophedon*, which meant a right-to-left and then left-to-right sweeping movement usually used to describe the alphabetic writing, or reading, of an ancient script or inscription. He had never enjoyed his schoolboy struggle with Ancient Greek and was grateful when Lugg, shuffling up beside him, broke his reverie.

'If that fella does find a mine, shouldn't we be standing further back out of range?'

'Don't fret, old son. I'll lay you a tenner against a bottle of brown ale that our friend down there doesn't detect anything made of metal.'

Almost immediately, Maurizio's metal detector began to emit a series of high-pitched rapid beeping noises.

'That'll be ten of your English pounds,' said Lugg smartly. 'I'll take cash.'

Things happened rapidly. Before the significance of those electronic beeps had registered with most of the onlookers, Daniela Petraglia was issuing instructions in Italian at breakneck speed and handing down a spade to Maurizio in exchange for the metal detector. Without hesitation he set to with a will, digging large spits of soil and flipping them casually behind him so they scattered along the length of the trench.

Precious Aird sucked in air between her teeth and clenched her fists. 'This isn't the way to do it.'

Perdita reached for her arm to comfort her, but before she could make contact there was a collective intake of breath from the crowd as Maurizio put his spade aside and bent down to pluck something from the earth. What he held up for the approval of his audience, just as a victorious gladiator would offer up a particularly grisly trophy to the baying crowd, appeared to be a piece of dirty brown fabric. There was a further collective gasp from the onlookers as something solid and grey fell out of the fabric and landed on to Maurizio's right boot, causing the startled Italian to jump a pace backwards.

Mr Campion decided it was time to intervene. '*Signora* Petraglia, I think we must take things at a more considered pace. This is not what you think it is.'

There was no doubt Campion had grabbed the attention of the Italian woman, and also that of everyone else gathered around the southern end of the trench.

'The machine says there is metal down there.' Daniela Petraglia reacted angrily as if defending herself from a vile accusation.

'It is not what you think it is,' Campion said with a severity which impressed all who heard him and surprised those who knew him well. 'We should allow Precious here to do some delicate trowelling and then we can see what we have. Are we agreed?'

Daniela Petraglia held Campion's gaze for an uncomfortable length of time and then simply nodded once and ordered Maurizio out of the trench. Campion bowed briefly to her then turned and jerked his head at Precious.

'Can you sort this out?' he asked and, without giving him an answer, Precious drew her trowel like a sword from the scabbard of her jeans pocket and jumped into the trench.

Sinking to her knees, Precious began to wield her trowel, scraping crumbs of earth from the flap of dirty brown material containing the small grey object which Maurizio had lifted and then dropped.

'It's bone all right, I'm sure of it, and there's more of it.' Head down and concentrating, Precious began to give a running commentary. 'The fabric could be leather, though I'm no expert and, if it is, it's pretty cool it's survived this long.'

'Thirty-five years,' said Campion as if thinking aloud. 'That's not unheard of in these conditions.'

'What are you talking about, Pa?' Rupert, transfixed by the activity in the trench, found his voice.

'Whatever is down there is within the backfill of the trench. That means it was put in there after the trench was opened and then closed in 1935. Whatever it is, it has nothing to do with an

Anglo-Saxon boat burial nor, for that matter, with any so-called treasure.'

Without taking her eyes off Precious working directly below her feet, Daniela Petraglia took issue with Mr Campion. 'How can you know? The detector says there is metal down there.'

'There may well be,' said Campion coolly, 'and it could well be valuable.'

There was a hush around the site. Lugg, his bushy eyebrows raised quizzically, pushed his face in front of that of his friend and mentor, the gesture asking the question for him.

'If I was a betting man,' said a smiling Campion, 'which clearly I am not, I would hazard some small change on the fact that there's a gold watch and chain down there.'

'You claiming to have X-ray vision now?'

'No, it's just a hunch, but I'm willing to bet that ten pounds you think I owe you.'

'Tut, tut,' Lugg admonished him, 'and you not a betting man; shame to take the money really. You're on.'

Mr Campion may not have been a gambler but he was sure he could have placed a winning bet on the fact that Precious, busy trowelling away at the bottom of the trench with her head bowed, would be doing so with a spur of pink tongue protruding from her lips in the universal habit of the young and innocent when they are deep in concentration.

There was no doubt that Precious was concentrating on her task and she now seemed oblivious to the fact that she had an audience, who were all leaning, sometimes at precarious angles, over the trench. She worked diligently and efficiently, lowering the level of the square yard she was scraping by a good inch until inconsistencies in the surface of the earth became visible even to those looking down from above. It would have taken a very practised eye to identify those small inconsistencies from that angle, and so Precious' running commentary was listened to intently and in reverent silence.

'There's more bone down here and something solid by my left knee. There's one sort of material – leather, I think – though it's badly stained by the soil, and there are tufts of other material, wool, maybe, disappearing off under the edge of the trench.'

'Is it animal skin or a . . .' Daniela Petraglia searched for the English word, '. . . a pelt?'

'Uh-huh, I'm sure it's man-made. I think there's even a pattern on it. Hold your horses, here's something for Maurizio. Can you see that?'

Precious leaned back on her haunches and, using her trowel as a pointer, indicated a spot in the middle of the trench about six inches from the end wall.

After a nod from his director, Maurizio reconnected his detector to his battery and lowered the sensor head on its shaft into the trench. Precious held her trowel above her head so as not to give the instrument a false signal and, when the circular head was two or three inches above the soil, the machine began to sound its beep-beep alarm.

Precious waved the detector away and looked to Campion for instructions. They came instead from Daniela Petraglia, who had dropped to her knees and was leaning, almost falling, into the trench, her face intimidatingly close to that of the American girl.

'Dig there, but be very careful.'

Only when Campion nodded agreement did Precious set to work with delicate movements of the trowel point, flicking tiny lumps of soil up and to the side. After five or six parries and thrusts, a worm-like sliver of yellow metal magically appeared.

Perdita was the first to break the hushed silence. 'Is that gold?'

Mr Campion held up a forefinger as if calling for a point of order. 'Can you move back about a foot, Precious, and clean the area more or less where your knees are? Do you need any help?'

'There's no room for more than one to work down here,' Precious replied. 'But somebody could get me a finds' tray or a bag or something to put stuff in.' She gave a self-deprecating laugh and shook her head. 'I didn't come on this dig expecting to find anything!'

It was the youngest member of the crowd, Cat, who was the first to respond. 'Will this do?' she asked, taking off her bowler hat and handing it down into the trench. 'I hate wearing the damn thing but it might be useful as a bucket.'

'How wonderfully inventive young people are,' Campion said to Lugg.

'But no sense of style,' the fat man replied gloomily.

Precious took the hat, placed it to the side and then edged backwards on her knees, scraping vigorously with the triangular edge rather than the point of her trowel as she shuffled. Occasionally she would straighten her upper body, resting her buttocks on the heels of her paratrooper boots and flex her right, trowelling arm while scooping loose soil out of the way with her left.

'Are you sure there's nothing we can do to help?' Rupert called down. 'We're all feeling very guilty standing around up here watching you do all the work.'

'Well, I'm not volunteering. I ain't at me best in confined spaces.'

Mr Campion peered over the top of his spectacles at the fat man. 'Don't worry, you are excused digging duties. You simply don't have the figure for it.'

'I'm sure we could squeeze you in here, Mr Lugg,' said Precious without looking up. 'There'll be plenty of room once we dig this guy out.'

When Precious got to her feet and stepped back a pace, shaking each leg to restore the circulation, it became clear that they were all looking at the skeletal frame of an upper torso; a body in one end of a thirty-foot-long grave.

Where she had been kneeling, something smooth and grey-white resembling a pumice stone or a rough pebble drew the eyes of each onlooker. It could have been something geological and was still half-covered in soil, but once studied closely a series of regular indentations, or rather protrusions, became clear and even the slowest brain realized that this particular piece of pumice stone had a set of upper teeth.

Perdita, transfixed, reached automatically for Rupert's hand, only to find it already on its way to meet hers. Cat, realizing on what she had been standing all morning, let out a small cry and sought solace in the arms of fellow digger Dave, much to the chagrin of fellow digger Simon. Lugg had his head on one side, gauging angles and distances. If that thing at the American girl's feet really was the skull, then the rest of the deceased must be between it and the trench end, the hips and legs still buried in the mound, roughly somewhere under the spot where the bossy Italian woman was kneeling and looking, even Lugg noticed, the most shocked of all the trench-side witnesses.

Mr Campion did not look shocked, or indeed particularly interested. To the outside observer, had there been one, he might well have appeared totally unconcerned by what had been uncovered in the base of the trench. Instead, he seemed to be fascinated by the reactions of Daniela Petraglia, Gianfranco and Maurizio. There was no doubt in Campion's mind that the Italian contingent had been taken completely by surprise by the discovery.

'This is not any sort of treasure, *Signora* Petraglia,' he said forcefully.

The Italian woman pointed a finger downwards like an Etruscan devil-goddess showing the way to hell. 'There is gold.'

'A small amount, hardly buried treasure. I think you will find that it is a gold chain, on the end of which will be a gold watch.'

Daniela Petraglia did not so much spring to her feet as uncoil her body, and when she stood erect, it was with menace. '*Impossible!*' As pronounced the Italian way, the word carried far more drama. 'You cannot know such things. It is trickery. *Truffatore! Imbroglione!*'

Campion remained serene. 'I am not a crook, *Signora*, though you are not the first to call me a trickster.'

He now had the full attention of the congregation standing at what was, beyond doubt, a graveside.

'I am convinced that we have uncovered the last remains of a local news hound, a journalist from the Hadleigh paper who was well-known in the area thirty-five years ago. His name was Samuel Salt.'

'That means nothing.'

'Perhaps not to you, *Signora*, but he is remembered as a regular customer at the King's Head in Sweethearting, and I am reliably informed that his most precious possessions were a motorbike and sidecar combination and a gold watch and chain. I am no expert on matters forensic but if the material our diggers have unearthed is leather, it is a reasonable assumption – or at least a jolly good guess – that it came from a leather flying helmet of the sort popular with bikers back in those days when no one bothered with crash helmets. That worm of gold glistening down there is, I suggest, part of a watch chain and will lead, if anyone has the stomach for it, to a Hunter or a half-Hunter dangling from the poor man's ribcage. A gruesome thought and you may say that all this is circumstantial if you were in the business of collating evidence, but I can add one more piece of corroboration.

'Samuel Salt covered the Sweethearting excavation for his newspaper, writing several articles about it. He was here on the day of the visit of the Prince of Wales and Mrs Simpson' – he turned to smile at Rupert and Perdita – 'the real ones, that is, although he never wrote anything about that day, or indeed anything after it, because he simply disappeared. One day this trench, or one as near as dammit exactly like it, was open to the elements awaiting the royal seal of approval. It was the end of the dig and once the distinguished visitors had departed, the trench was filled in – or backfilled as my American archaeological advisor tells me I must call it.

'I am convinced in my mind, small though it may be, that Samuel Salt, journalist of this parish, was already in the trench when the backfilling proper began. And he did not go in there voluntarily.'

'This has nothing to do with me!'

'I am not suggesting it has, *Signora*. In fact, I am fairly sure the name Samuel Salt, the late press hound, rings no bells at all with you. His was a very small part – almost that of an "extra" as you might say – in the real story of the Sweethearting Barrow and the subsequent fairy story which became known as the Abdication Treasure. Journalists are mostly annoying in life but, in death, this one has proved a real inconvenience to you.'

'How can that be? What are you saying?' *Signora* Petraglia's face was beginning to slowly contort in fury with the menace of lava oozing from a volcano. Mr Campion, on the other hand, presented a serene picture of tranquillity which would not have looked out of place in a pulpit.

'I am unilaterally declaring an end to all archaeology, filming and treasure hunting – by *all* parties – in Sweethearting and its environs until poor old Samuel Salt, if it is indeed he, is properly laid to rest. That will require contacting the local police immediately and then making ourselves available for the lengthy questioning which will no doubt follow. For that inconvenience I will apologize in advance but we must go through formal procedures. A crime has been committed here. Not by anyone present; in fact, it was done before most of you were even born, but murder – and I really do think it was murder – is a crime always and forever. Now I suggest we send an advance party to the hall to use the telephone there. I know there is a phone box in Sweethearting, which is nearer, but I really do not want to raise alarums and excursions in the village. After that, we leave a reception committee here to greet the police and I suggest the rest of us gather our equipment together and move up to the hall where Lavinia has sufficient supplies to provide everyone with a late lunch.'

The sermon over, the congregation began to disperse but no one had moved more than a yard from the trench when a sudden, shrill scream brought them to a halt. For most of those present, the assumption was that Precious Aird had discovered something even more unspeakable in the depths of the trench, but in fact the distress call had come from the youngest throat of all.

Daniela Petraglia had her left hand wrapped into young Cat's hair and was pulling so hard the girl was forced to lean back on her heels, her arms flailing and eyes streaming. In her right hand the Italian woman held a small black automatic pistol, the muzzle pressed hard up against Cat's temple.

'No police,' said *Signora* Petraglia, 'and everyone goes back to the hall right now. When we are there, you, *Signor* Campion, will tell me everything or your young friends will suffer. And then we will start on your family.'

SIXTEEN
The Evil Meal

Their predicament brought to Mr Campion's mind the story of the *Malamerenda* – the Evil Meal – an incident which took place in the Tuscan hill town of Siena in the early part of the fourteenth century. The Evil Meal was the climax of years of violence between two powerful clans, the Salimbeni and the Tolomei, whose rivalry some authorities have suggested formed the basis for another feud between Montagues and Capulets, dramatically transposed from Siena to Verona. In an attempt to solve the problem of those tiresome Tolomeis, the Salimbenis invited eighteen members of the rival family to a kiss-and-make-up dinner and then promptly massacred them. It was a blueprint for treacherous hospitality which was followed by the Campbells biting the Macdonald hand which fed them in Glencoe in 1692.

When Daniela Petraglia drew a pistol and pressed it against the temple of the terrified Cat, it had been the signal for Maurizio and Giancarlo also to draw guns and take up strategic positions around the site so that all those gathered around the trench were viable targets. Three armed Italians were instantly in total control of the destinies of seven uneasy Britons and one totally bemused American, who told herself that she would never get the hang of this country; a country where the archaeology wasn't really archaeology, treasure hunters went looking for treasure which everyone knew didn't exist connected to a king they didn't want, and even at gunpoint, standing over some poor guy's open grave, the Brits remained unbelievably relaxed – and so goddamn polite.

'And now everyone should please stay as calm as possible,' Mr Campion had announced as though asking for the collection plate to be circulated, 'for it has long been my experience that arguing with an angry lady with a pistol is almost as futile as arguing with an unarmed one.'

Not only was he staying cool, thought Precious Aird with not a little admiration, but that old stick Campion was somehow staying in control.

'How do you want us to proceed to the hall, *Signora*? I know there is little traffic on the road but a passing cyclist, for instance, may well find it odd to see a crocodile of prisoners being marched along at gunpoint – even in Suffolk. So do we tramp across the fields? There is little chance of anyone observing us that way, I'd wager.'

Without releasing her grip on the tearful Cat's hair, Daniela Petraglia did at least remove the muzzle of her gun from the girl's head. 'We take the cars. We leave all the equipment in the ditch and we go now.'

'A wise move, *Signora*. If there is no activity on the site it will not attract the casual visitor, but just in case it does, might I make a suggestion?'

A casual wave of her pistol gave permission.

'On the off-chance that a passing rambler or a nosey neighbour from Sweethearting might wander over here while we are elsewhere, might it not be advisable, if not decorous, to conceal the remains of our departed hound of the press down there in the trench? A thin layer of soil should be adequate and I think we can dispense with any funeral rites. It is, after all, rather late in the day for that. Lugg, would you do the honours?'

And the fat man did, with dignity, pick up a spade and shovel earth from the spoil heap into the end of the trench until all glimmers of skeletal bone and that faint twist of shining gold were extinguished.

The convoy of prisoners was then assembled at the roadside where three vehicles, conveniently as there were three gunmen, were parked. To each vehicle Daniela Petraglia allocated passengers and an armed guard. Campion would drive the film crew's Citroën with Rupert and *Signora* Petraglia as passengers. Precious would drive her VW under the supervision of Maurizio, with Lugg and the young diggers Cat and Dave, and Perdita would take Simon as a passenger and Giancarlo as a guard in her Mini. The Citroën would lead off, followed by the VW van and finally the Mini.

It was, Campion had to admit, a clever strategy. Campion himself would hardly try anything foolish with the *signora*'s gun pressed to his son's head and the son would behave knowing his wife was beyond rescue and similarly threatened in a following car. Precious, he was sure, would not act recklessly with two of her young diggers and the formidable Lugg in her charge, though she was probably more worried – needlessly, in Campion's opinion – about Lugg mounting a counterattack on their custodian. In his heyday Lugg would certainly have tried to disarm his guard, or at least jumped ship, so to speak. Even now, at his advanced age and girth, had he been the lone prisoner he might have tried, but not with three innocent bystanders sharing the same confined metallic space moving at thirty miles per hour. The Italian woman's plan was divide and control but they were not, Campion was sure, divided and conquered.

He started the unfamiliar left-hand-drive car and, when told by his captor sitting in the rear seat to proceed, he pulled out into the road at little more than a crawl in order to allow the other two vehicles – which he thought of as private prison vans or perhaps an unconventional funeral cortege – to manoeuvre into convoy formation.

'Do feel free to criticize my driving if I inadvertently stray over to the other side of the road. I'm not used to the steering wheel being this close to the hedgerow.' Campion kept his voice light for Rupert's sake but his son's face was deathly white and his eyes constantly flitting from the pistol aimed at his head to the Citroën's wing mirror to check that Perdita's red Mini was still following. 'But do not, under any circumstances, attempt to grab the steering wheel as that may be regarded as an aggressive move which could trigger – oh, dear, bad choice of words – our personal sword of Damocles in the back seat.'

Rupert attempted a thin smile and with some effort banished the nervousness from his voice. 'What happens when we get to the hall?'

'That, of course, is up to Donna Daniela,' said Mr Campion, 'but I do hope she allows us a decent lunch – I'm starving. It's been quite a busy morning.'

Oliver Grieg Bell answered the front door of the hall to find Mr Campion and Rupert standing sheepishly, side by side like a pair of naughty schoolboys pre-empted in a ring-the-bell-and-run-away prank. Oliver could not see that behind the two thwarted schoolboys Daniela Petraglia had her Beretta pushed into the small of Rupert's back.

'Albert, Rupert. I wasn't expecting you but please come in.' Oliver became aware of two more vehicles nosing to a halt behind the Citroën already parked at the top of the drive. 'Oh, you all seem to be here,' he said limply as the VW and the Mini disgorged their passengers, 'and hello, Daniela.'

The smile that had begun to blossom on Oliver's face was nipped in the bud when he realized that the object of his admiration was holding a gun, and then he frowned as he realized that his unexpected visitors were being herded towards the hall by two other armed Italians.

Daniela Petraglia nudged Rupert ahead of her across the threshold and gave Oliver a good view of the small automatic. 'Your telephone, Mr Bell.'

'Please, it's Oliver,' said Bell automatically and immediately bit his lower lip as he recovered his composure. 'You wish to use the telephone?'

'I think *Signora* Petraglia wants to make sure *no one* uses the telephone,' Campion intervened. 'I do apologize, Oliver, for descending upon you like this and somewhat mob-handed as I think the expression is, but there have been . . . developments . . . down at the dig.'

'You've found it? The Abdication Treasure?' Oliver's face lit up, all thoughts of armed invaders briefly banished, even as he was allowing them across the threshold and into the hallway.

'I'm afraid not, old man, but we did find something which has brought matters, shall we say, to a head. In fact, to plumb the depths of bad taste, you might say head and body, for what we found was, I am convinced, the body of Samuel Salt.'

'The reporter?'

'The very same, which would explain why he never filed any stories about, or more significantly after, a particular royal visit in 1935.'

'Enough!' commanded their captor, waving with her pistol. 'Inside! Everyone inside!'

As the intruders began to troop into the hall, Lavinia Bell appeared from the kitchen, drying her hands on a tea towel.

'Who is it, Oliver?'

'Lavinia, I'm so sorry to drop in on you unannounced,' said Campion, 'but could you possibly break out the iron rations and knock up a late lunch for . . .' he looked around and made a play of counting heads, '. . . eleven? A few cold cuts and some cheese would do nicely. It's a terrible imposition I know, but you see I am somewhat handicapped as my film crew seems to have mutinied.'

Before a stunned Lavinia could say anything, Rupert turned on his father.

'*Your* film crew?'

'Ah, yes, dear boy, I'm sorry. I should have said. I am a sort of investor in their film production, what I think they call an "angel" in show-business circles. But please don't tell your mother.'

Rupert, speechless, prompted by a metallic prod in his back, stumbled down the hallway.

'Would sandwiches do?' asked a similarly shell-shocked Lavinia.

'Perfectly acceptable, thank you,' said Campion before turning to Daniela Petraglia. 'Now, where do you want us? Somewhere we can sit down, preferably, as I suspect we have quite a lot to talk about and we might as well get comfortable.'

Daniela Petraglia brought her pistol close up to Mr Campion's face. 'You talk too much, but for once you might have something to say.'

There was another exercise in dividing and controlling. Precious, her three diggers and Lugg were ordered to the Orangery, guarded by Giancarlo while Maurizio marched Lavinia Bell and Perdita into the kitchen on food preparation duties. Campion, Rupert and Oliver were frog-marched into the front room, which was littered with loose music manuscript staff paper, some with inked notations but most with pencilled dots and scratchings.

'Sorry about the mess,' Oliver apologized and hurriedly scooped up an armful of sheets, knocked them together on his thigh and placed the pile on top of Hattie the harpsichord. After a moment's hesitation, he picked up the plaster bust of Lord Breeze and placed it on top of the pile to weigh the sheets down. 'I've been trying to do a bit of composing,' he said, sounding deflated.

'I have a feeling,' said Mr Campion, 'that we will not be requiring incidental music or a theme tune any longer.'

'That's a pity. What's happened?'

'As far as our televisual re-enactment goes I believe the term is "that's a wrap". Things were going splendidly, with Rupert here doing a pitch-perfect impersonation of a rather pampered prince undertaking yet another boring royal chore.'

Rupert, being an actor, was oblivious to danger or peril when praise was being given and placed a hand on his chest as he bowed in appreciation to his father.

'And then, in the bottom of our re-created trench, we discovered some old bones – the bones, I am convinced, of Samuel Salt, which would explain why in your researches you never found anything written by him after that royal visit in 1935. The Sweethearting Barrow trench was backfilled the day after the visit and I think Sam Salt was in it, with, say, a light sprinkling of soil to cover him. The diggers who did the filling probably never noticed anything and an ancient grave that had been empty suddenly had a body in it, but almost nobody knew about it.'

'Nobody?' Rupert asked, happy to play the Dr Watson character.

'Except the person or persons who put him there, which was quite clever really. Who would look for a body in a grave which had been opened and presented for royal inspection?'

'That had nothing to do with my people,' said *Signora* Petraglia grimly.

'I accept that, but a body in an unmarked grave in suspicious circumstances necessitates police intervention sooner or later. You were not prepared to risk that, were you, *Signora*? So you thought on your feet – rather too quickly, perhaps – and brought us all here, not to telephone the police but to make sure no one else did. Well, you have us all here under one roof but what now? I don't believe you plan on murdering all of us. I am not even sure if you have enough bullets in those little guns.'

The Italian woman cocked her head on one side and looked at Campion with disdain and just a hint of curiosity. 'We don't have to hurt all of you. Just his wife – and his.' The pistol in her hand flicked between Rupert and Oliver and then settled comfortably back on Campion's midriff. 'Now everyone will sit down and you' – the gun indicated Rupert – 'will sit there, nearest to me to prevent any foolish or dangerous actions.'

She indicated an armchair near the harpsichord and then she herself sat on the stool by the keyboard and rested her gun arm on the lid. Campion and Oliver she waved towards the sofa in front of the fireplace. Rupert was now seated only four feet from the muzzle of the Beretta and Campion and Oliver, though still well within range, were too far away to make a realistic grab for it.

'I can assure you,' Campion pleaded, 'that Rupert is only occasionally foolish and never dangerous. He is here solely as a jobbing actor and knows nothing about any so-called treasure or any . . . underlying matters.'

Daniela Petraglia offered Campion a thin smile. 'I do not consider your son dangerous at all, but I know you are and the best way to make you behave is for you to know that I will shoot your son without a moment's hesitation unless you tell me the truth.'

To his son's horror, Mr Campion put his head back slightly and placed a forefinger to his chin; an innocent in deep thought.

'Which particular truth would you like to hear?'

Perdita and Lavinia were marched in at gunpoint bearing trays of plates and sandwiches.

'They're only tinned ham and pickles, I'm afraid, and it's white bread,' said their hostess, conscious of the fact that her hair was

a mess and that the frilly apron she wore was doing nothing for
her sense of style.

'Delightful,' said Campion, receiving a plate. 'Am I the only
one?'

Signora Petraglia, Rupert and Oliver remained silent.

'Then forgive me for eating while talking, but I really am
famished.'

'Let them give food to the others,' Daniela Petraglia ordered
Maurizio in Italian, 'and put them in the Orangery too. Tell Giancarlo
to stay alert, then come back here – I have a job for you.'

Oliver and Lavinia and Rupert and Perdita exchanged confused
and anxious looks but no words as the women were lead away.

'Now, *Signor* Campion,' the instruction came as Campion was
in mid-bite, 'you will tell me what you know of the Heronhoe
Treasure.'

'My dear Donna Daniela, if only you had asked me that –
honestly – when you first sounded me out, then much of this
unpleasantness could have been avoided.'

'What do you mean "sounded out" Pa?' blurted Rupert.

'Be quiet!' snapped Daniela Petraglia. 'Let the grown-ups talk.'

'I was approached by a respectable Italian television company
to act as an advisor to a film they were making about the
Abdication, specifically because I was involved, tangentially, in
the Prince of Wales' visit to the Sweethearting excavation. Even
though I maintained that my involvement with that event was
purely transitory – Lugg and I were back in London when the
visit actually took place – it seemed that my involvement was
being insisted upon, almost as if I had been specially selected.
The visit of Edward and Mrs Simpson was going to be recon-
structed for the programme and for a small financial investment
I was able to have some say in the casting of those principal
roles as well as being as a sort of roving consultant to the project,
though I was denied the rather glamorous title of Executive
Producer, which was disappointing.

'It did not take a genius to work out that the object of the exercise
was the elusive Abdication Treasure or Heronhoe Horde or whatever
you want to call it, but for the life of me I couldn't work out how
an Italian television company would have come across these rather
dubious stories of treasure, let alone how they knew about the royal

visit here. It was not an official engagement and, as it involved Mrs Simpson, it was kept very quiet at the time.

'What I should have done was talked with old Wemyss-Grendle much earlier and discovered that the late, lamented Elspeth Brunt, or Elspeth Bolzano to use her married name, was the key to all this. It was Elspeth who set this particular hare running, wasn't it, *Signora*?'

Even though he had one eye on the gun levelled at him across the lid of the harpsichord, Rupert could not resist answering one question with another. 'Isn't she the sister of Sonia, the old dear who helps out at the King's Head?'

'Yes, she was; indeed, she worked there as well for a while, I believe, when Sonia – Mrs Aldous as she was then – was the landlady, but I have a feeling Elspeth was a little too flighty for bar work, perhaps too friendly with the customers, and she moved here to work at Heronhoe Hall for the Mad Major. She was in service here when Lugg and I stayed on the eve of the prince's visit, and to my acute embarrassment I cannot recollect her at all, but I have the feeling she remembered me.'

Daniela Petraglia banged the butt of her pistol on the lid of the harpsichord, producing a high-pitched squeak of anxiety from Oliver. 'Enough! You are telling me what I already know. Now tell me where the treasure is!'

Campion replaced his half-eaten sandwich on his plate and balanced the plate carefully on his knees before turning his spectacles fully on the Italian woman.

'My dear lady, the simple fact is there is no treasure. It is a myth, a story, a local legend. Goodness knows how many hours, days or even weeks Oliver here has spent researching the topic, often to the despair of his charming wife and his eminent father-in-law,' Mr Campion nodded politely to the bust of Lord Breeze which surveyed the room from the top of the harpsichord, 'who himself expended some energy on the matter when he purchased the estate. Neither of them came close to discovering what form this magical treasure took, let alone its worth or where it was supposed to be found. Is that not correct, Oliver?'

Oliver Bell nodded enthusiastically, quite content to deny, when threatened, the existence of something he had been convinced of up until now. 'I've even had the floorboards taken up in some rooms,' he gushed, keen to support Mr Campion, 'and found nothing, nothing at all.'

'Neither did our local burglar the other night, nor did he find anything at the King's Head, although admittedly he was disturbed on both occasions.' He turned his face back to *Signora* Petraglia. 'I assumed that you were behind those break-ins, but having chatted to Bill Crow this morning I find that he was acting as a self-employed entrepreneur, albeit a pretty useless one. He was inspired, however, by your arrival in Heronhoe which, in his tiny mind, gave some credence to the stories Elspeth Bolzano was so keen on. I would hazard a guess that when she was ill, towards the end of her life, Elspeth began to remember, or half-remember, events from her youth and concocted the story that King Edward had made some sort of parting gift to Sweethearting or Heronhoe, or both, at the time of his abdication, presumably in remembrance of good times had. However she put it, her husband Stephano believed her and, when he retired to his native Italy, I suspect he told those stories to others.'

Campion paused, delved into his trouser pocket to retrieve his handkerchief, then removed his spectacles and began to polish the lenses with precise circular movements of finger and thumb. 'Did Stephano pass on those stories to his brother, perhaps? Is Marco Bolzano still alive and also enjoying retirement in Italy? I'm afraid I've quite lost touch with the Bolzano brothers since they left Clerkenwell under something of a cloud fifteen years ago, and that was quite remiss of me.'

If the scene in the front room resembled the stage setting for a theatrical drama – a classy one given that a harpsichord was involved – then the Orangery at the rear of Heronhoe Hall resembled a transit camp for Displaced Persons. The young archaeologists who had been sleeping there on camp beds had, left to their own devices, naturally devoted little time to housekeeping. As a consequence, the floor area with a creeping moss comprising items of clothing, some of them even clean, shoes, dirty plates, cups and cutlery, books, a completed jigsaw of Constable's *The Hay Wain* and a game of Scrabble abandoned on the verge of a treble word score.

'I've seen worse prisons,' noted Lugg, being careful where he planted his feet as he was ushered in.

The three diggers gravitated to their camp beds and sleeping bags and sank on to them in shocked silence while Precious attempted to clear a space for Lugg on hers. Being familiar with the load-bearing properties of the ex-military canvas and metal rod construction of the bed, Lugg opted to sit on the floor if a snug corner spot could be found for him. Precious folded her sleeping bag to form a thick cushion and, using her boots, made a space for Lugg to lower his bulk on to it. With his back against the wall and after a considerable amount of wriggling, blowing and puffing, Lugg settled himself into a passable imitation of a very grumpy Pasha receiving bad news from some distant part of the Ottoman Empire.

He cheered visibly when Perdita and Lavinia were shown in bearing trays containing a small mountain of sandwiches, a bowl of pickled onions, some healthy sticks of celery in a glass of water and a pile of far more popular chocolate biscuits.

'Bin a while since breakfast,' he said to no one in particular as he loaded up a plate balanced on his drawn-up knees.

'You'll have to budge up a bit, Maggers,' said Perdita, gently nudging the big man's thigh with her shoe. 'Lavinia and I are joining all you other POWs here in Stalag 17, so make room for two little 'uns.'

'Pull up a piece of floor and make yerself at 'ome,' Lugg said magnanimously. 'To what do we owe this honour? I'd've thought you would have been put in the officers' camp in the front lounge.'

Lavinia bent over to offer more food from her tray and indicated with her eyes that Precious should lean in and also take something. 'There's a big pow-wow going on in there,' she said quietly, only just above a whisper, 'but I think it's coming to a head. The boss lady has told our personal guard to go and collect their luggage and their passports from Heronhoe.'

'That's good,' whispered Precious Aird.

Lavinia was suddenly indignant. 'Good that I speak Italian? Nobody bothered to ask before.'

'No,' hissed the American girl, 'good because now there are only two of them. I wasn't sure I could handle three.'

Oliver Grieg Bell cleared his throat nervously. 'Would someone care to tell me what is going on here?'

'I would like to second that motion,' said Rupert, still conscious of *Signora* Petraglia's gun arm laid across the harpsichord, the business end of the weapon pointing firmly in his direction.

'I have a confession to make,' said Mr Campion. 'Possibly more than one. I am partly responsible for the predicament we find ourselves in and for that I humbly apologize. My rather brilliant plan has not quite gone as expected.'

'You planned to keep the treasure for yourself!' The pistol trembled in Daniela Petraglia's hand, though her arm remained straight and pointing in Rupert's direction.

'My dear lady, how many times? There is no treasure and whether you call it the Heronhoe Horde or the Abdication Treasure or Sweethearting grave goods, it won't make it reality. It was all a dream, a fantasy, a myth; a piece of wish-fulfilment promulgated by a woman who, being charitable, was probably ill and, being less charitable, was wool-headed.

'Even if there was any truth in the rumour, which I stress is all we are dealing with here, then all logic would point to three places where something valuable – I will refrain from the word "treasure" from now on – might have been concealed for the last thirty-five years: here at Heronhoe Hall, at the King's Head or at Sweethearting at the site of the boat burial. Oliver has conducted a thorough search of the hall and found nothing likely to alleviate his financial concerns, if I may be so crude and bold as to put it that way. Similarly, the landlords of the King's Head, if appearances are anything to go by, do not seem to have prospered from any royal windfall. And we now know that the Sweethearting burial mound contained no Anglo-Saxon riches but rather a more recent body. Which is where my little plan went wrong.'

Campion paused and thoughtfully considered his reflection in the large oval mirror hanging over the fireplace before continuing.

'Although in some ways, that is where it all went right.'

'Fool! *Idiota!* You are talking crazy talk. You had no plan, unless it was to keep the treasure for yourself.'

Mr Campion shook his head slowly in despair and sighed dramatically. 'Is there a problem with my diction or your hearing, *Signora*? I know you speak English perfectly well, yet you persistently refuse to hear the phrase *there is no treasure*. Should you choose not to believe me, I can get official confirmation of that fact from the very highest authority in the land. Of course, that may take a while and I would have to consult the Court Circular, but I am sure it could be done.

'My plan had nothing to do with a fantasy treasure – it was to do with you, *Signora*. I did everything in my power to facilitate the visit of your spurious film crew, providing access to the hall and the Sweethearting Mound, archaeologists and even actors. I wanted to make it as easy as possible for you to get here so that all I had to do was wait until you did something stupid. And now you have, thanks to the late Samuel Salt, although I have to admit I did not plan that discovery.'

'I have told you, that body is nothing to do with us.'

Rupert flinched as he saw the woman's knuckles whiten as she tightened her grip on her Beretta.

'I know you had nothing to do with Mr Salt's death back in 1935, but failing to report finding his body is almost certainly an offence under English law,' said Campion calmly.

Signora Petraglia did not appear impressed or particularly worried and certainly not frightened. 'That is not a serious matter.'

Mr Campion shrugged his shoulders. 'It's certainly not as serious an offence as producing firearms in order to kidnap ten people and hold them captive against their will. I am fairly confident that even the most liberal member of our judiciary will take a dim view of that. You acted without thinking and brought things to a head rather sooner than I anticipated, but your obsession with treasure – your greed – was inevitably going to make you do something stupid, and you did.'

'So we have fallen into some sort of trap?'

'You could say that. Perhaps not exactly the trap I had in mind, but now it is sprung, it will do.'

'And yet I am the one holding the gun.'

'For the moment.'

The Italian woman's expression slowly changed from a haughty sneer to one of genuine puzzlement. 'You have gone to a lot of trouble, *Signor* Campion. You have put your friends and family in danger, and yet you say there is no treasure. So why are you doing this?'

'For Seraphina,' said Campion quietly.

SEVENTEEN
Hair in the Gate

G iancarlo Della Barba, who had never travelled further north than Rome, had been looking forward to his first visit to England, and especially Swinging London, with the enthusiasm of any red-blooded twenty-one-year-old Italian male whose outraged mother believed everything she read about miniskirts getting shorter and whose sombre parish priest had attempted to outlaw listening to the music of morally dubious pop groups such as The Beatles and The Kinks.

He had accepted the fact that he would be under the command of Donna Daniela, for he had seen older men, civic officials and even policemen offer her nothing but loyalty and respect for most of his life and it never crossed his mind to question any of her orders. The trip to England could only improve his standing within Donna Petraglia's organization and surely would offer the chance to sample delights not available to a young man from a small village in rural Campagna.

Giancarlo had even, secretly, paid for some basic English lessons from a retired schoolteacher from Salerno, but now he was beginning to regard that as a wasted investment. He had seen nothing of London apart from Clerkenwell, where he met only Italians who teased him when he attempted English and openly mocked his regional dialect. The East Anglian countryside had seemed drab and, above all, cold, as were the few inhabitants he had met, and Heronhoe, he discovered, was the least likely place in which to find 'a dolly bird' – a phrase he had often rehearsed in his head without ever being too sure of the circumstances in which he would use it. The only saving grace of the trip had been that in Clerkenwell and Heronhoe they had stayed in Italian restaurants which at least guaranteed that the food was worth eating.

Now Giancarlo was on sentry duty, standing guard over the prisoners in the Orangery and being studiously ignored by his prisoners, who were pre-occupied stuffing their faces with sand-wiches made of soft white bread and some sort of pink *prosciutto*, with the old fat man making loud, crunching sounds as he followed each mouthful of sandwich with a brown, vinegar-soaked onion. It was an affront to his masculinity that his seven prisoners were so unafraid of him, for he was the one with the gun, even though he had had to reassure himself that his Beretta had enough bullets in its magazine to cope with the worst-possible scenario. Thankfully Maurizio had been in charge of their arsenal and Giancarlo had managed to avoid revealing the fact that he had never fired a pistol in his life, his preferred weapons of choice being the switchblade or the Sicilian *Lupara* sawn-off shotgun which, to be honest, he had only used in anger against rabbits, not even wolves.

At least with the arrival of the lady of the house and the actress playing the royal mistress, there was something pleasant to look at. The two girl diggers were more his age, but the English one was timid and likely to burst into tears at any given moment, and the American one was too talkative and moved more like a soldier than a woman, plus both were dressed in layers of pullovers and padded coats, making it impossible to assess or appreciate their figures. The lady of the house was attractive enough, even if she was quite old – at least thirty – and clearly an aristo who, if she had noticed him at all, would have assumed he was a servant. The actress, on the other hand, was a treat. She was not dressed as Giancarlo had imagined a dolly bird to be dressed, but in her Thirties' costume she looked every centimetre the film star – a Claudia Cardinale or a Monica Vitti, perhaps – especially as she sat on a folded sleeping bag on the floor next to the fat man, her long skirt rucked up to show an enticing amount of stockinged leg.

And the American girl, in her muddy jeans and military boots, had noticed him watching the actress. Perhaps she was jealous.

'Seraphina who?'

'I was afraid you might say that,' sighed Campion wearily. 'Everyone seems to have forgotten poor Seraphina Vezzali but I remember her even though I never knew her.'

'Are you . . . all right, Pa?' ventured a concerned Rupert.

'I'm fine, just suffering feelings of guilt because I did nothing at the time. Seraphina Vezzali was an "Italian girl" in London back in 1955. She was exploited and manipulated by a gang of miscreants called Bolzano and, I am convinced, murdered by one of them. The favourite suspect was the elder brother Marco, though nothing could be proved and the Bolzano brothers disappeared from Clerkenwell. My theory is that Marco hot-footed it back to Italy, while the younger sibling Stephano ended up in Heronhoe running a restaurant and marrying a local girl called Elspeth Brunt.

'Elspeth died and Stephano retired to Italy where his stories – or rather his wife's stories – of some sort of treasure came to the attention of his overlords. And by that, I mean you, *Signora*, for the Bolzanos were always the foot soldiers for a more important family; the family at the head of their crime syndicate: the Petraglias.'

'Are you talking about the Mafia?' Rupert said in a loud, breathless whisper before turning nervously towards the harpsichord, the gun and Daniela Petraglia.

Mr Campion quickly drew attention back in his direction. 'I am told the word "Mafia" is reserved for Sicily. In Campagna the more familiar expression is *Camorra*, is it not?'

Daniela Petraglia said nothing but allowed the pistol in her hand to twitch slightly.

'I don't really expect you to answer that, *Signora*, as I am aware you have a code of silence to live by, and given your other . . . er . . . traditions . . . you of all people will appreciate my motive.'

'*Vendetta*,' said the woman respectfully, 'because the Vezzali girl meant something to you?'

'I'm afraid I never met her,' Campion admitted quietly. 'I was asked to help her and I did nothing. You might say I abdicated responsibility for her but I never forgot her. I made a few enquiries, of course, as did the police, but the Bolzanos had done a bunk and cleared out of London. It never occurred to me to look for one of them in my own backyard, as it were, here in Suffolk, although it was Marco who was supposedly the violent one, not Stephano, and it was Stephano who, in the end, was responsible for tempting the Petraglia clan back to England.'

Campion turned to Rupert and Oliver and spoke as if the woman was not there.

'The wonderful irony of this is that it was the Petraglias who came to me, to enlist my aid. When she was telling her stories about non-existent treasure, poor Elspeth must have rambled on about the visitors to Heronhoe Hall when she worked here and my name must have been mentioned. It would have meant nothing to her husband but, when he retired to Italy, Stephano began to repeat the stories and the Petraglias, their ears pricked at the word "treasure", had the resources to do some research.'

Daniela Petraglia, using the butt of her gun as a gavel, rapped on the harpsichord lid again; a judge calling for order in her courtroom.

'You were selected because you were involved in the visit of the prince and his lover and because your reputation suggests you would know about the treasure.' Her gun hand moved a few degrees until the muzzle was aimed directly at Campion. 'Now I ask you directly, for the first and last time, *where is it?*'

Giancarlo was leaning with his back against the door of the Orangery, his shoulder blades pressed into the wood, his left hand deep in the pocket of his leather jacket, his right elbow nestled into his right thigh, the gun held casually. A cigarette dangling from one corner of his mouth would have completed the pose and a hat with its brim pulled down would have been the epitome of cool.

He was hungry, but it would be a sign of weakness to ask for one of his prisoners' unappealing sandwiches, not that the old fat man was likely to leave any spare, and he could not order Lavinia Bell back to the kitchen to prepare him something, much as he would like to boss that one about, as Maurizio had left him alone on guard duty. Still, the actress, the one playing the king's mistress, was worth looking at. Looking at her legs and the way her tight pencil skirt rode up a millimetre or two every time she moved would take his mind off his echoing stomach.

Precious Aird had also noticed Perdita's legs and Giancarlo's interest in them.

As the others had made themselves comfortable and shared out the food, she had gradually moved to within two feet of Giancarlo and was standing casually, munching a sandwich, close to his right hand. She finished her sandwich and then unzipped her long parka,

making sure she was offering a full-frontal view to the young
Italian.

'Guess I'll make myself comfortable,' she said aloud as she
slipped off the coat and began to fold it before sinking on her
haunches and patting the cushion she had fashioned into place
against the skirting board. As she did, she made a point of turning
her head towards Perdita as they were now on the same eye level.
'Hey, tough break, Perdita, you've caught on something sharp.
That's one heck of a tear in those nice stockings.'

Perdita's instant reaction was to look as if she had been insulted
in a language she was not expecting to hear let alone understand.
Her second reaction was purely feminine. The palms of both hands
went to the hem of her skirt to smooth it higher up her thigh over
the silk of the stockings in order to assess the damage.

Giancarlo was transfixed and Precious Aird uncoiled like a
spring.

She came up off her haunches and stepped in towards Giancarlo
in a clinch as if they were about to launch on an exhibition of ball-
room dancing. Her left arm wrapped itself around Giancarlo's arm,
wrenching it against the shoulder socket as she leaned her weight on
it, which isolated the gun in his right hand behind her back.

Such a move in isolation might have caused only a brief distraction had it not come so suddenly and been accompanied by Precious
Aird's right hand whipping the trowel out of the back pocket of
her jeans and thrusting the point of it into the startled Italian's
neck between his Adam's apple and jaw bone.

'Drop the gun, wise guy,' she said into Giancarlo's face as a
single drop of blood ran down the blade of the trowel.

The three young archaeologists, Lavinia Bell and Perdita were
all open-mouthed in amazement at what they had just witnessed.
They were even more surprised when they realized that the first
person to react and offer assistance was Lugg.

The big man had got to his feet with alacrity if not grace, danced
his way around a camp bed and hopped over Perdita's legs to
clamp a meaty hand over the small pistol quivering aimlessly
behind Precious Aird's straining back. The small gun disappeared
into a mass of pink flesh and was, with magician's skill, transferred
to his jacket pocket.

'You can stop trying to remove his tonsils now, I've got him,'

Lugg said, twisting Giancarlo's arm professionally up his back, 'and remind me never to let you give me a wet shave. You're reckless, that's what you are; reckless.'

Precious unwound her left arm but kept the trowel point in place, forcing Giancarlo's head back against the door.

'He wasn't much of a risk. The safety catch was still on his gun. Somebody get something to gag him with,' she ordered. 'I don't want him shouting a warning to the Queen Bitch.'

Lavinia Bell got to her feet and untied the strings of her apron, pulling the garment away from her as if it burned. 'Use this. I've done enough kitchen work today.'

With the additional aid of his own belt and the strap from a shoulder bag, Giancarlo was gagged and bound and laid on the floor. Disarmed, outnumbered and, worst of all, defeated by a girl, Giancarlo offered little resistance.

'Now what?' Lugg asked, turning to Precious for orders.

She held out a hand. 'You give me the gun and I take care of the Queen Bitch.'

'You want the gun? Do you know how to use one?'

Precious Aird put her head on one side and gave Lugg a look of withering pity. 'I'm an American.'

'Fair enough.'

'I don't even know what it is supposed to be, let alone where it is,' said Campion, exasperated.

'You must know; you were here, the only one left who was,' snarled the woman.

'Oh, for the love of all that's holy, either shoot me or give it up. You really don't have any other option.'

The silence in the room was broken only by a loud intake of breath from Rupert until *Signora* Petraglia chose to speak.

'Yes, I do, but you do not. Once Maurizio returns with our passports, we will leave your awful country. You will remain here and you will keep everyone else here and not call the police because your daughter-in-law will be coming with us. If we are not prevented from leaving, then she will remain unhurt.'

Rupert began to rise from his chair.

'Sit down! If your father insists there is no treasure there is no reason to stay. I have no intention of waiting around to answer for the actions of the Bolzanos. Your wife will come with us as insurance and will be released as soon as we are safely on a boat to Europe.'

'A sea journey, *Signora*?' asked Campion, all innocence. 'I would have thought you would have opted for the British Air Ferries service from Southend – it's much closer and really very efficient. Just drive your car into the belly of a good old Bristol Superfreighter, take a seat in the tail section and then up, up and away. Before you know it you're coming in to land in Calais or perhaps Ostend. It's quite a good service, you know – several flights a day and out of season – you should get a flight easily enough.'

Mr Campion was aware that his son was staring at him, open-mouthed, clearly wondering why his father seemed to be offering useful advice on ways in which Italian gangsters could kidnap Perdita and make a clean getaway. But from where he sat, Rupert could not see what Mr Campion could, out the corner of his eye, in the mirror above the fireplace.

'I'm told the Superfreighter is an excellent workhouse of an aeroplane and happily hops across the Channel with two or three cars in its hold, though I always felt a little nervous driving up that ramp at the front and into the belly of the beast, as it were. Must be what being swallowed by a whale feels like.' He treated his audience to his widest, most vacuous grin. 'Of course, I have to be complimentary about the Superfreighter as I believe my wife was involved in certain design modifications to it in the early Fifties.'

'How did you know?'

'Know what, *Signora*?'

'Know that our plan was to leave through Southend airport?'

As he faced Daniela Petraglia, Campion's expression was suddenly vacant again, as if a switch had been flicked. 'I did not know, I merely assumed. From here, it is the quickest route to the Continent and the way I would go if I needed to make a quick exit.'

The Italian woman narrowed her eyes at Campion and, though her gun was still pointed at Rupert, it was clearly Mr Campion she had in her sights.

'I was told you were clever at being stupid. No, stupid is not the word, but you have the skill of persuading your enemies that you have the mind of a child.'

'If that is a compliment, then I will take it happily.'

Campion leaned forward, drawing the woman's eyes down and away from the fireplace mirror, as if he was hanging on her every word. It was a remarkably restrained performance as he had caught a glimpse of the reflection from the hallway where Precious Aird was down on one knee quietly undoing the laces of her black paratrooper boots.

'It was not. You pretend weakness to disguise weakness and sentimentality. Your sentimentality over the Vezzali girl has brought you to this. If anything happens to your son's wife, it is you he will blame. The Vezzali girl was not family, Perdita is. I think you could learn the true meaning of *vendetta*.'

The metallic click of the hammer may have gone unnoticed by the four people in the room, but the much louder crack of the shot most certainly did not, nor did the spectacular disintegration of the bust of Lord Breeze which scattered plaster and dust across the lid of Hattie the harpsichord.

'Put the gun down, lady,' commanded Precious Aird, 'or the next head to explode will be yours. Don't think I can't, lady. And don't for a second think I won't. Where I come from, ammunition ain't cheap so we don't waste it.'

Mr Campion was the first to react and he did so joyfully. 'The Americans have arrived! Late as usual, but very welcome nonetheless.'

The least-shocked person in the room at that moment was Daniela Petraglia. Rupert had flinched violently, gripped the arms of his chair and pushed himself backwards into the upholstery as if demonstrating the effect of G-force to a trainee astronaut; Oliver had appeared to melt into his chair, his limp frame collapsing in on itself like a deflating balloon; and even Mr Campion had taken automatic evasive action, folding his body forward off the sofa until his knees bumped into the carpet.

From his position of supplication, Campion glanced first into the mirror where he saw, reflected, the impressive sight of Precious Aird braced, her stockinged feet wide apart, in a pistol marksman stance, her left hand steadying her right, in which was a small, smoking automatic. *Signora* Petraglia, Campion was relieved to discover, was obeying orders.

Slowly and deliberately, the Italian woman placed her pistol flat on the lid of the harpsichord, raised her hand, turned the palm towards the doorway to prove it was empty then used it to lazily brush plaster dust from her hair and leather jacket.

'Remove the *signora*'s gun please, Rupert.' As he got to his feet, Campion realized his legs were shaking slightly and for reasons he could not dismiss as old age on weak bones. 'And get yourself a drink, Oliver – you really do look as if you need one.'

Rupert expelled himself from his chair and scooped up the pistol, pointing it unsteadily at Daniela Petraglia, who remained seated on the harpsichord stool, blowing dust from the shoulder of her jacket.

'I had no idea you were a dead shot,' Campion said, turning a smile on Precious, who showed no intention of relaxing her pose.

'Somehow it never came up,' she said, returning the smile.

'Where's young Giancarlo? I take it that's his gun?'

'It's not much of a gun and it wasn't hard to take it from him. Right now Lugg is sitting on him back in the Orangery.'

'Then he is certainly secure. Now we wait for Maurizio to return and, as we have him both outnumbered and outgunned, he shouldn't be a problem.'

'What about Mr Bell there?'

Campion turned his attention to Oliver, who was on his feet and staggering not to a cocktail cabinet but towards the harpsichord, mouthing the word 'Hattie . . .'

Being nearest, and quickest on the uptake, Rupert reassured him. 'Don't panic, old boy. Apart from the bust, which you might be able to glue back together, there's no damage to the harpsichord.'

'I wasn't aiming at Hattie,' said Precious confidently, 'and the bullet didn't even go on to crack the window glass. Told you it wasn't much of a gun. No stopping power. Sorry about the statue, though.'

Behind her, Lavinia Bell appeared from the hallway and headed in Oliver's direction. 'Don't be,' she said in passing. 'Daddy bought a job lot of those ghastly things.'

Fortuitously Campion's timing proved immaculate and the first police car to answer his telephone summons arrived thirty seconds after Maurizio had parked the Citroën in the drive and clambered out only to be greeted at gunpoint by Rupert, Precious and Oliver, who had remembered to retrieve his shotgun from the cupboard under the stairs. The confidence it gave him drained from his face when Precious, rather subversively, whispered to him, 'Now I could have made a real mess of Hattie with *that!*'

Faced with three brandished weapons, one of which seemed to be being brandished by someone who knew how to use it, Maurizio took the discretionary route away from valour and raised his hands in surrender.

The policemen in that first car were uniformed constables who were initially at a loss as to who to arrest or why, but at least they recognized Oliver and Lavinia Bell – one of them even addressed them as the new Lord and Lady of the manor – and so Campion offered their services as interpreters of an admittedly confusing situation. Fortunately the second police car, arriving only a few minutes after the first, contained Inspector Chamley of Suffolk CID, to whom Campion immediately made himself known.

Facing charges of failing to report a body (and preventing others to do so), aggravated assault (though Giancarlo might question exactly who had been assaulted), firearms offences and threatening behaviour, the Italian contingent were duly arrested and, showing a composure that suggested they had been through this experience before, all 'went quietly' as the best British police procedure required.

In handcuffs, Daniela Petraglia spoke for the first time since Precious Aird had demonstrated her marksmanship as she walked to the waiting police car, but then only in response to Campion's question.

'*Permesso, signora*; one last thing, for I doubt we will meet again, except perhaps in court.'

'If you must.'

'I know you do not, and probably never will, believe me when I say there is no hidden treasure hereabouts, but back there when you had us at your mercy, you said I was the only one left who was here in 1935. That was not strictly true, was it? Elspeth had a sister, Sonia.'

Daniela Petraglia tossed back her head and snorted. 'Sonia is a stupid old woman and a bigger fool than you pretend to be. She knows nothing. I asked her.'

'You didn't hurt her, did you?' Campion asked sharply.

The woman stared at him and said nothing as a policeman lead her away.

Back in the front room of the hall, Mr Campion called his troops together and introduced them to Inspector Chamley, who clearly felt outnumbered but insisted that he had reinforcements of his own on the way. He was, however, happy for Campion to give the orders in the interim.

'Precious, you have done sterling work being the hair in the gate as far as our nefarious film crew were concerned, and we are all in your debt. I would like you, please, to put yourself at the disposal of Inspector Chamley now and, when his crime-scene people get here, guide them round to the Sweethearting dig so that poor old Samuel Salt can be decently seen to.

'Lavinia, for goodness' sake get your husband a stiff drink and reassure him that his beloved Hattie is undamaged.

'Rupert and Perdita, you will come with me, please, and you will need your car keys.

'Lugg, somebody has to make a start on giving statements to the police, so it might as well be you.'

Lugg bridled as if accused on some unspeakable heresy. 'Hrrumph! Muggins 'ere gets the dirty jobs as per usual.'

Campion lead the way followed by his son and daughter-in-law, pulling on his hat and coat as he strode out of the hall and across the drive to Perdita's red Mini Cooper.

'Don't worry, old Lugg will confuse our noble officers of the law for hours. We have plenty of time.'

'Time for what?' Perdita asked, pulling open the driver's door.

'Time enough to find the treasure, of course,' said Mr Campion with an angelic grin.

EIGHTEEN
The Sweethearting Treasure

W as he being stupid? Was he just being slow? Was he just getting old and the first two were facets of the third? That Campion's mind allowed such treason was, he realized, because he had put family and friends in a place of danger and all to salve his own troubled conscience. The fact that no one had actually been hurt or traumatized as a result of his arrogant foolishness was due to the resourcefulness of a young American girl he hardly knew who had entered his world purely by chance. At least Lady Luck had not totally disowned him and he should be grateful that she had sent the formidable Precious Aird to act as guardian angel to them all; a precious asset indeed.

Rupert, scrunched up in the back seat of the Mini, his knees contorted almost to his chin, was also thinking about their unexpected saviour.

'Where did Precious learn to shoot like that?' he said over the noise of the Mini's engine being enthusiastically revved by Perdita's right foot.

'Almost certainly in the Americas,' said Mr Campion over his shoulder. 'Their archaeologists are trained to be more aggressive than ours, I'm told, as they have to deal with angry natives armed with poisoned arrows and blowpipes. Though of course there is always the possibility that she was aiming at Donna Daniela and hit the effigy of Lord Breeze by accident . . .'

'She knew what she was doing,' said Perdita, negotiating a bend with far more panache than her male passengers thought necessary. 'You should have seen the way she dealt with Giancarlo; the poor guy didn't stand a chance.'

'And all the time, there was I worried that Lugg would do something stupid.'

'We girls didn't need Lugg, though his weight did come in

useful afterwards, for sitting on the chap, once we'd distracted and disarmed him.'

Rupert strained his face nearer the front seats. 'How exactly did you manage to distract him, darling?'

Mr Campion noticed that Perdita's cheeks were glowing rosily and thought that might be a subject best explored without his presence.

'We'll have plenty of time to swap war stories later; now let's get to the King's Arms and disturb the licensee's holy hour of rest and recuperation.'

'I don't know what you expect to get out of Mr and Mrs Yallop,' said Rupert, his face glued to the side window observing the police Panda car which was drawing up alongside the Mound. A ruddy-faced man wearing a long, naval duffle coat and Wellington boots and with a broken shotgun in the crook of his arm was waving them into the side of the road like a bored flight controller on the deck of an aircraft carrier. 'That's Farmer Spark, isn't it? He seems to be on the ball.'

'Well, it is his land, after all,' said Campion, 'and he keeps an ever-watchful eye on it. I'm rather surprised the police didn't ride to our rescue before Precious had to, as I was sure Mr Spark would be observing our every movement at the dig. Perhaps he was feeding his pigs or inside giving his wife a perm or something when the guns appeared. Still, I'm sure he will tell the nice policemen what's been going on, and that will keep them busy and leave the coast clear for us.'

'Clear for exactly *what*?' asked Perdita, eyes on the road and accelerating again now the Panda car was out of both sight and mind.

Mr Campion clapped his hand together in flamboyant manner. 'Why, to find the Sweethearting Treasure, of course.'

'So you knew where it was all the time!' Rupert grabbed the back of Campion's seat so fiercely that it shook. 'Yet you kept telling Cruella that . . .'

'Cruella, that's very good,' Campion chuckled, 'but I was nothing less than honest with *Signora* Petraglia – well, not more than twenty per cent less than honest, but then she wasn't a very honest person.'

'But you do know where it is?'

'I wouldn't go that far. In fact, I wouldn't go so far as to say I know what it is, let alone where it is, but I think I know someone who may.' He pursed his lips and raised his eyebrows as though the thought had just occurred to him. 'Except I don't actually know them.'

'Who?'

'Sonia Brunt, of course. I've never met the lady but you two have. You can introduce me.'

'We've only met her once and we told you, she fainted at the sight of us! We're not exactly on social terms,' said Perdita.

'That should have given me my first clue, especially when you told me what Mr Yallop said.' Campion stared out of the window distractedly as the main street of Sweethearting flashed by.

'What did I say he said?'

'That Sonia was worth her weight in gold.'

'And that was significant?'

'In itself, a passing remark,' said Campion, 'but then Farmer Spark told me that Sonia was "really valued" by the brewery which owns the pub and then again, the odious Bill Crow referred to her as a "diamond". It was as if they were all, unconsciously, pointing me to the answer: gold, value, diamonds – all things associated with treasure.'

'I'm sorry, Albert, but it has been a long and eventful day and I'm not following.'

'Do not despair, daughter dear. I am probably not making much sense. It is something which comes with great age, but just think on this: what if Sonia Brunt *is* the Abdication Treasure?'

The trouble with resident guests, Joshua Yallop had long felt, was that they treated the place like a hotel and life would be a lot easier if the King's Head could do without them. There were occasions when he sincerely entertained the notion that running a country pub would be an ideal life were it not for customers in general, as they invariably proved more demanding than their custom was worth and showed little consideration for the private life of the licensee. Even this current party of Campions – admittedly a better class of visitor than one saw these days and certainly decent spenders in the bar – were taking liberties, and here they were interrupting his precious afternoon rest period yet again. If their persistent knocking on the front door woke Edna he knew he would suffer for it and so, as he clumped across the bar, he was determined to give them a piece of his mind and lay down a few rules of the house.

When he was close enough to register, through the glass panes in the door, that it was the senior Campion who was personally drumming his knuckles, Joshua Yallop had an instant change of heart. Mr Campion was a member of the Suffolk gentry by marriage and clearly of patrician stock in his own right – just the sort of customer worth cultivating. Secretly, Yallop had always dreamed that if he was going to be treated as a hotelier then he would prefer to run a nice, private hotel with a select clientele rather than a public house. A hotel in a location popular with the upper classes and one offering sea views from all rooms – somewhere like Torquay, perhaps.

'Mr Yallop, please accept my sincere apologies for troubling you out of hours. It is both inconsiderate and rude to intrude on your off-duty hours, but I would crave a few moments of your time.'

Now there was a gentleman for you. If only the King's Head could attract more like him.

'I hasten to say I am not making a plea for alcohol outside of lawful licensing hours.'

Yet Mr Campion would be just the sort of customer for whom Joshua Yallop might be tempted to break the law. The local Magistrates would surely appreciate that a man of Mr Campion's standing did not deserve to be shackled by petty bureaucratic legalities designed to keep the lower orders in check.

'I'm sure we could stretch a point,' he said, opening the door and bidding him enter with an elaborate swoop of his arm.

'My dear chap, I wouldn't dream of suggesting it. I feel guilty enough disturbing you as it is. I understand you had a break-in during the wee small hours. It must have been a terrible experience for you – and for Edna, of course.'

Again, the mark of a true gent: thinking of the plight of others. Remembering Edna's name and taking his hat off: those were also marks of class.

'Not much damage and no great loss to report, but thank you for asking,' said Yallop, rubbing his hands together as if expecting a tip.

'I understand the burglar made a beeline for your collection of historic bottled beers,' said Campion, surveying the bar. 'Did he take any?'

'Oh, surely they're not that valuable – are they?' Mr Yallop's unctuosity suddenly gave way to doubt. 'They weren't insured or anything . . . but I don't think any are missing.'

Campion said nothing but stared pointedly at the shelves behind the bar counter where there was an obvious gap in the display between the Maxim Stout and the large, wax-sealed bottle of King's Ale.

'There was a small amount of breakage,' admitted Yallop.

'I believe my son discovered that to his cost. Only a minor flesh wound, thankfully. I'm guessing the one he trod on was the Prince's Ale.'

'It was!' Joshua Yallop almost squealed with pleasure at his guest's detective abilities. 'But I don't think it was especially valuable, though of course Sonia was very upset.'

'Ah, yes, Sonia. It was Sonia Brunt who was the licensee here before you, I believe.'

'She was indeed, for many years, under her married name of Aldous, though when she took charge of the pub after he died in the war she held the licence in her maiden name. That bottle collection was started by Arthur Aldous, and technically it belongs to Sonia but she always seemed happy to have them displayed in the bar and she dusted them regular.'

'I was told she still works here,' said Campion. 'You say she took the breakage badly?'

'Very. She does a bit of cleaning around the place and occasionally helps out behind the bar. When she arrived this morning I thought I was going to have to send her home straight away.'

'And why was that?'

'She looked terrible, said she'd had a fall at home and was really badly bruised about the face but, Sonia being Sonia, she insisted on starting work. I think she needs the little bit of cash we give her more than she likes to admit,' Yallop confided. 'She got out her dustpan and brush and dusters and cleaning stuff and then saw the broken glass and started crying even as she was sweeping up the pieces. Proper distraught, she was, and her wailing woke up Edna, which meant I had two women in a state on my hands. I gave Sonia a small brandy to calm her down and insisted she take the day off.'

'Sonia lives in the village, doesn't she?' Campion asked, forgetting to ask how Mr Yallop had manged all on his own, which would have been the gentlemanly thing to do.

'Just along the High Street, number forty-nine; you must have passed it when you drove here. Well, really!'

Yallop was left speechless at the speed with which Campion replaced his hat, turned on his heels and raced from the pub.

'You looked just like them. It was like them being there again after all these years and it gave me a right shock. No wonder I fainted.'

Campion had shot out of the King's Head like a bullet and wrenched open the passenger door of the Mini Cooper with some force. Pushing his head into the interior, he ordered Rupert and Perdita to leave the car where it was and to follow him on foot. Rupert immediately began to unfold his legs and extract himself from the back seat but Perdita had remained seated firmly behind the steering wheel and demanded time to visit their room, get changed and 'get rid of all this make-up gunk'. Mr Campion softened his face and told his daughter-in-law that it was necessary for her to remain in character for a little longer as he could not possibly find another Wallis Simpson at such short notice, or at least not one as convincing as Perdita and she should think of it not as a chore but as a curtain call to an outstanding performance.

It may have been a curtain call but there was no applause from any audience in Sweethearting. The few local residents who saw the two figures in unseasonal Thirties' clothes walking down the High Street might have commented on their fashion sense but none made the connection to their historical inspiration. They were only a minor distraction on a dank winter's afternoon, but enough of a distraction to make sure that hardly anyone noticed the thin man in the fedora walking briskly a few paces in advance of them, checking the house numbers on gates and front doors.

At number 49, however, they were recognized and, if not welcomed, at least welcomed in.

'We are so sorry we frightened you.' Perdita gently touched the old lady's arm as she apologized. It was a tentative move, as if she were greeting a strange cat for the first time.

'Don't you mind this foolish old woman,' said Sonia Brunt. 'You do look the spit of her in those clothes but be thankful you don't sound like her. She had a terrible American twang I could never get on with.' She turned to Rupert and studied his face. 'He's not quite got it, though. Not enough sad lines under the eyes because he hasn't been bullied as much yet, but then he's a bit young for the part, isn't he?'

'Please don't compliment the actors on their performances, Mrs Aldous. You'll never see the back of them.'

'Nobody's called me that for thirty years,' the woman said to Mr Campion, 'at least not to my face.'

For the first time since they had entered the cottage directly into a cluttered sitting room from the front door, the Campions managed to get a good look at that face. There were no electric lights on in the cottage and the fading afternoon sunlight struggled to get in through windows, whose flanks were guarded by heavy green plush curtains anxious to be drawn. Even in the gloom, the bruising on Sonia's cheek and chin were visible and there was a dark blood bubble under her right eye.

'I know who did that to you, Sonia. They have been taken into custody by the police.'

'Good luck to them dealing with that woman, but you didn't come here to tell me that, did you?'

'No, Sonia, we did not. We came to ask about your treasure.'

Sonia Brunt was a small, square-ish woman, not a blue-rinsed hair's breadth above five feet tall and, in the shapeless, dark-blue house dress and apron she wore had something of the rag doll about her. There were liver spots on the backs of her hands and leathery wrinkles around her neck. Campion, who knew the perils of guessing the age of ladies, put her at seventy-five, and apart from a slight arthritic limp she seemed so solid on her feet that, he suspected, when those size-fours were planted they would be difficult to budge.

He was therefore mildly surprised when she replied in a matter-of-fact voice, 'You'd better come into the kitchen and have a look at it, then.'

In single file, the Campions followed Sonia through to her

cramped kitchen where she flicked a light switch to reveal a small Formica-topped table occupying most of the available floor space between larder cupboards, sink, gas oven and a battered washing machine.

Spread over the table top was a white tea towel on which was displayed the glass fragments of a bottle of Prince's Ale, the largest fragment being that held together by the oval orange and yellow label which still clearly displayed the Prince of Wales' feathers and the motto '*Ich Dien*'.

'*That* was it?' Rupert spoke before his father's stern glare could silence him.

Sonia Brunt took a deep, quivering breath. 'That's what the king sent me, what people have come to call the "treasure". And he was the king, not the prince, when he sent it. It might have been the last thing he did as king before he had to abdicate.'

'And hence the legend of the Abdication Treasure,' said Campion. 'It must have meant a lot to you for you to keep it hidden for so long.'

'But it was on display in pub for all to see!' Rupert complained, only to receive a second uncompromising glare from his father.

'Hiding in plain sight,' observed Perdita, 'is often the best way.'

'That's what I thought,' said Sonia, 'though there's not much point in keeping it secret now, is there?'

'Why did you keep it secret in the first place, Sonia?' Mr Campion asked gently.

'Because it *was* secret – and it was *mine*.'

'*A bottle of beer?*' Rupert was in danger of slipping into his party-piece Lady Bracknell impersonation, which drew another piercing look of disapproval from his father, yet it was Sonia's dignified response which proved the best reproof.

'It was a bottle of beer sent to me by my king.'

The old woman spoke with such sincerity that Campion allowed a long silence before he pressed for details.

'Sent towards the end of 1936, when the Abdication Crisis was coming to a head?'

Sonia nodded. 'When he had so much else on his mind he still remembered his little treasure here in Sweethearting.'

Her hands floated over the table top and with delicate reverence adjusted the positions of two pieces of broken glass as if trying to make sense of a difficult jigsaw puzzle. When she raised her face, it had a ghost of a smile, perhaps in relief from a burden lifted or a pain vanquished.

'Yes, that's what he used to call me,' she said proudly, 'and that's the treasure he sent his little treasure. It wasn't much and it was a bit silly – I mean, sending a bottle of beer to a publican! – but that's all it was and now it's in pieces.'

'It clearly meant a lot to you,' said Mr Campion, 'but I'm not quite clear why you concealed it. Oh, I appreciate you didn't physically conceal it – you put it on open public display in the King's Head – yet you must have been aware of all the rumours that your royal gift started running.'

'That was Elspeth, wasn't it? My flighty little sister, always batting her eyelashes at the prince when he used to come down here to go riding with the captain up at the hall. She convinced herself the king sent me jewels, a diamond tiara or an emerald necklace which he'd bought for Wallis but she'd turned her nose up at. It was all nonsense but it filled her head. I think she read too many trashy women's magazines, plus she'd always thought the prince fancied her. That was in the days before he'd met Mrs Simpson, when Elspeth used to help out in the pub.'

Her facial muscles ironed out any trace of a smile and her fingers touched the edges of the tea towel acting as a shroud for the smashed pieces of bottle.

'I kept it on display to spite Elspeth as much as anything. She'd come into the pub moaning and whining about how she was entitled to a share of whatever the king had sent, but I never let on she was standing next to it. I thought she'd forget about it, especially when she married that Italian from Heronhoe, but when she started to get ill it seemed to come back to her and she went on and on about it to her husband.'

'That would be Stephano Bolzano,' Campion said and Sonia nodded. 'Did he ever ask about the so-called treasure?'

'He had a go at me at Elspeth's funeral; at the graveside, would you believe. I told him she must have got her wires crossed when she worked at the hall and heard all the talk of treasure in the boat burial. Somehow, in her mind, she got things confused, what with the royal visit there and all the things in the papers at the time. He must have believed her, though, otherwise why would them other

Italians turn up out of the blue and start with their nastiness? Anyway, it don't matter any more; it's just broken glass now, not worth worrying about. Still, I'll have the memory of it.'

'So nobody else knew what it was the king had sent you? No one at all?'

The old woman hesitated before answering Campion. 'Only my late husband, Arthur Aldous. He didn't see it as anybody else's business either. He was killed in the war, you know, thirty years ago last year. That's why I didn't respond when you called me Mrs Aldous when you arrived.'

'Forgive me if I'm committing a terrible howler, Sonia, but I have a suspicion you never were Mrs Aldous, not legally.'

'Dad . . .' Rupert exhaled the word as a warning, but his father was undeterred.

'It was quite unusual back in the Forties for a widow, especially a war widow, to revert back to her maiden name even if they had plans to remarry. If, however, there was the question of taking on the licence of a public house, then the brewery and the local licensing bench would insist on a legal name. I suspect the same applied when it came to getting an identity card and ration books.'

The woman dropped her eyes back to the brown splinters on the table. 'You're right. Arthur and I were never properly married, not that anyone these days gives a fig about couples that live in sin, but they did back then. When I got the licence I told folk I had to use my maiden name as I would be the sole licensee now that Arthur had gone. There was a war on and nobody questioned it. Nobody knew we were never wed, not even Elspeth, not that she'd have turned a hair.'

'The king knew, didn't he, or did he guess? When he was the prince he brought his lovers to the King's Head whenever he came down to Heronhoe Hall, didn't he? Staying at the hall with that old rascal Wemyss-Grendle was hardly discreet, but you were. I do not wish to sound judgemental, but you kept their sinful secret because you had one of your own. You were good at keeping secrets, weren't you, Sonia?'

Perdita moved discreetly around the table closer to Sonia in case the small woman should be in need of support. It was a thoughtful but misguided action on Perdita's part, for instead of wilting Sonia Brunt adopted a stance of steely defiance.

'I was warned you were a slippery one, by that Italian bitch of all people. She said you were clever and that you'd come sniffing around.' She allowed herself a brief, scoffing laugh. 'Said you were the one I should be frightened of, not her! Hah! Well, maybe she was right, but I'm too old to be frightened now and there's nothing you can do to me. You've seen the great Sweethearting Treasure, now leave me alone.'

Campion turned the brim of his fedora between his fingers. It was a sign of nervousness Rupert had never seen before. 'I'm afraid I cannot, Sonia. Might I suggest we move into the other room and make ourselves comfortable while you tell us the rest of the story?'

NINETEEN
Stamp of Approval

E ven with the lights on and a one-bar 'realistic effect' electric fire glowing red, Sonia Brunt's front room would have met few definitions of 'cosy', although the chairs were not uncomfortable, the few paintings were passable popular repro- ductions of Constable's finest work and the collection of small china ornaments showed a harmless enthusiasm for Highland terriers. There were no other clues as to her personal interests apart from a set of small pewter tankards marching across the mantelpiece in single file which Campion recognized as spirit measures as used in a bar before the advent of the plastic 'optic' which dispensed liquor in a manner similar to an intravenous drip in a hospital operating theatre. They were the only indica- tions of Sonia Brunt's association with the pub trade and there were no other pointers at all to her life, past or present, outside the confines of the cottage. But it was not the fixtures and fittings which produced the chilly atmosphere in that room; it was the question, or accusation, which Mr Campion had left hanging in the air.

He had insisted they all sat down as he was conscious of the difference in height between himself and Sonia Brunt and loathed the notion that he would appear the bully in front of Rupert and Perdita.

'Sonia, I must press you on something, if only to get things straight in my own mind. You see, I am notoriously slow on the uptake.'

'I doubt that very much,' said Sonia, setting her jaw firmly.

Huddled together on the two-seater sofa, Perdita's hand patted Rupert's thigh in silent approval of Sonia's judgement.

'I get the impression that you and your husband Arthur hosted . . . shall we call them unofficial royal visits . . . at the King's Head before the prince became involved with Mrs Simpson. Whenever David came down to Heronhoe to go point-to-pointing with Captain Wemyss-Grendle, perhaps?'

'You won't get any details out of me.' In her lap, Sonia's hands twisted the hem of her apron as through she was wringing water from it. 'If I'd wanted to do that, I could have gone to the *News of the World* and earned myself a lot of money.'

'That's sadly very true,' said Campion, 'and very commendable, I'm sure. It was a secret you shared with no one else, except Arthur, of course. Is that correct?'

'Arthur would never say a word out of place – certainly not about that. He was very patriotic was Arthur, devoted to the monarchy, he was.'

'But someone else knew about these unofficial royal visits, didn't they? Or at least suspected.'

Perdita grabbed Rupert's knee and squeezed it, but Rupert had already noticed that Sonia's hands were now not so much twisting her apron as strangling it.

'Don't know what you mean,' the woman said sullenly.

'If I say the name Samuel Salt, perhaps you will.'

The liver-spotted hands ceased their manipulations and slowly began to smooth out the material of the apron. 'Sam Salt hasn't been round here for a long time.'

Rupert opened his mouth to speak but was discouraged by a glance from Mr Campion coupled with more pressure on his knee from Perdita.

'But he was a familiar face here in the Thirties or so I'm told, riding around in his motorbike and sidecar, reporting all the local news fit to print and, I believe, showing a great interest in your sister when she was your barmaid at the pub.'

'He had a thing for Elspeth but so did many a man. Elspeth never discouraged attention from a pair of trousers. Attracted men like ants at a picnic.'

'But Elspeth wasn't working at the King's Head in 1935, was she? She'd moved up to Heronhoe Hall by then. Did you encourage that?'

'It was best if she was out of the way when . . . when we had visitors. She wouldn't have been able to keep her mouth shut.'

'Sam Salt still frequented the King's Head, though, didn't he?'

'It was a pub.'

'And he was a journalist. I do appreciate the connection but I rather meant he was in Sweethearting quite a lot, especially when the digging of the boat burial started.'

Sonia's hands became fists. 'Nobody's seen Sam Salt for thirty-five years.' She glared at Campion, who held her gaze for what Perdita, counting silently to herself, recognized as the recommended four seconds needed for a good dramatic pause.

'I have, Sonia. I saw him only this morning. He did not look well.'

As she spoke, in a soft unemotional monotone, Mr Campion mentally rehearsed how Sonia Brunt's statement under caution to the police might have sounded.

> Sam Salt had been a customer of the King's Head since we took the tenancy. He was a reporter for the local newspaper and often took photographs to go with his stories. That summer in 1935, he was often in the village covering the dig at the Sweethearting Barrow, as the vicar told us to call it.
>
> He was there the day the Prince of Wales came to see the dig and took pictures with his camera of all the villagers standing proudly round the trench, even though the dig was finished by then and they hadn't found anything anyway.
>
> One of the prince's equerries had telephoned ahead to book a room in the name of Mr and Mrs David Boyle. That was the code we used and the name we put in our visitors' book in case the revenue ever asked about our bed-and-breakfast trade. We never accepted any other visitors when we had a booking from Mr Boyle, so they would have the

place to themselves and of course we never asked who 'Mrs Boyle' was, but it was rarely the same woman. That didn't matter to me and Arthur.

We always made sure that Mr and Mrs Boyle could get into our private quarters without having to go through the bar and be seen. Sometimes they'd arrive late at night after closing and would be gone before opening hours the next morning.

That afternoon, the afternoon of the visit to the dig, nobody had any idea who Mrs Simpson was – well, none of us locals anyway. She was just a face in the crowd out at the Barrow. The prince did his stuff, thanking the diggers and shaking hands, and then his driver and his bodyguard got him in his car and they drove off. Most of Sweethearting was down at the Barrow at the opposite end of the village to the pub and it was out-of-hours so nobody would have seen them.

Arthur let them in by a side door and we got them upstairs, where I'd put out some cold cuts and Arthur had laid on a bottle of wine as well some bottles of beer. We went downstairs and when it was six o'clock we opened up. We had a good crowd that night, celebrating the end of the dig, even the vicar and the vicar of Heronhoe. It made me smile to think they had no idea what was going on in the room right above their heads.

The prince's car and driver turned up before dawn the next morning, about five o'clock. I'd made a pot of tea but they didn't want any breakfast, though they were very polite about it and he even introduced me to her as his 'little Sweethearting treasure' and said he was sure he could always trust me.

It was that afternoon when Sam Salt came calling. We were just closing up after the lunchtime session, which had been quiet. After all the excitement of the royal visit there were probably a few hangovers in the village and the bar was empty when we heard Sam's motorbike pulling into the car park.

He came in and he looked a sight, all dishevelled and unshaven, so at first I thought he was drunk. I told him it was two minutes to closing time and he was cutting it fine, but he said he didn't want a drink, he wanted a story and there was a funny sort of leer on his face. He had a big envelope with him and he started to clear a space on the bar, got out his notebook as well. I didn't like his attitude so I called Arthur up out of the cellar where he'd been switching casks for the evening session.

By the time he arrived, Sam had laid out half-a-dozen pictures on the bar, pictures he'd taken the day before at the Barrow. He kept pointing to two which showed the crowd of onlookers and he kept jabbing a grubby finger at one face in particular. 'Do you recognize this woman?' he said, and he said it over and over again, just wouldn't stop. He was like a dog with a rat.

I said I didn't, though of course I did, and Arthur warned him to watch his mouth and not use that tone of voice with me, but that just got him more agitated. 'You should!' he said. 'She spent the night under your roof and not alone, if you get my meaning.'

Well, of course we got his meaning, stupid man, but Arthur said he had no idea what Salt was talking about and if he didn't change his tone he'd have to leave as the pub was now closed.

Salt wouldn't be moved. He kept stabbing a finger at the woman in the photograph and said he had seen her leaving by the side door at ten minutes past five that morning. He'd made a note of the time in his notebook for accuracy, he said. Turns out he'd spent most of the night in the hedgerow across the road spying on us and would have taken more pictures but it was too dark.

I tried to calm him by saying yes, we'd had residents last night and they had left early before breakfast, and he demanded to see the visitors' book. Arthur said that was confidential and none of his so-and-so business, but I said he could see it if it meant Salt would shut up and leave.

When I showed him, he just laughed when he read 'Mr and Mrs Boyle, London SW1', said that wouldn't fool anyone and it looked as if it was in my handwriting – which it was – but he'd make a note of it anyway.

While he was doing that, leaning on the bar, he was saying how this was his scoop, his big story; a story he would sell to the national newspapers and that would make his name. It would, he said 'be a bombshell'.

Arthur looked at me and I looked at Arthur and I knew we couldn't let that happen; it just wouldn't be loyal, would it?

When he'd come up from the cellar, Arthur had brought the wooden mallet we use for tapping casks with him and had put it on the bar. It only took a couple of whacks on the back of the head to shut Sam Salt up for good – and there was very little blood.

We hid the body in the cellar until the pub closed that night, then, after midnight, we loaded it into the sidecar of his motorbike and I rode pillion behind Arthur. Sam often left his bike in the car park when he did his rounds collecting village news, so nobody thought it odd to see it there for a few hours – if anybody did.

Arthur drove us through the village to the Barrow dig, which they'd already started to fill in. We put Sam in one end of the trench and shovelled a load of soil over him so he couldn't be seen. Arthur said the diggers would finish the job for us the next day and he was right.

The tide was out in the estuary but would come in before it got light, so we went to a place Arthur knew and ran the motorbike into the river. As far as I know, it has never surfaced, even though Sam Salt did.

We walked back to the pub, not seeing a soul, and burned Sam's notebook and those pictures in the fireplace. We burned the cask mallet, too.

Nobody ever asked us about Sam Salt. I don't think he was much missed.

'Arthur died serving king and country in 1939, not having said a word to anyone and until now, and neither have I. There's an end to it.'

'Not quite, I'm afraid,' said Mr Campion. 'I have to ask *when* you received that thank-you bottle of Prince's Ale.'

One moment Sonia Brunt had appeared exhausted; the next she was a tigress with glowing eyes and claws out.

'I know what you're suggesting, Mister Clever Clogs, but you're wrong. Nobody was buying our silence, not that a bottle of ale would be much of a price to pay. What was done was done. We never saw Mr and Mrs Boyle again, but *they* never knew anything about Samuel Salt. That Prince's Ale lying in pieces in the kitchen was my personal treasure, a private thank you sent by the king himself over a year later, during the Abdication. It was personal, addressed by the king himself, because we had kept his secret. He never knew our secret.'

A blanket of silence fell over the room, disturbed only by the ticking of a clock somewhere until Perdita cleared her throat and said, 'Well, Albert, what happens now?'

Mr Campion removed his spectacles and pinched the bridge of his nose with finger and thumb.

'I'm not terribly sure, but I fear much of it will be out of our hands. The police have a body on their hands and they tend to take things like that very seriously.'

'But it was so long ago.'

Campion replaced his glasses and focused not on Perdita but on Sonia Brunt, who was staring fixedly at her hands clasped in her lap.

'How long does it take to forget a murder? It's a very good question and one which has troubled me of late.'

'You don't forget,' said Sonia Brunt quietly. 'Sometimes you can forgive, or even be forgiven, but you never forget.' She raised her face to look at Campion. 'But at the time I didn't regret what we did. We were protecting the reputation of our lovely king.'

'And yet he didn't seem to care much about his own reputation.' Perdita extended a hand towards the old woman, but whether to comfort her or shake her Campion was not sure. 'He gave up the throne a year later without a thought for his loyal subjects.'

'That's not fair! He was in love. People said he was weak, but his only weakness was that he loved too much.' Sonia was becoming agitated, almost squirming in her chair. 'He proved it by marrying Mrs Simpson, and after all this time they're still together.'

'And therein lies another problem,' said Mr Campion. He spoke softly but his tone ensured he had their complete attention. 'The Duke and Duchess of Windsor are indeed still married, very much still with us and, as we know from recent experience, still of interest to newspapers and television companies, especially on the Continent.

'The police have a body and will soon confirm its identity. I'm afraid I have already given them a head start in that. They will soon make the connection – possibly they already have – between Samuel Salt's death and the royal visit to the Sweethearting Barrow dig, as it was the last time and place anyone saw him alive. How long before they start to sniff around the King's Head?

'It is unlikely they will follow the rather convoluted trail I have, but they are jolly thorough and will get there in the end. The one thing you might have going for you, Sonia, is that the Sweethearting Treasure no longer exists, except in pieces in your kitchen.'

'What are you suggesting, Pa?' asked Rupert, leaning forward in his seat.

'He's saying that we should keep the king out of things,' said Sonia.

'The duke,' corrected Campion, 'and to do that would mean getting rid of anything solid which could link him to the King's Head.'

'I'll put the bottle bits in the dustbin,' said the old woman. 'It's what I told Josh Yallop I was going to do anyway.'

Mr Campion nodded approval. 'You mentioned a visitors' book from when you ran the pub.'

'That got chucked out when I left the trade. It didn't have any real names in it that mattered or autographs of anyone important.'

'You're sure of that? Not even Mr and Mrs Boyle?'

'They were made-up names.'

'There was a David Boyle who was on the personal staff of the prince back in the Twenties. It might have rung a bell with an especially nosey nosey-parker.'

'I did not know that; I thought it was just an alias. But don't worry – the book went on a garden bonfire ten years ago. I saw it burn. I remember thinking that all I had left of them days was my bottle of Prince's Ale and now I don't even have that.'

'You are absolutely sure,' Campion pressed, 'there is nothing else which could link you to the prince? No souvenirs, mementoes, keepsakes? Your royal connection seemed to have meant a lot to you.'

Sonia Brunt stood up out of her chair and straightened her spine, but even then was only just taller than the seated Campion.

'You'll call me a sentimental old woman, I know, but when that bottle came in the post I kept the wrapping paper with all the stamps on. They had his portrait on them, you see. He was ever so handsome, even on a postage stamp.'

'May I see them?' asked Mr Campion.

Sonia shuffled across the room to a small chest of drawers guarded by a pack of china dogs. The top draw was clearly used as Sonia's domestic filing cabinet and, after sifting through a selection of parish magazines, bills and official-looking circulars, she pulled out a square of brown paper perhaps six inches square, looked at it and smiled, then handed it to Campion.

The paper was heavy duty brown parcel paper and had clearly been torn or roughly cut from a much larger piece. In the bottom corner there was a fragment of an address, handwritten in fountain pen black ink. Only the ends of the address lines were distinguishable and only someone who knew the context would recognize that 'Head' meant King's Head and that '. . . ting' referred to Sweethearting and '. . . olk' was Suffolk.

The bulk of the fragment held the stamps, two blocks of four 1½d, or 'three halfpence' as Campion knew them – red-brown stamps bearing the royal crown, the royal head in profile facing right and the word POSTAGE in capital letters. A distinct postmark identified that the stamps had been franked on the 11 December, 1936.

'That's it,' Sonia said, bitterness creeping into her voice. 'That's my last memory. Happy now?'

'I was worried that the address might prove incriminating, and to be honest it wouldn't take a genius to work it out. It has to be somewhere in Norfolk or Suffolk and I can't think of any place which ends in "ting" in Norfolk. It could, of course, have been destined for a Mr or a Mrs Head, but when looking at the king's head on those stamps, most people would make the subconscious connection to a pub called the King's Head.'

'Well, you take it and take what's left of the bottle as well. That way you'll be sure. The only connection left will be me and I won't say a word. Whatever happens to me, I'll take what I know to the grave.'

'I believe you will, Sonia. I believe you will.'

Campion folded the parcel paper carefully and tucked it into the inside pocket of his jacket, while in an old newspaper provided by Sonia, Rupert wrapped the fragments of glass that had once been the bottle of Prince's Ale. It was now dark outside and Campion asked his son if he and Perdita would mind fetching the car from the King's Head as he was sure their presence back at Heronhoe Hall was required. Even an accomplished raconteur such as Lugg could only keep the police baffled for so long.

The younger Campions, still unsure of the import and outcome of what they had heard, said an uncomfortable goodbye to Sonia Brunt and left Mr Campion at the door of the cottage.

When Rupert and Perdita were safely out of range, Campion closed the cottage door and turned back to face Sonia Brunt.

'Now we're alone, Sonia, please tell me. The wooden mallet which I suspect did for the late Samuel Salt – who actually picked it up off the bar and swung it, you or Arthur?'

Once again, Perdita drove and Rupert crouched in the back seat of the Mini, clutching the newspaper-wrapped parcel of broken glass to his chest as the car's headlights reflected from the incoming tide in the estuary on the short journey back to the hall. They passed the Barrow site where more police cars and vans were now parked and shadowy figures were setting up generator-powered floodlights.

'Would it be awfully boorish,' said Rupert, 'if I said that if I am now holding the treasure everybody's been after, then it's been a lot of wasted effort for not very much.'

'Possibly boorish,' said Mr Campion, 'but more importantly inaccurate.'

'Albert . . .' Perdita said threateningly. 'I'm quite willing to stop the car this very minute and we won't move an inch until you spill the beans. What did we miss?'

Even in the dark interior of the car, Perdita could sense that her father-in-law was smiling.

'You're not holding the Sweethearting Treasure, dear boy, I am.'

'The stamps,' said Perdita.

'Clever girl. Whether he meant to or not, the king sent Sonia something valuable when he stuck those stamps on that bottle of ale.'

'Of course!' Rupert enthused from the back seat. 'He was only king for a few months so the stamps with his head on them must be valuable.'

'Well, actually, no,' said his father. 'Didn't I encourage your stamp collecting when you were a lad? I'm sure I told you that philately will get you anywhere; I should have, it's a way of learning geography without the pain. Edward VIII stamps are not especially rare, *except when the king is facing the wrong way.*'

'Crikey O'Riley!' exclaimed Rupert. 'They're misprints? Mistakes?'

'I'm presuming so. It was common practice for a new monarch to approve the designs for new stamps and perhaps these were some early designs which didn't pass muster when someone spotted that the king should be facing left and not right. If the bottle was actually sent by the king, he could just have grabbed whatever was to hand. The postmark is significant as it shows the parcel was sent at the height of the Abdication Crisis – not that I'm suggesting that the king toddled down to the post office himself, but I can picture the scene. I think the bottle was sent on a whim and in great haste.'

'How many stamps are there?'

'Eight in total. I suspect someone had a rough guess at the postage and somebody thought that a shilling's worth of stamps would cover it; that sounds about right for those days.'

'So they will be rare?'

'I have no idea, but I've never seen or heard of anything like this. There was a famous American stamp from 1918 celebrating the wonders of flight called "the inverted Jenny" which showed a biplane but a batch had been printed with it upside down. They are supposed to be much sought-after by collectors.'

'So are they valuable?' Perdita asked as she steered the Mini into the drive of Heronhoe Hall.

'They may well be. When we get back to London I'll go and see that nice Mr Stanley Gibbons, who is wise beyond measure in all things to do with stamps, and he will advise us. We might be talking several thousand pounds.'

'So there was real treasure after all. That will be a nice surprise for Sonia.'

'No, it won't,' said Campion firmly and in the shadowy interior of the car his voice sounded positively menacing. 'My standards may have slipped with age and my moral compass is now decidedly skew-wiff, but I've never believed one should profit from a crime.'

'Oh,' said Perdita.

'Do you mean to say . . .?' Rupert started but Campion turned his head and put his forefinger to his lips.

'Now listen, you two, I would like you to forget everything you heard this afternoon. Could you do that for me? It would be purely for my own selfish reasons and naturally I would be fully responsible should there be consequences.'

'What are you saying, Pa?'

'I am saying that fifteen years ago I abdicated any responsibility for an innocent young Italian girl and have felt very bad about it ever since. Now I think I am going to abdicate from the question of the death of Samuel Salt and it will not trouble me, for I do not see how justice can be well-served at this distance in time. I will not hinder the wheels of law enforcement if they start turning, but will not oil them to help them crush a frail old woman. If either of you feel different, I will quite understand.'

Rupert and Perdita exchanged the briefest of glances and Perdita nodded in silent agreement.

'We'll follow your lead, Pa,' said Rupert, 'if you're sure in your own mind.'

'My mind is the one thing I'm never sure of,' said Mr Campion. 'So let us be as vague as possible – I'm told I'm rather good at that – when we get inside. There will be too many people floating round the hall, and anyway, we've had enough surprises for one day.'

'No, we haven't.'

As Perdita braked and the Mini slowed, she flicked on the main headlight beams, which illuminated a familiar grey Jaguar saloon neatly parked between two police cars outside the front door of the hall.

TWENTY
The Sermon Opposite the Mount

'**A**manda! You come with a chariot for which to carry me home!'

'Not before time, judging by the state you've put poor Lavinia's house in. There are policemen tramping everywhere, archaeologists in the Orangery and Lugg appears to have bought up half of Harrods' Food Hall. He's in the kitchen, by the way, and has put himself in charge of feeding the five thousand this evening, so I hope you remembered to pack your antacids. That's a lovely outfit, by the way, Perdita.'

In the doorway, Mr Campion leaned in to his son's shoulder. 'Have you noticed how your mother's hair glows even redder, just as coals glow when blown on, whenever she's annoyed? Now do the manly thing and go and give her a kiss. That may take some of the flak off me.'

Rupert did his dutiful son act with a kiss on each cheek and then Perdita greeted her mother-in-law in the traditional female manner, the two women joining hands then both leaning back just enough to admire each other's outfits and discovering that Perdita was warming to the longer skirt and pinched-waist look of Thirties' chic, although she was naturally jealous of Amanda's purple suede Jean Muir number with matching boots by Barbara Hulanicki, which must have knocked them dead at her business meeting in Birmingham.

'Birmingham . . .' Campion muttered to himself, '. . . it was Birmingham.'

When it was finally his turn to embrace his wife, he said, 'It is wonderful to see you, darling, though you've caught us on rather an unusual day. I assure you, it's not like this normally.'

Lady Amanda did not look convinced. Behind her, down the hallway, Precious Aird was leaning casually against the wallpaper talking to Inspector Chamley who was making copious notes in his regulation black notebook, uniformed policemen were passing between the front room and the door to the Orangery and a rather dishevelled Lavinia Bell was struggling to make headway in the direction of the kitchen while bearing a tray of dirty cups and mugs.

'I suspect it has been *exactly* like this since the day you arrived, Albert,' said Amanda. 'You should have visiting cards done which say "Fed up with conventional house parties? Invite Albert Campion: chaos and confusion guaranteed" or perhaps take out a small ad in *The Times*.'

Over his wife's shoulder, Campion saw the unmistakeable figure of Lugg appear from the kitchen, his Hitchockian outline surreally softened by the very feminine apron printed with vivid green and yellow flowers straining against his girth. He was clutching a large mixing bowl to his bosom and stirring the contents with contained aggression and a large wooden spoon. When he caught sight of Amanda in close contact with her husband, Lugg grimaced then carefully and quietly stepped back-wards, retreating into the kitchen.

'I will explain everything over dinner, my dear,' said Mr Campion, 'unless this turns out to be our *Malamerenda*, which if Lugg is cooking, may well be the case. Any idea what's on the menu?'

'His patent version of corned beef hash with mashed potatoes and baked eggs, or so he says, but you don't have to worry about dreaming up an explanation. I am fully aware of what's been going on and you should be ashamed of yourself.'

'You are – and I should?'

'You are too old for this sort of tomfoolery. Need I remind you that for your birthday this year we are going to have to find seventy candles from somewhere. We might have to send Lugg out to burgle a church.'

'Perish the thought. Not only would the crime be a sin and a disgrace but any church would have to think of the costs of re-consecration after a visit by Lugg.'

'Don't avoid the subject – you know what I meant. You've been seeking absolution from something which happened fifteen years ago for which you were in no way responsible. I suspected this television filming business was a subterfuge from the start and those fanciful stories of a missing treasure had your fingerprints all over them. When it came to break-ins, finding buried bodies and people pulling guns, I walked out of my business meetings and drove down here before you did anything stupid or dangerous or both. It appears I was too late, but thankfully it seems there are no serious casualties and the police are now restoring order.'

Mr Campion took a step back in order to appreciate his wife better and reached out to cup her chin in his hand.

'Dearest, it was stupid of me not to include you in my plans from the outset. I fully admit that and beg your forgiveness, but there was never really much danger. I may be too old for the rough house now but I had lots of resourceful young people to watch my back. Let me introduce you to one.'

'You mean Precious?'

'You've already met her?'

Amanda closed her eyes and opened them with a deliberate flutter. 'I thought she might come in useful,' she said with an air of pure innocence. 'Her father said she had certain skills which indicated that she was considering a career in the military and assured me she was perfectly capable of looking after herself. I merely proposed that she looked after you as well.'

Campion's gaze again shot towards Precious Aird who, even in the middle of an interview with Inspector Chamley, managed to flick a finger to her right eyebrow in a mock salute and give Campion a cheekily deliberate wink.

'She was my bodyguard?'

'Let's say she was watching over my own personal treasure,' Amanda smiled, 'my irreplaceable *antique* treasure. And she also had a watching brief over Rupert and Perdita, as well as being my only source of reliable information as to what was going on here.'

'So, bodyguard *and* spy, eh? I should have been quicker on the uptake when we spoke on the phone the other night. You hadn't rung the hall – Precious had called *you*. Lavinia mentioned that she had been making a lot of calls for someone who had only just arrived in the country and didn't know many people. She must have been quick off the mark today for you to make it down from Birmingham so fast. I'm assuming speed limits were not a hindrance.'

'The Jag did it in three hours dead and I didn't get stopped for speeding, though I probably should have been. Precious rang me immediately after the police were called this afternoon. I was probably on my way here before they were.'

'A resourceful girl indeed.'

'I was worried she would not be devious enough to slip under your radar. You're not cross, are you?'

Mr Campion, who had never been accused of having an icy personality, visibly melted in the crossfire of Amanda's endearing expression and Precious Aird's cheeky smile.

'Of course not, and I apologize most humbly for not keeping you fully briefed. I promise to always tell you everything in future.'

Amanda raised herself on tiptoe and her lips pecked her husband on the nose.

'Before you make any more promises you are unlikely to keep, you ought to apologize to these nice policemen who have been wondering where you've been and what you've been doing for the last few hours.'

Campion sighed. 'Yes, I must make a statement, I suppose, preferably over a stiff drink. Join me and get the story straight from the horse's mouth.'

'Oh, no,' said Amanda with a grin, 'you give the police your statement while I make sure that Lugg isn't totally destroying Lavinia's kitchen. I'll wait until we get home, then you can tell me the *real* story.'

They met outside the entrance to Farringdon Road tube station and walked at a leisurely pace up the hill into Clerkenwell. It was a month since Campion and Luke had met in a wintry churchyard at Pontisbright and there was a hint of damp spring attempting to penetrate the grime of London's fumes, so much so that Luke carried a smart new raincoat over his arm and Mr Campion was stepping out with a furled umbrella at shoulder-arms position.

They exchanged polite pleasantries and news of each other's friends, families and the odd mutual enemy, but it was not until they had reached the Exmouth Market and Spa Fields area and turned on to Roseberry Avenue that their chatter ceased to be chatter and became serious.

Crossing the road into Amwell Street, they stopped outside the loggia and portico with twin arches of the church of Saints Peter and Paul which to Luke, a Londoner, would always and only be 'The Italian Church'.

'This was where she was found, laid across the steps just here,' Luke said solemnly. 'Seraphina Vezzali, aged seventeen, not old enough to vote – not even these days. Beaten to death, assailant suspected but unknown. No arrests ever made. Case filed as unsolved though that *never* rests easy with me. Still, unsolved but not forgotten, eh, Albert?'

'Not here,' said Campion. 'Let's walk back to the Farringdon Road.'

'If you can't say it on the steps of a church, you can't say it anywhere. If you're worried about such things, I'm told they are big on forgiveness.'

'I know they are, Charlie, but I am not, which is what makes me uneasy being in close proximity to a higher authority.'

'The Vezzali girl was never your burden to bear, you know.'

'So everyone said, but she deserved to be someone's burden, even after fifteen years.'

Luke suddenly stopped dead in his tracks, his attention drawn to a small delivery van which had drawn up across the road on the corner of Exmouth Market. Campion recognized the signs as easily as if the policeman had sprouted antennae and they were waving, but then everything about Luke screamed 'never off-duty'. His friend stood immobile, memorizing the number plate of the van and watching the driver, who had decamped and was opening both rear doors to reveal an interior crammed to bursting with bulbous brown rubber 'spacehoppers' made even more ridiculous by their bendy rubber 'ears' which acted as handles for a rider to grasp and inane cartoon kangaroo faces.

'So much for the must-have toy last Christmas,' Luke snarled, 'already being touted round dodgy market traders. I hate 'em.'

'Bouncy spacehoppers or dodgy market traders?' Campion asked, closely observing his friend's reaction.

'Both, but it's mostly the thought of some wide boy trying to make a few bob out of surplus-to-requirement toys which could have been given to an orphanage or a kiddies' hospital. Mind you, those things probably put more kids into hospital than help with recovery.'

Campion patted Luke on his oak beam of a shoulder. 'Amanda would say you're just as much an old softie as I am.'

'I wouldn't last long in my job if I was. I certainly couldn't afford to wait fifteen years to get revenge for a crime which I took personally even though it had nothing to do with me.'

'It was a luxury I was able to indulge in, though I am not proud of myself for succumbing to the urge.' Campion began to walk on. 'Perhaps that's why I did not feel comfortable talking about it in the precincts of a church.'

'Well, you can sleep easy now,' said Luke, striding alongside. 'You got a result, of sorts, which is more than we did in 1955.'

'You've heard from the lawyers in Italy then?'

'Oh, yes – and how. Difficult to shut them up once they got started. Cost us a fortune in overtime for the Telex operators and the translation boys but it seems as if a deal has been done.'

'I'm all ears, old chum.'

'As long as Oliver and Lavinia Bell won't press for prosecution – and I'm assuming that you and your little army of film extras won't either – then we would be willing to agree to the extradition of Daniela Petraglia into the custody of the Naples police where she apparently is wanted for questioning on various matters, though the feeling is that she'll walk free before the key has turned in the lock on her cell door. She is what is known in the trade as "connected".'

'And in return?' Campion prompted.

'Stephano Bolzano returns to England of his own volition – and that's a laugh for a start – to answer questions about the murder of Seraphina Vezzali in Clerkenwell in 1955, very probably in the restaurant just round the corner up ahead. Best scenario is that we can get him on perverting the course of justice and failing to report a crime. There's no doubt he'll blame his mad brother Marco, who always got my vote for it, but nothing could be proved at the time because, to be honest, none of my lot looked hard enough and the thought of that gives me no pleasure at all.'

Campion felt his friend's simmering anger.

'I know, I know. What happened to Marco?'

'He's dead; caught a knife in the throat over a game of cards in a bar in Salerno in 1964. Doubtful if anyone mourned him, not even his brother, who now has to take the rap for him, even though it will probably not be much of a rap and he's doing it because he's more afraid of the Petraglia mob than he is of a British judge and jury.'

They continued side by side and had emerged on to the Farringdon Road once more, opposite the fire station, before Campion spoke again as they turned right.

'So we can draw a line, albeit a dotted one, under a murder from 1955, but what about the one from 1935?'

'That's a problem for East Suffolk I'm happy to say, and they're welcome to it. There was some initial doubt about identification of the body; the old dental records technique so beloved of detective story writers only works if you know the corpse went to a dentist, who he was and where he is now. The gold watch and chain helped. It wasn't inscribed but a few of the locals thought they recognized it as belonging to Samuel Salt.'

'And its presence strongly suggests that robbery was not a motive.'

'Agreed, plus there was a wallet on the corpse with a few pounds in it, though no documents, letters or press card, anything like that. All the stuff from the digs where he used to live is long gone.'

'But he was definitely murdered?'

'Unless he smashed the back of his own skull in and then buried himself, yes. The pathologist is still no wiser on the weapon used. It sounds like something for the archaeologists, not the boys in blue. And before you ask, the Suffolk boys in blue are nowhere near making an arrest. Don't suppose you'd like to make any contributions on that subject, would you, Albert?'

'I would prefer to change the subject,' Campion said swiftly. 'Heard any more from Lord Breeze?'

'Thankfully no. I believe there was an angry phone call from him to the chief constable demanding hanging, drawing and quartering for the gangsters who shot up the house he'd given his daughter as a wedding present.'

'Only one shot was fired,' said Campion with a smile, 'and the damage was minimal, though I can see why the noble lord took it personally.'

'Funnily enough there was only that one phone call and since then silence. I'm presuming you followed his advice not to find the non-existent Abdication Treasure?'

'Well . . . yes and no. I did find something valuable and it was vaguely connected to the Abdication, but not embarrassingly so if I might put it that way. I can't see it causing any problems for anyone who lives down The Mall, for which Lord Breeze will probably claim the credit. In fact, I happen to know he already has.'

'So it wasn't the Crown Jewels then?'

'Only to an avid philatelist. It was a set of unusual stamps, misprinted ones torn off an envelope or a parcel, which I found quite by accident jammed behind the skirting board in a bedroom at Heronhoe Hall. I understand that Stanley Gibbons, the stamp people, think they might fetch a couple of thousand pounds to a collector, which should pay for a new kitchen for Lavinia Bell after the destruction Lugg wrought upon it and a few other home improvements.'

Campion stopped on the corner of the side street which was their ultimate, if unspoken, destination and, using his umbrella, pointed across the Farringdon Road to a large complex of grey buildings guarded by impressive iron gates.

'Fancy a piece of whimsy, Charlie? If they had been in business here back in 1936, the Bolzano mob would have had those stamps right under their nose, just across the road as they went through the Mount Pleasant sorting office. One of life's little ironies, don't you think, the whole thing coming back to Little Italy in a way?'

Luke's face remained impassive as they turned the corner into the side street and almost immediately found themselves outside a small Italian restaurant with two card tables covered with checked tablecloths held down by salt-and-pepper cruets on the pavement guarding the door.

'Well, here's La Pergoletta,' said Luke. 'You sure you want to have lunch here?'

'Why not? It looks cheap and cheerful and your presence should guarantee nothing shady or illegal happens on the premises.'

'I'll lay odds they don't have the council's permission for these tables on the pavement, but if we sit inside we should be legal. This place has been a legitimate restaurant for quite a while now and has changed hands several times since the Bolzanos were here. I know – I checked.'

'Any thoughts on what might happen to Stephano?' Campion enquired, reaching for the door handle.

Luke shrugged his massive shoulders. 'Difficult to call. He could do a stretch inside, come out, get sent back to Italy and still be younger than you.'

'Thank you for reminding me of my mortality, Charlie. If that was a tactless way to get an invitation to my birthday party in May, then it worked. The invitation, like most things to be treasured, is in the post.'